HOLMES PUBLIC LIBRARY
470 Plymouth St.
Halifax, MA 02338

THE BLACK OBELISK

Books by Erich Maria Remarque

ALL QUIET ON THE WESTERN FRONT (1929)
THE ROAD BACK (1931)
THREE COMRADES (1937)
FLOTSAM (1941)
ARCH OF TRIUMPH (1946)
SPARK OF LIFE (1952)
A TIME TO LOVE AND A TIME TO DIE (1954)
THE BLACK OBELISK (1957)

The Black Obelisk

ERICH MARIA REMARQUE

TRANSLATED FROM THE GERMAN
BY DENVER LINDLEY

Harcourt, Brace and Company   New York

© 1957 BY
ERICH MARIA REMARQUE

All rights reserved, including the right to reproduce this book or portions thereof in any form.

first edition

LIBRARY OF CONGRESS CATALOG CARD NUMBER: 57-8840
PRINTED IN THE UNITED STATES OF AMERICA

To P. G.

THE BLACK OBELISK

Chapter One

The sun is shining in the office of Heinrich Kroll and Sons, Funeral Monuments. It is April, 1923, and business is good. The first quarter has been lively; we have made brilliant sales and grown poor in the process, but what can we do? Death is ineluctable, and such is human sorrow that it demands memorials of sandstone, marble, or even, when the sense of guilt or the inheritance is large, of costly black Swedish granite polished on all sides. Autumn and spring are the best seasons for dealers in the appurtenances of grief —more people die then than in summer or winter: in autumn because the sap has dried up, and in spring because it mounts and consumes the weakened body like too large a wick in too thin a candle. That at least is the conviction of our most active agent, Liebermann, the gravedigger at the municipal cemetery. And he ought to know: he is eighty years old, has buried upward of ten thousand corpses, has bought a house on the river and a trout hatchery with his commissions on tombstones and, through his profession, has become an enlightened brandy drinker. The one thing he hates is the city crematorium. It is unfair competition. We do not like it either. There is no profit in urns.

I look at the clock. It is a little before twelve, and since today is Saturday I prepare to close up. I slam the metal cover over the typewriter, carry the Presto mimeograph machine behind the curtain, clear away the stone samples, and take the photographic prints of war memorials and artistic funeral monuments out of the fixing bath. I am the advertising manager, draftsman, and bookkeeper for the firm; in fact, for a year now I have been the sole office employee in what is, after all, not even my own profession.

With anticipation I take a cigar out of the drawer. It is a black Brazilian. The salesman for the Württemberg Metal Works gave it to me this morning with the intention of foisting off on me later a consignment of bronze wreaths; so it is a good cigar. I look for a match, but as usual they have been mislaid. Fortunately a small fire is burning in the Dutch oven. I roll up a ten-mark bill, hold it in the flame and light the cigar with it. At the end of April there is no longer any real need for a fire in the oven; it is just a selling aid devised by my employer Georg Kroll. He believes that in time of sorrow when people have to hand out money they do it more willingly in a warm room than when they are cold. Sorrow in itself is a chilling of the soul, and if you add cold feet, it is hard to extract a decent price. Warmth has a thawing effect—even on the purse. Therefore our office is overheated, and our representatives have it dinned into them as an overriding principle never to attempt to close a sale in the cemetery when it is cold or rainy, but always in a warm room and, if possible, after a meal. Sorrow, cold, and hunger are bad business partners.

I throw the remnant of the ten-mark bill into the oven and stand up. At the same instant I hear a window thrown open in the house opposite. I don't need to look around to know what is going on. Cautiously I bend over the table as though I still had something to do to the typewriter. At the same time I peep into a little hand mirror which I have so arranged that I can observe the window. As usual it is Lisa, wife of Watzek, the horse butcher, standing there naked, yawning and stretching. She has just got up. The street is old and narrow; Lisa can see us and we can see her and she knows it; that is why she is standing there. Suddenly a quirk appears in her big mouth; she laughs, showing all her teeth, and points at the mirror. Her eagle eye has spied it. I am annoyed at being caught but act as though I had not noticed and retreat to the back of the room in a cloud of smoke. After a while I return. Lisa grins. I glance out, but not at her; instead I pretend to wave at someone in the street. As an extra flourish I throw a kiss into the void. Lisa falls for it; she is as inquisitive as a goat. She bends forward to see who is there. No one is there. Now I grin. She gestures angrily at her forehead with one finger and disappears.

I don't really know why I carry on this comedy. Lisa is what is called a terrific figure of a woman, and I know a lot of people who would gladly pay a couple of million to enjoy such a spectacle every morning. I, too, enjoy it, but nevertheless it irritates me that this lazy toad, who never climbs out of bed until noon, is so shamelessly certain of her effect. It would never occur to her that there might be men who would not instantly want to sleep with her. Besides, the question does not even greatly interest her. She only stands at the window with her black pony tail and her impertinent nose and swings her first-class Carrara marble breasts like an aunt waving a rattle in front of a baby. If she had a couple of toy balloons she would happily wave them; it is all the same to her. Since she is naked, she waves her breasts; she is just completely happy to be alive and to know that all men must be crazy about her, and then she forgets the whole thing and goes to work on her breakfast with her voracious mouth. Meanwhile, Watzek, the horse butcher, is slaughtering tired old carriage nags.

Lisa appears again. Now she is wearing a false mustache and is beside herself at this witty inspiration. She gives a military salute, and I assume that she is so shameless as to have her eye on old Knopf, the retired sergeant major whose house is next door. But then I remember that Knopf's bedroom window opens on the court. And Lisa is artful enough to know that she cannot be observed from the few other neighboring houses.

Suddenly, as though a reservoir of sound has burst its dike, the bells of St. Mary's begin to ring. The church stands at the end of our alley, and the strokes resound as though they fell straight from heaven into our room. At the same time I see outside the other office window, the one that faces on the court, my employer's bald head gliding by like a ghostly melon. Lisa makes a rude gesture and shuts her window. The daily temptation of Saint Anthony has been withstood once more.

Georg Kroll is barely forty, but his head is already as shiny as the bowling alley at Boll's Garden Restaurant. It has been shiny as long as I have known him, and that is over five years. It is so shiny that when we were in the trenches, where we belonged to the same regiment, a special order was issued that even at the quietest times Georg had to wear his steel helmet—such would have been the temptation, for even the kindliest of enemies, to find out by a shot whether or not his head was a giant billiard ball.

I pull myself together and report: "Company Headquarters, Kroll and Sons! Staff engaged in enemy observation. Suspicious troop movements in the Watzek sector."

"Aha," Georg says. "Lisa at her morning gymnastics. Get a move on, Lance Corporal Bodmer. Why don't you wear blinders in the morning like the drummer's horse in a cavalry band and thus protect your virtue? Don't you know what the three most precious things in life are?"

"How should I know that, Attorney General, when life itself is what I'm still searching for?"

"Virtue, simplicity, and youth," Georg announces. "Once lost, never to be regained! And what is more useless than experience, age, and barren intelligence?"

"Poverty, sickness, and loneliness," I reply, standing at ease.

"Those are just different names for experience, age, and misguided intelligence."

Georg takes the cigar out of my mouth. He examines it briefly and classifies it like a butterfly. "Booty from the metalworks."

He takes a beautifully clouded, golden-brown meerschaum cigar holder out of his pocket, fits the Brazilian into it and goes on smoking.

"I have nothing against your requisitioning the cigar," I say. "It is naked force, and that's all you noncoms know about life. But why the cigar holder? I'm not syphilitic."

"And I'm not homosexual."

"Georg," I say, "in the war you used my spoon to eat pea soup whenever I could steal it from the canteen. And the spoon stayed in my dirty boot and was never washed."

Georg examines the ash of the Brazilian. It is snow white. "The war was four and a half years ago," he informs me. "At that time infinite misery made us human. Today the shameless lust for gain has made us robbers again. To keep this secret we use the varnish of convention. Ergo! Isn't there still another Brazilian? The metalworks never tries to bribe an employee with just one."

I take the second cigar out of the drawer and hand it to him. "You know everything! Intelligence, experience, and age seem to be good for something after all."

He grins and gives me in return a half-empty package of cigarettes. "Anything else been happening?" he asks.

"Not a thing. No customers. But I must urgently request a raise."

"What, again? You got one only yesterday!"

"Not yesterday. This morning at nine o'clock. A miserable ten thousand marks. However, it was still worth something at nine this morning. Now the new dollar exchange rate has been posted and instead of a new tie all I can buy is a bottle of cheap wine. But what I need is a tie."

"Where does the dollar stand now?"

"Thirty-six thousand marks at noon today. This morning it was thirty-three thousand."

Georg Kroll examines his cigar. "Thirty-six thousand! It's a rat race. Where will it end?"

"In a wholesale crash. Meanwhile we have to live. Did you get some money?"

"Only a small suitcaseful for today and tomorrow. Thousands, ten thousands, even a couple of packages of hundreds. Something like five pounds of paper money. The inflation is moving so fast that the Reichsbank can't print money rapidly enough to keep up with it. The new hundred-thousand bills were only issued two weeks ago—soon we'll need million-mark notes. When will we be in the billions?"

"If it goes on like this, in a couple of months."

"My God!" Georg sighs. "Where are the fine peaceful times of 1922? Then the dollar only rose from two hundred fifty to ten thousand in a whole year. Not to mention 1921—when it went up a beggarly three hundred per cent."

I look out the window toward the street. Now Lisa is standing across the way in a printed silk dressing gown decorated with parrots. She has put a mirror on the window ledge and is brushing her mane.

"Look at that," I say bitterly. "She sows not neither does she reap, and our Father in Heaven supports her nevertheless. She didn't have that dressing gown yesterday. Yards of silk! And I can't scrape together the price of a tie."

Georg grins. "You're just an innocent victim of the times. But Lisa spreads her sails before the gale of the inflation. She is the fair Helen of the black marketeers. You can't get rich on tombstones. Why don't you go into the herring business or the stock market like your friend Willy?"

"Because I am a philosopher and a sentimentalist. I shall remain true to tombstones. Well, what about my raise? Even philosophers need to spend something on their wardrobes."

Georg shrugs his shoulders. "Can't you buy the tie tomorrow?"

"Tomorrow is Sunday. And I need it tomorrow."

Georg sighs and gets his bagful of money out of the vestibule. He reaches inside and throws me two packages. "Will that do?"

I see that they are mostly hundreds. "Hand over another pound of that wallpaper," I say. "This is not more than five thousand. Catholic profiteers put that much in the collection plate at Sunday mass and feel ashamed of being so stingy."

Georg scratches his bald skull, an atavistic gesture without meaning in his case. Then he hands me a third package. "Thank God tomorrow is Sunday," he says. "No dollar exchange rate. One day in the week the inflation stands still. God surely did not have that in mind when He created the Sabbath."

"How are we doing really?" I ask. "Are we ruined or in clover?"

Georg takes a long drag on the meerschaum holder. "I don't believe anyone in Germany knows that about himself. Not even the godlike Stinnes. People with savings are ruined, of course. So are all the factory workers and office workers. Also most of the small-business people, only they don't know it. The only ones who are making hay are the people with foreign exchange, stocks, or negotiable property. Does that answer your question?"

"Negotiable property!" I look out into the garden which serves as our warehouse. "We haven't much left. Mostly sandstone and poured concrete. Very little marble or granite. And what little we have your brother is selling at a loss. The best thing would be to sell nothing at all, wouldn't it?"

There is no need for Georg to answer. A bicycle bell rings outside. Someone mounts the ancient steps. There is an authoritative cough. It is the problem child of the family, Heinrich Kroll, Jr., the other owner of the firm.

He is a corpulent little man with a bristling mustache and dusty trousers, secured at the bottom with bicycle clips. His eyes sweep Georg and me with mild contempt. To him we are office hacks who loaf all day, while he is the man of action in charge of foreign affairs. He is indefatigable. Every day in the gray of dawn he goes to the railroad station and then by bicycle to the remotest villages: wherever our agents, the gravediggers and teachers, have reported a corpse. He is by no means inept. His corpulence inspires confidence; therefore he maintains it by diligent beer drinking early and late. Farmers like short thick men better than hungry-looking ones. His clothes help too. He does not wear a black frock coat, like our competitor Steinmeyer, nor a blue business suit like the travelers of Hollmann and Klotz—the one is too obvious, the other too unfeeling. Heinrich Kroll wears striped trousers with a dark jacket, together with a high old-fashioned wing collar and a subdued tie with a lot of black in it. Two years ago he hesitated for a while in choosing this outfit. He wondered whether a cutaway might not be more suitable, but then decided against it because of his height. It was a happy renunciation. Even Napoleon would have been ridiculous in a swallow tail. In his present outfit Heinrich Kroll looks like the dear Lord's diminutive receptionist—and that is exactly as it should be. The bicycle clips give the whole a cunningly calculated appearance of homeliness; in these days of automobiles, people believe they can get a better buy from a man who wears bicycle clips.

Heinrich takes his hat off and wipes his forehead. Outside it is fairly cool and he is not perspiring; he does this simply to show us what a hard worker he is in comparison with us office loafers.

"I have sold the memorial cross," he says with a modesty as unobtrusive as the roar of a lion.

"Which? The small marble one?" I ask hopefully.

"The big one," Heinrich replies, even more simply, and stares at me.

"What? The Swedish granite with double socle and bronze chains?"

"That's the one! Did you think we had any other?"

Heinrich clearly relishes his silly question as a triumph of sarcasm.

"No," I say. "We haven't any other. That's the trouble. It was the last. Our rock of Gibraltar."

"How much did you sell it for?" Georg Kroll now asks.

Heinrich straightens up. "For three-quarters of a million, without inscription and exclusive of freight and packing. They are additional."

"Good God!" Georg and I say at the same time.

Heinrich favors us with a glance full of arrogance; dead haddock sometimes wear a similar expression. "It was a hard battle," he proclaims and for some reason puts on his hat again.

"I wish you had lost it," I reply.

"What?"

"Lost it. Lost the battle."

"What?" Heinrich repeats in annoyance. I irritate him easily.

"He wishes you had not sold it," Georg Kroll says.

"What? What in the world does that mean? Hell and damnation, I slave from morning till night and when I make a brilliant sale all I get in this hole is reproaches! Go out to the villages yourselves and try—"

"Heinrich," Georg interrupts him mildly, "we know you work yourself to the bone. But today we're living in a time when every sale makes us poorer. For years there has been an inflation. Since the war, Heinrich. But this year the inflation has turned into galloping consumption. That's why figures no longer mean—"

"I know that myself. I'm no idiot."

No one says anything to that. Only idiots make such statements. And to contradict them is useless. That is something I have learned on the Sundays I spend at the insane asylum. Heinrich gets out a notebook. "The memorial cost us fifty thousand when we bought it. You would think that three-quarters of a million would mean a neat little profit."

He is dabbling in sarcasm again. He thinks he must use it on me because I was once a schoolteacher. That was shortly after the war, in an isolated village on the heath— nine long months until I made my escape, with winter loneliness howling like a dog at my heels.

"It would have been an even bigger profit if in place of the magnificent cross you had sold that damned obelisk out there," I say. "Your late father bought it for even less sixty years ago when the business was founded—for something like fifty marks, according to tradition."

"The obelisk? What's the obelisk got to do with this? The obelisk is unsalable, any child knows that."

"For that very reason," I say, "no tears would be shed if

you had got rid of it. But it's a pity about the cross. We'll have to replace it at great expense."

Heinrich Kroll snorts. He has polyps in his thick nose and gets stuffed up easily. "Are you by any chance trying to tell me that it would cost three-quarters of a million to buy a memorial cross today?"

"That's something we'll find out soon enough," Georg Kroll says. "Riesenfeld will be here tomorrow. We'll have to place a new order with the Odenwald Granite Works; there's not much left on inventory."

"We still have the obelisk," I suggest maliciously.

"Why don't you sell that yourself?" Heinrich snaps. "So Riesenfeld is coming tomorrow; well, I'll stay and have a talk with him myself. Then we'll see where prices stand."

Georg and I exchange glances. We know that we will keep Heinrich away from Riesenfeld even if we have to make him drunk or pour castor oil in his morning beer. That honest, old-fashioned businessman would bore Riesenfeld to death with his war experiences and stories of the good old times when a mark was still a mark and honesty was the mark of honor, as our beloved field marshal has so aptly put it. Heinrich dotes on such platitudes; not Riesenfeld. For Riesenfeld, honesty is what you demand from someone else when it's to his disadvantage, and from yourself when you can gain by it.

"Prices change daily," Georg says. "There's nothing to talk about."

"Really? Perhaps you, too, think I got a bad price?"

"That depends. Did you bring the money with you?"

Heinrich stares at Georg. "Bring it with me? What in blazes are you talking about? How could I bring the money when we haven't even made delivery? You know that's impossible!"

"It isn't impossible at all," I reply. "On the contrary, it's common practice today. It's called payment in advance."

"Payment in advance!" Heinrich's fat snout twitches contemptuously. "What does a schoolteacher like you know about it? In our business how can you demand payment in advance? From the sorrowing relatives when the wreathes on the grave haven't even begun to wilt! Are you going to demand money at such a moment for something that hasn't been delivered?"

"Of course! When else? That's when they're weak and it's easy to get money out of them."

"They're weak then? Don't make me laugh! That's when they're harder than steel! After all the expense for the coffin, the pastor, the grave, the flowers, the wake—why, you couldn't get so much as a ten-thousand advance, young man! First, people have to recover! Before they pay they have to see what they have ordered standing in the cemetery and not just on paper in the catalogue, even when it's been drawn by you with Chinese brushes and genuine gold leaf for the inscriptions and a few grieving relatives into the bargain."

Another example of Heinrich's personal tactlessness! I pay no attention. It is true that I not only drew the tombstones for our catalogue and reproduced them on the Presto mimeograph machine but also painted them to increase their effectiveness and provided them with atmosphere: with weeping willows, beds of pansies, cypresses, and widows in mourning veils watering the flowers. Our competitors almost died of envy when we produced this novelty; they had nothing but simple stock photographs, and Heinrich, too, thought the idea magnificent at the time, especially the use of gold leaf. As a matter of fact, to make the effect completely natural I had embellished the drawings of the tombstones with inscriptions emblazoned with gold leaf dissolved in varnish. I had had a splendid time doing it; I killed off everyone I hated and painted tombstones for them—for example, the beast who was my sergeant when I was a recruit and who is still living happily: "Here after prolonged and hideous sufferings, having seen all his loved ones precede him in death, lies Constable Karl Flümer." This was fully justified; Flümer had treated me outrageously and had sent me twice on patrols from which I had returned alive only by chance. I had ample reason to wish him the worst.

"Herr Kroll," I say, "allow us to give you another short analysis of the times. The principles by which you were raised are noble, but today they lead to bankruptcy. Anybody can earn money now; almost no one knows how to maintain its purchasing power. The important thing is not to sell but to buy and to be paid as quickly as possible. We live in an age of commodities. Money is an illusion; everyone knows that, but many still do not believe it. As long as this is so the inflation will go on till absolute zero is reached. Man lives seventy-five per cent by his imagination and only twenty-five per cent by fact—that is his strength and his weakness, and that is why in this witch's dance of numbers there are still winners and losers. We know that we cannot be absolute winners; but at the same time we don't want to be complete losers. If the three-quarters of a million marks you settled for today is not paid for two months, it will be worth what fifty thousand is worth now. Therefore—"

Heinrich's face has turned dark red. Now he interrupts me. "I am no idiot," he declares for the second time. "And you don't need to read me lectures. I know more of practical life than you do. And I would rather go down honorably than exist by disreputable profiteering methods. As long as I am sales manager of this firm the business will be conducted in the old, decent fashion—and that's all there is to it. I rely on my experience, and it has stood us in good stead so far; that's how it will continue in the future! It's a rotten trick to spoil a man's pleasure in a fine business deal! Why didn't you stick to your job of arse-drummer?"

He snatches up his hat and slams the door behind him. We see him vigorously stamping off, knock-kneed and bow-legged, a half-military figure with his bicycle clips. He is in formal retreat to his accustomed table at Blume's Restaurant.

"That bourgeois sadist wants to get fun out of his work," I say angrily. "Imagine that! How can we carry on our business except with pious cynicism if we want to save our souls? That hypocrite wants to get pleasure out of haggling over corpses and actually considers it his hereditary right!"

Georg laughs. "Take your money and let's be on our way. Weren't you going to buy a necktie? Get on with it! There'll be no more raises today!"

He picks up the suitcase with the money and casually puts it in the room next to the office, where he sleeps. I stow my packages of bills in a cardboard box with the inscription: Konditorei Keller, Finest Pastries, Home Deliveries.

"Is Riesenfeld really coming?" I ask.

"Yes. He telegraphed."

"What does he want? Money? Or has he something to sell?"

"We'll find out," Georg says and locks the office door.

Chapter Two

We step outside. The strong sun of late April pours down as though a gigantic golden basin full of light and wind were being emptied on us. We stop. The garden is aflame with green, spring rustles in the young foliage of the poplar tree as in a harp, and the first lilac is in bloom.

"Inflation," I say. "There you have one too—the wildest of all. It looks as if even nature knows that now you can only reckon in ten thousands and in millions. Look what the tulips are up to! And that white over there and the red and yellow everywhere! And what fragrance!"

Georg nods, sniffs, and takes a puff of his Brazilian; for him nature is doubly beautiful when he can smoke a cigar at the same time.

We feel the sun on our faces and we look at all the splendor. The garden behind the house is also the showroom for our monuments. There they are drawn up like a company behind Otto, the obelisk, who stands like a thin lieutenant at his post beside the door. It is Otto that I urged Heinrich to sell, Otto, the oldest tombstone of the firm, our trademark and a prodigy of tastelessness. Directly behind him come the cheap little headstones of sandstone and poured concrete with narrow pointed socles, for the poor, who live and slave in honesty and naturally get nowhere. Then come the larger but still inexpensive ones, with two socles, for those who are always trying to improve themselves, at least in death, since in life it was not possible. We sell more of these than of the perfectly plain ones, and one doesn't know whether to find this belated ambition on the part of the survivors touching or absurd. Next come the monuments of sandstone with inset plaques of marble, gray syenite, or black Swedish granite. These are already too expensive for the man who lives by the work of his hands. Small businessmen, foremen, artisans who own their own businesses are the clients—and of course that eternal bird of ill omen, the petty official who must always pretend to be more than he is, the honest white-collar proletarian of whom it is impossible to say how he manages to exist at all today since his raises always come far too late.

All these tombstones are still in the class of trifles—it is only behind them that you come to the blocks of marble and granite. First, those polished on one side, with front surfaces smooth but sides and backs roughhewn and socles rough all around. That is the sort for the more prosperous middle classes, the employer, the businessman, the larger store owner, and of course that diligent bird of ill omen, the higher official, who just like his lesser brother, must pay out more in death than he earned in life in order to preserve appearances.

But the aristocrats among the tombstones are those of marble and of black Swedish granite polished on all sides. Here there are no more rough surfaces and unfinished backs; everything has been brought to a high polish no matter whether one sees it or not, even the socles, of which there are not just one or two but often a third put in at an angle; and, if it is a showpiece in the real sense of the word, there is a stately cross of the same material on top. Today, of course, these are only for rich farmers, property owners, profiteers, and clever business people who deal in long-term promissory notes and so live on the Reichsbank, which keeps paying for everything with constantly replenished and unsupported paper currency.

Simultaneously we glance at the only one of these showpieces that, up to a quarter of an hour ago, still belonged to the firm. There it stands, black and glistening like the lacquer on a new car, the perfume of spring drifts around it, lilacs bend toward it; it is a great lady, cool, untouched, and, for one hour more, still virginal—then it will have the name of Otto Fleddersen, landowner, chiseled on its narrow waist in gilded Latin characters at eight hundred marks per letter. "Farewell, black Diana," I say. "Farewell!" and I raise my hat to it. "To the poet it's an eternal riddle that even perfect beauty is subject to the laws of fate and must perish miserably! Farewell! You will now become a shameless advertisement for the soul of the swindler Fleddersen, who cheated the poor widows of the city out of their last ten-thousand-mark bills for overpriced butter adulterated with margarine—not to mention his extortionate prices for calves' liver, pork cutlets, and roast beef! Farewell!"

"You're making me hungry," Georg remarks. "Off to the Walhalla! Or do you want to buy your tie first?"

"No. I have time before the stores close. There's no new dollar quotation Saturday afternoons. From noon today till Monday morning our currency is stable. Why? It sounds fishy to me. Why doesn't the mark fall over the week end? Does God hold it up?"

"Because the stock exchanges are shut. Any more questions?"

"Yes. Does man live from inside out or from outside in?"

"Man lives, period. There's goulash at the Walhalla, goulash with potatoes, pickles, and salad. I saw the menu as I was coming back from the bank."

"Goulash!" I pick a primrose and put it in my buttonhole. "Man lives, you're right! Whoever seeks further is already lost. Come along, let's annoy Eduard Knobloch."

We enter the big dining room of the Hotel Walhalla. At sight of us Eduard Knobloch, the owner, a fat giant with a brown toupee and a floating dinner coat, makes a face as though he had chewed on a bullet in his venison.

"Good morning, Herr Knobloch," Georg says. "Fine weather today. Gives one a great appetite!"

Eduard jerks his shoulders nervously. "Eating too much is unhealthy! It damages the liver, the gall bladder, everything."

"Not at your place, Herr Knobloch," Georg answers genially. "Your noonday meal is wholesome."

"Wholesome, yes. But too much of what is wholesome can be harmful too. According to the latest scientific investigations, too much meat—"

I interrupt Eduard by giving him a gentle slap on his soft belly. He leaps back as though someone had touched his privates. "Leave us alone and resign yourself to your fate," I say. "We won't eat you out of house and home. How's the poetry?"

"Gone begging. No time! In these times!"

I do not laugh at this idiotic word play. Eduard is not only an innkeeper, he is a poet too—but he'll have to do better than that. "Where's a table?" I ask.

Knobloch looks around. His face suddenly brightens. "I'm extremely sorry, gentlemen, but I've just noticed there's not a table free."

"That doesn't matter. We'll wait."

Eduard glances around again. "It looks as if none will be free for quite some time," he announces beaming. "The customers all seem to be just beginning their soup. Perhaps if you would care to try the Altstädter Hof or the Railroad Hotel. They say you can eat quite passably there."

Passably! The day seems to be dripping with sarcasm. First Heinrich and now Eduard. But we will fight for the goulash even if it takes an hour—it's the best dish on the Walhalla's menu.

But Eduard seems to be not only a poet but a mind reader as well. "No point in waiting," he says. "We never have enough goulash, we always run out of it early. Or would you like to try a German beefsteak? You can have it here at the counter."

"I'd rather be dead," I say. "We'll get goulash even if we have to cut you up."

"Really?" Eduard is all fat, skeptical triumph.

"Yes," I reply and give him a second slap on the belly. "Come, Georg, here's a table for us."

"Where?" Eduard asks quickly.

"Where that gentleman is sitting, the one who looks like a fashion plate. Yes, the redhead over there with the elegant lady. There, the one who's getting up and waving to us. My friend Willy, Eduard. Send a waiter. We want to order!"

Eduard emits a hissing sound behind us like a punctured tire. We go over to Willy.

The reason Eduard puts on this act is simple enough. Some time ago one could pay for meals at his place with coupons. One bought a book with ten tickets and thereby got the single meals somewhat cheaper. Eduard did this, at the time, to increase business. In the last weeks, however, the avalanche of the inflation has upset his calculations; if the first ticket still bore some relation to the price of a meal, by the

21

tenth the value had shrunk substantially. Eduard therefore decided to give up selling books of tickets. He was losing too much money. But here we had been clever. We found out about his plan in time and six weeks ago we invested the proceeds of a small war memorial in the wholesale purchase of tickets at the Walhalla. To keep Eduard from noticing what we were up to we employed a variety of people: the coffinmaker Wilke, the cemetery watchman Liebermann, our sculptor Kurt Bach, Willy, a few of our other friends and war comrades, and even Lisa. All of them bought books of tickets for us at the cashier's desk. When Eduard gave up selling coupons he expected that in ten days they would all be used up; each book contained ten tickets, and he assumed that any sensible man would buy one book at a time. But we each had over thirty books in our possession. Two weeks later Eduard became uneasy when we continued to pay with coupons; at the end of four weeks he had a slight attack of panic. At that time we were already eating for half-price; at the end of six weeks for the price of ten cigarettes. Day after day we appeared and handed over our coupons. Eduard asked how many we still had; we replied evasively. He tried to block the coupons; at the next meal we brought a lawyer with us whom we had invited to share a Wiener schnitzel. After dinner the lawyer gave Eduard a lesson in the laws governing contracts and obligations—and paid for his meal with one of our coupons. Eduard's lyricism took on a darker coloration. He proposed a compromise; we declined. He wrote a didactic poem on "Ill-gotten Gains," and sent it to the daily paper. The editor showed it to us; it was sprinkled with malicious references to "gravediggers of the nation"; there were references, too, to tombstones and "Kroll the Shyster." We invited our lawyer to share a pork cutlet with us at the Walhalla. He instructed Eduard in the concept of public slander and its consequences—and paid once more with one of our coupons. Eduard, who was formerly a simple floral lyricist, began now to write hymns of hate. But that was all he could do; the battle rages on uninterruptedly. Eduard is in daily hope that our supply will be exhausted; he does not know that we still have tickets for over seven months.

Willy rises. He is wearing a new dark green suit of first-rate material in which he looks like a redheaded tree toad. His tie is adorned with a pearl and on the index finger of his right hand he is wearing a heavy seal ring. Five years ago he was assistant to our company cook. He is the same age as I—twenty-five.

"May I present my friends and former buddies?" Willy asks. "Georg Kroll and Ludwig Bodmer—Mademoiselle Renée de la Tour of the Moulin Rouge in Paris."

Renée de la Tour nods in a reserved but not unfriendly way. We stare at Willy. Willy stares back proudly. "Sit down, gentlemen," he says. "I assume Eduard is trying to keep you from eating here. The goulash is good, though it could stand a few more onions. Sit down, we're happy to make room for you."

We arrange ourselves at the table. Willy knows about our war with Eduard and follows it with the interest of a born gambler. "Waiter!" I shout.

A waiter who is waddling by on flat feet four paces away is suddenly stricken deaf. "Waiter!" I shout again.

"You're a barbarian," Georg Kroll says. "You're insulting the man with his profession. Why did he take part in the 1918 revolution? *Herr Ober!*"

I grin. It is true the German revolution of 1918 was the least bloody there has ever been. The revolutionaries were so terrified by themselves that they at once cried for help from the magnates and the generals of the former government to protect them from their own fit of courage. The others did it. Generously too. A bunch of revolutionaries were executed, the princes and officers received magnificent pensions so that they would have time to plan future riots, the officials received new titles—high-school teachers became academic counselors, school inspectors became educational counselors, waiters were given the right to be addressed as *"Ober"* or headwaiter, former secretaries of the party became excellencies, the Social Democratic minister of the army, in seventh heaven, was entitled to have real generals under him in his ministry—and the German revolution sank back into red plush, *Gemütlichkeit,* and a yearning for uniforms and commands.

"Herr Ober!" Georg repeats.

The waiter remains deaf. It is one of Eduard's childish tricks; he tries to disconcert us by telling his waiters to ignore us.

Suddenly the dining room resounds to the thunder of a first-class Prussian barrack-room roar: *"Ober!* You there, can't you hear?" It has the instant effect of a trumpet call on an old war horse. The waiter stops as though shot in the back, and spins around; two others dash up to the table, somewhere there is the sound of heels clicking, a military-looking man at one of the nearby tables softly exclaims, "Bravo!"—and even Eduard Knobloch, with his dress coat streaming, rushes in to investigate this voice from the higher spheres. He knows that neither Georg nor I could sound so commanding.

We ourselves look around speechless at Renée de la Tour. She is sitting there, calm and maidenly, wholly uninvolved. But she is the only one who could have shouted—we know Willy's voice.

The waiter is standing at our table. "What may I do for you, gentlemen?"

"Noodle soup, goulash, and pie for two," Georg replies. "And be quick about it, otherwise we'll burst your eardrums, you slug."

Eduard arrives. He can't make out what is happening.

He glances under the table. No one is hidden there, and a ghost could hardly roar like that. Nor could we, as he knows. He suspects a trick of some sort. "I must urgently insist," he says finally, "that such an uproar must not occur in my establishment."

No one replies. We just look at him with empty eyes. Renée de la Tour is powdering her nose. Eduard turns around and departs.

"Innkeeper! Step over here!" The same thunderous voice suddenly summons him.

Eduard whirls around and stares at us. We still have the same empty smile on our mugs. He fixes Renée de la Tour with his eye. "Did you just—?"

Renée closes her compact with a click. "What's that?" she asks in a delicate silvery-clear soprano. "What is it you want?"

Eduard gapes. He no longer knows what to think. "You haven't been overworking, have you, Herr Knobloch?" Georg asks. "You seem to be suffering from hallucinations."

"But someone here just—"

"You're out of your mind, Eduard," I say. "You're not looking well either. Take a vacation. We have no wish to sell your relatives a cheap headstone of imitation Italian marble, and that's certainly all you're worth—"

Eduard blinks his eyes like an old horned owl. "You seem to be a strange sort of person," says Renée de la Tour in her flutelike soprano. "You hold your guests responsible for the fact that your waiters can't hear." She laughs, an enchanting swirl of bubbling silvery music like a forest brook in fairy tales.

Eduard clasps his forehead. His last support has collapsed. It cannot have been the young lady either. Anyone who laughs like that can't have a barrack-room voice. "You may go now, Knobloch," Georg remarks casually. "Or did you intend to join in our conversation?"

"And don't eat so much meat," I say. "Perhaps that's what's wrong. Remember what you were saying to us a few minutes ago? According to the most recent scientific investigations—"

Eduard turns quickly and rushes off. We wait till he is some distance away. Then Willy's great body begins to quiver with soundless laughter. Renée de la Tour smiles gently. Her eyes are sparkling.

"Willy," I say, "I'm a superficial sort of fellow and therefore this has been one of the finest moments of my young life—but now tell us what's going on!"

Willy, shaking with silent merriment, points to Renée. "*Excusez, Mademoiselle,*" I say. "*Je me—*"

Willy's laughter redoubles at my French. "Tell him, Lotte," he bursts out.

"What?" Renée asks with a gentle smile in a soft, growling bass.

We stare at her. "She is an artist," Willy gasps. "A duettist. She sings duets. Do you understand now?"

"No."

"She sings duets. But alone. One verse high, one low. One soprano and one bass."

A great light dawns. "But the bass—?" I ask.

"Talent!" Willy explains. "And then of course practice. You must hear her sometime when she does a spat between husband and wife. Lotte is fabulous."

We agree. The goulash appears. Eduard sneaks around at a distance watching our table. His mistake is that he always wants to find out why something happens. That spoils his poetry and makes him distrustful in life. At the moment he is brooding over the mysterious bass voice. He doesn't know what lies ahead of him. Georg Kroll, a cavalier of the old school, has invited Renée de la Tour and Willy to be his guests to celebrate our victory. Later, in payment for our excellent goulash, he will hand the infuriated Eduard four bits of paper whose combined worth today would hardly buy a couple of soup bones.

It is early evening. I am sitting beside the window in my room over the office. The house is low, angular, and old. Like this whole part of the street, it once belonged to the church that stands in the square at the foot. Priests and church officials used to live in it; but for sixty years it has belonged to Kroll and Sons. The property consists of two low houses joined by an arched entryway; in the second lives Knopf, the retired sergeant major, with his wife and three daughters. Then comes the beautiful old garden with our array of tombstones, and behind that at the left a kind of two-story wooden coach house on the ground floor of which Kurt Bach, our sculptor, has his workroom. He models mourning lions and mounting eagles for our war memorials and he draws the inscriptions on the tombstones which are later chipped out by the masons. In his free time he plays the guitar and wanders and dreams of the gold medals which at some future date will be awarded to the renowned Kurt Bach. He is thirty-two years old.

The upper floor of the coach house is rented to the coffin-maker Wilke. Wilke is an emaciated man, and nobody knows whether he has a family or not. Our relations with him are friendly, resting on mutual advantage. When we have a brand-new corpse not yet provided with a coffin, we recommend Wilke or tip him off; he does the same for us when he knows of a body that has not yet been snapped up by our competitors' hyenas; for the battle for the dead is bitter and is fought tooth and nail. Oskar Fuchs, the traveler for Hollmann and Klotz, even resorts to the use of onions. Before going into a house where there is a corpse, he gets out a couple of cut onions and smells them until his eyes are full of tears—then he marches in, proves his sympathy for the dear departed, and tries to make a sale. For this reason he is called Weeping Oskar. It's a strange fact that if the survivors had only paid half as much attention to many of the departed when they were still alive as they do when it no longer matters, then the corpses would most certainly have foregone the most expensive mausoleum—but that's what mankind is like: they only prize what they no longer possess.

Silently the street fills with the transparent smoke of twilight. There is already a light in Lisa's room, but this time the curtains are drawn, a sign that the horse butcher is home. Next to her house lies the garden of Holzmann, the wine merchant. Lilacs hang over the wall and from the cellars comes the fresh vinegary smell of the casks. Through the gate of our house marches the retired sergeant major, Knopf. He is a thin man and he wears a cap with a visor and carries a walking stick; despite his profession and although he has never read any book except the drill manual, he looks like Nietzsche. Knopf goes down Hakenstrasse and at the corner swings to the left into Marienstrasse. Toward midnight he will return, this time from the right—that will mean he has completed methodically, as befits an old military man, his circuit through the inns of the city. Knopf drinks nothing but corn schnaps, Werdenbrücker schnaps to be exact, nothing else. But on that subject he is the greatest connoisseur in the world. There are in the city some three or four firms that distill schnaps. To us they all taste more or less alike. Not so to Knopf; he can distinguish them even by smell. Forty years of unwearying application have so refined his taste that when it's a question of the same brand he can tell which inn it comes from. He maintains that there are differences between the inns' cellars and he can tell them apart. Naturally not with bottled schnaps, only with schnaps in the cask. He has won many a bet on it.

I get up and look around my room. The ceiling is low

and slanting and there is not much space, but I have what I need—a bed, a shelf of books, a table, a couple of chairs, and an old piano. Five years ago, when I was a soldier in the trenches, I never thought I would be so well off again. At that time we were in Flanders; it was the big attack on Kemmelberg, and we lost three-quarters of our company. On the second day, Georg Kroll was taken to the hospital with a stomach wound, but almost three weeks passed before I was knocked out by a shot in the knee. Then came the collapse, and I finally became a schoolmaster as my sick mother had wished and as I had promised her before she died. She was sick so often that she thought if I had an official position with life tenure nothing bad could happen to me any more. She died in the last months of the war, but I took my examinations just the same and was sent to a village on the heath, where I stayed till I grew sick of dinning into children things I did not believe myself and being buried alive amid memories I wanted to forget.

I try to read, but it is no weather for reading. Spring makes you restless, and in the twilight it is easy to lose yourself. There are no boundaries then and you feel breathless and confused. I turn on the light and at once feel more secure. On the table lies a yellow portfolio with the poems I have pecked out in triplicate on the Erika typewriter. From time to time I send a few of these to the newspapers. They either come back or there is no answer; then I peck out new copies and try again. I have only twice succeeded in publishing anything in our local newspaper, and then, to be sure, with Georg's help, for he knows the editor. Nevertheless, that was enough for me to be made a member of the Werdenbrück Poets' Club, which meets each week at Eduard Knobloch's in the Old German Room. Eduard recently tried to have me expelled because of the coupons, alleging moral turpitude; but the club declared, in opposition to Eduard, that I had behaved most honorably, just as the business and industrial leaders of our beloved fatherland had been doing for years—and, besides, art had nothing to do with morals.

I push the poems aside. They suddenly seem to me flat and childish, typical of the attempts almost every young man makes at one time or another. I began to write during the war, but then it made some sense—for minutes at a time it took me away from what I was seeing. It was like a little hut of protest and of belief that something else existed beyond destruction and death. But that was a long time ago; today I know that there exists a great deal more besides and I even know that both can exist simultaneously. I no longer need my poems for that; in the books on my shelf it has all been said much better and more convincingly. But what would become of us if that were a reason for giving something up? Where should we all be? So I go on writing, though what I write often seems gray and wooden in comparison with the evening sky which is now growing spacious and apple green above the roofs while twilight fills the streets with a drift of violet-colored ashes.

I go downstairs, past the darkened office and into the garden. The Knopfs' door is open, and inside the three daughters of the family sit around the lamp as though in a fiery cage, busy at their sewing machines. The machines whir. I glance at the window next to the office. It is dark; so Georg has already disappeared somewhere. Heinrich, too, has gone to the reassuring haven of his customary restaurant. I take a turn around the garden. Someone has been sprinkling it; the earth is damp and smells very strong. Wilke's coffin shop is empty, and there is no sound from Kurt Bach. His windows are open; a half-finished, mourning lion cowers on the floor as though it had a toothache, and beside it stand peacefully two empty beer bottles.

Suddenly a bird begins to sing. It is a thrush perched on top of the memorial cross that Heinrich Kroll has bartered away. Its voice is much too big for that little black ball with its yellow beak. It rejoices and mourns and moves my heart. For a moment I reflect that its song, which for me means life and future and dreams and everything undefined, strange, and new, no doubt means to the worms that are working their way up through the damp garden soil around the monument nothing but the dreadful signal of lacerating death from a murderous beak. Nevertheless, I cannot help myself; it carries me away, releasing everything within me; all at once I stand there helpless and lost, amazed that I am not torn apart or that I do not rise like a balloon into the evening sky—until finally I pull myself together and stumble back through the garden and the nocturnal fragrance, up the stairs to my piano, where I pound and caress the keys, trying to be something like the thrush and to pour out what I feel. But nothing much comes of it and in the end it is only a flood of arpeggios and shreds of sentimental ditties and folk songs and bits from the *Rosenkavalier* and *Tristan,* a hopeless medley till finally someone on the street shouts up: "Hey, you, why don't you learn to play?"

I stop abruptly and steal to the window. A dark figure is disappearing into the night; it is already too far away to hit. And why, after all? He is right. I cannot really play. Either at the piano or at life; never, never have I been able to. I have always been too hasty, too impatient; something always intervenes and breaks it up. But who really knows how to play, and if he does know, what good is it to him? Is the great dark less dark for that, are the unanswerable questions less inscrutable, does the pain of despair at eternal inadequacy burn less fiercely, and can life ever be explained and seized and ridden like a tamed horse or is it always a mighty sail that carries us in the storm and, when we try to seize it, sweeps us into the deep? Sometimes there is a hole in me that seems to extend to the center of the earth. What could fill it? Yearning? Despair? Happiness? What happiness? Fatigue? Resignation? Death? What am I alive for? Yes, for what am I alive?

Chapter Three

It is Sunday morning. Bells are ringing from all the steeples, and last night's will-o'-the-wisps have vanished. The dollar still stands at thirty-six thousand, time holds its breath, the crystal of the sky is as yet unmelted by the warmth of day, everything is clear and infinitely clean—it is the morning hour when even the murderer is forgiven and good and evil are empty words.

I dress slowly. Cool, sunny air sweeps through the open window. Like distant sawing, the snores of Sergeant Major Knopf reach me from next door. There is the steely flash of swallows darting through the arch. Like the office below it, my room has two windows—one opening on the courtyard, the other on the street. For a moment I lean against the rear window and look into the garden. Suddenly a dreadful scream breaks the stillness and is followed by gasping and groaning. It is Heinrich Kroll, who sleeps in the other wing. He is having his nightmare again. In 1918 he was buried by an explosion, and now, five years later, he still occasionally dreams about it.

I make coffee on my alcohol stove and pour a little kirsch

into it. That's something I learned in France, and despite the inflation I always manage to have schnaps. My salary is never enough for a new suit—I simply can't save up the money for that, it loses its value too fast—but it takes care of the small items and, of course, a bottle of brandy now and then for comfort.

I have margarine and plum preserve with my bread. The preserve is good; it comes from Mother Kroll's larder. The margarine is rancid, but that doesn't matter; during the war we all ate much worse. I survey my wardrobe. I have two uniforms remodeled into suits. One has been dyed blue, the other black—there wasn't much else to do with the gray-green material. Besides that I still have a suit from the time before I was a soldier. I have outgrown it a little, but it is a genuine civilian garment, not remodeled or adapted, and so I put it on. It goes with the tie that I bought yesterday afternoon and that I am going to wear today so that Isabelle will see it.

I walk contentedly through the streets of the city. Werdenbrück is an ancient town of sixty thousand, with wooden buildings and baroque structures interspersed with dreadful new developments. I cross it and go out along an avenue lined with horse chestnuts, then up a little hill to the big park where the insane asylum stands. There it is, in Sabbath peace, with birds twittering in the trees. I go there to play the organ at Sunday mass in the little church attached to the institution. I learned to play it when I was studying to be a teacher, and a year ago I snapped up the post here as a secondary job. I have a number of them. Once a week I give piano lessons to the rowdy children of Karl Brill, the shoemaker, and in return get my boots resoled and a little money —and twice a week I tutor the idiot son of Bauer, the bookseller, and as a reward I am allowed to read all the new books and am given a discount when I want to make a purchase. Naturally this discount is exploited by the entire membership of the Poets' Club, even by the shameless Eduard Knobloch, who on these occasions suddenly becomes my friend.

The mass begins at nine o'clock. I sit down at the organ and watch the last inmates coming in. They move forward silently and take their places in the pews. A few attendants and nurses sit between them and on the sides. Everything is done softly, much more silently than in the country churches where I played when I was a schoolmaster. There is no sound except the scuffling of shoes on the stone floor; they scuffle, they do not tramp. These are the footsteps of people whose thoughts are far away.

In front of the altar the candles have been lit. The radiance from outside falls through the stained-glass window, mixing with the candle glow in a soft red and blue, transfused with gold. In this glow stands the priest in his brocaded vestments, and on the steps of the altar his assistants kneel in their red gowns and white tunics.

I pull out the stops for flutes and *vox humana* and begin to play. With a jerk the heads of the inmates in the front rows turn around all at once as though pulled by a string. The pale faces and dark eyes stare expressionlessly upward toward the organ. In the dim golden light they float like bright, flat disks; sometimes in winter when it is dark they look like large consecrated wafers waiting for the Holy Ghost to descend upon them. These people never grow accustomed to the organ; they have no past and no memory. Every Sunday the flutes and violins and basses strike their alienated minds as unexpected and new. Then the priest at the altar begins, and they turn toward him.

Not all the inmates follow the mass. In the rear rows there are many who do not move. They sit there as though shrouded in nameless sorrow and surrounded by an infinite void—but perhaps that is only the way it seems. Perhaps they are in different worlds where there has been no word of the crucified Saviour; perhaps they are absorbed harmlessly and innocently in a music by contrast with which the organ sounds pale and crude. Or maybe they are thinking of nothing at all, as indifferent as the sea or life or death. Only we give meaning to nature. What it may be in itself, perhaps those heads down there know, but they cannot betray the secret. What they see has made them dumb. They could be the last descendants of the builders of the Tower of Babel. Their tongues have been twisted and they cannot communicate what they have seen from the highest terraces.

I peer toward the front rows. On the right side in a flicker of rose and blue I see Isabelle's dark head. She is kneeling in her pew very straight and slim. She did not look around when the organ began. Often she does look around, but today she seems so withdrawn into herself that she hears nothing. Her narrow head is inclined to one side like a Gothic statue. She is not praying, she is some place whither no one can follow her. I push back the basses and the *vox humana* and pull out the *vox caelestis*. That is the softest and most rapturous of the organ registers. We are approaching the divine transformation. Bread and wine are becoming the flesh and blood of God. It is a miracle like that other one, the creation of man out of dust and clay. Riesenfeld maintains that the third is man's failure to do anything with that miracle except to exploit and kill his fellow man in increasingly wholesale fashion and to crowd into the brief interval between death and death as much egoism as possible—although only one fact is really certain from the start: that he must die. That's what Riesenfeld says, Riesenfeld of the Odenwald Granite Works, one of the sharpest, most enterprising manipulators in the business of death. *Agnus Dei qui tollis peccata mundi.*

After mass the nurses of the institution give me breakfast of eggs, cold cuts, bouillon, bread, and honey. That's part of my salary. It takes care of the midday meal, for Eduard's coupons are not good on Sunday. In addition, I receive two thousand marks, a sum just sufficient to pay my streetcar fare there and back, if that's what I wanted to use it for. I have never asked for a raise. Why, I do not know; when it comes to Karl Brill and the tutoring lessons for the son of Bauer, the bookseller, I fight for one like a wild goat.

After breakfast I go for a walk in the asylum park. It is a handsome, spacious estate with trees, flowers, and benches surrounded by a high wall; one might think he was in a rest home if he did not notice the bars at the windows.

I love the park because it is quiet and I don't have to talk to anyone about war, politics, or the inflation. I can sit in silence and do such old-fashioned things as listen to the wind and the birds and watch the light filtering through the bright green of the treetops.

Those of the inmates who are allowed out are strolling by. Most are quiet, a few are talking to themselves, one or two carry on lively discussions with one another or with visitors and attendants, and many sit silent and alone, heads bowed and motionless as though turned to stone in the sun—until they are herded back into their cells.

It took me some time to get used to this sight—and even now there are moments when I stare at the madmen as I did in the beginning, with a mixture of curiosity, dread, and a nameless third emotion that reminds me of the first time I saw a corpse. I was twelve then, and the body was that of Georg Hellmann; a week before, I had been playing with him, now he lay there amid wreaths and flowers, a thing unspeakably alien, made of yellow wax, a thing that, in a horrible way, had nothing more to do with us, that had departed for an unthinkable eternity and yet was still there, a speechless, strange, chill threat. Of course, later, in the war,

I saw countless dead men and felt scarcely any more emotion than if I had been in a slaughterhouse—but that first one I never forgot, just as one never forgets any first time. He was death. And it is this same death that sometimes peers at me from the extinguished eyes of the madmen, a living death, more bewildering, almost, and more incomprehensible than that other, silent one.

Only with Isabelle it is different.

I see her coming toward me along the path from the women's pavilion. A yellow dress billows around her like a bell of shantung silk, and in her hand she is carrying a broad, flat straw hat.

I get up and go to meet her. Her face is narrow, and one really sees only the eyes and mouth. The eyes are gray and green and very transparent; the mouth is as red as that of a consumptive or as though it were heavily painted. The eyes, however, can suddenly become shallow, slate-colored, and small, and the mouth narrow and bitter like that of an old maid. When she is that way, she is Jennie, a distrustful, unattractive person, discontented with everything you do —otherwise she is Isabelle. Both are illusions, for in reality she is Geneviève Terhoven and is suffering from an illness that has the ugly and rather spectral name of schizophrenia —a division of consciousness, a split personality—and that is the reason she considers herself either Isabelle or Jennie —someone other than she really is. She is one of the youngest patients in the asylum. Her mother is said to live in Alsace and to be quite rich but to pay little attention to her. In any event, I have not seen her here since I have known Geneviève, and that is now six weeks.

Today she is Isabelle, as I see immediately. At such times she lives in a dream world divorced from reality and seems light and weightless and I would not be surprised if the sulphur butterflies, playing around us, came and settled on her shoulders.

"There you are again!" she says, smiling. "Where have you been all this time?"

When she is Isabelle she says *du* to me. This is no particular distinction; at such times she says *du* to everyone. "Where have you been?" she asks again.

I make a gesture in the direction of the gate. "Somewhere—out there—"

She looks at me for an instant inquiringly. "Out there? Why? Are you looking for something?"

"I guess so—if I only knew what!"

She comes close to me. "Give it up, Rolf. One never finds anything."

I recoil at the name Rolf. Unfortunately, she often calls me that, for just as she takes herself for someone else, so, too, does she me, and not always for the same person. She alternates between Rolf and Rudolf, and once a certain Raoul turned up. Rolf is a boring fellow whom I cannot stand; Raoul seems to be a sort of gay deceiver—what I like best is when she calls me Rudolf, then she is enthusiastic and in love. My real name, Ludwig Bodmer, she ignores. I have told it to her often, but it simply does not make any impression.

During the first weeks this was all very confusing, but now I am accustomed to it. At that time I had the common conception of mental illnesses: nothing but continuous violence, attempts at murder, and gibbering idiots. They exist, of course, and they are more frequent than the other; but just by contrast Geneviève is all the more surprising. At first I could hardly believe that she was sick at all, so playful seemed her alternations of name and personality, and even now that still sometimes happens to me. Finally I realized, however, that in the silence, behind these fragile structures, was a quivering chaos. It did not quite penetrate, but it was close at hand, and this, combined with the fact that Isabelle was just twenty and, because of her illness, sometimes of an almost tragic beauty, gave her a strange fascination.

"Come, Rolf," she says, taking my arm.

I try again to escape the hated name. "I am not Rolf," I explain. "I'm Rudolf."

"You are not Rudolf."

"Oh yes, I'm Rudolf. Rudolf, the unicorn."

She called me that once. But I have no success. She smiles, as one does at a stubborn child. "You're not Rudolf and you are not Rolf. But neither are you what you think you are. Now come, Rolf!"

I look at her. For a moment I again have the feeling that she is not sick at all and is only pretending. "Don't be boring," she says. "Why do you always want to be the same person?"

"Yes, why?" I reply in surprise. "You're right! Why does one want to be? What is there so precious about a person? And why does one take oneself so seriously?"

She nods. "You and the doctor! But in the end the wind blows over everything. Why won't you two yield to it?"

"The doctor too?" I ask.

"Yes, the man who calls himself that. The things he wants to find out from me! But he knows nothing at all. Not even how the grass looks at night when no one is watching."

"How can it look? Gray, probably, or black. And silvery when the moon is shining."

Isabelle shakes her head. "Just as I thought! Just like the doctor!"

"How does it look then?"

She stops. A gust of wind blows over us laden with bees and the smell of flowers. The yellow dress billows like a sail. "It isn't there at all," she says.

We walk on. An old woman in asylum clothes comes past us along the *allée*. Her face is red and glistening with tears.

Two helpless relatives walk beside her. "What *is* there, then, if the grass isn't?" I ask.

"Nothing. It's only there while you're watching. Sometimes if you turn around very fast you can still catch it."

"What? The grass not being there?"

"No—but the way it scurries back to its place. That's how they all are—the grass and everything that's behind you. Like servants who have gone to a dance. You just have to be very quick in turning around. Then you can catch them —otherwise they're already there, acting as innocent as if they'd never been away."

"Who, Isabelle?" I ask very cautiously.

"Things. Everything behind you. They're just waiting for you to turn around so they can disappear!"

I consider that for a moment. It would be like having an abyss behind you all the time. "Am I not there either when you turn around?" I ask.

"You aren't there either. Nothing is."

"Really?" I say somewhat bitterly. "But for me I am always there. No matter how fast I turn around."

"You turn around in the wrong direction."

"Are there different directions too?"

"For you there are, Rolf."

I recoil once more at the hated name. "And for you? What about you?"

She looks at me, smiling absently as though she did not know me. "I? But I'm not here at all!"

"Really? You certainly are for me."

Her expression changes. She knows me again. "Is that true? Why then don't you say it to me more often?"

"But I say it to you all the time."

"Not enough." She leans against me. I feel her breath and her breasts under the thin silk. "Never enough," she says with a sigh. "Why doesn't anyone know that? Oh, you statues!"

Statues, I think. What other role is left for me? I look at her. She is beautiful and exciting, I am aware of her, and every time I am with her it is as if a thousand voices were telephoning through my veins; then suddenly all are cut off as though they had a wrong number, and I find myself helpless and confused. One cannot desire a madwoman. Perhaps some can, not I. It is as though you were to desire a clockwork doll. Or someone hypnotized. But that does not alter the fact that you are aware of her.

The green shadows of the *allée* part, and in front of us beds of tulips and narcissuses lie in the full sun. "You must put your hat on, Isabelle," I say. "The doctor wants you to."

She throws her hat among the flowers. "The doctor! What doesn't he want! He wants to marry me, but his heart is starved. He's a sweating owl."

I don't think that owls can sweat, but the image is convincing nevertheless. Isabelle steps among the tulips like a dancer and crouches there. "Can you hear them?"

"Of course," I reply in relief. "Anyone can hear them. They're bells. In F sharp."

"What is F sharp?"

"A musical note. The sweetest of all."

She throws her wide skirt over the flowers. "Are they ringing in me now?"

I nod, looking at her slender neck. Everything rings in you, I think. She breaks off a tulip and looks at the open blossom and the fleshy stem from which sap is oozing. "They are not sweet."

"All right—then they're bells in C sharp."

"Must it be sharp?"

"It could be flat."

"Can't it be both at the same time?"

"Not in music. There are certain rules. It can be only one or the other. Or one after the other."

"One after the other!" Isabelle looks at me with mild contempt. "You always use these pretexts, Rolf. Why?"

"I don't know either. I wish things were otherwise."

Suddenly she straightens up and throws away the tulip she has picked. With a leap she is out of the bed and is vigorously shaking her dress. Then she pulls it up and looks at her legs. Her face is twisted with disgust. "What happened?" I ask in alarm.

She points at the bed. "Snakes—"

I glance at the beds. "There aren't any snakes there, Isabelle."

"Yes there are! Those there!" She points at the tulips. "Don't you see what they want?"

"They don't want anything. They are flowers," I say uncomprehendingly.

"They touched me!" She is trembling with disgust and staring at the tulips.

I take her by the arm and turn her around so that she can no longer see the bed. "Now you're turned around," I say. "Now they're not there any more, Isabelle."

She is breathing heavily. "Don't permit it! Stamp on them, Rudolf."

"They're not there any more. You have turned around and now they're gone. Like the grass at night and the things."

She leans against me. Suddenly I am no longer Rolf. She presses her face against my shoulder. She doesn't have to explain anything more to me. I am Rudolf and must know. "Are you sure?" she asks, and I feel her heart beating against my hand.

"Perfectly sure. They're gone. Like servants on Sunday."

"Don't permit it, Rudolf."

"I won't permit it," I say, not knowing what she means. But that's unimportant. She is already growing calmer.

We walk back slowly. Almost without transition she becomes tired. A nurse marches up on flat heels. "You must come and eat, Mademoiselle."

"Eat," Isabelle says. "Why must one eat all the time, Rudolf?"

"So that you won't die."

"You're lying again," she says wearily, like a helpless child.

"Not this time. This time it's true."

"Really? Do stones eat?"

"Are stones alive?"

"Of course. More intensely than anything. So intensely that they are eternal. Don't you know what a crystal is?"

"Only from my physics lessons. That's sure to be wrong."

"Pure ecstasy," Isabelle whispers. "Not like those over there—" She makes a gesture back toward the flower bed.

The attendant takes her arm. "Where is your hat, Mademoiselle?" she asks after a few steps, looking around. "Wait a moment, I'll get it."

She goes to retrieve the hat from among the flowers. Behind her Isabelle comes over to me hastily, her expression distraught. "Don't abandon me, Rudolf!" she whispers.

"I won't abandon you."

"And don't go away! I have to leave. They are taking me! But don't you go away!"

"I won't go away, Isabelle."

The attendant has rescued the hat and now marches up to us like fate on broad soles. Isabelle stands there looking at me. It is as though it were farewell forever. It's always as though it were a farewell forever. Who knows how she will be when she returns?

"Put your hat on, Mademoiselle," says the attendant.

Isabelle takes it and lets it hang loose from her hand. The light in her eyes goes out. She turns and goes back to the pavilion. She does not look around.

It all began one day early in March when Geneviève suddenly came up to me in the park and began to talk to me as though we had known each other for a long time. There was nothing unusual about that—in the asylum you don't need to be introduced; you are beyond formalities here, and people speak to each other when they feel like it, without lengthy preambles. They speak at once about whatever comes into their heads, and it makes no difference if the other does not understand—that's unimportant. One doesn't want to persuade or to explain; one is there and one speaks, and often two people talk to each other splendidly because neither listens to what the other is saying. Pope Gregory VII, for example, a little man with bandy legs, does not argue. He does not need to persuade anyone that he is pope. He is, and that's the end of it. He is having serious troubles with Henry IV; Canossa is not far off, and sometimes he talks about it. It doesn't matter that his interlocutor is a man who believes he is made entirely of glass and begs everyone not to jostle him because he is already cracked—the two talk together, Gregory about the king who must do penance in his shirt, and the glass man about how he cannot stand the sun because it is reflected in him —then Gregory bestows the papal blessing, the glass man for an instant takes off the cloth that protects his transparent head against the sun, and both take leave of each other with the courtesy of past centuries. So I was not surprised when Geneviève came up to me and began to talk; I was only surprised at how beautiful she was, for at that moment she was Isabelle.

She talked to me for a long time. She was wearing a light cape of blond fur that was worth at least ten or twenty memorial crosses of the best Swedish granite; with it she wore an evening dress and gold sandals. It was eleven o'clock in the morning, and in the world beyond the walls this costume would have been surprising. Here, however, it was simply exciting; as though someone had drifted down in a parachute from some happier planet.

It was a day of sun, showers, wind, and sudden stillness. They whirled together in confusion; one hour it was March, the next April, and then without transition a day in May or June. Into this confusion came Isabelle from God knows where—from somewhere beyond boundaries, where the light of reason penetrates only in distorted streams, like the aurora borealis, across skies that know neither day nor night, only their own echoing beams and the echoes of those echoes and the pale light of the Beyond and of timeless vastness.

She confused me from the start, and all the advantages were on her side. I had, to be sure, got rid of many bourgeois concepts in the war, but this had only made me cynical and a little desperate, not superior and free. So I sat there and stared at her as though she were a creature without weight hovering in the air while I stumbled awkwardly after her. Moreover, a strange wisdom often flickered in what she said; it was only displaced and then, astoundingly, it would reveal vistas that made one's heart pound; but when one tried to hold onto it, veils of mist intervened, and Isabelle was already somewhere else.

She kissed me on that first day, and she did it so naturally that it seemed to mean nothing at all; but that did not keep me from feeling it. I felt it, it excited me, and then it struck like a wave against the barrier reef—I knew she did not mean me at all; she meant someone else, some figure of her fantasy, Rolf or Rudolf; and perhaps she did not mean them either, perhaps they were just names thrown up from dark, subterranean streams, without roots or connections.

From then on she came into the garden almost every

Sunday; when it was raining she came to the chapel. The Mother Superior allowed me to practice on the organ after mass when I felt like it. I did it on rainy days. I did not really practice, my playing was not good enough to be called that; I simply played for myself, as I did on my piano, vague fantasies of one sort or another, dreams and yearning for the unknown, for the future, for fulfillment, and for my own self; to do that one does not have to play especially well. Sometimes Isabelle came with me and listened. On those days she would sit below me in the half-dark, the rain would beat against the stained-glass windows, and the organ tones would go out over her dark head—I did not know what she was thinking, and it was strange and rather touching, but suddenly in the background loomed the question Why, the screaming terror, the fear, and the silence. I felt all that and I felt, too, something of the incomprehensible loneliness of the creature when we were in that empty church with the twilight and the organ tones, only we two alone as though we were the last creatures, held together by the half-light, the music, and the rain, and nevertheless separated forever, without a bridge, without understanding, without words, with only the strange glow of the little campfires on the outskirts of the life within us which we saw and misunderstood, she in her fashion, I in mine, blind and deaf and dumb without being either dumb or deaf or blind, and for that reason much poorer and more bereft. What was it in her that had made her come up to me? I did not know and would never know —it was buried under the rubble of a landslide—nor did I understand why this strange relationship should confuse me so since I knew what was wrong with her and that she did not mean me. Nevertheless, it filled me with undefined yearning and disturbed me and sometimes made me happy and unhappy without rhyme or reason.

A little nurse comes up to me. "Mother Superior would like to speak to you."

I get up and follow her, feeling uncomfortable. Perhaps one of the nurses has been spying and the Mother Superior is going to tell me that I am not to speak to inmates under sixty, or she may even dismiss me, although the physician in charge has said that it is a good thing for Isabelle to have company.

The Mother Superior receives me in her reception room. It smells of floor wax, virtue, and soap. Not a breath of spring has penetrated here. The Mother Superior, a gaunt, energetic woman, greets me cordially; she considers me a model Christian who loves God and believes in the Church. "Soon it will be May," she says, looking me straight in the eye.

"Yes," I reply, examining the snowy white curtains and the bare, shining floor.

"We have been wondering whether we could not hold some May devotions."

I am silent and relieved. "In the city churches there are devotions every evening at eight during May," the Mother Superior explains.

I nod. I know those May devotions. Incense wells up through the twilight, the monstrance gleams, and after the devotion young people wander about in the squares for a time under the old trees where the June bugs buzz. To be sure, I never attend; but I know about them from the time before I was a soldier. That was my first experience with girls. It was all very exciting and secret and harmless. But I wouldn't think of coming up here every evening for a month to play the organ.

"We would like to have a devotion at least on Sunday evenings," says the Mother Superior. "I mean a formal one with organ music and the *Te Deum*. There are simple prayers every evening for the nuns as it is."

I reflect. Sunday evenings are tiresome in the city, and the devotion lasts barely an hour. "We can pay you very little," the Mother Superior explains. "The same as for the mass. That's probably not much now, is it?"

"No," I say. "It's not much now. We have an inflation outside."

"I know." She stands there undecided. "The Church's way of dealing with requests is unfortunately not adapted to these times. The Church thinks in centuries. We must accept that. After all, one works for God and not for money. Don't you agree?"

"One can work for both," I reply. "That's a particularly happy situation."

She sighs. "We are bound by the decisions of the Church authorities. They are taken once a year, no oftener."

"For the salaries of the pastors, the cathedral chaplains, and the bishop too?" I ask.

"I don't know about that," she says, flushing a little. "But I think so."

Meanwhile, I have made up my mind. "This evening I haven't time," I explain. "We have an important business meeting."

"But today is still April. Now, next Sunday—or if you can't do it on Sundays perhaps some day of the week. After all, it would be nice to have proper May devotions. The Divine Mother will certainly reward you."

"Unquestionably. Then there is only the problem of supper. Eight o'clock is just in between. Afterward is too late and beforehand it would be a scramble."

"Oh, as far as that is concerned, of course you could eat here if you liked. His Reverence always eats here too. Perhaps that's a solution."

It is exactly the solution I wanted. The food here is almost as good as at Eduard's, and if I eat in company with the priest there is certain to be a bottle of wine as well. Since

Eduard refuses to accept tickets on Sunday, this is indeed a splendid solution.

"All right," I say. "I'll try to do it. We don't need to say any more about the money."

The Mother Superior sighs with relief. "God will reward you."

I walk back. The garden paths are empty. For a time I wait for the yellow sail of shantung silk. Then the bells of the city ring for midday, and I know it's time for Isabelle's nap and after that the doctor; there is nothing more to be done until four o'clock. I walk through the big gate and down the hill.

Beneath me lies the city with its steeples green with verdigris and its smoking chimneys. On both sides of the *allée,* beyond the horse chestnut trees, stretch the fields where on weekdays the nondangerous inmates work. The institution is part public, part private. The private patients, of course, do not have to work. Beyond the fields are woods, streams, ponds, and clearings. When I was a boy I used to fish there and catch salamanders and butterflies. That was only ten years ago, but it seems to belong to a different life —to a vanished time in which existence proceeded in orderly organic sequence and everything belonged together, from childhood on. The war changed that; since 1914 we live scraps of one life and then scraps of a second and a third; they do not belong together and we are not able to put them together. For this reason it is really not so hard for me to understand Isabelle and her different lives. Only she is almost better off in this respect than we are; when she is in one, she forgets all the others. With us they are hopelessly confused—childhood, cut short by the war, the time of hunger and fraud, of trenches and lust for life— something of all these has been left over and remains with us even now, making us restless. You cannot simply push it away. It keeps bobbing back disconcertingly, and then you are confronted by irreconcilable contrast: the skies of childhood and the science of killing, lost youth and the cynicism of knowledge gained too young.

Chapter Four

We are sitting in the office waiting for Riesenfeld. For supper we had pea soup so thick a spoon would stand up in it; in addition, we ate the meat cooked in the soup—pigs' feet, pigs' ears, and a very fat piece of side meat for each of us. We need the fat to coat our stomachs against alcohol; we must not on any account get drunk before Riesenfeld does. And so Frau Kroll has done the cooking for us herself and as dessert has forced on us a helping of fat Dutch cheese. The future of the firm is at stake. We must wring a shipment of granite out of Riesenfeld even if we have to crawl home in front of him on our hands and knees to do it. Marble, shell lime, and sandstone we still have, but we are in bitter need of granite, the caviar of sorrow.

Heinrich Kroll has been removed from the scene. Wilke, the coffinmaker, has done us this service. We gave him two bottles of schnaps and he invited Heinrich to a game of skat with free drinks before dinner. Heinrich was taken in; he can never resist getting something for nothing, and on such occasions he drinks as fast as he can; moreover, like every nationalist, he considers himself a very clearheaded drinker. In reality he can't stand anything at all, and drink overtakes him suddenly. One moment he is ready to drive the Social Democratic party out of the Reichstag singlehanded and the next he is snoring openmouthed, not even to be aroused by the command On your feet, forward march! This is particularly true when he has been drinking on an empty stomach, as we have arranged for him to do. Now he is innocently sleeping in Wilke's workshop in an oak coffin, comfortably bedded down on wood shavings. In our concern about waking him, we did not carry him back to his own bed. Wilke is now in the ground-floor studio of our sculptor, Kurt Bach, playing dominoes with him, a game both love because it gives them so much time for thought. They are engaged in drinking up the bottle and a quarter of schnaps left over from Heinrich's defeat and claimed by Wilke as an honorarium.

The shipment of granite we want to extract from Riesenfeld is something we cannot, of course, pay for in advance. We never have that much money at one time and it would be madness to try to accumulate it in the bank—it would melt away like snow in June. Therefore we want to give Riesenfeld a promissory note payable in three months. That means we want to pay practically nothing.

Naturally, Riesenfeld must not lose on the transaction. That shark in the ocean of human tears needs to make a profit like every honest businessman. And so on the day he receives the note from us he must take it to his bank or ours and have it discounted. The bank ascertains that both Riesenfeld and we are good for its face value, deducts a few per cent for discounting the note, and pays out the money. We pay back to Riesenfeld the amount of the bank's commission. Thus, he receives full payment for the shipment just as though we had paid in advance. Nor does the bank lose. It immediately sends the note to the Reichsbank, which in turn pays just as the bank paid Riesenfeld. And there in the Reichsbank it remains until, on the expiration date, it is presented for payment. What it will be worth then is easy to imagine.

We have only known about all this since 1922. Before then we tried to transact business in the same way as Heinrich Kroll and almost went broke doing it. We had sold out almost our entire inventory and, to our amazement, had nothing to show for it except a worthless bank account and a few suitcases full of currency not even good enough to paper our walls with. We tried at first to sell and then buy again as quickly as possible—but the inflation easily overtook us. The lag before we got paid was too long; while we waited, the value of money fell so fast that even our most profitable sale turned into a loss. Only after we began to pay with promissory notes could we maintain our position. Even so, we are making no real profit now, but at least we can live. Since every enterprise in Germany is financed in this fashion, the Reichsbank naturally has to keep on printing unsecured currency and so the mark falls faster and faster. The government apparently doesn't care; all it loses in this way is the national debt. Those who are ruined are the people who cannot pay with notes, the people who have property they are forced to sell, small shopkeepers, day laborers, people with small incomes who see their private savings and their bank accounts melting away, and government officials and employees who have to survive on salaries that no longer allow them to buy so much as a new pair of shoes. The ones who profit are the exchange kings, the profiteers, the foreigners who buy what they like with a few dollars, kronen, or zlotys, and the big entrepreneurs, the manufacturers, and the speculators on the exchange whose property and stocks increase without limit. For them practically everything is free. It is the great sellout of thrift, honest effort, and respectability. The vultures flock from all sides, and the only ones who come out on top are those who accumulate debts. The debts disappear of themselves.

It was Riesenfeld who at the last instant instructed us in these matters and turned us into small-time participants in the great sellout. He accepted our first ninety-day note, although at the time we were by no means good for the sum on the face of it. But the Odenwald Granite Works was, and that was enough.

Naturally we were grateful. We tried to entertain him like an Indian rajah when he came to Werdenbrück—that is, insofar as an Indian rajah could be entertained in Werdenbrück. Kurt Bach, our sculptor, made a colorful portrait of Riesenfeld which we solemnly presented to him. Unfortunately, he did not like it. It makes him look like a country preacher, which is exactly what he does not want. He wants to look like a dark seducer and he assumes that that is the effect he makes—a remarkable example of self-deception, considering his pointed belly, and short, bandy legs. But who does not live by self-deception? I, with my innocuous, average talents, do I not cherish, especially at night, the dream of becoming a better man with ability enough to find a publisher? In these circumstances who is to throw the first stone at Riesenfeld's parenthetical legs, especially when they, at a time like this, are clad in genuine English tweeds?

"What in the world are we going to do with him, Georg?" I ask. "This time we haven't a single attraction! Riesenfeld won't be satisfied with just getting drunk. He has too much imagination and too restless a character for that. He wants something he can see and hear, or, better yet, grab hold of. Our choice of women is hopeless. The few pretty ones we know haven't the slightest desire to spend a whole evening listening to Riesenfeld in his role of Don Juan of 1923. Unfortunately, helpfulness and understanding are only to be found among the older and homely dames."

Georg grins. "I don't even know whether our cash will last out the night. When I got the stuff I made a mistake about the dollar rate; I thought it was still the same as at ten o'clock. When the twelve o'clock quotation was announced, it was too late."

"On the other hand there's been no change today."

"There has at the Red Mill, my boy. On Sundays they're two days ahead of the dollar rate there. God knows what a bottle of wine will cost tonight!"

"God doesn't know either," I say. "The proprietor himself doesn't know. He only decides on the price when the electric light goes on. Why doesn't Riesenfeld have a passion for the arts? That would be a lot cheaper. Admission to the museum still costs only two hundred and fifty marks. For that we could show him pictures and plaster heads for hours. Or music. There's an organ concert at St. Catherine's today—"

Georg chokes with laughter. "Well, all right," I admit, "it's absurd to picture Riesenfeld in such a setting; but why doesn't he at least love operettas and light music? We could take him to the theater, and it would still be much less than that damn night club!"

"Here he comes," Georg says. "Ask him."

We open the door. Through the early spring evening Riesenfeld comes sailing up the steps. We see at once that the enchantment of spring twilight has had no effect on him. We greet him with false camaraderie. Riesenfeld notices it, squints at us, and drops into a chair. "Quit the play acting," he growls in my direction.

"That's just what I was going to do," I reply. "It's not easy for me. What you call play acting is known elsewhere as good manners."

Riesenfeld grins briefly and evilly. "Good manners won't get you far these days—"

"They won't? Then what will?" I ask to draw him out.

"Cast-iron elbows and a rubber conscience."

"But, Herr Riesenfeld," Georg says reassuringly, "you yourself have the best manners in the world! Perhaps not the best in the bourgeois sense—but certainly the most elegant—"

"Really? There's just a chance you might be mistaken!" Despite his disclaimer Riesenfeld is flattered.

"He has the manners of a robber," I remark, exactly as Georg expects. We play this game without rehearsal, as though we knew it by heart. "Or rather those of a pirate. Unfortunately, they bring him success."

Riesenfeld has recoiled a little at the word robber; the shot went too near home. But "pirate" reassures him. Exactly as intended. Georg gets a bottle of Roth schnaps out of the cupboard where the porcelain angels stand and pours. "What shall we drink to?" he asks.

Ordinarily people drink to health and success in business. With us it's a bit difficult. Riesenfeld's too sensitive a nature for that; he maintains that in the tombstone business such a toast is not only a paradox but the equivalent of wishing that as many people as possible may die. One might as well drink to cholera, war, and influenza. Since then we have left the toasts to him.

He stares at us sidewise, his glass in his hand, but does not speak. After a while he says suddenly in the half-darkness: "What actually is time?"

Georg puts his glass down in astonishment. "The pepper of life," I reply. The old rascal can't catch me so easily with his tricks. Not for nothing am I a member of the Werdenbrück Poets' Club; we are used to big questions.

Riesenfeld disregards me. "What's your opinion, Herr Kroll?" he asks.

"I'm a simple man," Georg says. *"Prost!"*

"Time," Riesenfeld continues doggedly. "Time, this uninterrupted flow—not our lousy time! Time, this gradual death."

Now I, too, put down my glass. "I think we'd better have some light," I say. "What did you eat for dinner, Herr Riesenfeld?"

"Shut up, youngster, when grownups are talking," Riesenfeld replies, and I notice that I have been inattentive for a moment. He did not intend to disconcert us—he means what he says. God knows what has happened to him this afternoon! I am tempted to reply that time is an important factor in the note we want him to accept—but content myself with my drink instead.

"I'm fifty-six now," Riesenfeld says, "but I remember the time when I was twenty as though it were only a couple of years ago. What's become of everything in between? What's happened? Suddenly you wake up and find you're old. What about you, Herr Kroll?"

"Much the same," Georg replies. "I'm forty but I often feel sixty. In my case it was the war."

He is lying to support Riesenfeld. "It's different with me," I explain. "Also because of the war. I went in when I was a little over seventeen. Now I am twenty-five; but I still feel like seventeen. Like seventeen and seventy. The War Department stole my youth."

"With you it was not the war," Riesenfeld replies. "You're simply a case of arrested intellectual development. That would have happened to you if there'd never been a war. As a matter of fact, the war really made you precocious; without it you would still be at the twelve-year-old level."

"Thanks," I say. "What a compliment! At twelve everyone is a genius. He only loses his originality with the onset of sexual maturity, to which you, you granite Casanova, attribute such exaggerated importance. That's a pretty monstrous compensation for loss of spiritual freedom."

Georg fills our glasses again. We see that it is going to be a tough evening. We must get Riesenfeld out of the depths of cosmic melancholy, and neither one of us is especially keen on being involved in philosophical platitudes tonight. We should prefer to sit quietly under a chestnut tree and drink a bottle of Moselle instead of in the Red Mill commiserating with Riesenfeld over his lost youth.

"If you're interested in the relativity of time," I say, briefly hopeful, "then I can introduce you to a society where you can meet experts in that field—the Poets' Club of this dear city. Hans Hungermann, the writer, has elucidated the problem in an unpublished sequence of sixty poems. We can go there right now; there's a meeting every Sunday night with a social hour afterward."

"Are there women there?"

"Naturally not. Women poets are like calculating horses. With the exception, of course, of Sappho's pupils."

"Well then, what's the social hour?" Riesenfeld asks.

"It consists of running down other writers. Especially the successful ones."

Riesenfeld grunts contemptuously. I am ready to give up. Suddenly the window in the horse butcher's house across the street lights up like a brightly lit painting in a dark museum. Behind the curtains we see Lisa. She is just getting dressed and has nothing on except a brassière and a pair of very short white silk panties.

Riesenfeld emits a snort like a ground hog. His cosmic melancholy has disappeared like magic. I get up to turn on the light. "No light!" he snaps. "Have you no feeling for poetry?"

He creeps to the window. Lisa begins to draw a tight dress over her head. She writhes like a serpent. Riesenfeld snorts aloud. "A seductive creature! *Donnerwetter,* what a rear end! A dream! Who is she?"

"Susanna in the bath," I explain, trying to intimate delicately that at the moment we are in the role of the old goats watching her.

"Nonsense!" The voyeur with the Einstein complex never moves his eyes from the golden window. "I mean what's her name."

"I haven't the slightest idea. This is the first time we've seen her. She wasn't even living there at noon today," I say to whet his interest.

"Really?" Lisa has got her dress on and is now smoothing it down with her hands. Behind Riesenfeld's back Georg fills his glass and mine. We toss off the drinks. "A woman of breeding," Riesenfeld says, continuing to cling to the window. "A lady, that's easy to see. Probably French."

As far as we know, Lisa comes from Bohemia. "It might be Mademoiselle de la Tour," I reply. "I heard someone mention that name yesterday."

"You see!" Riesenfeld turns around to us for an instant. "I told you she was French! One can tell right away—that *je ne sais quoi!* Don't you think so too, Herr Kroll?"

"You're the connoisseur, Herr Riesenfeld."

The light in Lisa's room goes off. Riesenfeld pours his drink down his time-parched throat and once more presses his face against the window. After a while Lisa appears at the door and goes down the steps into the street. Riesenfeld stares after her. "An enchanting walk! She does not mince; she takes long strides. A lithe, luscious panther! Women who mince are always a disappointment. But I give you my guarantee for that one."

At the words "lithe, luscious panther" I have quickly downed another drink. Georg has sunk into his chair, grinning silently. We have turned the trick. Now Riesenfeld whirls around. His face shimmers like a pale moon. "Light, gentlemen! What are we waiting for? Forward into life!"

We follow him into the mild night. I stare at his froglike back. If only, I think enviously, it were as easy for me to bob up from my gray hours as it is for this quick-change artist.

The Red Mill is jam packed. All we can get is a table next to the orchestra. The music is too loud anyway, but at our table it is completely deafening. At first we shout our observations into one another's ears; after that we content ourselves with signs like a trio of deaf mutes. The dance floor is so crowded that the dancers can hardly move. But that doesn't matter to Riesenfeld. He spies a woman in white silk at the bar and rushes up to her. Proudly he propels her with his pointed belly across the dance floor. She is a head taller than he and stares in boredom at the balloon-hung ceiling. Lower down, Riesenfeld seethes and smolders like Vesuvius. His demon has seized him. "How would it be if we poured some brandy into his wine to make him tight quicker?" I ask Georg. "The boy is drinking like a spotted wild ass! This is our fifth bottle! In two hours we'll be bankrupt if it goes on like this. I estimate we've already drunk up a couple of imitation marble tombstones. Here's hoping he doesn't bring that white ghost to our table so that we'll have to quench her thirst too."

Georg shakes his head. "That's a bar girl. She'll have to go back."

Riesenfeld returns. He is red in the face and sweating. "What does all this amount to compared to the magic of fantasy!" he roars at us through the confusion. "Tangible reality, well and good! But where's the poetry? That window tonight against the dark sky—that was something to dream about! A woman like that, even if you never see her again, is something you'll never forget. Understand what I mean?"

"Sure," Georg shouts. "What you can't get always seems better than what you have. That's the origin of all human romanticism and idiocy. *Prost,* Riesenfeld!"

"I don't mean it so coarsely," Riesenfeld roars against the fox trot "Oh, if St. Peter Knew That." "I mean it more delicately."

"So do I," Georg roars back.

"I mean it even more delicately!"

"All right! As delicately as you like!"

The music rises to a mighty crescendo. The dance floor is a variegated sardine box. Suddenly I stiffen. Laced into the trappings of a monkey in fancy dress, my sweetheart Erna is pushing her way through the swaying mob to my right. She does not see me, but I recognize her red hair from afar. She is hanging shamelessly on the shoulder of a typical young profiteer. I sit there motionless, but I feel as though I had swallowed a hand grenade. There she is dancing, the little beast to whom ten of the poems in my unpublished collection "Dust and Starlight" are dedicated, the girl who has been pretending for a week that she is not allowed out of the house because of a mild case of concussion. She says she fell in the dark. Fell indeed, but into the arms of this young man in the double-breasted tuxedo, with a seal ring on the paw with which he is supporting the small of Erna's back. A fine case of concussion! And I, imbecile that I am, sent her just this afternoon a bunch of rose-colored tulips from our garden with a poem in three stanzas entitled "Pan's May Devotions." Suppose she read it aloud to this profiteer! I can see the two doubled up with laughter.

"What's the matter with you?" Riesenfeld roars. "Are you sick?"

"Hot!" I roar back and feel sweat running down my back. I am furious; if Erna turns around she will see me perspiring and red in the face—when more than anything I should like to appear superior and cool and at my ease like a man of the world. Quickly I wipe my face with my handkerchief. Riesenfeld grins unsympathetically. Georg notices this. "You're sweating quite a bit yourself, Riesenfeld," he says.

"That's different! This sweat comes from the joy of life!" Riesenfeld roars.

"It's the sweat of fleeting time," I snarl maliciously and feel the salt water trickling into the corners of my mouth.

Erna is near us now. She is staring out over the orchestra in vacant happiness. I give my face a mildly reproachful, superior, and smiling expression while the sweat wilts my collar. "What's the matter with you anyway?" Riesenfeld shouts. "You look like a moon-struck kangaroo!"

I ignore him. Erna has finally turned around. I look toward the dancers, examining them coolly until at last, with an expression of surprise, I pretend accidentally to recognize her. Casually I lift two fingers in greeting. "He is *meschugge*," Riesenfeld howls through the syncopation of the fox trot *"Himmelsvater."*

I do not reply. I am literally speechless. Erna has not seen me at all.

Finally the music stops. Slowly the dance floor empties. Erna disappears into a booth. "Were you seventeen or seventy just now?" Riesenfeld howls.

Since at this moment the orchestra is silent, his question thunders through the room. A couple of dozen heads turn to look at us, and even Riesenfeld is startled. I want to creep quickly under the table; but then it occurs to me that the people around us may have taken the question for a business offer and I reply coldly and loudly: "Seventy-one dollars apiece and not a cent less."

My reply awakens immediate interest. "What's the merchandise?" asks a man with a child's face at the next table. "Perhaps I'll get into the act. I'm always interested in good items. Cash, of course. Aufstein is the name."

"Felix Koks," I complete the introduction, happy to be able to pull myself together. "The items were twenty bottles of perfume. Unfortunately, the gentleman over there has just bought them."

"Sh—" whispers an artificial blonde.

The entertainment has begun. A master of ceremonies is talking nonsense and is furious because nobody likes his jokes. I pull my chair back and disappear behind Aufstein; masters of ceremonies, bent on attacking the audience, always love to pick on me, and tonight that would be bad because of Erna.

Everything goes fine. The master of ceremonies disappears in disgust, and who should suddenly appear in a white bridal dress and veil but Renée de la Tour. Relieved, I pull my chair back and wonder how I can use my acquaintance with Renée to impress Erna.

Renée begins her duet. Docilely and modestly she trills a few verses in a high, maidenly soprano—then comes the bass and makes an immediate sensation. "How do you like the lady?" I ask Riesenfeld.

"Lady?"

"Would you like to meet her? Mademoiselle de la Tour."

Riesenfeld is taken aback. "La Tour? Are you going to pretend that this absurd freak of nature is the enchantress in the window opposite you?"

That's just what I am about to pretend, in order to see how he reacts, when I notice a sort of angelic glow hovering about his elephantine snout. Without a word he gestures toward the entrance with his thumb. "There—over there—there she is! That walk! You recognize it instantly!"

He is right. Lisa has entered. She is in the company of two middle-aged playboys and is behaving like a lady of the most cultivated society, at least according to Riesenfeld's conceptions. She hardly seems to breathe and listens to her cavaliers with haughty distraction. "Am I right?" Riesenfeld asks. "You recognize women instantly by their walk, don't you?"

"Yes. Women and policemen," Georg says grinning; but he, too, looks appreciatively at Lisa.

The second number begins. A girl acrobat stands on the dance floor. She is young, with an impudent face, short nose, and beautiful legs. She does an adagio with somersaults, handstands, and leaps. We go on watching Lisa. She apparently wants to leave the place again. That, of course, is pretense; there's only this one night club in the city; the rest are cafés, restaurants, or dives. That's why one meets everyone here who has enough cash to get in.

"Champagne!" roars Riesenfeld in a dictator's voice.

I am alarmed; Georg, too, is worried. "Herr Riesenfeld," I say, "the champagne here is very bad."

At that moment a face looks at me from the floor. I look back in amazement and see that it is the dancer, who has bent over backward so far that her head protrudes from between her legs. For a second she looks like an extremely deformed dwarf. "I'm ordering the champagne!" Riesenfeld exclaims, motioning to the waiter.

Georg winks at me. He plays the role of cavalier, while I'm there to look after awkward situations; that's the arrangement between us. "If you want champagne, you shall have it," he says now. "But of course you're our guest, Riesenfeld."

"Impossible! I'm taking care of this! Not another word!" Riesenfeld is now the complete Don Juan of the upper classes. He looks with satisfaction at the golden neck in the ice bucket. Various ladies immediately exhibit a strong interest. I, too, feel gratified. The champagne will show Erna that she threw me overboard too soon. With satisfaction I drink to Riesenfeld, who responds formally.

Willy turns up. That was to be expected; he is a regular patron of the place. Aufstein and his friends leave, and Willy sits down at the table next to ours. Almost immediately he gets up to greet Renée de la Tour. With her is a pretty girl in a black evening dress. After a while I recognize her as the acrobat. Willy introduces us. Her name is Gerda Schneider. She throws an appraising glance at the champagne and at us three. We watch to see whether Riesenfeld will catch fire; then we'd be rid of him for the evening. But Riesenfeld is committed to Lisa. "Do you think I could invite her to dance?" he asks Georg.

"I wouldn't advise you to just now," Georg replies diplomatically. "But perhaps we'll meet her later in the evening."

He looks at me reproachfully. If I had not said in the office that we did not know Lisa, everything would be simple. But who could have guessed Riesenfeld would turn romantic? Now it is too late to explain. Romantics have no sense of humor.

"Don't you dance?" the acrobat asks me.

"Badly. I have no sense of rhythm."

"Nor have I. Let's try it together."

We wedge our way into the mass on the dance floor and are slowly pushed forward. "Three men without women in a night club," Gerda says. "Why?"

"Why not? My friend Georg maintains that anyone who takes a woman into a night club is inviting her to put horns on his head."

"Who is your friend Georg? The one with the big nose?"

"The one with the bald head. He is a believer in

the harem system. Women should not be exhibited, he says."

"Of course," Gerda replies. "And you?"

"I haven't any system. I'm just chaff in the wind."

"Don't step on my feet," Gerda says. "You're not chaff at all. You weigh at least one fifty."

I pull myself together. We are just being pushed past Erna's table, and this time, thank God, she recognizes me although her head is resting on the shoulder of the profiteer with the seal ring and his arm is around her waist. How can I watch at such a moment? I smile sweetly down at Gerda and pull her closer to me, keeping an eye on Erna the while.

Gerda smells of lily of the valley. "Oh, let go of me!" she says. "This won't get you anywhere with that redhead. That's what you're trying for, isn't it?"

"No," I lie.

"You oughtn't to have noticed her at all. But you had to keep on staring over at her and then you suddenly start this ridiculous comedy with me. What a beginner you are!"

I still try to keep the false smile on my face; the last thing I want is for Erna to notice what's going on. "I didn't arrange this," I say lamely. "I didn't want to dance."

Gerda pushes me away. "Evidently you're a cavalier as well. Let's stop. My feet hurt."

I wonder whether to explain that I did not mean it that way; but who knows what would come of it? Instead I keep my mouth shut and follow her back to the table, head high, but plunged in shame.

Meanwhile, the alcohol has taken effect. Georg and Riesenfeld are calling each other *du*. Riesenfeld's first name is Alex. In another hour at most he will invite me, too, to call him *du*. Tomorrow morning, of course, it will all be forgotten.

I sit there rather dejected, waiting for Riesenfeld to get tired. The dancers drift past, borne by the music on a lazy current of noise, bodily proximity, and herd instinct. Erna, too, comes by, provocatively ignoring me. Gerda jabs me in the ribs. "Her hair is dyed," she says, and I have the sickening feeling that she is trying to comfort me.

I nod and become aware that I have had enough to drink. Finally Riesenfeld shouts for the waiter. Lisa has left; now he wants to go too.

It takes a while before we are finished. Riesenfeld actually pays for the champagne; I'd expected that we would be stuck with the four bottles he has ordered. We say good-by to Willy, Renée de la Tour, and Gerda Schneider. The place is closing anyway; the musicians are putting away their instruments. Everyone crowds around the exit and the hat-check counter.

Suddenly I am standing beside Erna. Her cavalier, at the hat-check counter, is wrestling with his long arms to get her coat. Erna measures me icily. "I would catch you here! That's something you probably didn't expect!"

"You catch me?" I say, taken aback. "I've caught you!"

"And in what company!" she goes on as though I had not spoken. "With dance-hall girls! Don't touch me! Who knows what you've caught already!"

I have made no move to touch her. "I'm here on business," I say. "And you? How do you come to be here?"

"On business!" she laughs cuttingly. "Business here? Who's dead?"

"The backbone of the state, the man with small savings," I reply, considering myself witty. "He gets buried daily, but his memorial is not a cross—it's a mausoleum called the Stock Exchange."

"To think that I trusted such a worthless loafer!" she says

as though I had made no reply. "It's all over between us, Herr Bodmer!"

Georg and Riesenfeld are at the counter fighting for their hats. I realize that I have been tricked into defending myself. "Listen," I hiss. "Who told me this very afternoon that she could not go out because she had a raging headache? And who is hopping around here with a fat profiteer?"

Erna gets white around the nose. "Vulgar poetaster!" she whispers as though spewing vitriol. "You probably think you're superior because you can copy dead men's poems, don't you? Why don't you learn instead to make enough money to take a lady out in proper style! You with your walks in the country! 'To the silken banners of May!' Don't make me sob with pity!"

The silken banners are from the poem I sent her this afternoon. I reel inwardly; outwardly I grin. "Let's stick to the subject," I say. "Who is leaving here with two honest businessmen? And who with a cavalier?"

Erna looks at me big-eyed. "You expect me to go out on the streets at night by myself like a bar whore? What do you take me for? Do you think I intend to allow myself to be accosted by any loafer? What are you thinking of anyway?"

"You oughtn't to have come here at all in the first place!"

"Indeed? Just listen to that! Giving orders already! Forbidden to leave the house while the gentleman goes gallivanting! Any more commands? Shall I darn your socks?" She laughs cuttingly. "The gentleman drinks champagne, but seltzer and beer were good enough for me, or a cheap wine of no vintage!"

"I didn't order the champagne! That was Riesenfeld!"

"Of course! Always the innocent, you miserable failure of a schoolteacher. Why are you still standing here? I'll have nothing more to do with you! Stop molesting me!"

I can hardly speak for rage. Georg comes up and hands

me my hat. Erna's profiteer also appears. They go off together. "Did you hear?" I ask Georg.

"Part of it. Why are you fighting with a woman?"

"I didn't intend to get into a fight."

Georg laughs. He is never entirely drunk, even after pouring it down by the bucket. "Never let them get you into it. You always lose. Why do you want to be right?"

"Yes," I say. "Why? Probably because I'm a son of the German soil. Don't you ever get into arguments with women?"

"Of course. But that doesn't keep me from giving good advice to my friends."

The cool air hits Riesenfeld like a hammer tap. "Let's call each other *du*," he says to me. "After all, we're brothers. Exploiters of death." His laugh is like the barking of a fox. "My name is Alex."

"Rolf," I reply. I wouldn't dream of using my real first name for this drunken, one-night brotherhood. Rolf is good enough for Alex.

"Rolf?" Riesenfeld says. "What a silly name! Have you always had it?"

"Since my military service I've had the right to use it on leap years. Besides, Alex is nothing special."

Riesenfeld staggers a bit. "It doesn't matter," he says generously. "Children, it's been a long time since I've felt so fine! Could we get some coffee at your place?"

"Of course," Georg says. "Rolf is a first-class coffee cook."

We wobble through the shadows of St. Mary's to Hackenstrasse. In front of us paces a lonely wanderer with a storklike gait. He turns in at our gateway. It is Sergeant Major Knopf, just returning from his tour of inspection of the inns. We follow him and catch up just as he is urinating against the black obelisk beside the door. "Herr Knopf," I say, "that's improper conduct!"

"At ease," Knopf mutters, without turning his head.

"Sergeant Major," I repeat, "that's improper conduct! It's disgusting! Why don't you do it in your own house?"

He turns his head briefly. "You want me to piss in my parlor? Are you crazy?"

"Not in your parlor! You have a perfectly good toilet in your house. Use it! It's only about ten yards from here."

"Drivel!" Knopf replies.

"You're soiling the trade-mark of our firm. Besides, you're committing sacrilege. That's a tombstone. A holy object."

"Not till it's put in the cemetery," Knopf says and stalks off to the door of his house. "Good night to all of you, gentlemen."

He makes a half-bow at random, striking his forehead against the doorpost. Growling, he disappears. "Who was that?" Riesenfeld asks me, while I look for the coffee.

"Your opposite. An abstract drinker. He drinks without imagination. He needs no help at all from outside. No wishful fantasies."

"That's something too!" Riesenfeld takes his place at the window. "Just a hogshead for alcohol then. Man lives by dreams. Haven't found that out yet?"

"No. I'm too young."

"You're not too young. You're just a product of the war—emotionally immature and with too much experience in murder."

"*Merci,*" I say. "How's the coffee?"

Apparently the fumes have cleared. We are now back to formal terms of address. "Do you think the lady over there is already home?" Riesenfeld asks Georg.

"Probably. It's all dark."

"That could be because she hasn't come back yet. We can wait a few minutes, can't we?"

"Of course."

"Perhaps we can get our business out of the way in the meantime," I say. "All that's needed is a signature to the contract. Meanwhile I'll get some fresh coffee from the kitchen."

I go out, giving Georg time to work on Riesenfeld. This sort of thing goes better without witnesses. I sit down on the steps outside. From Wilke's carpenter shop come peaceful snores. Heinrich Kroll must still be there, for Wilke lives elsewhere. The national businessman will get a fine shock when he wakes up in a coffin. I debate whether to wake him up, but I'm too tired and it's already getting light—let the shock serve that fearless warrior as an icy bath to strengthen him and reveal to him the end result and aim of any war. I look at my watch, waiting for Georg's signal, and then stare into the garden. Morning is rising silently from the blossoming trees as though from a soft bed. In the lighted second-story window of the house opposite stands Sergeant Major Knopf in his nightgown taking a last gulp from the bottle. The cat rubs against my legs. Thank God, I say to myself, Sunday is over.

Chapter Five

A woman in mourning slips unobtrusively through the gate and stands irresolute in the courtyard. I go out. Someone shopping for a small tombstone, I think, and ask: "Would you like to look at our exhibition?"

She nods, but then says immediately: "No, no, that's not really necessary."

"You can look around at leisure. You don't have to buy. If you like I'll leave you alone."

"No, no! It's just—I simply wanted—"

I wait. Pressure has no place in our business. After a while the woman says: "It's for my husband—"

I nod and continue to wait. At the same time I turn toward the row of little Belgian headstones. "These are very much in demand," I say finally.

"Yes— It's just that—"

She breaks off again and looks at me almost beseechingly. "I don't know whether it's permissible—" she finally forces herself to say.

"What, to put up a tombstone? Who could possibly forbid that?"

"The grave is not in the churchyard—"

I look at her in surprise. "Our pastor will not allow my husband to be buried in the churchyard," she says softly and quickly with averted face.

"But why not?"

"He committed—because he did violence to himself," she bursts out. "He took his own life. He could not stand it any longer."

She stands there staring at me. She is still frightened by what she has said. "You mean because of that he may not be buried in the churchyard?" I ask.

"Yes. Not in the Catholic cemetery. Not in consecrated earth."

"But that's nonsense!" I say angrily. "He should be buried in doubly consecrated earth. No one takes his own life except in despair. Are you quite sure that's right?"

"Yes. Our pastor says so."

"Pastors talk a lot. That's their business. Where is he to be buried then?"

"Outside the cemetery. On the other side of the wall. Not on the consecrated side. Or in the municipal cemetery. But that won't do at all! All sorts of people are buried there."

"The municipal cemetery is more beautiful than the Catholic one. And there are Catholics buried there too."

She shakes her head. "He was pious," she whispers. "He must—" Her eyes are suddenly full of tears. "He can't possibly have remembered that this way he would not be allowed to lie in consecrated earth."

"He probably didn't think about it at all. But don't grieve at what your pastor says. I know thousands of very pious Catholics who lie in unconsecrated earth."

She turns to me. "Where?"

"On the battlefields in Russia and France. They lie there all together in mass graves, Catholics and Jews and Protestants, and I don't think it makes a bit of difference to God."

"They fell in battle. But my husband—"

Now she is weeping openly. In our business tears are taken for granted, but these are different. Besides, the woman is a little bundle of straw; she looks as though the wind could sweep her away. "Very likely at the last minute he repented," I say just to say something. "In that case everything is forgiven."

She looks at me. She is so hungry for a bit of comfort. "Do you really think so?"

"I certainly do. Of course the priest would not know. Only your husband knows. And he cannot tell you now."

"The pastor says that mortal sin—"

"Dear lady," I interrupt her, "God is far more compassionate than the priests, believe me."

I know now what torments her. It is not so much the unconsecrated grave; it is the thought that her husband, as a suicide, must burn in hell for all eternity and that he could perhaps get off with a couple of hundred thousand years in purgatory if he could be buried in the Catholic cemetery.

"It was on account of the money," she says. "It was in the savings bank, a guaranteed deposit for five years; he could not withdraw it. It was the dowry for my daughter by my first marriage. He was her guardian. When he withdrew the money two weeks ago, it was not worth anything at all, and her fiancé broke off the engagement. He thought we would have a good dowry. Two years ago it would still have been enough, but now it's not worth anything. My daughter did nothing but weep. That's what he couldn't stand. He thought it was his fault; he should have paid stricter attention. But after all, it was a guaranteed deposit; we couldn't withdraw it. That way the interest was higher."

"How was he expected to pay stricter attention? This sort of thing happens to lots of people nowadays. After all, he wasn't a banker—"

"No. A bookkeeper. The neighbors—"

"Don't bother about what the neighbors say. They're all malicious gossips. Just leave everything to God."

I feel that I am not very convincing, but what can one say to a woman in such circumstances? Certainly not what I really think.

She dries her eyes. "I ought not to tell you all this. What concern is it of yours? Forgive me! Sometimes one doesn't know where to—"

"It doesn't matter," I say. "We are used to it. All the people who come here have lost somebody."

"Yes—but not the same way as—"

"Oh yes," I explain. "In these times that happens much oftener than you think. Seven in the last month alone. They were people who no longer knew which way to turn. Respectable people, I mean; the disreputable ones get by."

She looks at me. "You think that one can put up a tombstone even when it's not in consecrated ground?"

"If you have a permit for a grave, you certainly can. Unquestionably in the municipal cemetery. If you wish you can pick one out now. You don't need to take it until everything is arranged."

She looks around. Then she points to the third smallest headstone. "What does one like that cost?"

It's always the same. The poor never ask the price of the smallest ones first: it's as though they avoided doing it out of a strange courtesy toward death and the dead. They do not want to ask about the cheapest first; whether they take it later on is another matter.

There's nothing I can do to help her; that piece of stone costs one hundred thousand marks. She opens her tired eyes in alarm. "We can't afford that. It's much more than—"

I can well imagine it is more than is left of the inheritance. "Then take this small one," I say. "Or simply a plaque without a stone. Look, here is one—it costs forty thousand marks and is very handsome. After all, what you want is for people to know where your husband is buried, and a plaque is just as good for that as a stone."

She examines the sandstone plaque. "Yes—but—"

She probably has barely enough for the next month's rent. Nevertheless, she doesn't want to buy the cheapest—as though that made any difference at all to the poor devil! If, instead, she had had more understanding earlier and had carried on less about her daughter, perhaps he would still be alive. "We could gild the inscription," I say. "Then it will look very dignified and distinguished."

"Will the inscription cost extra?"

"No. It's included in the price."

That is not true. But I can't help myself; she is so sparrow-like in her black clothes. Now if she wants a long quotation from the Bible I am sunk; the cutting would cost more than the plaque. But all she wants is the name and the dates 1875-1923.

She pulls a package of bills out of her pocket; they have been crumpled and then carefully smoothed out and tied in a bundle. I take a deep breath—payment in advance! That hasn't happened for a long time. Earnestly she counts out two piles. There is not much left over. "Forty thousand. Will you count it?"

"I don't need to. I'm sure it's correct."

It must be correct. She has certainly counted it over many times. And who but she would stoutly pay in advance? Why else had her husband committed suicide? "I'll tell you something," I say. "We'll give you a cement grave enclosure too. Then it will look very neat and separate."

She looks at me anxiously. "For nothing," I say.

The ghost of a sad little smile flits across her face. "That's the first time anyone has been kind to me since it happened. Not even my daughter—she says the disgrace—"

She wipes the tears away. I am very much embarrassed

and feel like the actor Gaston Münch in Sudermann's *Honor* at the city theater. Once she is gone, I pour myself a drink of schnaps as a bracer. Then I remember that Georg has not yet returned from his interview with Riesenfeld at the bank and I become suspicious of myself; perhaps I have been kind to this woman simply to bribe God. One good deed in return for another—a grave enclosure and an inscription against Riesenfeld's acceptance of a ninety-day note and a fat shipment of granite. This cheers me up so much that I have a second drink. Then I see on the obelisk outside the traces left by Sergeant Major Knopf, and I get a pail of water to wash them away, cursing him aloud. Knopf, however, in his bedroom is sleeping the sleep of the just.

"Only six weeks," I say in disappointment.

Georg laughs. "A six-week note is not to be sneezed at. The bank wouldn't stand for any more. Who knows where the dollar will be then? Besides, Riesenfeld has promised to come by again in a month. Then we can make a new agreement."

"Do you believe he will?"

Georg shrugs his shoulders. "Why not? Perhaps Lisa will draw him here again. He was raving about her at the bank like Petrarch about Laura."

"Good thing he didn't see her close up in the daylight."

"That's true of a lot of things." Georg stops short and looks at me. "But why Lisa? She really doesn't look so bad."

"In the morning she sometimes has regular sacks under her eyes. And she certainly doesn't look romantic. Vulgar rather. In a vigorous style."

"Romantic!" Georg snorts contemptuously. "What does

that mean? There are different kinds of romanticism! And robustness and vulgarity have their own charm!"

I look at him sharply. Can he by any chance have his own eye on Lisa? He is strangely secretive about his personal affairs. "I think what Riesenfeld means by romanticism is an adventure in high society," I say. "Not an affair with a horse butcher's wife."

Georg waves my objection aside. "Where's the difference? High society often behaves more vulgarly than a horse butcher."

Georg is our expert on high society. He subscribes to the *Berliner Tageblatt* and reads it principally for the news about art and society. He is extremely well informed. No actress can marry without his knowing it; every important divorce in the aristocracy is diamond-scratched in his memory; he never makes a mistake even after three or four marriages; it's as though he were a bookkeeper of society. He keeps track of all the theatrical performances, reads the critics, knows precisely about the high life on the Kurfürstendamm. And not only that: he follows international social life as well: film stars and the queens of society—he reads the movie magazines, and a friend in England sometimes sends him the *Tatler* and a few other elegant periodicals. Then he is exhilarated for days. He himself has never been in Berlin and has been abroad only as a soldier in France. He hates his profession, but he had to take it over after his father's death; Heinrich was too simpleminded. The magazines and pictures help to assuage his disappointment; they are his weakness and his recreation.

"A vulgar lady of high society is for connoisseurs," I say. "Not for Riesenfeld. That cast-iron devil has the sensitiveness of mimosa."

"Riesenfeld!" Georg makes a contemptuous face. He considers the director of the Odenwald Works, with his superficial fancy for French ladies, a miserable upstart. What does he know about the delicious scandal involved in the divorce of the Countess Homburg? Or about Elizabeth Bergner's last *première*? He doesn't even know their names! But Georg knows the Almanach de Gotha and the artist's lexicon almost by heart. "We really ought to send Lisa a bouquet of flowers," he says. "She helped us without knowing it."

Once more I look at him sharply. "Do it yourself," I reply. "And tell me, did Riesenfeld throw in a memorial cross polished on all sides?"

"Two. We have Lisa to thank for the second. I told him we would put it where she couldn't help seeing it. It seemed to be important to him."

"We could put it here in the office window. Then when she gets up in the morning it will make a strong impression. I could paint 'Memento Mori' on it in gold. What's the lunch at Eduard's today?"

"German beefsteak."

"Hacked meat, eh? Why is hacked meat German?"

"Because we're a warlike people and even in time of peace we hack up each other's faces in duels. You smell of schnaps. Why? Surely not because of Erna?"

"No. Because we all must die. Sometimes that fact staggers me even though I've known it for some time."

"That's very creditable. Especially in our profession. Do you know what I'd like?"

"Of course. You would like to be the mate on a whaler, or a copra dealer in Tahiti, or the discoverer of the North Pole, an explorer in the Amazon, Einstein or Sheik Ibrahim with a harem of women of twenty different nationalities, including the Circassians, who are supposedly so fiery you have to put on an asbestos mask to embrace them."

"That of course. But in addition I'd like to be

dumb; beaming and dumb. That's the greatest gift in our times."

"Dumb like Parsifal?"

"A bit less of the savior. Credulously, peacefully, healthily dumb."

"Come along," I say. "You're hungry. Our mistake is that we are neither dumb nor clever. Always betwixt and between like monkeys in the branches. That makes us weary and sometimes sad. Man needs to know where he belongs."

"Really?"

"No," I reply. "That only makes him lazy and fat. But how would it be if we went to a concert this evening to make up for the Red Mill? They're playing Mozart."

"I'm going to sleep early tonight," Georg explains. "That's my Mozart. You go alone. Expose yourself bravely and alone to the onslaught of the good. That is not without danger and often creates more havoc than simple evil."

"Yes," I say, thinking of the sparrow-like woman of this morning.

It is late afternoon. I am reading the family items in the newspapers and cutting out the death notices. That always cheers me and restores my faith in humanity—especially after the evenings when we have had to entertain our suppliers or agents. If things went according to the death notices, man would be absolutely perfect. There you find only first-class fathers, immaculate husbands, model children, unselfish, self-sacrificing mothers, grandparents mourned by all, businessmen in contrast with whom Francis of Assisi would seem an infinite egotist, generals dripping with kindness, humane prosecuting attorneys, almost holy munitions makers—in short, the earth seems to have been populated by a horde of wingless angels without one's having been aware of it. Pure love, which in reality is to be found so seldom, shines on all sides in death, and is the commonest thing of all. The highest virtues are to be found in abundance, sincere concern, profound piety, selfless devotion; even the survivors know what parts to play—they are bowed with grief, their loss is irreparable, they will never forget the dear departed—it is elevating to read all this, and one can feel proud to belong to a race possessed of such noble feelings.

I cut out the death notice of Niebuhr, the baker. He is described as a kindly, conscientious, and well-loved husband and father. I myself have seen Frau Niebuhr rushing from the house with flying braids when the kindly Niebuhr was after her with his leather belt; and I have seen son Roland's broken arm which his conscientious father inflicted by throwing him out of a second-story window in a sudden attack of rage. Nothing better could have happened to the careworn widow than for that blustering tyrant finally to be carried off by a stroke as he was baking breakfast rolls and pastry; nevertheless, she does not think so now. All the woe that Niebuhr caused her has suddenly disappeared. He has become an ideal. Man, the eternal liar, finds brilliant scope for his particular talent when death occurs and calls it piety, and the astonishing thing about it is that he believes as firmly in it as though he had put a rat into a hat and then drawn out a snow-white rabbit.

Frau Niebuhr has undergone this magical transformation at the moment when that clod of a baker, who beat her daily, was being dragged upstairs to their apartment. Instead of falling on her knees and thanking God for her deliverance, there began in her immediately the transfiguration through death. She cast herself weeping on the corpse, and since then her eyes have not been dry. When her sister reminded her of the frequent beatings and of Roland's crookedly set arm, she announced indignantly that these trifles were due to the heat of the baking oven; Niebuhr, in his never-wearying consideration for his family, had worked too hard and the heat of the oven had resulted in something like a sunstroke. Thereupon she showed her sister the door and went on mourning. In other respects she is a sensible, diligent, and alert woman who knows what's what; but now she suddenly sees Niebuhr as he never was and firmly believes in the picture—that's what's so marvelous about it. Man is not only an eternal swindler but also eternally credulous; he believes in the good, the beautiful, and the perfect even when they are not to be found or only in very rudimentary form—and that is the second reason why I find reading the death notices uplifting and why it makes me an optimist.

I put the Niebuhr notice with the seven others I have cut out. On Mondays and Tuesdays we always have a few more than usual. That's a result of the week end; a celebration, eating, drinking, quarreling, excitement—and this time the heart, the arteries, or the brain cannot hold out any longer. I put Frau Niebuhr's notice in the pigeonhole for Heinrich Kroll. It's a case for him. He is a straightforward fellow without irony and he has the same conception of the transfiguring effect of death that she has, provided she orders the tombstone from him. It will be easy for him to talk about the dear, unforgettable departed, especially since Niebuhr was a fellow habitué of Blume's Restaurant.

My work for the day is finished. Georg Kroll has retired into his den beside the office with the new issues of the *Berliner Tageblatt* and the *Elegant World*. I could do some more work with colored chalk on the drawing of a war memorial that I have made, but tomorrow is time enough for that. I shut the typewriter and open the window. A phonograph is playing in Lisa's apartment. She appears fully dressed this time, waves a tremendous bouquet of red roses out the window, and throws me a kiss. Georg, I think. What a sly one! I point toward his room. Lisa leans out of the window and shouts across the street in her hoarse voice: "Many thanks for the flowers! You may be vultures but you're cavaliers too!"

She shows her predatory teeth and trembles with laughter at her joke. Then she gets out a letter. " 'My lady,' " she caws. " 'An admirer of your beauty takes the liberty of laying these roses at your feet.' " She catches her breath with a hoot. "And the address! 'To the Circe of Hackenstrasse 5.' What is a Circe?"

"A woman who turns men into swine."

Lisa rocks with laughter. The little house seems to rock with her. That's not Georg, I think. He hasn't completely lost his mind. "Who's the letter from?" I ask.

"Alex Riesenfeld," Lisa croaks. "By courtesy of Kroll and Sons. Riesenfeld!" She is almost choking. "Is that the little runt you were with in the Red Mill?"

"He is not little and not a runt," I reply. "He's a giant sitting down and very virile. Besides, he's a billionaire!"

A thoughtful expression crosses Lisa's face. Then she waves and smiles again and disappears. I close the window. Suddenly for no reason I remember Erna. I begin to whistle uncomfortably and wander across the garden to the shed where Kurt Bach's studio is.

He is sitting on the front steps with his guitar. Behind him shimmers a sandstone lion which he has just completed for a war memorial. It is the same old cat, dying of toothache.

"Kurt," I say, "if you could have a wish instantly fulfilled what would you wish?"

"A thousand dollars," he replies without reflection, and strikes a resounding chord on his guitar.

"*Pfui Teufel!* I thought you were an idealist."

"I am an idealist. That's why I wish I had a thousand dollars. I don't need to wish idealism for myself. I have that in abundance already. What I need is money."

There is no possible reply to that. It's perfect logic. "What would you do with the money?" I ask, still hopeful.

"I would buy a block of houses and live on the rent."

"You couldn't live on the rent," I say. "It's too low and you're not allowed to raise it. You couldn't even pay for repairs and you would soon have to sell your houses again."

"Not the houses I'd buy. I'd keep them until the inflation is over. Then they would earn proper rents again and all I'd have to do is rake them in." He strikes another chord. "Houses," he says thoughtfully as though he were speaking of Michelangelo. "For as little as a hundred dollars you can buy a house that used to be worth forty thousand gold marks. What a profit you could make on that! Why haven't I a childless uncle in America?"

"Kurt," I say in disappointment, "you're a disgusting materialist. A house owner, that's all you want to be! And what's to become of your immortal soul?"

"A house owner and a sculptor." Bach executes a glissando. Upstairs, Wilke, the carpenter, is keeping time with his hammer. He is working hard on a white coffin for a child and is getting paid overtime. "Then I'd never need to make another damn dying lion or ascending eagle for you! No more animals! Never any more animals. Animals are something to eat or shoot or tame or admire. Nothing else! I have had enough of animals. Especially heroic ones."

He begins to play the "Hunter from the Kurpfalz." I see that I will get no decent conversation out of him tonight. Especially not the sort to make a man forget unfaithful women. "What is the meaning of life?" I ask as I leave.

"Eating, sleeping, and intercourse."

I dismiss the idea with a gesture and wander back. Unconsciously I walk in time with Wilke's hammering; then I notice it and change the rhythm.

Lisa is standing in the gateway. She has the roses in her hand and holds them out to me. "Here! Take them! I have no use for them."

"Why not? Haven't you any feeling for the beauty of nature?"

"No, thank God. I'm no cow. Riesenfeld!" She laughs in her night-club voice. "Tell the boy I'm not the sort of person you give flowers to."

"What then?"

"Jewelry," Lisa replies. "What did you think?"

"Not clothes?"

"Only when you're on more intimate terms." She squints at me. "You look miserable. Want me to cheer you up?"

"No thanks," I reply. "I'm cheerful enough. Go along by yourself to the cocktail hour at the Red Mill."

"I didn't mean the Red Mill. Do you still play the organ for those crazy people?"

"Yes," I say in surprise. "How did you know about that?"

"Word gets around. Do you know, I'd like to go with you to that loony bin sometime."

"You'll get there soon enough without me."

"Well, we'll just see which of us is the first," Lisa says carelessly, laying the flowers on the curb. "Here, take these vegetables! I can't keep them in the house. My old man is jealous."

"What?"

"Jealous as a razor! And why not?"

I do not know what is jealous about a razor; but the image is convincing. "If your husband is jealous, how can you keep on disappearing at night?" I ask.

"He does his butchering at night. I make my own arrangements."

"And when he isn't butchering?"
"Then I have a job as hat-check girl in the Red Mill."
"Have you really?"
"God, are you stupid!" Lisa replies.
"And the clothes and jewelry?"
"All cheap imitations." Lisa grins. "Every husband believes that! You can persuade men of anything! Well then, take your green groceries. Send them to some calf. You look as though you sent flowers."
"Never."

Lisa throws me an abysmal glance over her shoulder. Then without replying she walks back across the street on her beautiful legs. She is wearing shabby red slippers; one has a pom-pom, on the other it is missing.

The roses gleam in the twilight. It is an impressive bouquet. Nothing shabby about Riesenfeld. Fifty thousand marks, I estimate. Glancing around cautiously, I pick them up like a thief and go to my room.

Upstairs the window is red with sunset. The room is full of shadows and reflections; suddenly loneliness falls upon me as though from ambush. I know it's nonsense; I am no more lonely than an ox in a herd of oxen, but I cannot help myself. Loneliness has nothing to do with lack of company. It occurs to me that perhaps I was too hasty with Erna last night. Quite possibly there could be an innocent explanation for everything that has happened. She was jealous; that was clear in everything she said. And jealousy is love. Everyone knows that.

I stare through the window, realizing that jealousy is not love but possessiveness—but what does it matter? The twilight distorts your thoughts, and you ought not to argue with women, Georg says. But that's exactly what I have been doing! Full of remorse I smell the fragrance of the roses, which have transformed my room into a Venusberg. I realize that I am melting into universal forgiveness, universal conciliation and hope. Quickly I write a few lines, seal the envelope without even rereading them, and go into the office to get the tissue paper in which the last shipment of porcelain angels was sent. I wrap up the roses and go to look for Fritz Kroll, the youngest sprig of the firm. Fritz is twelve years old. "Fritz," I say, "do you want to earn two thousand?"

"You bet," Fritz replies. "Same address?"

"Yes."

He disappears with the roses—the third clearheaded person this evening. They all know what they want, Kurt, Lisa, Fritz—I alone have no idea. It's not Erna either; I realize that the minute it's too late to call Fritz back. But what is it? Where are the altars, where the gods and where the sacrifices? I decide to go to the Mozart concert—even though I shall be alone and the music will make it still worse.

The sky is full of stars when I come back. My steps reverberate in the street and I am full of excitement. Quickly I open the office door, turn on the light, and stop short. There are the roses beside the Presto mimeographing machine and there, too, is my letter, unopened, and beside it a scrap of paper with a message from Fritz. "The lady says to go bury yourself. Sincerely, Fritz."

Bury myself! A thoughtful joke! There I stand, disgraced to the marrow, full of shame and rage. I put Fritz's note into the cold grate. Then I sit down in my chair and brood. My rage outweighs my shame, as always happens when one is really ashamed and knows he ought to be. I write another letter, pick up the roses, and go to the Red Mill. "Please give these to Fräulein Gerda Schneider," I say to the doorman. "The acrobat."

The man in the braided uniform looks at me as though I had made him an immoral proposal. Then he gestures haughtily over his shoulder with his thumb. "Give them to a page."

I find a page and tell him to present the bouquet during the performance.

He promises to do so. I hope Erna will be there to see it. Then I wander for a while through the city until I grow tired and go home.

I am greeted by a melodious tinkle. Knopf is once more standing in front of the obelisk relieving himself. I say nothing; I want no more arguments. I take a pail, fill it with water, and empty it at Knopf's feet. The Sergeant Major gapes. "Inundation," he mutters. "Had no idea it had rained." And he staggers into the house.

Chapter Six

Over the woods hangs a dusky, red moon. The evening is sultry and very still. The glass man walks past silently. Now he can venture out; there is no danger that the sun will turn his head into a burning glass. However, he is wearing heavy rubbers as a precaution—there might be a thunderstorm and that is even more dangerous for him than the sun. Isabelle is sitting beside me on one of the garden benches in front of the pavilion for incurables. She is wearing a tight black dress and there are high-heeled golden shoes on her bare feet.

"Rudolf," she says, "you abandoned me again. Last time you promised to stay. Where have you been?"

Rudolf, I think, thank God! I couldn't have stood being Rolf tonight. I have had a depressing day and feel as though I had been shot at with rock salt.

"I have not abandoned you," I say. "I was away—but I have not abandoned you."

"Where were you?"

"Somewhere out there—"

Out there with the madmen is what I almost said, but I caught myself in time.

"Why?"

"I don't know, Isabelle. People do so many things without knowing why—"

"I was looking for you last night. There was a moon—not that one up there, the red, restless, lying one—no, the other moon, the cool, clear one that you can drink."

"It would certainly have been better for me to be here," I say, leaning back and feeling peace flood into me from her. "How can you drink the moon, Isabelle?"

"In water. It's perfectly easy. It tastes like opal. You don't really feel it in your mouth; that comes later on—then you feel it beginning to shimmer inside you. It shines out of your eyes. But you mustn't turn on a light. It wilts in the light."

I take her hand and lay it against my temple. It is dry and cool. "How do you drink it in water?" I ask.

Isabelle withdraws her hand. "You hold a glass of water out the window—like this." She stretches out her arm. "Then the moon is in it. You can see it, the glass lights up."

"You mean it's reflected in it?"

"It is not reflected. It is in it." She looks at me. "Reflected—what do you mean by reflected?"

"A reflection is an image in a mirror. You can see your reflection in all sorts of things that are smooth. In water too. But you are not in it."

"Things that are smooth!" Isabelle smiles, politely incredulous. "Really? Just imagine!"

"But of course. If you stand in front of a mirror you see yourself in it too."

Isabelle takes off one of her shoes and looks at her foot. It is narrow and long and unmarred by calluses. "Well, perhaps," she says, still politely uninterested.

"Not perhaps. Certainly. But what you see isn't you. It is only a mirror image. Not you."

"No, not me. But where am I when it is there?"

"You're standing in front of it. Otherwise you couldn't see your reflection."

Isabelle puts her shoe on again and glances up. "Are you sure of that, Rudolf?"

"Perfectly sure."

"I'm not. What do the mirrors do when they're alone?"

"They reflect whatever is there."

"And if nothing is there?"

"That's impossible. Something is always there."

"And at night? In the dark of the moon—when it's perfectly black, what do they reflect then?"

"The darkness," I say, no longer completely sure of my ground, for how can there be a reflection in complete darkness? It always requires some light.

"Then they are dead when it is completely dark?"

"Perhaps they are asleep—and when the light comes again they wake up."

She nods thoughtfully and draws her dress close about her legs. "And when they dream?" she asks suddenly. "What do they dream about?"

"Who?"

"The mirrors."

"I think they dream all the time," I say. "That is what they do all day long. They dream us. They dream us the other way around. What is our right is their left, and what is left is right."

Isabelle turns around to me. "Then they are our other side?"

I reflect. Who really knows what a mirror is? "There, you see," she says. "Just before, you said there was nothing in them. But now you admit they have our other side."

"Only as long as we are standing in front of them. Not when we go away."

"How do you know that?"

"You can see it. When you go away and look back your image is no longer there."

"What if they just hide it?"

"How can they hide it? You know they reflect everything! That's the very reason they are mirrors. A mirror can't hide anything."

A crease appears between Isabelle's brows. "What becomes of it then?"

"Of what?"

"The image! Our other side! Does it jump back into us?"

"That I don't know."

"It can't just get lost!"

"It doesn't get lost."

"What becomes of it then?" she asks more insistently. "Is it in the mirror?"

"No. There's nothing left in the mirror."

"It might be there just the same! What makes you so sure? After all, you can't see it when you are away."

"Other people can see that it's no longer there. They only see their own image when they stand in front of a mirror. Not someone else's."

"They cover it with their own. But where is mine? It must be there after all!"

"It is there, of course," I say, regretting that we have got on this subject. "When you step in front of the mirror again it appears there too."

Isabelle is suddenly very excited. She kneels on the bench and bends forward. Her silhouette is black and slender against the narcissus, whose color looks sulphurous in the sultry night. "So it is there after all! Just now you said it wasn't."

She clings to my hand trembling. I don't know what to say to calm her. I can't get anywhere with the laws of physics; she would reject them contemptuously. And at the moment I am no longer so sure about them myself. All at once mirrors really seem to hold a mystery.

"Where is it, Rudolf?" she whispers, pressing herself against me. "Tell me where it is! Has a piece of me been left behind everywhere? In all the mirrors I have looked into? I have seen lots of them, countless ones! Am I scattered everywhere in them? Has each of them taken some part of me? A thin impression, a thin slice of me? Have I been shaved down by mirrors like a piece of wood by a carpenter's plane? What is still left of me?"

I take her by the shoulders. "All of you is still here," I say. "On the contrary, mirrors add something. They make it visible and give it to you—a bit of space, a lighted bit of yourself."

"Myself?" She continues to cling to my hand. "But suppose it is not that way? Suppose myself is buried all over in thousands and thousands of mirrors? How can I get it back? Oh, I can never get it back! It is lost! Lost! It has been rubbed away like a statue that no longer has a face. Where is my face? Where is my first face? The one before all the mirrors? The one before they began to steal me!"

"No one has stolen you," I say in desperation. "Mirrors don't steal. They only reflect."

Isabelle is breathing heavily. Her face is pale. The red glow of the moon shimmers in her transparent eyes. "What has become of it?" she whispers. "What has become of everything? How can we tell where we are, Rudolf? Everything is running, rushing, sinking, sinking out of sight! Hold me tight! Don't let me go! Can't you see them?" She is staring toward the misty horizon. "There they come flying! All the dead mirror images! They come seeking blood! Can't you hear them? The gray wings! They dart like bats! Don't let them touch me!"

She presses her head against my shoulder and her quivering body against mine. I hold her and look into the twilight which is growing deeper and deeper. The air is still, but now the darkness is slowly advancing from the trees of the *allée* like a noiseless company of shadows. It seems to be trying to outflank us and cut off our retreat. "Come along," I say. "Let's go over there. It's brighter beyond the drive. There's still light there."

She resists, shaking her head. I feel her hair on my face; it is soft and smells of hay. Her face, too, is soft, and I feel the delicate bones, her chin and the curve of her brow, and suddenly I am once more deeply astonished that behind this narrow hemisphere there lives another world with wholly different laws and that this head, which I can so easily hold in my hand, sees everything differently, every tree, every star, every relationship, and itself too. A different universe is shut up inside it, and for a moment everything seems confused and I no longer know what is real—what I see or what she sees or what is there when we are not and is unknowable because it is like the mirrors: they are there when we are and yet they never give anything back to us but our own image. Never, never shall we know what they are when they are alone or what is behind them; they are nothing and yet they hold reflections and must be something; but they will never reveal their mystery.

"Come along," I say. "Come, Isabelle. No one knows what he is or whence he comes and where he goes—but we are together, that is all we can know."

I draw her with me. Perhaps there is really nothing else when everything is falling to pieces, I think, except this bit of togetherness and even that is a sweet deception, for when someone else really needs you you cannot follow him or stand by him. I have noticed that often enough in the war when I looked into the face of a dead comrade. Each of us has his own death and must suffer it alone; no one can help him then.

"You won't leave me alone?" she whispers.

"I won't leave you alone."

"Swear it," she says, stopping.

"I swear," I reply.

"All right, Rudolf." She sighs as though many of her problems were now lessened. "But don't forget. You forget so often."

"I won't forget."

"Kiss me."

I draw her to me. I have a very slight feeling of horror and am uncertain what to do. I kiss her with dry, closed lips.

She raises her hand to my head and holds it. Suddenly I feel a sharp bite and push her back. My lower lip is bleeding. She has bitten into it. I stare at her. She is smiling. Her face has changed. It is mean and sly. "Blood!" she says softly and triumphantly. "You were going to betray me again. I know you! But now you can't do it. It is sealed. You cannot go away again!"

"I cannot go away," I say soberly. "All right! But that's no reason to attack me like a cat. How it bleeds! What am I to say to the Mother Superior if she sees me like this?"

Isabelle laughs. "Nothing," she replies. "Why do you always have to say something? Don't be such a coward!"

I taste the warm blood in my mouth. My handkerchief is no good—the wound will have to close itself. Isabelle is standing in front of me. Now she is Jennie. Her mouth is small and ugly and she wears a sly, malicious smile. Then the bells begin to ring for the May devotion. An attendant comes along the path. Her white coat shimmers dimly in the twilight.

During the devotion my wound stopped bleeding, I have received my thousand marks, and I am now sitting at table with Vicar Bodendiek. Bodendiek has taken off his silk vestments in the little sacristy. Fifteen minutes ago he was still a mythical figure—shrouded in the smoke of incense he stood there in the candlelight clothed in brocade, raising the golden monstrance with the body of Christ in the Host above the heads of the pious sisters and the skulls of those of the insane who had received permission to attend devotion—but now in his shabby black coat and slightly sweat-stained white collar, which fastens behind instead of in front, he is just a simple agent of God, good-natured, powerful, with red cheeks and a red nose whose burst veins reveal the wine lover. He does not know it but for many years before the war he was my confessor, in the days when the school made us confess and take communion every month. Those of us who were smart went to Bodendiek. He was hard of hearing, and since one whispers at confession, he could not understand what sins we were admitting to. Therefore, he gave the lightest penances. A couple of Our Fathers and you were free of all sin and could go and play football or try to get forbidden books out of the public library. It was a different story with the cathedral pastor to whom I went once because I was in a hurry and there was a line standing in front of Bodendiek's booth. The cathedral pastor gave me a crafty penance: I was to come to him for confession in one week, and when I did so he asked me why I was there. Since you can't lie in the confessional, I told him and he gave me a dozen rosaries as penance and the command to appear at the same time next week. That went on until I was almost in despair—I saw myself chained for life to the cathedral pastor by these weekly confessions. Fortunately in the fourth week the holy man came down with measles and had to stay in bed. When my day for confession came, I went to Bodendiek and explained the situation to him—the cathedral pastor had instructed me to confess that day but he was sick. What was I to do? I could not go to his house since measles are contagious.

Bodendiek decided that I might just as well confess to him; a confession is a confession and a priest a priest. I did it and was free. From then on, however, I avoided the cathedral pastor like the plague.

We are sitting in a little room near the big assembly hall used by the inmates who are not under restraint. It is not really a dining room; there are bookcases in it, a pot with white geraniums, a few straight and easy chairs, and a round table. The Mother Superior has sent us a bottle of wine and we are waiting for the meal. Ten years ago I would never have dreamed that someday I would be drinking a bottle of wine with my father confessor—but then, neither would I have dreamed that I would someday kill men and be decorated for it instead of being hanged—nevertheless, that is what happened.

Bodendiek samples the wine. "A Schloss Reinhartshausener from the estate of Prince Heinrich von Preussen," he remarks reverently. "The Mother Superior has sent us something very good. Do you know anything about wine?"

"Very little."

"You ought to learn. Food and drink are gifts of God. They should be enjoyed and understood."

"Death is surely a gift of God also," I reply, glancing through the window into the dark garden. It has grown windy and the black treetops are tossing. "Ought one to enjoy and understand it too?"

Bodendiek looks at me with amusement over the rim of his wine glass. "For a Christian death is no problem. He doesn't exactly have to enjoy it; but he can understand it without difficulty. Death is entrance into eternal life. There's nothing to fear there. And for many it is a release."

"Why?"

"A release from sickness, pain, loneliness, and misery." Bodendiek takes an appreciative sip and swirls it inside his red cheeks.

"I know," I say. "Release from this earthly vale of tears. Why did God create it in the first place?"

At the moment Bodendiek does not look as though he were finding the earthly vale of tears hard to bear. He is comfortably replete and has spread the skirts of his priest's robe over the arms of his chair so that they will not be creased by the weight of his ponderous bottom. Thus he sits, an expert on wine and the beyond, his glass firm in his hand.

"Why really did God create this earthly vale of tears?" I repeat. "Couldn't He have admitted us at once to eternal life?"

Bodendiek shrugs his shoulders. "You can read about that in the Bible. Man, paradise, the fall—"

"The fall, the eviction from paradise, original sin, and with it the curse of one hundred thousand generations. The God of the longest wrath on record."

"The God of forgiveness," Bodendiek replies, holding his wine up to the light. "The God of love and of justice Who is always ready to forgive and Who has given His own son to redeem mankind."

"Herr Vicar Bodendiek," I say suddenly very angry, "why really did the God of love and justice make people so unequal? Why is one miserable and sick and another healthy and mean?"

"He who is humiliated here will be exalted in the next life. God is compensatory justice."

"I'm not so sure of that," I reply. "I knew a woman who had cancer for ten years, who survived six frightful operations, who was never without pain, and who finally doubted God when two of her children died. She gave up going to mass, to confession, and to communion, and according to the rules of the Church she died in a state of mortal sin. According to those same rules she is now burning for all eternity in the hell which the God of love created. Is that justice?"

Bodendiek looks for a while into his wine. "Was it your mother?" he asks then.

I stare at him. "What has that to do with it?"

"It was your mother, wasn't it?"

I swallow. "Suppose it was my mother—"

He is silent. "A single second is enough to reconcile oneself with God," he says then cautiously. "One second before death. A single thought. It doesn't even have to be spoken."

"I said that a couple of days ago too—to a woman who was in despair. But suppose the thought was not there?"

Bodendiek looks at me. "The Church has rules. She has rules for prevention and for education. God has none. God is love. Which of us can fathom His judgment?"

"Does He judge?"

"We call it so. It is love."

"Love," I say bitterly. "A love full of sadism. A love that torments people and makes them miserable and pretends to compensate for the horrible injustice of this world by the promise of an imaginary heaven."

Bodendiek smiles. "Don't you think that other people before you have thought about that too?"

"Yes, countless people. And smarter than I am."

"I think so too," Bodendiek replies comfortably.

"That doesn't prevent me from doing it too."

"Certainly not," Bodendiek fills his glass. "Only do it thoroughly. Doubt is the other side of faith."

I look at him. There he sits, a tower of security which nothing can shake. Behind his strong head stands the night, Isabelle's unquiet night, which blows and tosses and is endless and full of unanswerable questions. Bodendiek, however, has an answer for everything.

The door opens. Our meal is brought in round dishes stacked on top of one another on a big tray. They fit into one another the way they do in hospitals. The kitchen nurse spreads a cloth over the table, lays out the knives, forks, and spoons and disappears. Bodendiek lifts the top dish. "What do we have tonight? Bouillon," he says delicately. "Bouillon with marrow balls. First class! And red cabbage with *Sauerbraten*. A revelation!"

He fills his own plate and begins to eat. I am annoyed at myself for having argued with him and I feel his obvious superiority although that has nothing to do with the problem. He is superior because he is not seeking anything. He knows. But what does he really know? He can prove nothing. Nevertheless, he can play with me as he wishes.

The doctor comes in. It is not the director; it is the resident physician. "Will you eat with us?" Bodendiek asks. "In that case you'll have to go to it. Otherwise there'll be nothing left."

The doctor shakes his head. "I haven't time. There's going to be a thunderstorm. That's when the patients are always most restless."

"There's no sign of a storm."

"Not yet. But it will come. The patients feel it in advance. We've already had to put some of them in baths. It will be a difficult night."

Bodendiek divides the rest of the *Sauerbraten* between us. He takes the larger portion for himself. "All right, Doctor," he says. "But at least have a glass of wine with us. It's a 1915. A gift of God! Even for this young heathen here."

He winks at me, and I would like to pour my *Sauerbraten* gravy down his slightly greasy collar. The doctor sits down with us and accepts a glass. The pale nurse puts her head through the door. "I won't eat now, Nurse," the doctor says. "Put a couple of sandwiches and a bottle of beer in my room."

He is a man of about thirty-five, dark, with a narrow face, close-set eyes, and big, projecting ears. His name is Wernicke, Guido Wernicke, and he hates his first name as much as I hate Rolf.

"How is Fräulein Terhoven?" I ask.

"Terhoven? Oh yes—not especially well, unfortunately. Didn't you notice anything today? Any change?"

"No. She was the same as ever. Perhaps a little excited, but you just said that was due to the thunderstorm."

"We'll see. You can never tell much in advance up here."

Bodendiek laughs. "Certainly not. Not here."

I look at him. What a rude Christian, I think. But then it occurs to me that he is a guardian of souls by profession; in such cases there is always some loss of sensibility in the interests of competence—just as with doctors, nurses, and tombstone salesmen.

I hear him conversing with Wernicke. Suddenly I have no more desire to eat and I get up and go to the window. Beyond the tossing, black treetops all at once there has risen a wall of pale-edged cloud. I stare out. All at once everything is very strange, and behind the familiar scene of the garden another, wilder one silently forces its way forward, pushing the old one aside like an empty husk. I recall Isabelle's cry: "Where is my first face? My face before all the mirrors?" Yes, where is the first face of all? I think. The first landscape before it was turned into the landscape of our senses, into parkland and wood and house and man— where is Bodendiek's face before it became Bodendiek, where is Wernicke's before it had a name? Do we still know anything about that? Or are we caught in a net of concepts and words, of logic and deceptive reasoning, behind which lie the lonesome, glowing primeval fires to which we no longer have access because we have transformed them into utility and warmth, into kitchen fires and central heating and deceit and certainty and respectability and walls and, most of all, into a Turkish bath of sweaty philosophy and science? Where are they? Do they still stand, ever unseizable and pure and unattainable, behind life and death, before they became life and death for us, and are the only persons still close to them maybe those who now crouch in this house in their barred rooms and creep and stare and feel the thunderstorm in their blood? Where is the boundary between chaos and order and who can cross it and return, and if anyone could what would he then know of it? Would not the one wipe out the memory of the other? Who are the unbalanced, the branded, the excluded—we with our boundaries, our reason, our orderly picture of the world or the others through whom chaos rages and flashes and who are exposed to infinity like rooms with three walls into which lightning strikes and storm and rain pour while we others sit proudly enclosed in rooms protected by four walls and doors and think we are superior because we have escaped from chaos? But what is chaos? And what is order? And who possesses them? And why? And who will ever escape?

A pale light darts high above the garden wall and after a time is answered by soft rumbling. Our room seems like a cabin full of light afloat in a night which has become uncanny, as though somewhere captive giants were straining at their chains to leap up and annihilate the race of dwarfs that has for a time confined them. A cabin of light in the darkness, books and three orderly minds in a house like a beehive where the uncanny is locked up in cells and flashes lightning-like in the disturbed brains around us! What if in the next second a flash of recognition should run through them all and they should find their way together in revolt, what if they broke the locks, forced open the bars, and foamed up the stairs like a gray wave to sweep away the lighted room, this cabin of sound, well-grounded reason, into the night and into what stands, nameless and mighty, behind the night?

I turn around. The man of faith and the man of science are sitting in the full brilliance of the ceiling light. For them the world is not a vague, quivering unrest, it is not a muttering from the depths or a lightning flash in the icy spaces of the void—they are men of faith and of science, they have sounding lines and plummets and scales and measures, each of them a different set but that does not matter, they are sure, they have names to put on everything like labels, they sleep well, they have a goal that contents them, and even horror, the black curtain in front of suicide, has a well-recognized place in their existence, it has a name, it has been classified and thereby rendered harmless. Only what is nameless or has burst its name is deadly.

"There's lightning," I say.

The doctor looks up. "Really?"

He has just been explaining the nature of schizophrenia, Isabelle's ailment. His dark face is slightly flushed with excitement. He describes how patients of this sort leap lightning-like from one personality to another in a matter of seconds and how this may be the reason that in ancient times they were regarded as seers and holy men and in later times as possessed of the devil and were looked upon by the people with superstitious respect. He philosophizes about the causes, and suddenly I wonder how he comes to know all this and why he describes it as a sickness. Could it not equally well be regarded as a particular asset? Doesn't every normal person have a dozen personalities in him too? And isn't the distinction simply that the healthy person suppresses them and the sick one gives them scope? Who then is sick?

I walk over to the table and empty my glass. Bodendiek watches me benevolently, Wernicke as a doctor might watch a wholly uninteresting case. For the first time I feel the wine; I feel it is good, self-contained, mature, and not unsettled. It no longer has chaos in it, I think. It has transformed chaos, transformed it into harmony. But transformed it, not replaced it. It has not disappeared. Suddenly, for a second's time, I am unreasonably, unspeakably happy. So it can be done, I think. One can transform chaos! It does not have to be one or the other. It can also be one through the other.

Another pale flash lights the window and expires. The doctor gets up. "Now it's starting. I must go over to the confined cases."

The confined cases are the patients who never come out. They remain locked up until they die in rooms where the furniture is screwed down, the windows barred, and the doors can only be opened from outside with a key. They are in cages like dangerous beasts and no one likes to talk about them.

Wernicke looks at me. "What's the matter with your lip?"

"Nothing. I bit myself in my sleep."

Bodendiek laughs. The door opens and the little nurse brings in another bottle of wine and three glasses. Wernicke leaves with the nurse. Bodendiek reaches for the bottle and fills his glass. Now I understand why he invited Wernicke to drink with us; the Mother Superior thereupon sent a new bottle. A single one would not have been enough for three men. That sly fellow, I think. He has repeated the miracle of the loaves and fishes. From a single glass for Wernicke he has made a whole bottle for himself. "You probably won't be drinking any more, will you?" he asks.

"Yes I will!" I reply, seating myself. "I've acquired the taste. You taught me. Many thanks."

Bodendiek draws the bottle out of the ice with a bittersweet smile. He regards the label for a moment before pouring—a quarter glass for me. His own he fills almost to the rim. I calmly take the bottle out of his hand and fill my own glass as full as his. "Herr Vicar," I say, "in many ways we are not so very different."

Bodendiek suddenly laughs. His face unfolds like a peony. "To health and happiness," he says unctuously.

The thunder rumbles near and far. The lightning falls like silent saber blows. I am sitting at the window in my room with the scraps of all Erna's letters in front of me in a hollow elephant's foot which the world traveler Hans Ledermann gave me a year ago for a wastebasket.

I am through with Erna. I have counted up all her unattractive qualities; I have rooted her out of me emotionally and humanly; as dessert I have read a couple of chapters of Schopenhauer and Nietzsche. Nevertheless, I should prefer to have a tuxedo, a car, and a chauffeur so that I could now turn up at the Red Mill, accompanied by two or three famous actresses and with several hundred millions in my pocket so that I could deal that serpent the blow of her life. I dream for a time of how it would be if tomorrow morning she should read in the paper that I had won the sweepstakes or had been gravely injured while rescuing children from a burning house. Then I see a light in Lisa's room.

She opens the window and signals. My room is dark; she cannot see me; therefore I'm not the one. She says something silently, points at her breast and then at our house, and nods. The light goes out.

I lean out cautiously. It is twelve o'clock, and the windows round about are dark. Only Georg Kroll's is open.

I wait and see Lisa's door move. She steps out, looks quickly in both directions, and runs across the street. She is wearing a light, brightly colored dress and is carrying her shoes in her hand so as not to make any noise. At the same time I hear the door of our house being opened cautiously. It must be Georg. The door has a bell above it and in order to open it without making a noise you have to get on a chair, hold the clapper, press down on the latch with your foot, and draw the door open, an acrobatic feat for which you have to be sober. Tonight I know that Georg is sober.

There is the sound of murmuring; the click of high heels. Lisa, that vain creature, has put on her shoes again to appear more seductive. The door of Georg's room sighs softly. Well, well! Who would have thought it? Still waters!

The storm returns. The thunder grows louder, and suddenly, like a cascade of silver coins, the rain pours down upon the pavement. It rebounds in dusty fountains and a breath of coolness ascends from it. I lean out of the window and look into the watery tumult. The rain is already running off through the rain pipes, lightning flares, and in its intermittent flashes I see Lisa's bare arm reaching out of Georg's window into the rain, then I see her head and hear her husky voice. I do not see Georg's bald dome. He is no nature lover.

The gate to the courtyard opens under the blow of a fist. Soaking wet, Sergeant Major Knopf staggers in. Water is dripping from his cap. Thank God, I think, in weather like this I won't have to follow up his misdemeanors with a pail of water! But Knopf disappoints me. He doesn't pay any attention to his victim, the black obelisk. Cursing and slapping at the raindrops as though they were mosquitos he flees into the house. Water is his great enemy.

I pick up the elephant's foot and empty its contents into the street. The rain quickly washes away Erna's protestations of love. Money has won, I think, as always, though it is worth nothing. I go to the other window and look into the garden. The great festival of the rain is in full swing, a green nuptial orgy, shameless and innocent. In the flare of the lightning I see the plaque for the suicide. It has been put to one side; the inscription has been carved and gleams with gold. I shut the window and turn on the light. Below, Georg and Lisa are murmuring. My room suddenly seems horribly empty. I open the window again and listen to the anonymous rushing and decide to request from Bauer, the bookseller, as honorarium for my last week's tutoring, a book on yoga, renunciation and self-sufficiency. Adepts are said to achieve fabulous results through simple breathing exercises.

Before I go to sleep I pass a mirror. I stop and look into it. What is there really? I think. Whence comes the perspective which is not a perspective, the deceptive depth, the space which is a plane? And who is that who peers out questioningly and is not there?

I look at my lip swollen and crusted with blood. I touch it and someone opposite me touches his ghostly lip which is not there. I grin and the not-I grins back. I shake my head and the not-I shakes his not-head. Which of us is which? And what am I? The one there or the one clothed in flesh standing in front? Or something else, something behind both? I feel a shudder and turn out the light.

Chapter Seven

Riesenfeld has kept his word. The courtyard is full of monuments and pedestals. The ones polished on all sides are in crates and wrapped in sacking. They are the prima donnas among tombstones and must be handled with extreme care to avoid damaging their edges.

The whole crew are in the courtyard to help and to watch. Even old Frau Kroll is wandering around, examining the blackness and quality of the granite and now and again casting a melancholy glance at the obelisk beside the door—the single remaining item of her late husband's purchases.

Kurt Bach is directing the moving of a huge sandstone block into his workroom. A dying lion is to be created out of it, but this time not one bowed with toothache but roaring a last defiance, a broken spear in his flank. It is to be a war memorial for the village of Wüstringen where there is a particularly belligerent veterans' organization under the command of Major Wolkenstein, retired. The sorrowing lion was too much like a washrag for Wolkenstein. What he would really like is one with four heads spewing fire from all its mouths.

A shipment from the Württemberg Metal Works, which arrived at the same time, is also being unpacked. Four eagles taking flight have been arranged in a row on the ground, two of bronze and two of cast iron. They are to become the crowning decorations for other war memorials to inspire the youth of the land to a new war—for, as Major Wolkenstein has so persuasively declared: "We must win sometime, and then woe to the vanquished!" For the moment, to be sure, the eagles look like nothing so much as giant roosters trying to lay eggs—but this will be quite different once they are enthroned on the monuments. Even generals without their uniforms are likely to look like grocers' apprentices, and Wolkenstein himself in civilian clothes could be taken for a fat athletic director. Costume and perspective are important in our beloved fatherland.

As advertising director I supervise the arrangement of the monuments. They are not to be placed haphazardly in rows but aristically located about the garden in intimate groups. Heinrich Kroll is against this. He would like to see the stones placed like soldiers in formation; anything else seems to him effeminate. Fortunately he is outvoted. Even his mother is against him. Indeed, she is always against him. Even now she cannot understand why Heinrich belongs to her and not to the wife of Major Wolkenstein, retired.

The day is blue and beautiful. Over the city the sky hangs like a giant silken tent. The cool of morning still lingers in the crowns of the trees. Birds are twittering as though nothing existed except early summer, their nests, and their young. It doesn't matter to them that the dollar, like an ugly, spungy toadstool, has puffed itself up to fifty thousand. Nor that the morning paper contains the notices of three suicides—all people of small independent means, all committed in the favorite fashion of the poor by an open gas jet. Frau Kubalke was found in her living room with her head in the gas heater; the pensioned government clerk Hopf, freshly shaved, in his last, faultlessly brushed, much-mended suit, grasping in his hand four worthless red-seal thousand-mark notes like tickets to heaven; and the widow Glass on the floor of her kitchen, her bankbook, showing deposits of fifty thousand marks, torn in two beside her. Hopf's red-seal thousand-mark notes were his last banner of hope; for a long time there has been a belief that they would sometime or other be redeemed at full value. Whence this rumor came no one knows. They were never officially payable in gold, and even if they had been, the State, that immune betrayer, which embezzles billions and jails anyone who defrauds it of as much as five marks, would find some pretext for not paying. Only day before yesterday there was a notice in the paper that these notes would not receive preferential treatment. That's the reason Hopf's death notice is in the paper today.

From the workroom of Wilke, the coffinmaker, come the sounds of hammering, as though a giant, cheerful woodpecker lived there. Wilke's business is booming; everyone needs a coffin sooner or later, even a suicide—the time of mass graves and burial in canvas bags has passed with the war. Now once more one decays fittingly in slowly moldering wood, in shroud or backless frock coat or in a burial dress of white crepe de Chine. Niebuhr, the baker, even in all the glory of his orders and fraternal insignia; his wife insisted on it. In addition, he has been provided with a facsimile of the Harmony Singing Club's flag. He was their second tenor, and every Saturday roared his way through *"Schweigen im Walde"* and *"Stolz weht die Flagge Schwarzweissrot,"* drank almost enough beer to burst, and then went home to beat his wife—an upright man, as the pastor said at his funeral.

Fortunately at ten o'clock Heinrich Kroll disappears with his bicycle and his striped pants to visit the villages. All this new granite makes his salesman's soul restless; he has to be on his way to let the sorrowing survivors know about it.

Now we can become more expansive. First of all we give ourselves a recess and are served liverwurst sandwiches and coffee by Frau Kroll. Lisa appears in the gateway. She is wearing a blazing red silk dress. Old Frau Kroll scares her away with a glance. She can't stand Lisa, although she is no prude herself. "That dirty tramp," she exclaims with emphasis.

Georg promptly falls into the trap. "Dirty? What do you mean dirty?"

"Can't you see she's dirty? Unwashed under all that finery."

I see Georg involuntarily grow thoughtful. Dirt is not something you like to think of in connection with your beloved—unless you're a decadent. For an instant there is a kind of flash of triumph in his mother's eyes; then she changes the subject. I look at her in admiration; she is a general of mobile units—she strikes swiftly, and when her opponent gets ready to defend himself she is already somewhere else. Lisa may be a tramp; she is certainly not obviously dirty.

The three daughters of Sergeant Major Knopf come flitting out of the house. They are seamstresses like their mother, small, roly-poly, and nimble. Their machines whir all day long. Now they dart off, carrying bundles of exorbitantly costly silk shirts for profiteers. Knopf, the old soldier, does not hand over one pfennig of his pension for household expenses; that's something for the four women to see to.

Cautiously we unpack the two black war memorials. They really ought to stand at the entrance to make an impressive effect, and in winter we would place them there; but it is May and, strange though it may seem, our courtyard is an arena for cats and lovers. The cats begin to scream from the monuments in February and chase each other behind the cement grave borders; the lovers, however, put in their appearance as soon as it is warm enough to make love in the open—and when is it too cold for that? Hackenstrasse is a quiet, remote street, our gate is inviting, and our garden old and large. The somewhat macabre display does not disturb the lovers; on the contrary, it seems to stir them to particular frenzy. Only two weeks ago, a chaplain from the village of Halle, who like all men of God was accustomed to rise with the roosters, came to see us at seven in the morning to order four of the smallest headstones for the graves of four charitable nuns who had died during the preceding year. As I, drunk with sleep, was leading him into the garden I was able to remove, just in time, a rose-colored stocking of artificial silk that was floating like a flag from our last memorial cross, left there by some enthusiastic nocturnal pair. Unquestionably there is something conciliatory, in the broad, poetic sense, about sowing life in a place of death, and Otto Bambuss, the poet schoolmaster of our club, when I told him about it, promptly stole my idea and worked it up into an elegy with cosmic humor—on the other hand it can be rather disturbing, especially when an empty brandy bottle stands there too, gleaming in the morning sun.

I supervise the display. It makes a pleasant effect, as far as one can say that of tombstones. The two crosses stand on their pedestals shimmering in the sunlight, symbols of eternity, hewn fragments of a once-glowing earth, now cooled, polished, and ready to preserve forever the name of some successful businessman or rich profiteer—for even a scoundrel does not like to depart from this planet without leaving some trace behind.

"Georg," I say, "we'll have to take care your brother doesn't sell our Werdenbrück Golgotha to some miserable farmer who won't pay until after the harvest. On this lovely day, amid the song of birds and the aroma of coffee, let us take a holy oath not to sell these two crosses except for cash on the line!"

Georg smiles, undismayed. "It's not as dangerous as that. We have to redeem our note in three weeks. As long as we get the money before that we are ahead of the game—even if we sell at cost."

"Ahead of the game!" I reply. "An illusion until the next dollar quotation."

"Sometimes you're too commercial." Georg meticulously lights a cigar worth five thousand marks. "Instead of complaining, you should rather regard the inflation as a reversed symbol of life. At the end of each day your life has one day's duration less. We live our life on capital, not income. Each day the dollar rises, but each night your life is quoted at one day less. There you have the subject for a sonnet."

"That's a theme for Eduard Knobloch." I look at the self-satisfied Socrates of Hackenstrasse. Small beads of sweat adorn his bald head like pearls on a bright dress. "It's amazing how philosophical a fellow can be when he has not slept by himself," I say.

Georg does not move an eyelash. "What would you expect?" he asks me calmly. "Philosophy ought to be serene, not tormented. To mix it up with metaphysical speculation is just like mixing sensual pleasure with what the members of your Poets' Club call ideal love. It makes an intolerable mishmash."

"Mishmash?" I say, somehow hurt. "Hold on a minute,

you bourgeois adventurer! You butterfly collector, trying to impale everything on needles! Don't you know that without what you call mishmash you're as good as dead?"

"Absolutely not. I just keep things separate." Georg blows cigar smoke into my face. "I prefer to endure the transitoriness of life with dignified philosophic melancholy rather than commit the vulgar error of confusing some Minna or Anna with the chilly secret of existence and of assuming that the world would come to an end if Minna or Anna preferred some other Karl or Josef. Or if an Erna preferred some overgrown infant in English tweeds."

He grins. I stare coldly into his disloyal eye. "A cheap crack, worthy of Heinrich!" I say. "You simple connoisseur of what's available! Will you please tell me then why you read with so much passion the magazines that are crammed full of unattainable sirens, scandals of high society, great ladies of the theater, and movie queens?"

Georg once more blows three hundred marks' worth of smoke into my eyes. "I do that for purposes of fantasy. Have you never heard of heavenly and earthly love? Only a short time ago you were trying to combine them in your Erna and learned a sound lesson, you simple-minded delicatessen dealer in love, trying to keep sauerkraut and caviar on the same shelf! Haven't you found out yet that then the sauerkraut will never taste like caviar but the caviar will always taste like sauerkraut? I keep them carefully separated, and so should you! It makes life comfortable. Now come, let's go and torment Eduard Knobloch. Today he's serving beef stew with noodles."

I nod and go without a word to get my hat. Inadvertently Georg has dealt me a heavy blow—but I'm damned if I'm going to let him know it.

When I return Gerda Schneider is sitting in the office. She

is wearing a green sweater, a short dress, and big earrings with artificial stones. On the left side of her sweater she has pinned one of the roses from Riesenfeld's bouquet, which must be extraordinarily durable. Pointing at it, she says: *"Merci!* Everyone was envious. That was a bush for a prima donna."

I look at her and think: very likely there sits exactly what Georg means by earthly love—clear, determined, young, and without affectation. I sent her flowers, and she has come, and that's all there is to it. She has interpreted the flowers as any intelligent person should. Instead of acting a tedious part, here she is. She has accepted, and there is really nothing more to talk about.

"What are you doing this afternoon?" she asks.

"I'm working until five. Then I'm going to give a tutoring lesson to an idiot."

"What in? Idiocy?"

I grin. "Come to think of it, yes."

"That would be until six. Come to the Altstädter **Hof** afterward. I exercise there."

"All right," I say without pausing to consider.

Gerda gets up. "Well then—"

She holds up her face to me. I am surprised. I hadn't expected so much from my gift of flowers. But why not, really? Very likely Georg is right: one oughtn't to combat the pains of love with philosophy—only with another woman. Cautiously I kiss Gerda on the cheek. *"Dummkopf!"* she says and kisses me warmly on the mouth. "Traveling artistes don't have time for foolery. In two weeks I must be off. Well then, till tonight."

She walks out, erect, with her firm, strong legs and strong shoulders. On her head she has a red Basque beret. She seems to love color. Outside she stops beside the obelisk and glances at our Golgotha. "That's our inventory," I say.

She nods. "Does it bring you any income?"

"So-so—in these times—"

"And you're employed here?"

"Yes. Funny, isn't it?"

"Nothing's funny," Gerda says. "What about me spending my time in the Red Mill sticking my head backward between my legs? Do you think God had that in mind when he made me? Well, till six."

Old Frau Kroll comes out of the garden with a sprinkling can in her hand. "That's a respectable girl," she says, glancing after Gerda. "What is she?"

"She's an acrobat."

"Well, an acrobat!" she says in surprise. "Acrobats are mostly respectable people. She's not a singer, too, is she?"

"No. A regular acrobat. She can do *saltos,* handstands, and dislocations like a human serpent."

"You seem to know quite a lot about her. Did she want to buy something?"

"Not yet."

She laughs. Her spectacles glitter. "My dear Ludwig," she says, "you can't imagine how silly your present way of life will seem to you some day when you're seventy."

"I'm not so very sure about that," I tell her. "It seems pretty silly to me right now. What, by the way, is your opinion of love?"

"Of what?"

"Love. Heavenly and earthly love."

Frau Kroll laughs heartily. "That's something I've forgotten long since, thank God!"

I am in Arthur Bauer's bookstore. This is payday for the tutor. Arthur, Jr. has seized the opportunity to put a few tacks on my chair by way of greeting. I wanted to stick his sheep's head in the goldfish bowl that decorates their plush-upholstered living room, but I had to control myself—otherwise Arthur, Sr. would not have paid, and Arthur, Jr. knows this.

"So it's yoga," says Arthur, Sr., jovially pushing toward me a stack of books. "I've put aside all we have. Yoga, Buddhism, asceticism, omphaloskepsis—do you plan to become a fakir?"

I look at him disapprovingly. He is a little man with a pointed beard and nimble eyes. Another shot, I think, aimed at my beleaguered heart! But I'll get the best of you, you cheap mockingbird; you're no Georg! I say to him sharply: "What's the meaning of life, Herr Bauer?"

Arthur looks at me as expectantly as a poodle. "Well?"

"Well what?"

"What's the point? You're making a joke, aren't you?"

"No," I reply coolly. "That's a test question for the salvation of my young soul. I'm putting it to a lot of people, especially those who ought to know."

Arthur plucks at his beard as though it were a harp. "So you seriously ask a nonsensical question like that on a Monday afternoon at the busiest time in this shop and expect an answer too?"

"Yes, I do," I say. "But admit it at once! You don't know either! Despite all your books!"

Arthur relinquishes his beard to run his hands through his hair. "Good God, the things people think of to worry about! Take the matter up in your poetry club!"

"In the poetry club there's nothing but poetical evasion. What I want is the truth. Otherwise why am I alive and not a worm?"

"The truth?" Arthur bleats. "That's something for Pontius Pilate! It has nothing to do with me. I am bookseller, husband, and father; that's enough for me."

I look at the bookseller, husband, and father. He has a mole on the right side of his face beside his nose. "So that's enough," I say cuttingly.

"That's enough," Arthur replies firmly. "Indeed, sometimes it's too much."

"Was it enough when you were twenty-five?"

Arthur opens his blue eyes as wide as he can. "When I was twenty-five? No. I still wanted to become it at that time."

"What?" I ask hopefully. "A human being?"

"Owner of this bookstore, husband, and father. A human being I am anyway. But not yet a fakir."

He waddles quickly away after this harmless second shot to wait on a lady with a copious, drooping bosom who is looking for a novel by Rudolf Herzog. I quickly leaf through the books about the happiness of renunciation and promptly lay them aside. During the day one is considerably less receptive to this sort of thing than at night when one is alone and there is nothing else available.

I walk over to the shelves that contain the works on religion and philosophy. They are Arthur Bauer's pride. Here he has, collected in one place, pretty much everything that humanity has thought in a couple of thousand years about the meaning of life, and so it should be possible for a couple of hundred thousand marks to become adequately informed on the subject—for even less really, let us say for twenty to thirty thousand marks; for if the meaning of life were knowable, a single book should suffice. But where is it? I glance up and down the rows. The section is very extensive, and this suddenly makes me distrustful. It seems to me that with truth and the meaning of life the situation is the same as with hair tonics—each firm praises its own as the only satisfactory one, and yet Georg Kroll, who has tried them all, still has a bald head just as he should have known from the beginning he would have. If there were a hair tonic that really grew hair, there would be only that one and all the others would long ago have gone out of business.

Bauer comes back. "Well, found something?"

"No."

He looks at the volumes I have pushed aside. "So then, there's no point in being a fakir, eh?"

I do not directly contradict the silly joker. Instead I say: "There's no point in any books at all. If you look at everything that is written here and then at the way things are in the world, all you'll want to read is the menu in the Walhalla and the family notes in the daily paper."

"What's that?" asks the bookseller, husband, and father in quick alarm. "Reading is education! Everyone knows that."

"Really?"

"Of course! Otherwise what would become of us booksellers?"

Arthur rushes off again. A man with a closely trimmed mustache is asking for a work entitled *Undefeated in the Field*. It is the great success of the postwar period. In it an unemployed general proves that the German army was victorious in battle to the end.

Arthur sells him the gift edition in leather with gold edges. Gratified by the sale he returns. "How would you like something classical? Second hand of course!"

I shake my head and point silently at a book I have found in the meantime on the display table. It is called *The Man of the World, a Breviary of Good Manners for All Walks of Life*. Patiently I wait for the inescapable, shallow jokes about fakir-cavaliers and the like. But Arthur cracks no jokes. "A useful book nowadays," he tells me earnestly. "It should come out in a large, cheap edition. Well then, we're quits, eh?"

"Not quite. You still owe me something." I lift a thin volume—Plato's *Symposium*. "I'll take this too."

Arthur does some mental arithmetic. "It doesn't quite come out, but all right. We'll call the *Symposium* second hand."

I have him wrap up the *Breviary of Good Manners,* for

I would not for the world be caught with it. Nevertheless, I determine to study it that very night. A little polish harms no one, and Erna's contemptuous comments still ring in my ears. The war made savages of us, but today one can only afford coarse manners if one has a thick wallet to make up for them. That, however, is something I do not have.

Full of contentment I step out into the street. The uproar of existence greets me instantly. Willy roars by in a fiery red town car, without seeing me. I press the breviary for men of the world firmly under my arm. Forward into life! I think. Here's to earthly love! Away with dreams! Away with ghosts! That goes for Erna as well as for Isabelle. As for my soul, I still have Plato.

The Altstädter Hof is an inn frequented by wandering actors, gypsies, and carters. On the second floor there are a dozen rooms for rent and behind there is a large room with a piano and gymnastic equipment where variety artists can practice their numbers. The chief business, however, is the bar. It not only serves as a meeting place for traveling actors but is frequented by the underworld of the town as well.

I open the door to the back room. Renée de la Tour is standing beside the piano practicing a duet. In the background a man with a bamboo cane is training two white spitzes and a poodle. To the right two muscular women are lying on a mat smoking. And on the trapeze, her feet inserted beneath the bar and between her hands, her back thrust through, Gerda Schneider swings at me like the winged figurehead of a galleon.

The two muscular women are in bathing suits. As they loll about, their muscles play. No doubt they are the lady wrestlers on the program of the Altstädter Hof. Renée roars good evening to me in a first-class drill sergeant's voice and comes over. The dog trainer whistles. The dogs throw somersaults in the air. Gerda whishes smoothly back and forth on the trapeze, reminding me of the moment in the Red Mill when she looked up at me from between her legs. She is wearing black tights and has a red cloth knotted around her hair.

"She's practicing," Renée explains. "She wants to go back to the circus."

"The circus?" I look at Gerda with new interest. "Was she ever in the circus?"

"Of course. She grew up there. But the circus went broke. It couldn't go on paying for the lions' meat."

"Was she in the lion act?"

Renée laughs like a sergeant major and looks at me mockingly. "That would be exciting, wouldn't it? No, she was an acrobat."

Gerda whooshes over us again. She looks at me with staring eyes as though she wanted to hypnotize me. But she is not seeing me at all; her eyes stare from exertion.

"Is Willy really rich?" Renée de la Tour asks.

"I believe he is. What people call rich today. He has various enterprises and a pile of stocks that go up every day. Why?"

"I like men to be rich." Renée gives her soprano laugh. "All women like that," she roars then as though on the drill field.

"I've noticed that," I tell her bitterly. "A rich profiteer is better than a poor but honest employee."

Renée shakes with laughter. "Wealth and honesty don't go together, baby! Not these days! Probably they never did."

"Only if you inherit it or win it in a lottery."

"Not even then. Money ruins character, don't you know that?"

"I know. But then why do you consider it so important?"

"Because I don't care about character," Renée chirps in a prim, old-maid's voice. "I love comfort and security."

Gerda whirls toward us in a perfect *salto*. She comes to rest half a yard in front of me, rocking back and forth on her toes and laughing. "Renée is lying," she says.

"Did you hear what we were saying?"

"All women lie," Renée says in her angel's voice. "When they don't they're not worth bothering about."

"Amen," the dog trainer replies.

Gerda smooths back her hair. "I'm through here. Wait till I change."

She goes to a door marked Dressing Room. Renée looks after her. "She's pretty," she remarks impartially. "Look how she carries herself. She walks properly, and that's the most important thing in a woman. Bottom in, not out. Acrobats learn how."

"I heard that once before," I say. "From a connoisseur of women and granite. How do you walk properly?"

"When you feel as if you were holding a five-mark piece with your tail—and then forget about it."

I try to picture that and fail. It has been too long since I have seen a five-mark piece. But I know a woman who can yank a fair-sized nail out of the wall that way. She is Frau Beckmann, the girl friend of Karl Brill, the shoemaker. She's a powerful woman, made of iron. Karl Brill has won many a bet on her, and I myself have had an opportunity to admire her act. A nail is driven into the workshop wall, not too deep, of course, but deep enough so that it would take a good jerk by hand to pull it out. Then Karl goes to awaken Frau Beckmann. She appears among the drinkers in the shop wearing a light dressing gown, sober, serious, and matter-of-fact. A little cotton is wound around the head of the nail so she won't hurt herself, then Frau Beckmann takes up her position behind a low screen with her back to the wall, leaning slightly forward, her dressing gown discreetly wrapped around her, her hands resting on the screen. She maneuvers a little to get hold of the nail with her hams, suddenly tenses, straightens up, then relaxes—and the nail falls to the floor. Usually a little chalk trickles after it. Without a word or any sign of triumph Frau Beckmann turns around, disappears up the stairs, and Karl Brill collects the bets from his astounded drinking companions. It is strictly a sporting event; no one looks upon Frau Beckmann's performance from any but a purely professional point of view. And no one ventures a loose word about it. She would beat his head in. She is as strong as a giant; the two lady wrestlers are anemic children by comparison.

"Well, make Gerda happy," Renée says laconically. "For two weeks. Simple, isn't it?"

I stand there, somewhat embarrassed. The vade mecum for high society assuredly contains no rules for such a situation. Fortunately Willy appears. He is elegantly dressed and has a Borsalino on the side of his head; nevertheless, he looks like a cement block draped with artificial flowers. With a courtly gesture he kisses Renée's hand, then reaches in his pocket and brings out a small jewel box. "For the most fascinating woman in Werdenbrück," he announces with a bow.

Renée emits a small, soprano scream and looks at Willy incredulously. Then she opens the box. A gold ring set with an amethyst sparkles up at her. She puts it on the middle finger of her left hand, stares at it in rapture and then throws her arms around Willy. Willy stands there very proud and smiling, listening to the trills and the bass; in her excitement Renée can't keep control of them. "Willy!" she chirps, and then thunders, "I am so happy!"

Gerda comes out of the dressing room in a bathrobe. She has heard the scream and wants to know what's happening. "Get ready, children," Willy says. "We'll be on our way."

The two girls disappear. "Couldn't you have given Renée the ring later on when you were alone, you show-off?" I ask. "What am I to do now about Gerda?"

Willy breaks into good-natured laughter. "Damn it all, I never thought about that! What can we do? Come along and have dinner with us."

"So that all four of us can spend our time staring at Renée's amethyst? Not on your life."

"Listen to me," Willy says. "Things are not the same with Renée and me as with Gerda and you. I am serious. Believe it or not, I'm crazy about Renée. Seriously crazy. She's a magnificent creature!"

We sit down in two old cane chairs by the wall. The white spitzes are now practicing walking on their front legs. "Imagine," Willy explains. "It's her voice that drives me crazy. At night it's fabulous. As though you had two different women. First a tender one and a minute later a fishwife. And it goes farther than that. When it's dark and she cuts loose with that drill sergeant's voice of hers, cold shivers run up my back. It's damned odd. I'm not a pansy, but sometimes I feel as if I were defiling a general or that bastard Sergeant Flümer, who used to make life miserable for us when we were recruits. It's only for an instant and then everything's straight again, but—you understand what I mean?"

"More or less."

"All right, so she has me hooked. I want her to stay here. I'm going to fix up a little home for her."

"Do you think she'll give up her profession?"

"She doesn't need to. Once in a while she can accept an engagement. I'll go with her. My business is movable."

"Why don't you marry her? You're rich enough."

"Marriage is something else again," Willy explains. "How can you marry a woman who's capable at any minute of roaring at you like a general? You can't help jumping to attention when that happens unexpectedly; that's something in our blood. No, someday I'll marry a calm plump little thing who is a first-class cook. Renée, my boy, is the typical mistress."

I look with admiration at this man of the world. He smiles in a superior fashion. The *Breviary of Good Manners* is superfluous for him. I forgo wisecracks. Wit wears thin against someone able to give amethyst rings. The lady wrestlers get up lazily and try a couple of holds. Willy looks at them with interest. "Capital women," he whispers to me like a first lieutenant of the Kaiser's time.

"What's the matter with you? Attention! Eyes right!" a resonant voice roars behind us.

Willy jumps. It is Renée, exhibiting her ring and smiling. "See now what I mean?" Willy asks.

I see it all right. The two leave. Outside, Willy's car is waiting, the red town car with leather upholstery. I'm glad Gerda is taking longer to dress. At least she won't see that car. I wonder what I can offer her tonight. The only thing I have besides the breviary for men of the world is tickets for Eduard Knobloch's restaurant—and they unfortunately aren't valid in the evening. I decide to try them, nevertheless, and to pretend to Eduard that they are the last two.

Gerda comes in. "Do you know what I'd like, my pet?" she says before I can open my mouth. "Let's go into the country for a while. We'll take a streetcar. I want to go for a walk."

I stare at her, not trusting my ears. A walk in the country —exactly what Erna, that poison-tongued serpent, reproached me for. Has she mentioned it to Gerda? She would be quite capable of it.

"I thought we might go to the Walhalla," I say cautiously and mistrustfully. "They have magnificent food there."

Gerda shakes her head. "Why? It's much too nice for that. I made some potato salad this afternoon. Here!" She holds up a package. "We'll eat it in the country and we can buy sausages and beer to go with it. All right?"

I nod silently, more suspicious than ever. Erna's reproach about the seltzer water, sausage, beer, and cheap wine of no vintage still sticks in my mind. "I have to be back at nine in that stinking hole, the Red Mill," Gerda explains.

Stinking hole? I stare at Gerda once more. But her eyes are clear and innocent, with no trace of irony. And suddenly I understand! What's paradise for Erna is nothing but a place of employment for Gerda! She hates the dive that Erna loves. Rescued, I think. Thank God! The Red Mill with its fantastic prices sinks out of my mind like Gaston Münch as the ghost in Hamlet disappearing through the trap door at the city theater. Instead, the vision of priceless quiet days with sandwiches and homemade potato salad rises before me! The simple life! Earthly love! Peace of soul! At last! Sauerkraut, if you like, but sauerkraut, too, can be magnificent! With pineapple, for example, cooked in champagne. To be sure, I've never eaten it that way, but Eduard Knobloch says it's a dish fit for reigning kings and poets.

"All right, Gerda," I say casually. "If that's what you really want, we'll go for a walk in the woods."

Chapter Eight

The village of Wüstringen is gay with flags and bunting. We are all assembled—Georg and Heinrich Kroll, Kurt Bach, and I. The war memorial has been delivered and is now to be dedicated.

This morning the ministers of both denominations celebrated their rites in church; each for his own dead. In this the Catholic minister had the advantage; his church is bigger, it is brightly painted, has stained-glass windows, incense, brocaded vestments, and acolytes clad in white and red. The Protestant has no more than a chapel with sober walls and plain windows; now, standing beside the Catholic man of God, he is like a poor relation. The Catholic is attired in a lace tunic and is surrounded by his altar boys; the other is wearing a black coat, his single splendor. As a professional advertising man I have to admit that in these things Catholicism has an enormous advantage over Martin Luther. It appeals to the imagination and not to the intellect. Its priests are arrayed like native witch doctors; a Catholic service with its colors, its atmosphere, its incense, its picturesque usages is incomparable as a performance. The

Protestant feels this; he is thin and wears spectacles. The Catholic is red-cheeked, plump, and has beautiful white hair.

Each of them has done what he could for his dead. Unfortunately, among the fallen are two Jews, sons of Levi, the cattle merchant. For them no spiritual comfort has been provided. The two rival men of God join forces in opposing the presence of the rabbi—supported by the president of the veterans' organization, Major Wolkenstein, retired, an anti-Semite who firmly believes the war was lost because of the Jews. If you ask him why, he straightway brands you as a traitor. He was even against having the names of the two Levis engraved on the memorial tablet. He maintained they had beyond question fallen far behind the front. Finally, however, he was outvoted. The mayor exerted his influence. His own son died of grippe in 1918 in the reserve hospital in Werdenbrück without ever having been in the field. The mayor wanted him, too, to appear as a hero on the memorial tablet and so he declared that death is death and a soldier a soldier—thus the Levis got the two lowest places on the back of the tablet where, no doubt, the dogs will piss.

Wolkenstein is wearing complete imperial uniform. That, to be sure, is forbidden, but who is going to do anything about it? The strange transformation that began shortly after the armistice has gone forward steadily. The war which almost every soldier hated in 1918 has slowly become, for those who survived intact, the great adventure of their lives. They came back to the everyday life that had seemed a paradise to them when they lay in the trenches and cursed the war. Now it has become commonplace again, filled with cares and vexations, and at the same time the war has gradually risen on the horizon—far off, survived, and for that very reason, without their intention and almost without their co-operation, changed, transfigured, falsified. Mass murder has become an adventure from which they have escaped. The despair is forgotten, the misery glorified, and death, which did not strike them, has become what it is most of the time to the living—something abstract and no longer real. It only gains reality when it strikes close by or reaches out and seizes you. The veterans' organization, now drawn up in front of the memorial under the command of Wolkenstein, was pacifistic in 1918. Now it has become strongly nationalistic. Wolkenstein has adroitly transformed the memories of the war and the feelings of comradeship, which almost all of them had, into pride in the war. Anyone who is not nationalistic desecrates the memory of our fallen heroes—those poor, mistreated, fallen heroes who would all have loved to go on living. How they would sweep Wolkenstein from the platform where he is now speaking if they but could! But they are defenseless and have become the possession of thousands of Wolkensteins who use them for their selfish ends concealed under such words as patriotism and national pride. Patriotism! For Wolkenstein that means wearing a uniform again, becoming a colonel, and once more sending people to death.

He thunders mightily from the tribunal, warming to his theme: the inner cur, the dagger in the back, the unconquered German army, and the oath to our dead heroes, to honor them, to avenge them, and to rebuild the German army.

Heinrich Kroll listens reverently; he believes every word. Kurt Bach, who as creator of the lion with the lance in his flank has been included in the invitation, stares dreamily at the shrouded memorial. Georg looks as though he would give his life for a cigar; and I, wearing a borrowed morning coat that is too small for me, wish I were at home in bed with Gerda in our vine-draped room while the orchestra in the Altstädter Hof bangs out the "Song of the Siamese Guards."

Wolkenstein ends with three cheers. The band strikes up "The Good Comrade." The choir sings in two-part harmony.

We all join in. It is a neutral song, innocent of politics and revenge—a simple lament for a dead comrade.

The ministers step forward. The shroud falls from the memorial. Kurt Bach's roaring lion crouches on top of it. Four bronze eagles with lifted wings are poised on the edges. The memorial tablets are of black granite, the other stones of highest workmanship. It is a very costly memorial, and we expect to be paid for it this afternoon. That was the agreement and that is why we are here. We shall be practically bankrupt if we do not get the money. In the last week the dollar rate has almost doubled.

The ministers consecrate the memorial; each for his own God. During the war when we had to attend divine services and the ministers of the various denominations prayed for the victory of German arms, I often reflected that in just this way the English, French, Russian, American, Italian, and Japanese men of God were praying for the victory of their armies and I used to picture God as a kind of hurried and embarrassed club president, especially when He had to listen to the prayers of the same denomination from enemy countries. For which should He decide? For the one with the most inhabitants? Or the one with the most churches? And what of His justice if He let one country win and the other, where the prayers were no less diligent, lose? Sometimes He seemed to me like a harassed, elderly emperor, ruling over many countries and forced to keep changing his uniform to receive different deputations—now the Catholic, now the Protestant, the Evangelical, the Anglican, the Episcopalian, the Reformed, according to which divine service happened to be going on at the moment. Or like an emperor reviewing the Hussars, the Grenadiers, the Artillery, and the Navy.

The wreaths are put in place. One of them is ours, with the name of the firm on it. In his high falsetto Wolkenstein strikes up the song *"Deutschland, Deutschland über alles."*

Apparently this was not provided for on the program; the band is silent and only a few voices are lifted. Wolkenstein flushes and turns round in a rage. The trumpeter and then the English horn take up the melody. Both drown out Wolkenstein, who is now gesticulating violently. The other instruments come to life and about half the crowd gradually joins in; but Wolkenstein has begun too high and it all becomes rather squeaky. Fortunately the women take a hand. They, to be sure, are standing in the background but they save the situation and bring the song to a triumphant close. For some reason I think of Renée de la Tour—she could have done it all by herself.

The social activities begin in the afternoon. We have to stay because we have not yet received our money. Due to Wolkenstein's long patriotic speech we have missed the noon dollar exchange rate—no doubt a substantial rise, and a loss for us. The day is hot. My borrowed morning coat is too tight around the chest. There are thick, white clouds in the sky, and on the tables stand thick goblets of Steinhäger schnaps and beside them tall glasses of beer. Faces are red and glittering with sweat. The feast for the dead was rich and abundant. That evening there is to be a great patriotic ball in the Niedersächsischer Hof. Paper garlands hang everywhere and flags—black, white, and red, of course—and wreathes of evergreen. A single black, red, and gold flag hangs from the garret window in the last house in the village. Those are the colors of the German republic. Black, white, and red were those of the old empire. They have been forbidden, but Wolkenstein has declared that the dead fell under those glorious old colors and anyone who exhibits black, red, and gold is a traitor. That means that Beste, the cobbler, who lives there is a traitor. He was shot in the lungs during the war, but he is a traitor. In our beloved fatherland it is easy to be denounced as a traitor. Only the Wolkensteins are not. They are the law. They decide who is a traitor.

Excitement increases. The older people disappear. A good many of the veterans as well. Work in the fields summons them. The Iron Guard, as Wolkenstein calls the others, remain. The ministers have long since departed. The Iron Guard consists of younger men. Wolkenstein, who despises the republic but accepts the pension it gives him and uses it to agitate against it, makes another speech which begins with the word "Comrades." That is too much for me. No Wolkenstein ever called us comrades when we were in the army. Then we were filth, *schweinehunde,* idiots and, at best, men. Only once, on the evening before an attack, were we called comrades—by that slave driver Helle, a former commissioner of forests, who was our first lieutenant. He was afraid he would get a bullet in the back next morning.

We go to the mayor's house. He is sitting at ease over coffee, cakes, and cigars, and he refuses to pay. We were prepared for something of the sort. Fortunately Heinrich Kroll is not with us; he has stayed behind to admire Wolkenstein. Kurt Bach has gone out into the grain fields with a muscular village beauty to enjoy nature. Georg and I stand facing Mayor Döbbeling, who is supported by his hunchbacked clerk, Westhaus. "Come back next week," Döbbeling says comfortably, offering us cigars. "Then we'll have the whole thing straightened out and we'll pay you at once. In all this confusion it wasn't possible today."

We accept the cigars. "That may well be," Georg replies. "But we need the money today, Herr Döbbeling."

The clerk laughs. "Everyone needs money."

Döbbeling winks at him. He pours schnaps. "Let's drink to it!"

It was not he who invited us to the celebration; it was Wolkenstein, who gives no thought to gross commercial matters. Döbbeling would have liked none of us to be present—or at most, Heinrich Kroll. He would have had no trouble in handling him.

"It was agreed that we were to get the money at the dedication," Georg says.

Döbbeling raises his shoulders equably. "This is practically the same thing—next week. If you were paid everywhere as promptly as that—"

"We are paid, otherwise we don't deliver."

"Well this time you have delivered. *Prost!*"

We do not refuse the schnaps. Döbbeling winks again at his admiring clerk. "Good schnaps," I say.

"Have another?" the clerk asks.

"Why not?"

The clerk pours. We drink. "Well then—" Döbbeling says. "Next week."

"Well then," Georg says, "today! Where is our money?"

Döbbeling is offended. We have accepted his schnaps and cigars and yet we are still rebellious. That is against the rules. "Next week," he says. "Have another schnaps for the road?"

"Why not?"

Döbbeling and the clerk grow animated. They think they have won. I glance through the window. Outside, as though in a framed picture, lies the late afternoon landscape—the courtyard gate, an oak tree, and beyond them, infinitely peaceful, extend the fields in bright chrome and light green. Why, I wonder, do we sit here quarreling? Isn't life itself out there, golden and green and silent, in the rising and falling breath of the seasons? What have we turned it into?

"It pains me," I hear Georg say, "but we must insist. You know that next week the money will be worth much less. We have already lost money on the job. It took three weeks longer than we expected."

The mayor looks at him craftily. "Well then, one week more or less won't make any difference."

The little clerk suddenly bleats. "What do you expect to

do, then, if you don't get your money? You can't take the memorial away with you!"

"Why not?" I reply. "There are four of us and one is a sculptor. We could easily take the eagles with us and even the lion if that proves necessary. Our workmen can be here in two hours."

The clerk smiles. "Do you really think you could take apart a memorial that has been dedicated? There are several thousand people in Wüstringen."

"Not to mention Major Wolkenstein and the veterans," the mayor adds. "Enthusiastic patriots."

"Besides, if you should try it, it would be hard for you ever to sell another tombstone here." The clerk is grinning openly now.

"Another schnaps?" Döbbeling asks, grinning also. They have us in a trap. There's nothing we can do.

At this moment a man comes racing across the courtyard. "Mayor!" he shouts through the window. "You must come at once. There has been an accident!"

"What?"

"Beste! The carpenter—they have—they were going to pull down his flag and that's when it happened!"

"What? Did Beste shoot? That damned socialist!"

"No! Beste is—he's bleeding—"

"No one else?"

"No, just Beste—"

Döbbeling's face brightens. "Well then! No reason to shout so loud!"

"He can't get up. He's bleeding from the mouth."

"Got punched in his fresh snout," the little clerk explains. "Why does he always have to be so irritating? We're coming. Just take it easy."

"You will excuse me, I feel sure," Döbbeling says with dignity to us. "This is official business. I have to investigate the matter. We must postpone our business."

He puts on his coat, sure that he is now through with us for good. We go out with him. He is in no great hurry, and we know why. When he arrives no one will remember who beat up Beste. It is an old story.

Beste is lying in the narrow hallway of his house. The flag of the republic lies beside him torn in two. A number of people are standing in front of the house. None of the Iron Guard is present. "What happened?" Döbbeling asks a policeman, standing beside the door, notebook in hand.

The policeman is about to report. "Were you present?" Döbbeling asks.

"No. I was called later."

"Very good. So you know nothing. Who was present?"

No one replies. "Aren't you going to send for a doctor?" Georg asks.

Döbbeling gives him a hostile glance. "Is that necessary? A little water—"

"It is necessary. The man is dying."

Döbbeling turns around hastily and bends over Beste. "Dying?"

"Dying. He has a bad hemorrhage. Perhaps there are broken bones as well. It looks as though he had been thrown down the stairs."

Döbbeling gives Georg a slow look. "That is simply your supposition, Herr Kroll, and nothing more. We'll let the medical examiner decide the matter."

"And what about a doctor for this man?"

"Let me take care of that. I happen to be the mayor and not you. Fetch Doctor Bredius," Döbbeling says to two boys with bicycles. "Tell him there has been an accident."

We wait. Bredius comes up on the bicycle of one of the boys. He jumps off and goes into the hall. "The man is dead," he says, straightening up.

"Dead?"

"Yes, dead. It's Beste, isn't it? The one who was wounded in the lungs."

The mayor nods uncomfortably. "It's Beste. I know nothing about any wound in the lungs. But perhaps he had a shock—no doubt his heart was weak—"

"You don't get a hemorrhage from that," Bredius declares dryly. "What happened?"

"We're just looking into that. Will everyone please leave except those who can give evidence as witnesses." He looks at Georg and me.

"We'll come back later," I say.

Almost all the people who have been standing around leave with us. There won't be many witnesses.

We are sitting in the Niedersächsischer Hof. Georg is angrier than I have seen him in a long time. A young workman comes in and sits down at our table. "Were you there?" Georg asks.

"I was there when Wolkenstein was egging the crowd on to pull down the flag. Wiping out that stain of infamy, he called it."

"Did Wolkenstein go along?"

"No."

"Of course not. What about the others?"

"A whole bunch went storming over to Beste's house. They had all been drinking."

"And then?"

"I think Beste tried to defend himself. They probably really didn't intend to kill him. But then it just happened. Beste was trying to hold onto the flag and they pushed him and it down the stairs together. Perhaps they gave him a few clouts as well. When you've been drinking you often don't know your own strength. They certainly didn't intend to kill him."

"They just wanted to give him something to remember them by?"

"Yes. Exactly that."

"That's what Wolkenstein told them to do, eh?"

The workman nods and then looks alarmed. "How do you know that?"

"I can imagine. That's how it was, wasn't it?"

The workman is silent. "If you know, why do you ask me?" he says finally.

"There ought to be a precise record. Homicide is something for the prosecuting attorney. And so is incitement to homicide."

The workman recoils. "I'll have nothing to do with that. I don't know anything."

"You know a lot. And there are other people who know what happened too."

The workman finishes his beer. "I haven't said anything," he announces with determination. "And I don't know anything. What do you think would happen to me if I didn't keep my trap shut? No sir, not I! I have a wife and a child and I have to live. Do you think I could find a job if I started to babble? No sir, look for someone else! Not me!"

He disappears. "That's how it will be with all of them," Georg says.

We wait. Outside we see Wolkenstein walking by. He is no longer in uniform and is carrying a brown handbag. "Where is he going?" I ask.

"To the station. He no longer lives in Wüstringen. He has moved to Werdenbrück. Now he's district president of the veterans' organizations. He only came here for the dedication. He has his uniform in that suitcase."

Kurt Bach appears with the girl. They have brought flowers in with them. The girl is inconsolable when she hears what has happened. "Then they're sure to cancel the ball."

"I don't think so," I say.

"Yes, they will. When there is an unburied body. What luck!"

Georg gets up. "Come along," he says to me. "It's no good. We'll have to go and talk to Döbbeling again."

The village is suddenly quiet. The sun shines down at an angle from behind the war memorial. Kurt Bach's marble lion is aglow. Döbbeling has now become entirely an official personage.

"You're not going to start talking about money again in the presence of death?" he remarks at once.

"Yes I am," Georg says. "That's our profession. We are always in the presence of death."

"You must be patient. I have no time now. You know what has just happened."

"Yes, we know. And since we saw you we have found out the rest. You can put us down as witnesses, Herr Döbbeling. We're going to stay here until we get our money and so we'll be glad to report to the Homicide Department tomorrow morning."

"Witnesses? What kind of witnesses? You weren't even there."

"Witnesses. Just let us attend to that. After all, you must want to find out everything connected with the killing of Beste, the carpenter. The killing and the incitement thereto."

Döbbeling stares at Georg for a while. Then he says slowly: "Are you trying to blackmail me?"

Georg gets up. "Will you be so kind as to tell me exactly what you mean by that?"

Döbbeling makes no reply. He continues to stare at Georg. Georg returns his glance. Then Döbbeling goes to the safe, opens it, and lays several packages of notes on the table. "Count them and give me a receipt."

The money lies on the red-checked tablecloth amid the empty schnaps glasses and the coffee cups. Georg counts it and writes a receipt. I glance through the window. The yellow and green fields are still shimmering; but they are no longer the harmony of existence; they are less and more.

Döbbeling takes Georg's receipt. "I hope you understand that you will not be putting up any more tombstones in our cemetery," he says.

Georg shakes his head. "That's where you're mistaken. As a matter of fact we're going to put one up very soon. For the carpenter Beste. Gratis. And that has nothing to do with politics. If you should decide to add Beste's name to the war memorial, we're perfectly willing to do it for nothing."

"I hardly think it will come to that."

"I imagine not."

We walk to the station. "So the fellow had the money right there," I say.

"Of course. I knew he had it. He's had it for eight weeks and he's been speculating with it. Made a handsome profit and was going to make a few hundred thousand more. We wouldn't have got it next week either."

At the station Heinrich Kroll and Kurt Bach are waiting for us. "Did you get the money?" Heinrich asks.

"Yes."

"That's what I expected. They're very respectable people here. Reliable."

"Yes. Reliable."

"The ball has been canceled," says Kurt Bach, the nature boy.

Heinrich straightens his tie. "That carpenter brought it on himself. It was a nasty provocation."

"What? Putting up the official flag of our country?"

"It was a provocation. He knew how the others feel. He

ought to have realized there'd be a row. It's only logical."

"Yes, Heinrich, it's logical," Georg says. "And now do me the favor of shutting your logical trap."

Heinrich Kroll gets up, offended. He is about to say something but changes his mind when he sees Georg's face. He methodically brushes the dust from his dark jacket with his hand. Then he spies Wolkenstein, who is also waiting for the train. The retired major is sitting on a remote bench and looks as if he wished he were already in Werdenbrück. He shows no sign of joy when Heinrich goes up to him. Nevertheless, Heinrich sits down beside him.

"What will come of this?" I ask Georg.

"Nothing. None of the culprits will be found."

"And Wolkenstein?"

"Nothing will happen to him either. The carpenter is the only one who would be punished if he were still alive. Not the others. Political murder, when it strikes from the right, is honorable and surrounded by mitigating circumstances. We have a republic, but we have taken over the judges, officials, and officers from the old days. So what do you expect?"

We stare at the sunset. The train goes puffing toward it, black and lost, like a funeral coach. It's strange, I think, all of us have seen so many dead in the war and we know that over two million of us fell uselessly—why, then, are we so excited about a single man, when we have practically forgotten the two million already? But probably the reason is that one dead man is death—and two million are only a statistic.

Chapter Nine

"A mausoleum!" Frau Niebuhr says. "A mausoleum or nothing!"

"All right," I reply. "Let it be a mausoleum."

In the short time since Niebuhr's death the timid little woman has changed remarkably. Now she is caustic, talkative, and quarrelsome and has really become pretty much of a pest. I have been dickering with her for two weeks about a memorial for the baker, and each day I think less harshly of the departed. Many people are brave and kind as long as things go badly with them and become intolerable when things improve, especially in our beloved fatherland; the most timid and obsequious recruits here often become the worst-tempered noncoms.

"You haven't any on display," Frau Niebuhr says pointedly.

"Mausoleums," I explain, "are not put on display. They are made to order like the ball dresses of queens. We have a few drawings of them here and perhaps we'll have to make one especially for you."

"Of course! It must be something quite special. Otherwise I shall go to Hollmann and Klotz."

"I hope you have been there already. We like our clients to visit the competition. In mausoleums quality is the thing of paramount importance."

I know that she has been there long since. The traveler for Hollmann and Klotz, Weeping Oskar, has told me about it. We ran into him a short time ago and tried to bribe him away. He is still undecided, but we have offered him a higher percentage than Hollmann and Klotz pay, and to show us that he is well disposed during this period of reflection he is temporarily working for us as a spy. "Show me your drawings!" Frau Niebuhr commands like a duchess.

We have none, but I get out a few renderings of war memorials. They are effective, forty-five inches high, drawn with charcoal and colored chalk and embellished with appropriate backgrounds.

"A lion," Frau Niebuhr says. "He was a lion! But a leaping lion, not a dying one. It must be a leaping lion."

"How would a leaping horse do?" I ask. "A few years ago our sculptor won the Berlin-Teplitz challenge trophy with that subject."

She shakes her head. "An eagle," she says thoughtfully.

"A true mausoleum should be a kind of chapel," I explain. "Stained glass like a church, a marble sarcophagus with bronze laurel wreaths, a marble bench for your repose and silent prayer, around the outside flowers, cypresses, gravel paths, perhaps a bird bath for our feathered songsters, an enclosure for the plot of short granite columns with bronze chains, a massive iron door with the monogram, the family coat of arms, or the hallmark of the Bakers' Guild—"

Frau Niebuhr listens as though Moritz Rosenthal were playing a Chopin nocturne. "Sounds all right," she says then. "But haven't you anything original?"

I stare at her angrily. She stares back coldly—the prototype of the eternal rich client.

"There are original things, to be sure," I reply softly and venomously. "For example, like those in the Campo Santo in Genoa. Our sculptor worked there for years. One of the showpieces is by him—the figure of a weeping woman bending over a coffin, in the background the risen dead, being led heavenward by an angel. The angel is looking backward and with his free hand blesses the mourning widow. All this in white Carrara marble, the angel with wings either folded or spread—"

"Very nice. What else is there?"

"Very often the vocation of the departed is represented. For example, one could have a statue of a master baker kneading bread. Behind him stands death, tapping him on the shoulder. Death can be represented with or without a scythe, either wearing a pall or naked, that is as a skeleton, a very difficult undertaking, for a sculptor, especially in the matter of the ribs, which have to be chiseled out separately and very carefully so that they won't break."

Frau Niebuhr is silent as though waiting for more. "Of course the family can be added too," I continue. "Praying at one side or cowering in terror before death. These, naturally, are objects that will run into the billions and will require a year or two of work. A big advance and consultation fees would be absolutely necessary."

Suddenly I fear she will accept one of my proposals. A twisted angel is the height of Kurt Bach's attainments; his art does not go beyond that. Nevertheless, at need we could give the sculpture to a subcontractor.

"And then?" Frau Niebuhr asks inexorably.

I wonder whether to tell this heartless devil something about the tomb in the form of a sarcophagus with the lid pushed a little to one side and a skeleton hand reaching out—but I decide against it. Our positions are unequal; she

144

is the buyer and I am the seller; she can torment me, but not the other way about—and perhaps she will buy something after all.

"That's all for the present."

Frau Niebuhr waits a moment longer. "If you have nothing more, I must go to Hollmann and Klotz."

She looks at me with June bug eyes. She has thrown her mourning veil back over her black hat. Now she is waiting for me to make a desperate plea. I do not do it. Instead, I explain coldly, "That will please us very much. It is our principle to draw in the competition so that people can see how capable our firm is. In commissions involving so much sculpture the artist is, of course, extremely important, otherwise you may suddenly have, as happened recently in the case of one of our competitors whose name I should prefer not to mention, an angel with two left feet. Squinting madonnas have turned up, too, and a Christ with eleven fingers. When it was noticed it was already too late."

Frau Niebuhr brings down her veil like a theater curtain. "I'll be on my guard!"

I am convinced she will be. She is a greedy connoisseur of her own mourning, drinking it in full draughts. It will be a long time before she places her order; for until she makes up her mind she can torment all the monument builders—but afterward only one, the one on whom she has settled. Now she is something like a footloose bachelor of sorrow—later she will be like a married man who must remain faithful.

Wilke, the coffinmaker, comes out of his workroom. There are wood shavings hanging in his mustache. In his hand he has a box of appetizing smoked sprats which he is eating with relish.

"What do you think about life?" I ask him.

He pauses. "One way in the morning and another in the evening, one way in winter and another in summer, one way before eating and another afterward, and probably one way in youth and another in age."

"Right. Finally a sensible answer!"

"All right, if you know the answer why go on asking?"

"Asking is educational. Besides, I ask one way in the morning and another in the evening, one way in winter and another in summer, and one way before intercourse and another afterward."

"After intercourse," Wilke says thoughtfully. "Right you are, everything is different then! I had completely forgotten about that."

I bow before him as though before an abbot. "Congratulations on your asceticism! You have conquered the prick of the flesh already! I wish I were as far advanced!"

"Nonsense! I'm not impotent! But women are funny when you're a coffinmaker. They get the horrors. Don't want to come into your workroom when there's a coffin there. Not even if you serve Berlin pancakes and port wine."

"Where do you serve them?" I ask. "On an unfinished coffin? You certainly don't on a polished one; port wine leaves rings."

"On the bench by the window. You can sit on the coffin. Besides, it isn't even a coffin. It doesn't become a coffin until there's a dead body in it. Until then it's only a piece of carpentry work."

"Correct. But sometimes it's hard to make the distinction!"

"It all depends. Once in Hamburg I had a girl who was equal to it. Even enjoyed it. She was keen to try. I filled a coffin half full of those soft white pine shavings that always smell so woodsy and romantic. Everything went fine. We had magnificent fun until we wanted to get out again.

Some of the damned glue on the bottom hadn't quite dried, the shavings had been pushed aside and the girl's hair was stuck fast. She pulled a couple of times and then started to scream. She thought it was death who had got hold of her hair. She screamed and screamed, and people came running, including my boss; she was pulled out and I lost my job in a hurry. Too bad—it might have become a beautiful relationship! Life isn't easy for people like us."

Wilke throws me a despairing glance, then grins briefly and grubs appreciatively in the box without offering it to me. "I've heard of two cases of sprat poisoning," I say. "It's a particularly horrible and lingering death."

Wilke dismisses the thought. "These are freshly smoked. And very tender. A delicacy. I'll share them with you if you'll get me a nice, unprejudiced girl—like the one in the sweater who sometimes comes to visit you."

I stare at the coffinmaker. He undoubtedly means Gerda. Gerda for whom I am waiting at this moment. "I'm no procurer," I say sharply. "But I'll give you a piece of advice. Take your women someplace else, not into your workshop."

"Where would you suggest?" Wilke is picking bones out of his teeth. "That's just the hitch! To a hotel? Too expensive. Besides, there's the danger of police raids. Into the city parks? The police again! Or here in the yard? My shop is better than that."

"Haven't you an apartment?"

"My room isn't safe. My landlady is a dragon. Years ago I had an affair with her. In extreme need, you understand. Only for a short time—but even today, after ten years, that bitch is still jealous. All I have left is my shop. Well, how about an office of friendship? Introduce me to the lady in the sweater!"

I point silently at the empty box of sprats. Wilke throws

it into the court and goes to the faucet to wash his paws. "I have a bottle of first-class blended port upstairs," he volunteers.

"Keep the stuff for your next orgy!"

"It will turn into ink before that. But there are more sprats where these came from."

I point to my forehead and go into the office to get a drawing pad and a folding chair so that I can sketch a mausoleum for Frau Niebuhr. I sit down beside the obelisk —there I can listen for the telephone and at the same time keep an eye on the street and the courtyard. I plan to adorn the drawing of the memorial with this inscription: HERE, AFTER SEVERE AND PROLONGED SUFFERING, LIES MAJOR WOLKENSTEIN, RETIRED. DEPARTED THIS LIFE MAY, 1923.

One of the Knopf girls comes out and admires my work. She is a twin and can hardly be told from her sister. Their mother can do it by smell; Knopf doesn't care, and the rest of us can never be sure. I begin to speculate about what it would be like to be married to a twin if the other were living in the same house.

Gerda interrupts me. She is standing laughing at the entrance to the court. I put my drawing aside. The twin disappears. Wilke stops washing. Behind Gerda's back he points to the sprat box which the cat is pushing across the courtyard, then to himself and lifts two fingers. Silently he whispers: "Two."

Today Gerda is wearing a gray sweater, a gray skirt, and a black beret. She no longer looks like a parrot; she looks pretty and athletic and cheerful. I look at her with new eyes. A woman who is desired by someone else, even a love-starved coffinmaker, immediately becomes more precious than before. Man, as it happens, lives by relative rather than absolute values.

"Were you at the Red Mill today?" I ask.

Gerda nods. "That stinking hole! I was rehearsing there. How I hate these dives full of stale cigar smoke!"

I look at her approvingly. Behind her, Wilke is buttoning his shirt, combing the shavings out of his mustache, and adding three fingers to his bid. Five boxes of sprats! A handsome offer, but I pay no attention to it. Before me stands a week's happiness, clear and definite, a happiness without pain—the simple happiness of the senses and of the disciplined imagination, the short happiness of a two weeks' night-club engagement, already half over, a happiness that has freed me from Erna and has even made Isabelle what she should be, a painless fata morgana awakening no unrealizable desires.

"Come, Gerda," I say, suddenly filled with an upwelling of natural gratitude. "Let's go and have a first-rate meal today! Are you hungry?"

"Yes, very. We can get—"

"No potato salad today and no sausages! We're going to have a splendid meal and celebrate our jubilee, the midpoint of our life together. A week ago you came here for the first time; in another week you will wave me farewell from the station. Let's celebrate the former and not think about the latter!"

Gerda laughs. "As a matter of fact, I wasn't able to make any potato salad. Too much to do. The circus is not the same as that silly cabaret."

"Fine, then today we'll go to the Walhalla. Do you like to eat goulash?"

"I like to eat," Gerda replies.

"That's the thing! Let's stick to it! And now forward to the celebration of the high mid-point of our short life!"

I toss the drawing pad through the open window onto the office desk. As we leave I see Wilke's infinitely disappointed face. With a hopeless look he is holding up both hands—ten boxes of sprats—a fortune!

"Why not?" Eduard Knobloch says obligingly, to my amazement. I had expected bitter opposition. The coupons are only good at noon, but, after a glance at Gerda, Eduard is ready to accept them and he even lingers beside our table: "Won't you please introduce me?"

I am forced to do it. He has accepted the coupons, and so I must accept him. "Eduard Knobloch, hotelkeeper, restaurateur, poet, billionaire, and miser," I explain casually. "Fräulein Gerda Schneider."

Eduard bows, half flattered, half annoyed. "Don't believe a word he says, *gnädiges Fräulein.*"

"Not even your name?" I ask.

Gerda smiles. "Are you a billionaire? How interesting!"

Eduard sighs. "Only a businessman with all a businessman's worries. Don't pay any attention to this silly character! And you! A beautiful, resplendent image of God, carefree as a trout swimming above the dark abysses of melancholy—"

I can't believe my ears and gape at Eduard as though he had spit up gold. Today Gerda seems to have a magical attraction. "Never mind the plaster-cast phrases, Eduard," I say. "The lady is an artist herself. Am I supposed to be the dark abyss of melancholy? Where is the goulash?"

"I think Herr Knobloch speaks very poetically!" Gerda is looking at Eduard with innocent admiration. "How can you find time for it? With such a big establishment and so many waiters! You must be a happy man! So rich and talented too—"

"I manage, I manage!" Eduard is beaming. "So you are an artist too—"

I see a sudden doubt lay hold of him. Unquestionably the

shadow of Renée de la Tour has slipped in like a cloud across the moon. "A serious artist, I assume," he says.

"More serious than you," I reply. "Fräulein Schneider is no singer as you suspect. She can make lions jump through hoops and ride on tigers. And now forget the policeman that's in you as in all true sons of our beloved fatherland and serve us our dinner!"

"Well, lions and tigers!" Eduard's eyes have grown big. "Is that true?" he asks Gerda. "You can't believe a word this fellow says."

I kick her foot under the table. "I was in the circus," Gerda replies, not understanding the reason for this byplay. "And I'm going back to the circus again."

"What is there for dinner, Eduard?" I ask impatiently. "Or do we have to give you our whole life story in installments first?"

"I'll go and see myself," Eduard says gallantly to Gerda. "For such a guest! The magic of the sawdust ring! Ah! Forgive Herr Bodmer's erratic behavior. He grew up during the war with bogtrotters and got his education from his sergeant, a hysterical postman."

He waddles away. "A fine figure of a man," Gerda says. "Is he married?"

"He was, but his wife ran away from him because he is so stingy."

Gerda runs her fingers over the damask tablecloth. "She must have been a silly woman," she says dreamily. "I like thrifty people. They save their money."

"That's the silliest thing you can do in the inflation."

"Of course you have to invest it wisely." Gerda looks at her knife and fork of heavy silver plate. "I imagine your friend here does that all right—even if he is a poet."

I look at her in some amazement. "That may be," I say. "But others get no advantage from it. Least of all his wife. He made her work like a slave from morning till night.

Having a wife means to Eduard having someone to work for him for nothing."

Gerda smiles ambiguously like the Mona Lisa. "Every safe has its combination, don't you know that, baby?"

I stare at her. What's going on here? I wonder. Is this the same girl who was dining with me last night on sandwiches and milk for a modest five thousand marks, admiring the view and talking about the magic of the simple life? "Eduard is fat, dirty, and incurably stingy," I announce firmly. "I've known him for years."

Riesenfeld, that expert on women, has told me once that this combination would scare off any woman. But Gerda seems not to be an ordinary woman. She examines the big chandeliers hanging from the ceiling like transparent stalactites, and sticks to her dream. "Probably he needs someone to take care of him. Not like a hen of course! He seems to need someone who appreciates his good qualities."

I am now openly alarmed. Are my peaceful two weeks of happiness already slipping away? Why did I, fool that I am, have to drag Gerda here, to this place of silver and crystal? "Eduard has no good qualities," I say.

Gerda smiles again. "Every man has some. You just have to bring them out."

Fortunately at this moment the waiter Freidank appears, pompously bearing a *pâté* on a silver platter. "What in the world is that?" I ask.

"Goose liver *pâté*," Freidank announces haughtily.

"But it says potato soup on the menu!"

"This is the menu Herr Knobloch himself ordered," says Freidank, a former lance corporal in the Commissary Department, slicing two pieces—a thick one for Gerda, a thin one for me. "Or would you rather have potato soup according to your constitutional rights?" he inquires cordially. "It can be done."

Gerda laughs. Angered at Eduard's cheap attempt to

win her with food, I am about to order potato soup when Gerda kicks me under the table. On top she graciously exchanges plates with me. "That's how it should be," she says to Freidank. "A man must always have the larger portion, don't you think?"

"Well, yes," Freidank stutters, suddenly confused. "At home—but here—" The former lance corporal doesn't know what to do. He has had orders from Eduard to give Gerda a generous slice but me a mere sliver and he has followed those orders. Now he sees the reverse happening and almost has a nervous breakdown; he must assume responsibility and doesn't know what to do. Prompt obedience to orders has been bred into our proud blood for centuries—but to decide something by one's self is another matter. Freidank does the one thing he knows: he looks about for his master, hoping for new orders.

Eduard appears. "Go ahead and serve, Freidank, what are you waiting for?"

I pick up my fork and quickly cut a piece of the *pâté* in front of me, just as Freidank, true to his original orders, tries to change the plates. Freidank freezes. Gerda bursts into laughter. Eduard takes command like a general in the field, appraises the situation, pushes Freidank aside, cuts a second good-sized piece of *pâté,* lays it with a gallant gesture in front of Gerda, and asks me in a bittersweet tone: "Do you like it?"

"It's all right," I reply. "Too bad it's not goose liver."

"It is goose liver."

"It tastes like calf's liver."

"Have you ever in your life eaten goose liver?"

"Eduard," I reply, "I have eaten so much goose liver that I vomited it."

Eduard laughs through his nose. "Where?" he asks contemptuously.

"In France, during the advance, while I was being

trained to be a man. We conquered a whole store full of goose liver. Strasbourg goose liver in tureens with black truffles from Périgord which are missing in yours. At that time you were peeling potatoes in the kitchen."

I do not go on to say that I got sick because we also found the owner of the store—a little old woman plastered in shreds on the remnant of the wall, her gray head torn off and stuck on a store hook as though impaled on the lance of some barbarian tribesman.

"And how do you like it?" Eduard asks Gerda in the melting tones of a frog squatting happily beside the dark abysses of melancholy.

"Fine," Gerda replies, going to work.

Eduard makes a courtly bow and withdraws like a dancing elephant. "You see," Gerda says beaming at me. "He isn't so stingy after all."

I put down my fork. "Listen, you circus wonder with your sawdust halo," I reply, "you see before you a man whose pride is still severely injured, to speak in Eduard's jargon, because he was left flat by a lady who ran off with a rich profiteer. Is it now your intention to pour boiling oil in the still unhealed wounds, to borrow Eduard's baroque prose again, by doing the same thing to me?"

Gerda laughs and goes on eating. "Don't talk nonsense, my pet," she commands with her mouth full. "And don't be an injured liverwurst. Make more money than the others if that's what's bothering you."

"Fine advice! How am I to make it? By magic?"

"The way the others do. They've managed somehow."

"Eduard inherited this hotel," I say bitterly.

"And Willy?"

"Willy is a profiteer."

"What is a profiteer?"

"A man who knows all the angles. Who deals in everything from herrings to steel shares. Who does business where he can with whom he can and how he can as long as he manages to stay out of jail."

"Well, there you see!" Gerda says, helping herself to the rest of the *pâté*.

"Do you want me to be one?"

Gerda cracks a roll with her strong teeth. "Be one or don't just as you like. But don't get in a stew if you don't want to be one and the others do. Anyone can complain, my pet!"

"That's right," I say, perplexed and suddenly very sober. A mass of soap bubbles suddenly seem to be bursting inside my skull. I look at Gerda. She has a damnably reasonable way of looking at things. "You're perfectly right, you know," I say.

"Of course I'm right. But just look what's coming! Do you think that can be for us?"

It is for us. A roast chicken and asparagus. A meal for munitions makers. Eduard supervises the serving himself. He lets Freidank carve. "The breast for madame," he commands.

"I'd rather have a leg," Gerda says.

"A leg and a piece of the breast for madame," Eduard directs gallantly.

"Go right ahead," Gerda replies. "You are a cavalier, Herr Knobloch! I knew you were!"

Eduard smirks with self-satisfaction. I cannot understand why he is putting on this act. I can't believe he likes Gerda so much as to make her presents of this sort; more likely he is trying to snatch her away from me out of rage over our coupons. A retaliatory act of justice. "Freidank," I say. "Take this skeleton off my plate. I don't eat bones. Give me the other leg in return. Or is your chicken a one-legged victim of the war?"

Freidank looks at his master like a sheep dog. "That's the tastiest of all," Eduard explains. "The breast bones are very delicate to nibble."

"I'm no nibbler. I'm an eater."

Eduard shrugs his heavy shoulders and reluctantly gives me the other leg. "Wouldn't you rather have some salad?" he asks. "Asparagus is very injurious to drunkards."

"Give me the asparagus. I am a modern man with a strong tendency to self-destruction."

Eduard floats off like a rubber rhinoceros. Suddenly I have an inspiration. "Knobloch!" I roar after him in the thunderous tones of Renée de la Tour.

He whirls around as though struck in the back by a lance. "What's the meaning of that?" he asks me indignantly.

"What?"

"To roar like that."

"Roar? Who's roaring except you? Or don't you want Miss Schneider to have some salad? If not, why offer it to her?"

Eduard's eyes become enormous. One can see in them a monstrous suspicion growing into a certainty. "You—" he asks Gerda. "Was it you who called me?"

"If there is any salad, I'd like to have some," Gerda answers, not knowing what it is all about. Eduard continues to stand beside our table. Now he firmly believes that Gerda is Renée de la Tour's sister. I can see how he regrets the liver *pâté,* the chicken, and the asparagus. He feels that he has been horribly tricked. "It was Herr Bodmer," says Freidank, who has crept up. "I saw him."

But Freidank's words make no impression on Eduard. "Speak when you're spoken to, waiter," I say to him carelessly. "You should have learned that from the Prussians! On your way now—go on spilling goulash sauce down the necks of unsuspecting guests. And you, Eduard, since you're here, tell me whether this magnificent meal is a gift or are you going to want our coupons for it?"

Eduard looks as though he were about to have a stroke. "Hand over the coupons, you scoundrel," he says dully.

I tear them out and lay the bits of paper on the table. "Who's been playing the scoundrel here is open to question, you incapable Don Juan," I say.

Eduard does not pick up the coupons himself. "Freidank," he says, now almost voiceless with rage. "Throw this rubbish into the wastebasket."

"Wait," I say, reaching for the menu. "If we are going to pay, we are still entitled to dessert. What would you like, Gerda? *Rote grütze* or compote?"

"What do you recommend, Herr Knobloch?" asks Gerda, unaware of the drama going on inside Eduard.

Eduard makes a despairing gesture and departs. "Well then, compote!" I shout after him.

He jerks slightly and then goes on as though he were treading on eggs. Each second he expects to hear the drill sergeant's voice again. I hesitate and then decide against it, as a more effective tactic. "What's going on here all of a sudden?" Gerda asks.

"Nothing," I reply, dividing the chicken bones between us. "Nothing but a small illustration of the great Clausewitz's thesis on strategy: Attack when your opponent thinks he has won, and then at the point where he least expects it."

Gerda nods uncomprehendingly and begins to eat the compote that Freidank has rudely slapped down in front of us. I look at her thoughtfully and decide never to bring her to the Walhalla again, but from now on to follow Georg's iron law: Never take a woman to a new place, then she won't insist on going there and won't run away from you.

It is night. I am leaning on the window sill of my room. The moon is shining, the heavy scent of lilacs drifts up from the garden. It's an hour since I came home from the

Altstädter Hof. A pair of lovers flits along the street in the shadow of the moon and disappears into our garden. I do nothing about it; when you are not thirsty yourself you are generous toward others—and now the nights are irresistible. Just to prevent accidents, I have put signs on the two precious memorial crosses with the inscription: "Warning! May fall! Avoid broken toes!" For some reason or other the lovers seem to prefer the crosses when the ground is wet; no doubt because they can hold onto them more firmly, although you would think the medium-sized monuments would do equally well. I had the notion of putting up another sign recommending them, but I gave it up. Sometimes Frau Kroll rises early and, for all her tolerance, she would box my ears for frivolity before I could explain to her that before the war I was a prudish fellow—a characteristic that disappeared during the defense of our beloved fatherland.

Suddenly I see a square black figure coming along through the moonlight. I freeze. It is Watzek, the horse butcher. He disappears into his house two hours ahead of time. Perhaps he has run out of nags; horseflesh is much in demand these days. I watch the window. It lights up, and Watzek's shadow wanders about. I wonder whether to tell Georg Kroll; but disturbing lovers is a thankless task and, besides, it may be that Watzek will go to sleep without noticing anything. That, however, does not seem to be happening. The butcher opens the window and stares right and left along the street. I hear him snort. He closes the shutters and after a while appears at the door with a chair in his hand, his butcher's knife in the leg of his boot. He sits down on the chair as though to await Lisa's return. I look at the clock; it is eleven thirty. The night is warm, and Watzek may sit there for hours. Lisa, on the other hand, has been with Georg for quite a while; the hoarse panting of love has already subsided. If she runs into the butcher's arms she will no doubt find some plausible explanation and he no doubt will be taken in. Just the same, it would be better if nothing happened.

I creep down the stairs and tap out the beginning of the "Hohenfriedberger March" on Georg's door. His bald head appears. I tell him what has happened. "Damn it," he says. "Go and **try** to get him away."

"At this hour?"

"Try it! Exercise your charm."

I wander out, yawn, pause, and then stroll over to Watzek. "Nice evening," I say.

"Nice evening, shit," Watzek replies.

"Well, of course," I concede.

"It won't last much longer," Watzek says suddenly and fiercely.

"What won't?"

"What? You know exactly what! This filthiness! What else?"

"Filthiness?" I ask in alarm. "What do you mean?"

"Well, what do you think? Don't you see it yourself?"

I glance at the knife in his boot and I already see Georg lying with throat cut among the monuments. Not Lisa, of course; that's man's old idiocy. "It depends on how you look at it," I say diplomatically. I can't understand why Watzek hasn't already climbed through Georg's window. It's on the ground floor and open.

"All that will be atoned for," Watzek declares grimly. "Blood will flow. The guilty will pay."

I look at him. He has long arms and a thickset frame; he looks very strong. I could catch him in the chin with my knee and when he staggered to his feet kick him between the legs—or if he tried to run I could trip him up and then pound his head on the pavement. That would do for the moment—but what about later on?

"Did you hear him?" Watzek asks.

"Who?"

"You know! Him! Who else? There's only one after all!"

I listen. I haven't heard a thing. The street is quiet. Georg's window has now been cautiously closed.

"Who did you expect me to hear?" I ask loudly to win time and warn the others so that Lisa can disappear into the garden.

"Man alive, him! The *Führer!* Adolf Hilter!"

"Adolf Hitler!" I repeat in relief. "Him!"

"What do you mean, him?" Watzek asks challengingly. "Aren't you for him?"

"And how! Especially just now! You can't imagine how much!"

"Then why didn't you listen to him?"

"But he wasn't here."

"He was on the radio. We heard him at the stockyard. A six-tube set. He will change everything! Marvelous speech! That man knows what's wrong. Everything must be changed."

"That's obvious," I say. There, in one sentence, lies the whole stock in trade of the world's demagogues. "Everything must be changed! How about a beer?"

"Beer? Where?"

"At Blume's, around the corner."

"I'm waiting for my wife."

"You can wait for her just as well at Blume's. What did Hitler talk about? I'd like to know. My radio is caput."

"About everything," the butcher says, getting up. "That man knows everything! Everything, I tell you, comrade!"

He puts his chair back in the hall and we wander companionably off toward the Dortmunder beer in Blume's Garden Restaurant.

Chapter Ten

In the mild twilight the glass man is standing motionless in front of a rose bed. Gregory VII is strolling along the avenue of chestnut trees. A middle-aged nurse is taking a bent old man for a walk; he keeps trying to pinch her muscular posterior and after each attempt giggles happily. Two men are sitting beside me on a bench, each explaining to the other why he is mad and neither paying the slightest attention. Three women in striped dresses are watering the flowers, moving silently through the evening with their tin cans.

I am perched on a bench beside the rose bed. Here everything is peaceful and right. No one is disturbed because the dollar has risen twenty thousand marks in a single day. No one hangs himself on that account, as an elderly couple did last night in the city. They were found this morning in the wardrobe—each on a length of clothesline. Except for them there was nothing in the wardrobe; everything had been sold or pawned, even the bed and the wardrobe itself. When the purchaser of the furniture came to get it he discovered the bodies. They were clinging together and their swollen, bluish tongues were pointed at each other. They were very light and could be taken down quickly. Both were freshly washed, their hair brushed, and their clothes clean and neatly mended. The purchaser, a full-blooded furniture dealer, vomited when he saw them and announced that he did not want the wardrobe. It was not until evening that he changed his mind and sent for it. By then the bodies were lying on the bed and had to be removed because the bed, too, was to be taken. Neighbors loaned a couple of tables which served as biers for the old people, their heads covered with tissue paper. The tissue paper was the only thing in the apartment that still belonged to them. They left a letter in which they said they had originally intended to kill themselves by gas, but the gas company had turned it off because the bill was so long overdue. And so they asked the furniture dealer's pardon for the trouble they were causing him.

Isabelle approaches. She is wearing blue shorts that leave her knees bare, a yellow blouse, and an amber necklace.

I have not seen her for some time. After devotion in church I have slipped away each time and gone home. It was not easy to forgo the fine meal and the wine with Bodendiek and Wernicke, but I preferred peace and quiet with sandwiches and potato salad and Gerda.

"Where have you been?" Isabelle asks me as she always does.

"Out there," I say vaguely. "Where money is the one thing of importance."

She sits down on the arm of the bench. Her legs are very brown, as though she had spent a lot of time in the sun. The two men beside me look up ill-temperedly, then rise and walk away. Isabelle slides down onto the bench. "Why do children die, Rudolf?" she asks.

"I don't know."

I do not look at her. I am determined never again to become involved with her; it is bad enough that she is sitting there beside me with her long legs and her tennis shorts as though she had guessed that from now on I intend to live by Georg's recipe.

"Why are they born if they are going to die right away?"

"You must ask Vicar Bodendiek about that. He maintains that God keeps a record of every hair that falls from everyone's head and that all of it has a meaning and a moral lesson."

Isabelle laughs. "God keeps a record? Of whom? Of Himself? Why? After all, He knows everything, doesn't He?"

"Yes," I say, suddenly angry without knowing why. "He is omniscient, just, kind, and filled with love—nevertheless, children die and the mothers they need die and no one knows why there is so much misery in the world."

Isabelle turns toward me with a start. She is no longer laughing. "Why isn't everyone simply happy, Rudolf?"

"I don't know. Perhaps because then God would be bored."

"No," she says quickly. "That's not the reason."

"What is it then?"

"Because He is afraid."

"Afraid? Of what?"

"If everyone were happy, there would be no more need of God."

Now I am looking at her. Her eyes are very transparent. Her face is brown and thinner than before. "He only exists for unhappiness," she says. "That is when you need Him and pray to Him. That's why He causes it."

"There are people, too, who pray to God because they are happy."

"Really?" Isabelle smiles incredulously. "Then they pray because they are afraid they won't stay happy. Everything is fear, Rudolf. Don't you know that?"

The cheerful old man is led past us by his muscular nurse. From a window in the main building comes the high whine of a vacuum cleaner. I look around. The window is open but barred, a black hole out of which the vacuum cleaner screams like a damned soul.

"Everything is fear," Isabelle repeats. "Aren't you ever afraid?"

"I don't know," I reply, still on my guard. "I guess so. I was often afraid in the war."

"That's not what I mean. That is reasonable fear. I mean nameless fear."

"Of what? Of life?"

She shakes her head. "No. An earlier fear."

"Of death?"

She shakes her head again. I ask no further questions. I don't want to become involved. We sit in silence for a time in the twilight. Once more I have the feeling that Isabelle is not sick, but I suppress the thought. If it arises, confusion will follow, and I don't want that. Finally Isabelle moves. "Why don't you say something?" she asks.

"What do words amount to?"

"A great deal," she whispers. "Everything. Are you afraid of them?"

I consider the question. "Very likely we are all a little afraid of big words. They have been used to tell such dreadful lies. Perhaps we're afraid of our feelings too. We no longer trust them."

Isabelle draws her legs up on the bench. "But you need them, darling," she murmurs. "Otherwise how can you live?"

The vacuum cleaner has stopped whining. Suddenly it is very quiet. The cool smell of damp earth rises from the flower beds. A bird calls in the chestnut trees, always the same call. The evening is suddenly a scale with an equal weight of the world on both sides. I feel as though it were balanced weightlessly on my breast. Nothing can happen to me, I think, as long as I go on breathing quietly.

"Are you afraid of me?" Isabelle whispers.

No, I think, shaking my head; you are the one human being I am not afraid of. Not even in words. In your presence they are never too big and they are never ridiculous. You always understand them, for you still live in a world where words and feelings and lies and vision are one and the same thing.

"Why don't you say something?" she asks.

I shrug my shoulders. "Sometimes you can't say anything, Isabelle. And often it is hard to let go."

"Let go of what?"

"One's self. There are many obstacles."

"A knife can't cut itself, Rudolf. Why are you afraid?"

She is perched on the bench, beautiful and confiding and completely strange. "It can only grow dull," she says, "if you don't use it. Is that what you want?"

"I don't know, Isabelle."

"Don't wait too long, darling. Otherwise it will be too late. One needs words," she murmurs.

I make no reply. "Against fear, Rudolf," she says. "They are like lamps. They help. Do you see how gray everything is getting? Blood is not red any more. Why don't you help me?"

I stop resisting. "You sweet, strange, and beloved heart," I say. "If only I could help you!"

She bends forward and puts her arms around my shoulders. "Come with me! Help me! They are calling!"

"Who is calling?"

"Can't you hear them? The voices. They are always calling!"

"No one is calling, Isabelle. Only your heart. But what is it calling?"

I feel her breath brushing my face. "Love me, then it won't call any more," she says.

"I love you."

She lets herself sink down beside me. Now her eyes are closed. It grows darker and I see the glass man once more slowly strutting past. A nurse is bringing in a few old people who have been sitting on the benches, bent and motionless, like dark bundles of woe. "It's time," she says in our direction.

I nod and stay where I am. "They're calling," Isabelle whispers. "You can never find them. Who has so many tears?"

"No one," I say. "No one in the world, beloved heart."

She makes no reply. She is breathing like a tired child at my side. Then I pick her up and carry her along the *allée* to the pavilion where she lives.

As I set her down she wavers and clings to me. She murmurs something I cannot understand and lets me lead her indoors. The entry is bright with a shadowless, milky light. I put her in a cane chair in the hall. She lies there with closed eyes as though she had been taken down from an invisible cross. Two nuns in black come by. They are on their way to chapel. For a moment they seem to be coming to remove Isabelle and bury her. Then the attendant in white arrives and leads her off.

The Mother Superior has sent us a second bottle of Moselle. Nevertheless, Bodendiek, to my amazement, left directly after the meal. Wernicke is still at table. The weather is calm and the patients are as quiet as they ever are.

"Why aren't the completely hopeless cases killed?" I ask.

"Would you kill them?" Wernicke asks in return.

"I don't know. It's the same as when someone is dying slowly and hopelessly and you know he is suffering. Would you give him an injection to save him days of pain?"

Wernicke makes no reply.

"Fortunately Bodendiek is not here," I say. "So we don't have to indulge in a moral and religious discussion. I had a comrade whose belly was ripped open like a butcher shop. He pleaded with us to shoot him. We took him to the field hospital. There he screamed for three days, then he died. Three days is a long time when you're roaring with pain. I have seen many people perish. Not die—perish. All of them would have been helped by an injection. My mother among them."

Wernicke remains silent.

"All right," I say. "I know: to put an end to life in any creature is always like murder. Since my war experience I don't even like to kill a fly. Nevertheless, my portion of veal tasted fine tonight, and yet a calf had to be killed so that we could have it. Those are the old paradoxes, the incomplete logic. Life is a miracle, even in a calf or a fly. Particularly in a fly, that acrobat with its thousand-faceted eyes. It is always a miracle. But it always comes to an end. Why in time of peace do we kill a sick dog and not a suffering human being? And yet we murder millions in useless wars."

Wernicke still makes no reply. A big June bug is buzzing around the lamp. It strikes the bulb, falls, scrambles up, and flies once more, circling the light afresh. Experience has taught it nothing.

"Bodendiek, that son of the Church, naturally has an answer for everything," I say. "Animals have no soul; human beings do. But what becomes of that bit of soul when some convolution in the brain is injured? Where is it when someone becomes an idiot? Is it already in heaven? Or is it waiting somewhere for the twisted remnant that still causes a human body to slaver, eat, and defecate? I've seen some of your cases in the closed wards—animals are gods by comparison. What has become of the soul of an idiot? Is it divisible? Or is it hanging like an invisible balloon over the poor, muttering skull?"

Wernicke makes a gesture as though brushing away an insect.

"All right," I say. "That's a question for Bodendiek, who will answer it with the greatest ease. Bodendiek can solve everything with the great unknown God, with heaven and hell, the reward for suffering and the punishment for wickedness. No one has ever had any proof—faith alone makes one blessed, according to Bodendiek. But then why have we been given reason, the critical faculty, and the yearning for proof? Just in order not to use them? That's a strange game for the great Unknown to play! And what is reverence for life? Fear of death? Fear, always fear! Why? And why can we ask questions when there are no answers?"

"Finished?" Wernicke asks.

"No—but I'm not going to ask you anything more."

"Good. I couldn't answer anyway. You know that at least, don't you?"

"Of course. Why should it be just you who could when all the libraries in the world have only speculations for answer?"

The June bug has come to grief on its second flight. It scrambles to its legs again and begins a third. Its wings are like polished blue steel. It is a beautiful utilitarian machine; but faced by light it is like an alcoholic with a bottle of schnaps.

Wernicke pours the remainder of the Moselle into our glasses. "How long were you in the war?"

"Three years."

"Remarkable!"

I make no reply. I can guess what he is thinking and I

have no desire to go into all that again. Instead he asks: "Do you believe that reason is a part of the soul?"

"I don't know. But do you believe that the debased creatures creeping about and soiling themselves in the closed wards still have souls?"

Wernicke reaches for his glass. "All that is simple for me," he says. "I'm a scientist. I don't believe in anything at all. I simply observe. Bodendiek, on the other hand, believes a priori! Between the two you flutter about in uncertainty. Do you see that June bug?"

The June bug is engaged in its fifth attack. He will go on doing it until he dies. Wernicke turns off the lamp. "There, that will help."

The night comes in, big and blue, through the open window, bringing with it the smell of earth, of flowers, and the sparkling of the stars. Everything I have said immediately seems to me dreadfully silly. The June bug makes one more buzzing circuit and then steers safely through the window. "Chaos," Wernicke says. "Is it really chaos? Or is it only so for us? Have you ever considered how the world would be if we had one more sense?"

"No."

"But with one sense less?"

I reflect. "Then you would be blind, or deaf, or you couldn't taste. It would make a big difference."

"And with one sense more? Why should we always be limited to five? Why couldn't we perhaps develop six someday? Or eight? Or twelve? Wouldn't the world be completely different? Perhaps with the sixth our concept of time would disappear. Or our concept of space. Or of death. Or of pain. Or of morality. Certainly our present concept of life. We wander through our existence with pretty limited organs. A dog can hear better than any human being. A bat finds its way blind through all obstacles. A butterfly has a radio receiver that enables it to fly for miles directly to its mate. Migrating birds are vastly superior to us in their orientation. Snakes can hear with their skin. There are hundreds of such examples in natural history. So how can we know anything for certain? The extension of one organ or the development of a new one—and the world changes, life changes, and our concept of God changes. *Prost!*"

I lift my glass and drink. The Moselle is tart and earthy. "And so it's better to wait till we have a sixth sense, eh?" I say.

"That's not necessary. You can do what you like. But it's a good thing to know that one more sense would knock all our conclusions into a cocked hat. That puts an end to too much solemnity, doesn't it? How's the wine?"

"Good. How is Fräulein Terhoven? Better?"

"Worse. Her mother was here; she didn't recognize her."

"Perhaps she didn't want to."

"That's practically the same thing; she didn't recognize her. She screamed at her to go away. A typical case."

"Why?"

"Do you want to listen to a long lecture on schizophrenia, mother complexes, flight from one's self, and the effects of shock?"

"Yes," I say. "Today I do."

"You won't hear it. Only the essentials. A split personality is usually flight from one's self."

"What is one's self?"

Wernicke looks at me. "We'll not go into that today. Flight into another personality. Or into several. Usually, however, the patient keeps returning for a shorter or longer period into his own. Not Geneviève. Not for a long time. You, for example, have never seen her as she really is."

"She seems quite reasonable as she is now," I say without conviction.

Wernicke laughs. "What is reason? Logical thought?"

I think about the two new senses we are to have and make no reply. "Is she very sick?" I ask.

"According to our experience, she is. But there have been quick and often amazing cures."

"Cures—from what?"

"From her sickness," Wernicke says, lighting a cigarette.

"She is often quite happy. Why don't you leave her the way she is?"

"Because her mother is paying for the treatment," Wernicke explains dryly. "Besides, she is not happy."

"Do you believe she would be happier if she were healthy?"

"Probably not. She is sensitive, intelligent, obviously full of imagination, and probably the bearer of a hereditary taint. Qualities that do not necessarily make for happiness. If she had been happy, she would hardly have taken flight."

"Then why isn't she left in peace?"

"Yes, why not?" Wernicke says. "I have often asked myself that question. Why operate on the sick when you know the operation will not help? Shall we write down a list of whys? It would be long. One of the whys would be: Why don't you drink your wine and shut up? And why don't you pay attention to the night instead of to your immature brain? Why do you talk about life instead of living it?"

He stands up and stretches. "I must make my evening rounds in the closed wards. Want to come along?"

"Yes."

"Put on a white gown. I'll take you to a special ward. Afterward you'll either be sick or able to enjoy your wine with profound thankfulness."

"The bottle's empty."

"I have another in my room. Perhaps we'll need it. Do you know what's remarkable? For your twenty-five years you've seen a considerable amount of death, suffering, and human idiocy—nevertheless, you seem to have learned nothing from all of it except to ask the silliest questions imaginable. But probably that's the way of the world—when we have finally learned something we're too old to apply it—and so it goes, wave after wave, generation after generation. No one learns anything at all from anyone else. Come along!"

We are sitting in the Café Central—Georg, Willy, and I. This night I did not want to stay at home alone. Wernicke has shown me a ward in the insane asylum I had never seen before—where the war casualties are, men with head wounds, men who were buried, and men who went to pieces. In the mild summer evening this ward stood there like a dark dugout amid the song of nightingales. The war, which has already been almost forgotten by everyone, still goes on ceaselessly in these rooms. Grenades explode in these poor ears; the eyes reflect, just as they did four years ago, an incredulous horror; bayonets continue to bore into defenseless stomachs; hourly, tanks crush the screaming wounded, flattening them like flounders; the noise of battle, the crash of hand grenades, the splitting of skulls, the roar of mines, the suffocation in collapsing dugouts, they all have been preserved here through a horrible black magic and go on silently in this pavilion in the midst of roses and summer. Orders are given and inaudible orders are obeyed. Beds are trenches and dugouts, constantly buried and constantly excavated anew; there is dying and killing, strangling and suffocation; gas sweeps through these rooms and agonies of terror find expression in shouts and creeping and horrified groans and tears and often simply in a silent cowering in a corner, compressed into the smallest possible space, with faces pressed hard against the wall—

"Stand up!" youthful voices suddenly shout behind us. A

number of guests spring up smartly from their tables. The café orchestra is playing *"Deutschland, Deutschland über alles."* This is the fourth time tonight.

It is not the orchestra that is so nationalistic, nor the host. It is a group of young ruffians trying to make themselves important. Every half-hour one of them goes to the orchestra and commands the national anthem. He does this as though he were riding forth to battle. The orchestra does not dare to refuse, and so the anthem rolls out instead of the overture to *"Dichter und Bauer."* Then each time comes the command "Stand up!" from all sides—for one has to rise from one's seat when the national anthem is played, especially since it has brought two million dead, a lost war, and the inflation.

"Stand up!" screams a seventeen-year-old ruffian who could not have been more than twelve at the end of the war.

"Kiss my ass," I reply, "and go back to school."

"Bolshevist!" shouts the youngster, who almost certainly doesn't know what that means. "Here are some Bolshevists, comrades!"

The purpose of these good-for-nothings is to start a row. They keep ordering the national anthem, and each time a number of people do not get up because it seems so silly. Then with blazing eyes the brawlers descend on them, looking for a fight. Somewhere a couple of cashiered officers are directing them and feeling important too.

A dozen are now standing around our table. "Stand up or there'll be trouble!"

"What trouble?" Willy asks.

"You'll see soon enough! Cowards! Betrayers of your country! Up!"

"Get away from our table," Georg says. "Do you think we need directions from minors?"

A man of about thirty pushes his way through the

crowd. "Have you no respect for your national anthem?"

"Not in cafés when it's being used to start a brawl," Georg replies. "And now cut out this nonsense and leave us in peace!"

"Nonsense? Do you call a German's most sacred feelings nonsense? You'll pay for that! Where were you during the war, you shirker?"

"In the trenches," Georg replies, "unfortunately."

"Anyone can say that! Prove it!"

Willy gets up. He is a giant. The music has just stopped. "Prove it?" Willy says. "Here!" He lifts one leg a little, turns his posterior lightly toward the speaker and there is an explosion like a medium-sized cannon. "That," Willy says conclusively, "is all I learned from the Prussians. Formerly I had nicer manners."

The leader of the crowd has sprung back involuntarily. "You said coward, didn't you?" Willy asks grinning. "You seem a little jumpy yourself!"

The host has come up accompanied by three husky waiters. "Quiet, gentlemen, I must insist! No arguments here!"

The orchestra is now playing "Birdsong at Evening." The defenders of the national anthem retire with dark threats. It's possible that they will fall on us outside. We look them over; they're sitting together close to the door. There are about twenty of them. The battle will be pretty hopeless for us.

But suddenly unexpected help arrives. A dried-up little man approaches our table. He is Bodo Ledderhose, a dealer in hides and old iron. We were with him in France. "Children," he says, "I've just noticed what's going on. Am here with my club. Over behind those columns. We're a full dozen and can give you a hand if those ass-faces want to start anything. Agreed?"

"Agreed, Bodo. You were sent by God."

"Not that. But this is no place for respectable people. We just dropped in for a glass of beer. Unfortunately the host here has the best beer in the city. Otherwise he's an unprincipled ass-hole."

It strikes me that Bodo is going a bit far to demand principles from so simple a human organ; but it is elevating just the same. In bad times one ought to make impossible demands. "We're going soon," Bodo continues. "Are you?"

"Right away."

We pay and get up. Before we reach the door the guardians of the national anthem are already outside. As though by magic they suddenly have cudgels, stones, and brass knuckles in their hands. They stand in a half-circle in front of the entrance.

Bodo suddenly is between us. He pushes us to one side and his twelve men walk through the door in front of us. "Something you want, you snot faces?" Bodo asks.

The guardians of the Reich stare at us. "Cowards!" says the leader finally, the man who was about to fall on three of us with twenty men. "We'll catch you yet!"

"Very likely," Willy says. "That's why we spent a couple of years in the trenches. But see to it that you always have odds of three or four on your side. Superior force is very reassuring to patriots."

We walk down Grossestrasse with Bodo's club. The sky is full of stars. There are lights in the store windows. Sometimes when you are with wartime comrades it still seems strange and splendid and breathtaking and incomprehensible that you can wander about this way, free and alive. Suddenly I understand what Wernicke meant about thankfulness. It is a thankfulness not directed toward anyone— a simple gratitude at having escaped for a while longer— for eventually, of course, no one really escapes.

"What you need is another café," Bodo says. "How would ours do? We haven't any roaring apes there. Come along, we'll show it to you!"

They show it to us. Downstairs they serve coffee, seltzer water, beer, and ice cream—upstairs are the assembly rooms. Bodo's club is a singing society. The city crawls with clubs, which all have their weekly meetings, their statutes and bylaws, and are very serious and self-important. Bodo's club meets Thursdays on the second floor. "We have a good polyphonic male choir," he says. "Only we're a little weak in first tenors. It's a funny thing, but probably a lot of first tenors fell during the war. And the rising generation isn't old enough yet—their voices are just starting to change."

"Willy is a first tenor," I tell him.

"Really?" Bodo looks at him with interest. "Sing this, Willy."

Bodo flutes like a thrush. Willy flutes in turn. "Good material," Bodo says. "Now try this!"

Willy manages the second too. "Join our club," Bodo now urges him. "If you don't like it you can always resign later."

Willy demurs a little, but to our astonishment swallows the bait. He is immediately made treasurer of the club. In return he pays for two rounds of beer and schnaps and adds pea soup and pigs' knuckles for everyone. Bodo's club is politically democratic; but among the first tenors they have a conservative toy dealer and a half-communistic cobbler; one cannot be choosy in the matter of first tenors, there are so few of them. During the third round Willy announces that he knows a lady who can also sing first tenor and bass as well. The members of the society are silent, doubtfully chewing their pigs' knuckles. Georg and I take a hand and explain Renée de la Tour's accomplishments as duettist. Willy swears that she is not really a bass but by nature a pure tenor. There ensues a hugely enthusiastic response. Renée is elected to membership *in absentia* and is thereupon immediately made an honorary member. Willy pays for the necessary drinks. Bodo is dreaming of inserting mysterious soprano parts that will drive the rival singing clubs crazy at the yearly contest because they will think Bodo's club contains a eunuch, especially since Renée will naturally have to appear in male attire since otherwise the club would be classified as a mixed choir. "I'll tell her this very evening," Willy announces. "Children, how she will laugh! In every key!"

Georg and I finally leave. Willy keeps watch over the square from the second-story window; like an old soldier he reckons on the possibility of an ambush by the guardians of the national anthem. But nothing happens. The market square lies peaceful under the stars. Around it the windows of the bars stand open. From Bodo's meeting place come the melodious strains of *"Wer hat dich, du schöner Wald, aufgebaut so hoch dort oben?"*

"Tell me, Georg," I ask as we turn into Hackenstrasse, "are you happy?"

Georg Kroll lifts his hat to an unseen presence in the night. "I'll ask you another question," he says. "How long can one sit on the point of a needle?"

Chapter Eleven

Rain pours from the sky. Mist steams up from the garden to meet it. The summer is drowned, it is cold, and the dollar stands at a hundred and twenty thousand marks. With a mighty crash a section of our gutter breaks from the roof and falls; water shoots across the window like a wall of gray glass. I sell two angels of bisquit porcelain and a wreath of immortelles to a frail woman whose two children have died of grippe. Georg lies in the next room coughing. He, too, has grippe, but I have fixed a mug of mulled wine for him. Besides, he has a half-dozen magazines lying around and is making use of this chance to inform himself about the latest marriages, divorces, and scandals in the great world of Cannes, Berlin, London, and Paris. The indefatigable Heinrich Kroll comes in wearing striped trousers, bicycle clips, and an appropriate dark raincoat. "Would you mind if I dictated a few orders?" he asks with incomparable sarcasm.

"By no means. Go right ahead."

He gives me the commissions. They are for small tombstones of red granite, a marble plaque, a couple of grave enclosures—the commonplaces of death, nothing special. Then he stands for a time, irresolute, warming his backside at the cold oven, looking at the collection of rock samples that for the past twenty years has been lying on the shelves of the office, and finally bursts into speech. "If difficulties like this are going to be put in my way, it won't be long before we're broke!"

I say nothing, just to annoy him. "Broke, I say," he explains. "And I know what I'm talking about."

"Really?" I look at him encouragingly. "Then why defend yourself? Everyone believes you."

"Defend myself? I don't need to defend myself! But what happened in Wüstringen—"

"Have they found the murderer?"

"Murderer? What's that to us? Why talk about murder in a case like that? It was an accident. The man has only himself to blame! What I'm talking about is the way you treated Mayor Döbbeling! And on top of that to offer the carpenter's widow a tombstone gratis!"

I turn toward the window and gaze into the rain. Heinrich Kroll is one of those people who never have any doubt about their own views—this makes them not only tiresome but dangerous as well. They are the bronze core of our beloved fatherland that makes it possible to keep on starting wars again and again. They are incapable of learning; they are born with their hands at the seams of their trousers and are proud to die that way too. I don't know whether the type exists in other countries—but surely not in such numbers.

After a while I listen again to what the little muttonhead is saying. It seems that he has had a long interview with the mayor and has cleared the matter up. Thanks solely to his personality, we are once more permitted to sell tombstones in Wüstringen.

"And what are we supposed to do now?" I ask him. "Worship you?"

He throws me a venomous glance. "Look out, you'll go too far someday!"

"How far?"

"Too far. Don't forget you're an employee here."

"I forget it all the time. Otherwise you'd have to give me a triple salary—as draftsman, office manager, and advertising manager. Moreover, we are not on a military footing or you'd have to stand at attention in front of me. But if you like I can always give our competitors a ring—Holmann and Klotz would take me on instantly."

The door opens and Georg appears in bright red pajamas. "Were you talking about Wüstringen, Heinrich?"

"About what else?"

"Then go down to the cellar and stand in the corner. A man was killed in Wüstringen! A life was ended. Someone's world was destroyed. Every murder, every killing, is the first killing in the world. Cain and Abel repeated again and again! If you and your fellows could only understand that, there'd be fewer battle cries on this otherwise blessed earth!"

"There would be servants and slaves, groveling before the inhuman Treaty of Versailles!"

"The Treaty of Versailles! Of course!" Georg takes a step forward. The smell of mulled wine is strong around him. "If we had won the war, then of course we would have deluged our enemies with love and gifts, wouldn't we? Have you forgotten what you and your friends wanted to annex? The Ukraine, Brie, Longwy, and the whole iron and coal basin of France? Has the Ruhr been taken away from us? No, we still have it! Are you going to maintain that our treaty of peace would not have been ten times harsher if we had been in a position to dictate one? Didn't I myself hear you jabbering about it as recently as 1917?

France was to be reduced to a third-rate power, huge slices of Russia were to be annexed, and all enemies were to pay in goods and treasure until they were bled white! That was you, Heinrich! But now you join in the chorus roaring against the injustice that has been done us. Your self-pity and your cries for vengeance are enough to make one sick! Always someone else is to blame, not you. You stink of self-righteousness, you Pharisees! Don't you know that the first mark of a man is that he stands for what he has done? But with you and your fellows it is always some tremendous injustice that has befallen you, and the only difference between you and God is that God knows everything but you know everything better."

Georg glances about as though waking up. His face is now as red as his pajamas and even his bald head is rosy. Heinrich has recoiled in alarm. Georg follows him. He is furious. Heinrich retreats farther. "Don't come near me!" he screams. "You're blowing your germs right in my face! What would happen if we both had grippe?"

"Then no one would dare die," I say.

The battling brothers make a fine picture. Georg in red satin pajamas, sweating with rage, and Heinrich in his little morning suit, terrified of catching the grippe. There is another witness to the scene: Lisa in a print dressing gown decorated with sailing ships is leaning far out the window in spite of the weather. In Knopf's house the door is open. In front of it the rain hangs like a curtain of glass beads. It is so dark inside that the girls have turned on the light. It would be easy to take them for Wagner's Rhine Maidens swimming there. Under a huge umbrella Wilke, the carpenter, wanders around the courtyard like a black mushroom. Heinrich Kroll disappears, literally pushed out of the office by Georg. "Be sure to gargle," I shout after him. "Grippe is deadly to people of your constitution."

Georg stands still and laughs. "What an idiot I am," he

says. "As though you could ever tell people like that anything!"

"Where did you get the pajamas?" I ask. "Have you joined the Communist party?"

Applause comes from across the street. Lisa is expressing her approval of Georg—a serious disloyalty toward Watzek, the loyal National Socialist and future director of the stockyards. Georg bows, his hand on his heart. "Get into bed, you clown," I say. "You've turned into a fountain of sweat!"

"It's healthy to sweat! Just look at the rain! The sky out there is sweating. And across the street that sample of life, in its open dressing gown, with white teeth and full of laughter! What are we doing here? Why don't we explode like fireworks? If we really knew what life is, we would explode! Why am I selling tombstones? Why am I not a comet? Or the great roc, sailing over Hollywood and snatching the most delectable women out of their swimming pools? Why must we live in Werdenbrück and do battle in the Café Central instead of fitting out a caravan for Timbuktu and setting forth with mahogany-colored bearers into the spacious African morning? Why don't we own a bordello in Yokohama? Answer me! It is important to know at once! Why aren't we racing with purple fish in the red evenings of Tahiti? Answer me!"

He reaches for the bottle of schnaps. "Hold on!" I say. "There's still wine. I'll heat it up at once on the alcohol stove. No schnaps now! You're feverish! Hot red wine with spices from the Indies and the Sunda Islands!"

"Fine! Heat it. But why aren't we ourselves on the Islands of Hope, sleeping with women who smell of cinnamon and whose eyes turn white when we mate with them under the Southern Cross and cry out like parrots and like tigers? Answer me!"

The flame of the alcohol stove burns like the blue light of adventure in the semidarkness of the office. The rain roars like the sea. "We are on our way, Captain," I say, taking a hefty swig of the whisky to catch up with Georg. "The caravel is just passing Santa Cruz, Lisbon, and the Gold Coast. The slaves of the Arabian Mohammed Ben Hassan Ben Watzek are staring out of their cabins and waving to us. Here is your hookah!"

I hand Georg a cigar out of the box kept for our best agents. He lights it and blows a couple of perfect smoke rings. His pajamas show dark wet spots. "On our way," he says. "Why aren't we there yet?"

"We are there. One is there always and everywhere. Time is a prejudice. That is the secret of life. People just don't know it. They keep trying to arrive someplace!"

"Why don't they know it?" Georg asks in commanding tones.

"Time, space, and causality are the veils of Maia which prevent open vision."

"Why?"

"They are the whips God uses to keep us from becoming His equals. He drives us through a panorama of illusions and through the tragedy of duality."

"What duality?"

"The I and the world. The duality of being and living. Object and subject are no longer one. Birth and death are the consequences. The chain rattles. Whoever breaks free of it also breaks free of birth and death. Let us try it, Rabbi Kroll!"

The wine steams, smelling of lemon and spice. I add sugar, and we drink. Applause comes from the cabin of the slave ship of Mohammed Ben Hassan Ben Jussuf Ben Watzek on the other side of the gulf. We bow and put down our glasses. "And so we are immortal?" Georg asks with sudden impatience.

"Only hypothetically," I reply. "In theory—for immortal is the opposite of mortal, and therefore, unfortunately, already again half of a duality. Only when the veil of Maia has been entirely torn away does duality completely go by the board. Then one is home again, no more subject and object, but both in one, and all questions die."

"That's not enough!"

"What more is there?"

"Man is. Period."

"That, too, is part of a pair: man is, man is not. Always a duality, Captain! We must transcend it!"

"How? The instant we open our mouths we have hold of part of another pair. That can't go on! Are we to go through life dumb?"

"That's the opposite of not-dumb."

"Damn it! Another trap! What to do, Helmsman?"

I am silent and lift my glass. A red reflection gleams in the wine. I point to the rain and I lift a piece of granite from among the stone samples. Then I point to Lisa, to the reflection in the glass, the most transitory thing in the world, to the granite, the most enduring in the world, put the glass and the granite aside and close my eyes. For all this hocus-pocus, something like a shudder suddenly runs along my spine. Have we perhaps unwittingly caught the scent? Have we in our cups laid hold of the magic key? Suddenly where is the room? Is it rushing through the universe? Where is the world? Is it just now passing the Pleiades? And where is the red reflection of the heart? Is it Pole Star, axis, and center in one?

Frenetic applause from the other side of the street. I open my eyes. For a moment there is no perspective. Everything is flat and far and near and round at the same time and has no name. Then it whirls back into place and stands still and is once more what it has always been called. When did this happen to me before? It did once! I am perfectly sure of it, but I can't remember when.

Lisa waves a bottle of crème de cacao out of the window.

At that moment the bell on the door rings. We hastily wave to Lisa and close the window. Before Georg can disappear, the office door opens and Liebermann, the gravedigger at the municipal cemetery, comes in. With a single glance he takes in the alcohol stove, the mulled wine, and Georg's pajamas. "Birthday?" he croaks.

"Grippe," Georg replies.

"Congratulations!"

"Why congratulations?"

"Grippe brings business. I've noticed it out there. Considerable increase in deaths."

"Herr Liebermann," I say to the hearty octogenarian. "We're not talking about business. Herr Kroll has a serious, cosmic attack of grippe, against which we are taking measures. Will you have a glass of the medicine?"

"I'm a schnaps drinker. Wine just sobers me."

"We have schnaps too."

I pour him a tumblerful. He takes a good swallow, opens his knapsack and gets out four trout wrapped in big, green leaves. They smell of the river and rain and fish. "A gift," Liebermann says.

The trout lie on the table, their eyes dull. Their gray-green skin is covered with red flecks. We stare at them. Softly and suddenly death has stolen into the room again where a moment ago immortality held sway—softly and silently, with the creatures' reproach toward that murderer and omnivore, man, who talks of peace and love, cuts the throats of lambs and lets fish gasp out their lives in order to have strength to go on talking about peace and love— not excepting Bodendiek, the man of God and fancier of red meat.

"A fine supper," Liebermann says. "Especially for you, Herr Kroll. A light diet for the sick."

I carry the dead fish into the kitchen and give them to Frau Kroll, who appraises them with the eye of an expert.

"With fresh butter, boiled potatoes, and salad," she announces.

I glance around. The kitchen is gleaming, pots and pans reflect the light, a kettle is hissing, and there is a good smell. Kitchens are always a comfort. The reproach disappears from the eyes of the trout. Instead of dead creatures they have suddenly become food, which can be prepared in various ways. It almost seems as though they had been hatched for that purpose. What traitors we are, I think, to our nobler feelings!

Liebermann has brought us a few addresses. The grippe is indeed taking its toll. People are dying because they have little resistance left. They were weakened to begin with by the food shortage during the war. I decide suddenly to look for another profession. I am tired of death. Georg has fetched his dressing gown. He sits there like a sweating Buddha. The dressing gown is of a poisonous green. At home Georg loves loud colors. Suddenly I know what it was that our former conversation reminded me of. It was something Isabelle said a while ago. I do not remember it exactly, but it had to do with the deceptiveness of things. But in our case was it really deception? Or were we for an instant one centimeter closer to God?

The Poets' Den in the Hotel Walhalla is a small, paneled room. A bust of Goethe stands on a bookshelf, and photographs and etchings of German classical and romantic writers, together with a few moderns, hang on the walls. This spot is the meeting place of the Poets' Club and of the intellectual elite of the city. There is a gathering every week. Even the editor of the daily paper appears occasionally and is openly flattered and secretly hated depending on whether he has accepted or rejected some contribution. He pays no attention. Like a kindly uncle he drifts through the tobacco smoke, slandered, attacked, and venerated; on only one point is everyone in agreement about him: that he knows nothing about modern literature. According to him, after Theodor Storm, Eduard Mörike, and Gottfried Keller the great wasteland begins.

A couple of provincial judges and pensioned officials, interested in literature, attend too; so do Arthur Bauer and some of his colleagues; the poets of the city come, of course, a few painters and musicians, and occasionally a guest from outside. At the moment, Arthur Bauer is being courted by that lickspittle Mathias Grund, who hopes that Arthur will print his seven-part "Book of Death." Eduard Knobloch, founder of the club, appears. He throws a quick look around the room and brightens. Some of his critics and enemies are not there. To my amazement he sits down beside me. I had not expected that after the episode with the chicken. "How goes it?" he asks quite humanly and not in his dining-room voice.

"Brilliantly," I say because I know that will irritate him.

"I am planning a new sonnet sequence," he announces without further explanation. "I hope you have no objection."

"Why should I? I hope they rhyme."

I have the edge on Eduard because I have had two sonnets printed in the paper whereas he has only had two didactic poems. "It's a cycle," he says, to my astonishment slightly embarrassed. "The thing is this: I'd like to call it 'Gerda.'"

"Call it whatever—" I interrupt myself. "Gerda, did you say? Why Gerda? Gerda Schneider?"

"Nonsense! Simply Gerda."

I regard the fat giant suspiciously. "What's that supposed to mean?"

Eduard gives a false laugh. "Nothing. Only poetic license. The sonnets have something to do with the circus. Distantly, of course. As you know, it's stimulating to the imagination if you can find—even theoretically—a concrete point of departure."

"Stop talking nonsense," I say. "What does this mean, you cheat!"

"Cheat?" Eduard replies with feigned indignation. "It would be fairer to call you that! Didn't you act as though the lady were a singer like Willy's disgusting friend?"

"Never. You just thought so."

"Anyway," Eduard announces, "the thing tormented me. I investigated and found out you had lied. She's not a singer at all."

"Did I ever say she was? Didn't I tell you she was with the circus?"

"You did. But you used the truth to make me disbelieve you. And then you imitated the other lady."

"How did you find out all this?"

"I met Mademoiselle Schneider accidentally on the street and asked her. One's allowed to do that, I presume?"

"Supposing she tricked you?"

Suddenly Eduard has a smile of disgusting self-assurance on his baby face; he makes no reply. "Listen to me," I say, alarmed and therefore very calm. "This lady is not to be won with sonnets."

Eduard does not react to this. He continues to show the superiority of a poet who in addition to his poems owns a first-class restaurant. And I have seen that in this matter Gerda is vulnerable. "You scoundrel," I exclaim in rage. "All this won't do you any good. The lady is leaving in a couple of days."

"She is not leaving," Eduard replies, showing his teeth for the first time since I have known him. "Her contract was renewed today."

I stare at him. This clod knows more than I. "So you met her today?"

Eduard begins to stammer slightly. "Accidentally today—that was it! Just today."

The lie is written plain on his fat cheeks. "So you instantly had the inspiration for the dedication?" I say. "Is that how you repay our months of faithful patronage? With the jab of a kitchen knife in the genitals, you dishwasher?"

"You can take your damned patronage and—"

"You've sent her the sonnets already, haven't you, you impudent peacock?" I interrupt him. "Oh stop it, lies won't help you! She'll show them to me anyway, you maker of dirty beds!"

"What do you mean?"

"Your sonnets, you matricide! Didn't I teach you how to write them? Nice thanks! Couldn't you at least have had the decency to send her villanelles or odes? But no, my own weapons—well, Gerda will show me the stuff so I can translate it to her!"

"Why, that would be—" Eduard stutters, his self-confidence shaken for the first time.

"It would be nothing," I reply. "Women do such things. As I know. But since I value you as a restaurant keeper, I will reveal something more: Gerda has a giant of a brother who keeps watch over the family honor. He has already crippled two of her admirers. And he is especially fond of beating up people with flat feet. That means you."

"Nonsense," Eduard says. Nevertheless, I see he has grown thoughtful. No matter how improbable an assertion is, if it is made with enough assurance it has an effect. That's something I learned from Watzek's political idol.

The poet Hans Hungermann comes up to the sofa where we are sitting. He is the author of the unpublished volume of poetry "Wotan's Death" and the dramas "Saul," "Baldur," and "Mohammed." "How fairs art, my friends?" he asks.

"Have you read the ordure that Otto Bambuss printed yesterday in the *Tecklendorfer Kreisblatt*? Buttermilk and phlegm! To think that Bauer publishes that slimy bastard!"

Otto Bambuss is the most successful poet in the city. We all envy him. He writes sentimental verses about picturesque nooks, country villages, street corners in the evening, and his own melancholy soul. He has had two thin volumes published by Arthur Bauer—one, indeed, is in a second printing. Hungermann, the stalwart writer of runes, hates him, but tries to exploit his connections. Mathias Grund despises him. I, on the other hand, am Otto's intimate. He longs to visit a bordello sometime but does not dare. He thinks it would impart a mighty, full-blooded *élan* to his somewhat anemic verse. As soon as he sees me he comes up. "I've heard that you know a circus lady! The circus, what a subject! Do you really know one?"

"No, Otto. Eduard has been boasting. The only one I know sold tickets to the circus three years ago."

"Tickets—nevertheless, she was there! She must still have some of the atmosphere. The smell of carnivores, the ring. Couldn't you introduce me to her sometime?"

Gerda really has a future in literature! I look at Bambuss. He is a tall, stringy fellow, pale, chinless, with an insignificant face adorned with spectacles. "She was in the flea circus," I say.

"Too bad!" He takes a step backward in disillusionment. Then he murmurs, "I must do something. I know what I lack—blood."

"Otto," I reply. "Couldn't it be someone unconnected with the circus? Some simple bed rabbit?"

He shakes his narrow head. "That's not so easy, Ludwig. I know all about love. Spiritual love, I mean. I need no more of that; I possess it. What I need is passion, wild, brutal passion. Ravening, purple forgetfulness. Delirium!"

He is practically gnashing his tiny teeth. He is a teacher

in a small village near the city, and of course he can't find delirium there. Everyone there is interested in getting married or in marrying Otto to some honest girl with a good dowry and the ability to cook. But Otto doesn't want that. He believes that a poet must experience life. "The difficulty is that I can't bring the two together," he explains darkly. "Heavenly and earthly love. For me love immediately becomes soft, full of devotion, sacrifice, and kindness. The sex drive grows soft and domesticated. Every Saturday night, you understand, so you can get a good sleep Sunday. But what I need is pure sex, nothing else, something you can get your teeth into. Too bad. I heard that you knew a trapeze artist."

I observe Bambuss with new interest. Heavenly and earthly love—he too! The sickness seems to be more widespread than I thought. Otto drinks a glass of Waldmeister lemonade and looks at me out of his pale eyes. Very likely he expects me to give up Gerda at once so that his heart may grow genitals. "When are we ever going to a bordello?" he asks sadly. "You did promise me, you know."

"Soon. But that's no purple sink of iniquity, Otto."

"I only have two weeks more of vacation. Then I'll have to go back to the village and it's all over."

"We'll do it before that. Hungermann would like to go too. He needs it for his new drama 'Casanova.' We could make a joint expedition."

"For God's sake, I mustn't be seen! Think of my profession!"

"For that very reason! An expedition is harmless. The crib has a couple of public rooms on the lower floor. Anyone can go there."

"Of course we'll go," Hungermann says behind me. "All of us together. We'll make an expedition of discovery. Purely scientific. Eduard wants to go along too."

I turn toward Eduard with the intention of pouring a

sauce of sarcasm over that superior sonnet cook—but it's no longer necessary. Eduard suddenly looks as though he had seen a snake. A slim fellow has just tapped him on the shoulder. "Eduard, old comrade!" he says cordially. "How goes it? Rejoicing that you're still alive, eh?"

Eduard stares at him. "Nowadays?" he says in a strangling voice.

He has blanched. His chubby cheeks suddenly sag, his shoulders droop, his lips, his hair, even his belly hang down. In the twinkling of an eye he has become a fat weeping willow.

The man who has caused all this is called Valentin Busch. Together with Georg and me he makes the third pest in Eduard's existence, and more than that—he is pest, cholera, and paratyphus all in one. "You look blooming, my boy," Valentin declares cheerfully.

Eduard laughs hollowly. "Appearances are deceptive. I'm consumed by cares, taxes, rents, and thieves—"

He is lying. Rents and taxes mean nothing in the inflation; you pay them after a year, that amounts to not paying at all. The sums have long since lost all value. And the only thief Eduard knows is himself.

"At least there's something to eat on your bones," Valentin replies, smiling pitilessly. "That's what the worms in Flanders thought when they scurried out to get you."

Eduard squirms. "What's it to be, Valentin?" he asks. "A beer? Beer is the best thing in this heat."

"I don't think it's too warm. But the best is just good enough to celebrate the fact that you're alive, you're right there. Give me a bottle of Johannisberger Langenberg, from the Mumm estate, Eduard."

"That's sold out."

"It is not sold out. I have just inquired from your wine waiter. You have more than a hundred bottles left. What luck that it's my favorite!"

I laugh. "What are you laughing at?" Eduard screams in rage. "You're a fine one to laugh! Bloodsucker! You're all bloodsuckers! You bleed me white! You, your *bon vivant* of a tombstone dealer friend, and you, Valentin! You bleed me white! A trio of parasites!"

Valentin winks at me and goes on solemnly, "So that's your thanks, Eduard! And that's the way you keep your word! If I had but known at that time—"

He rolls back his sleeve and stares at a long, jagged scar. In 1917 he saved Eduard's life. Eduard, the K.P. noncom, had been transferred at that time and sent to the front. On one of his first days there a shot caught him in the calf of the leg while he was on patrol in no man's land. Shortly after, he was hit again and was losing blood fast. Valentin found him, tied him up, and dragged him back to the trenches. In doing so he got a shell fragment in his arm. But he saved Eduard's life, who otherwise would certainly have bled to death. Eduard, overflowing with gratitude, offered Valentin as reward the right to eat and drink whatever he liked in the Walhalla as long as he lived. Valentin, with his uninjured left hand, shook with Eduard in agreement. Georg Kroll and I were witnesses.

That all seemed harmless enough in 1917. Werdenbrück was far away, the war was near, and who knew whether Valentin and Eduard would ever return to the Walhalla? They did return; Valentin after being wounded twice more, Eduard round, fat, and reinstated as mess boss. At first Eduard was really grateful, and when Valentin came to visit him he occasionally even went so far as to serve flat German champagne. But the years began to wear on him. The trouble was, Valentin established himself in Werdenbrück. Formerly he had lived in another city; now he moved into a little room near the Walhalla and appeared punctually at Eduard's for breakfast, lunch, and dinner. The latter soon bitterly regretted his ill-considered promise. Valentin was a hearty eater, especially now that he had no more cares. Perhaps Eduard would have been able to console himself to some extent for the food; but Valentin drank too, and gradually he developed a connoisseurship in wine. Formerly he had drunk beer; now he drank only the finest vintages and thereby contributed to Eduard's desperation far more than we did with our miserable coupons.

"Oh, all right," Eduard says in despair as Valentin holds out the scar for his inspection. "But eating and drinking means drinking at meals, not between times. Drinking between meals is something I did not promise."

"Just look at this miserable shopkeeper," Valentin replies, nudging me. "In 1917 he didn't think that way. Then it was: Valentin, dearest Valentin, rescue me and I'll give you everything I have!"

"That's not true! I never said that!" Eduard screams in falsetto.

"How do you know? You were half crazy with fear and half dead from loss of blood when I dragged you back."

"I couldn't have said that! Not that! Even if it had meant instant death. It's not in my character."

"That's right," I say. "That skinflint would rather have died."

"That's what I mean," Eduard explains, sighing with relief at finding aid. He wipes his forehead. His locks are wet from alarm at Valentin's last threat. He is already picturing the Walhalla up for sale. "Very well, for this one time," he says quickly so as not to be pushed further. "Waiter, a half-bottle of Moselle."

"Johannisberger Langenberg, a whole bottle," Valentin corrects him. And, turning to me, "May I invite you to have a glass?"

"And how!" I reply.

"Stop!" Eduard says. "That was definitely not in the agreement! It was for Valentin alone! As it is, Ludwig costs me a lot of money every day, that bloodsucker with his worthless coupons!"

"Quiet, you poisoner," I reply. "This is the working out of karma. You open fire on me with sonnets, and so I bathe my wounds in your Rhine wine. Would you like me to send a certain lady a twelve-line poem in the manner of Aretino about this situation, you defrauder of the man who saved your life?"

Eduard swallows the wrong way. "I need fresh air," he mutters in a rage. "Extortioner! Pimp! Have you no sense of shame?"

"We save our shame for more serious matters, you harmless dealer in millions." Valentin and I touch glasses. The wine is splendid.

"How about our visit to the house of sin?" Otto Bambuss asks, sideling up timidly.

"We'll go without fail, Otto. We owe that much to art."

"Why is it more fun to drink in the rain?" Valentin asks, refilling his glass. "It really ought to be the other way around."

"Do you have to have an explanation for everything?" I say.

"Of course not. What would become of conversation then? It just occurred to me."

"Perhaps it's just herd instinct, Valentin. Liquids to liquids."

"Maybe so. But I piss more too, on days when it's raining. That at least is strange."

"You piss more because you drink more. What's strange about that?"

"You're right." Valentin nods in relief. "I'd never thought of it. Are there more wars, too, because more people are born?"

Chapter Twelve

Bodendiek swoops through the mist like a big, black crow. "Well," he asks jovially, "are you still busy improving the world?"

"I'm observing it," I reply.

"Ah ha! The philosopher! And what have you found out?"

I look into his cheerful face, red and shiny under the broad-brimmed hat. "I've found out that Christianity hasn't substantially improved the world in two thousand years," I reply.

For an instant the benevolent superiority of his mien is altered, then it is restored. "Don't you think you're a trifle young for judgments like that?"

"Yes—but don't you think that blaming someone for his youth is a poor argument? Can't you think of anything better?"

"I can think of a great deal. But not to confute absurdities like that. Don't you know that all generalization is a sign of superficiality?"

"Yes," I reply wearily. "I only said that because it's raining. Besides, there's something in it. I've been studying history the last few weeks when I couldn't sleep."

"Why? Also because of the rain?"

I ignore this harmless quip. "Because I want to guard myself against premature cynicism and provincial despair. Simple faith in the Trinity can't blind everyone to the fact that we're busily preparing for another war—after just losing one, which you people and your reverend colleagues of the various Protestant denominations blessed and consecrated in the name of God and love of one's neighbor—you, I must admit, with some reserve and embarrassment, but your colleagues more cheerfully, in uniforms, rattling the cross and shouting for victory."

Bodendiek shakes the rain from his black hat. "We gave final consolation to the dying, on the battlefield—you seem to have forgotten that."

"You shouldn't have let it go so far! Why didn't you declare a strike? Why didn't you forbid the faithful to go to war? That's where your duty lay. But the time of martyrs is past. And so, when I had to attend divine service during the war I had to hear prayers for the victory of our arms. Do you think Christ would have prayed for the victory of the Gallileans over the Philistines?"

"The rain," Bodendiek replies in measured tones, "seems to have made you unusually emotional and demagogic. You seem to have found out that by a little adroitness, omission, distortion, and one-sided presentation you can attack anything at all and make it questionable."

"I know. That's the very reason I'm studying history. When we were studying religion at school, we were always being told about the dark, primitive, cruel pre-Christian times. I've been reading up about that and I've discovered that we are not much better off now—aside from certain technical and scientific triumphs which, moreover, are used principally to kill more people."

"It's possible to prove anything you like if you're determined to do it, dear friend. And the opposite too. Proofs can be found for every preconceived opinion."

"I know that too," I say. "The Church gave a brilliant example of it when it wiped out the Gnostics."

"The Gnostics! What do you know about them?" Bodendiek asks in offensive surprise.

"Enough to suspect they were the more tolerant part of Christianity. And all I have learned in my life so far is to prize tolerance."

"Tolerance—" Bodendiek says.

"Tolerance!" I repeat. "Consideration for others. Understanding of others. Letting each live in his own fashion. Tolerance, which in our beloved fatherland is a foreign word."

"Anarchy, in short," Bodendiek replies, softly and with sudden sharpness.

We are standing in front of the chapel. The lights are burning and the stained-glass windows shimmer comfortingly in the eddying rain. Through the open door comes the faint smell of incense. "Tolerance, Herr Vicar," I say. "Not anarchy, and you know the difference! But you don't dare admit it! No one possesses heaven but you! No one can give absolution but you! You have a monopoly. There is no religion but yours! You are a dictatorship! So how can you be tolerant?"

"We don't need to be. We possess the truth."

"Naturally," I say, pointing to the lighted windows. "There you are! Comfort for those afraid of life. Stop thinking, I'll do it for you! The promise of heaven and the threat of hell—playing on the simplest emotions—what has that to do with truth, that unattainable fata morgana of our brains?"

"Fine words," Bodendiek exclaims, long since at ease again, superior and mildly derisive.

"Yes, that's all we have—fine words," I say, angered at myself. "And you have nothing more—just fine words."

Bodendiek walks into the chapel. "We have the Holy Sacraments—"

"Yes—"

"And faith, which to simpletons like you, whose addled brains upset their stomachs, seems nothing but stupidity and flight from the world, you harmless earthworm in the fields of triviality."

"Bravo!" I say. "At last you, too, are waxing poetic. Late baroque, to be sure."

Bodendiek laughs suddenly. "My dear Bodmer," he explains, "many a Saul has become a Paul in the nearly two thousand years that the Church has existed. And during that time we have encountered more formidable dwarfs than you and survived them. Go on busily groping. At the end of every path God stands, waiting for you."

He disappears with his umbrella into the sacristy, a well-nourished man in a black frock coat. In half an hour, garbed as fantastically as a general of Hussars, he will reappear and be a representative of God. It's the uniform, as Valentin Busch was saying after the second bottle of Johannisberger while Eduard Knobloch lapsed into melancholy and plans for murder, simply the uniform. Take away their costumes, and nobody will want to be a soldier any more.

After the devotion I go for a walk with Isabelle along the *allée*. Here it is raining irregularly—as though the shadows, crouching in the trees, were sprinkling themselves with water. Isabelle is wearing a dark raincoat, buttoned up around her throat, and a small cap that hides her hair. Nothing of her is visible but her face which shines in the darkness like a thin moon. The weather is cold and windy; no one else is in the garden. I have long since forgotten Bodendiek and the black rage that sometimes wells up in me without reason, like a dirty fountain. Isabelle is walking close beside me; I hear her footsteps in the rain and I feel her movements and her warmth; it seems to me the only warm thing left in the whole world.

Suddenly she stops. Her face is pale and determined and her eyes look almost black. "You don't love me enough," she blurts out.

I look at her in surprise. "It's the best I can do," I say.

She stands in silence for a while. "Not enough," she murmurs then. "Never enough. It is never enough."

"Yes," I say, "very likely it is never enough. Never in our lives, never with anyone. Very likely it is always too little, and that is the misery of the world."

"It is not enough," Isabelle repeats as though not hearing me. "Otherwise we would not still be two."

"You mean otherwise we would be one?"

She nods.

I think of my conversation with Georg while we were drinking mulled wine. "We'll always have to remain two, Isabelle," I say cautiously. "But we can love each other and believe that we are no longer two."

"Do you think once upon a time we were one?"

"I don't know. No one can know a thing like that. One wouldn't be able to remember it."

She looks at me fixedly out of the darkness. "That's it, Rudolf," she whispers. "One doesn't remember. Not anything. Why not? You seek and seek. Why is everything gone? There was so much! You only remember that and nothing more. Why don't you remember? You and I, didn't all this happen once before? Tell me! Tell me! Where is it now, Rudolf?"

The wind whirls past sprinkling us with raindrops. One often feels as though something had happened before, I remember. It comes quite close to you and stands there and you know it was just this way once before, exactly so; for an instant you almost know how it must go on, but then it disappears as you try to lay hold of it like smoke or a dead memory. "We could never remember, Isabelle," I say. "It's like the rain. That also has become one, out of two gasses, oxygen and hydrogen, which no longer remember they were once gasses. Now they are only rain and have no memory of an earlier time."

"Or like tears," Isabelle says. "But tears are full of memories."

We walk on for a time in silence. I am thinking of those strange moments when unexpectedly a kind of second sight like a deceptive memory seems suddenly to give us glimpses of many earlier lives. The gravel crunches under our shoes. Behind the garden wall there is the prolonged blowing of a car horn like a signal to someone about to escape. "Then it's like death," Isabelle says finally.

"What is?"

"Love. Perfect love."

"Who knows, Isabelle? I think no one can ever know. We only recognize things as long as each of us is still an I. If our I's were blended, it would be like the rain. We should be a new I and unable to remember the earlier separate I's. We should be something different, as different as rain is from air—no longer an I heightened by a you."

"And if love were perfect so that we blended together, then it would be like death?"

"Perhaps," I say hesitantly. "But not like annihilation. No one knows what death is, Isabelle. And so it can't be compared with anything. But we should certainly no longer feel our former selves. We should simply become once more another lonely I."

"Then love must always be incomplete?"

"It's complete enough," I say, cursing myself because in my pedantic schoolmaster's way I have become too involved again.

Isabelle shakes her head. "Don't evade me, Rudolf! It must be incomplete, I see that now. If it were complete, there would be a flash of lightning and then nothing."

"There would be something left, though—but beyond our powers of perception."

"Just like death?"

I look at her. "Who knows?" I say cautiously so as not to excite her further. "Perhaps death has a completely wrong name. We can only see it from one side. Perhaps it is perfect love between God and us."

The wind tosses a shower of rain onto the leaves of the trees and they toss it on with ghostly hands. Isabelle is silent for a time. "Is that why love is so sad?" she asks then.

"It isn't sad. It only makes us sad because it cannot be fulfilled and cannot be retained."

Isabelle stops. "Why, Rudolf?" she says, suddenly very emphatic, stamping her foot. "Why must it be so?"

I look into her pale, intent face. "It's our fate," I say.

She stares at me. "That is fate?"

I nod.

"It can't be! It's misery!"

She throws herself against me and I hold her tight. I feel her sobs against my shoulder. "Don't cry," I say. "What's to become of us if we cry about something like that?"

"What else is there to cry about?"

Yes, what else? I think. Everything else, the wretchedness on this accursed planet, only not about that. "It's no misfortune, Isabelle," I say. "It is good fortune. We simply have silly names for it like perfect and imperfect."

"No, no!" She shakes her head violently and won't be comforted. She weeps and clings to me and I hold her in my arms and feel that it is not I but she who is right, she who knows no compromises; that in her still burns the first, the only *why,* which existed before all the accumulated trash of existence, the first question of the awakening self.

"It is no misfortune," I say nevertheless. "Misfortune is something entirely different, Isabelle."

"What is it?"

"Misfortune is not the fact that two can never become wholly one. Misfortune is the fact that we must continually abandon each other, every day and every hour. You know it and you cannot stop it, it runs through your hands and it is the most precious thing there is and yet you cannot hold onto it. There is always one who dies first. Always one who remains behind."

She looks up. "How can one abandon what one does not have?"

"One can," I reply bitterly. "Can't one though! There are many stages of abandonment and being abandoned and each is painful and many are like death."

Isabelle's tears have stopped. "How do you know that?" she says. "You are not old enough."

I am old enough, I think. Part of me had grown old by the time I came back from the war. "I know," I say. "I found it out."

I found it out, I think. How often had I had to abandon the day and the hour, and my existence, the tree in the morning light and my hands and my thoughts, and each time it was forever and when I came back I was a different person. One can abandon a great deal and one must always leave everything behind one when one goes to meet death; faced with that one is always naked, and if one finds the way back, one must reacquire everything one left behind.

Isabelle's face shimmers before me in the rainy night, and I am suddenly overwhelmed by tenderness. I sense again in what loneliness she lives, undismayed, alone with her visions, threatened by them and surrendered to them, with no roof for shelter, without surcease or diversion, exposed to all the winds of the heart, without help from anyone, without complaint and without self-compassion. Beloved fearless heart, I think, untouched and aiming straight as an arrow at the essential alone, even if you do not reach it and go astray—but who does not go astray? And hasn't almost everyone given up long since? Where is the beginning of error, of stupidity, of cowardice, and where the beginning of wisdom and the final courage?

A bell begins to ring. Isabelle gives a start. "It's time for you to go in," I say. "They're waiting for you."

"Are you coming with me?"

"Yes."

We walk toward the house. As we step out of the *allée,* we are greeted by a squall of rain driven around us in short gusts like a wet veil. Isabelle presses against me. I look down the hill toward the city. Nothing is to be seen. Mist and rain have isolated us. Nowhere is there a light; we are entirely alone. Isabelle walks beside me as though she belonged to me forever and as though she had no weight, and once more it seems to me as if she really had none and were like the figures in legends and dreams, obedient to different laws from those of everyday existence.

We stand in the doorway. "Come with me!" she says.

I shake my head. "I can't. Not today."

She is silent, looking at me with straight, clear eyes, without reproach and without disillusionment; but suddenly something seems to have gone out in her. I lower my eyes feeling as though I had struck a child or killed a swallow. "Not today," I say. "Later. Tomorrow."

She turns away without a word and walks into the hallway. I see the nurse go up the stairs with her and suddenly I feel as though I had irrevocably lost something one finds but once in a lifetime.

I stand there bewildered. What could I have done? And how did I once more become involved in all this? It wasn't my intention at all! This accursed rain!

Slowly I walk toward the main building. Wernicke, wearing a white coat and carrying an umbrella, comes out. "Have you taken Fräulein Terhoven back?"

"Yes."

"Good. Pay a little more attention to her, won't you? Visit her now and then during the day if you have time."

"Why?"

"You'll get no answer to that," Wernicke replies. "But she is calmer when she has been with you. It's good for her. Is that enough?"

"She takes me for someone else."

"That makes no difference. I don't care about you—only about my patient." Wernicke squints through the shower. "Bodendiek praised you this evening."

"What?—He certainly had no cause!"

"He maintains that you are on the road back. To the confessional and communion."

"What an idea!" I exclaim, genuinely incensed.

"Don't underestimate the wisdom of the Church! It is the only dictatorship that has not been overthrown in two thousand years."

I walk down to the city. Mist waves its pennants in the rain. My thoughts are haunted by Isabelle. I have left her in the lurch; that's what she believes now, I know. I ought not to go there any more, I think. It simply confuses me, and I am confused enough already. But how would it be if she were no longer there? Wouldn't it be like losing the most important thing, the thing that can never grow old or stale or commonplace because one never possesses it?

I arrive at the house of Karl Brill, the shoemaker. The sounds of a phonograph come from the workroom. I have been invited here tonight for a stag evening. It is one of the famous occasions when Frau Beckmann is to exhibit her acrobatic art. I hesitate for a moment—I really am not in the mood—but then I go in. For that very reason.

I am greeted by a wave of tobacco smoke and the smell of beer. Karl Brill gets up and embraces me, staggering slightly. His head is just as bald as Georg Kroll's, but to make up for it he wears all his hair under his nose in a huge mustache. "You've come at just the right moment," he exclaims. "The bets are down. All we need is some better music than this miserable phonograph! How about the 'Beautiful Blue Danube'?"

"It's a deal!"

The piano has already been brought in and is standing beside the resoling machines. In the front of the room the shoes and leather have been pushed to one side and straight and easy chairs have been placed wherever possible. A cask of beer stands ready; several bottles of schnaps are already empty. A second battery stands in readiness on the workbench. There, too, lies a big nail wrapped in cotton beside a large cobbler's hammer.

I pound out the "Blue Danube." Karl Brill's drinking companions stagger about through the haze. They are already well loaded. Karl puts a glass of beer and a double Steinhäger schnaps on the piano. "Clara is getting ready," he says. "We have over three million in bets. I only hope she's in top form; otherwise I'll be half bankrupt."

He squints at me. "Play something very spirited when the time comes. That always warms her up. You know she's crazy about music."

"I'll play the 'March of the Gladiators.' But how about a small side bet for me?"

Karl glances up. "Dear Herr Bodmer," he says in an injured voice, "surely you're not going to bet against Clara! How could you play with any conviction then?"

"Not against her. On her. A side bet."

"How much?" Karl asks quickly.

"A measly eighty thousand," I reply. "It's my whole fortune."

Karl thinks it over for a moment. Then he turns around. "Is there anyone here who wants to bet another eighty thousand? Against our piano player?"

"I do!" A fat man steps forward. Taking some bills out of a small suitcase, he slaps them down on the workbench.

I put my money beside them. "May the God of thieves defend me," I say. "Otherwise lunch is all I'll have tomorrow."

"Let's get going!" Karl Brill says.

The nail is shown around. Then Karl steps to the wall, places the nail at the height of the human buttocks, and drives it a third of the way in. He pounds less vigorously than his gestures would suggest. "It's driven in good and strong," he says, pretending to give the nail a powerful tug.

"We'll just see about that."

The fat man who has bet against me steps forward. He moves the nail and grins. "Karl," he says, laughing contemptuously, "I could blow that out of the wall. Just give me the hammer."

"First blow it out of the wall."

The fat man does not blow. He gives a strong tug and the nail comes out. "I can drive a nail through a table top with my hand," Karl Brill says. "But not with my rear end. If you make conditions like that, let's call the whole thing off."

The fat man makes no reply. He takes the hammer and drives the nail into another place in the wall. "Now, how's that?"

Karl Brill tests it. Some six or seven centimeters of the nail still protrude from the wall. "Too hard. You can't even pull it out with your hand."

"Take it or else," the fat man declares.

Karl tries again. The fat man puts the hammer on the

workbench, overlooking the fact that each time Karl tests the nail he loosens it a little. "I can't take an even-money bet on that," Karl says finally. "Only two to one and I'll lose anyway."

They agree on six to four. A pile of money rises on the workbench. Karl has tugged indignantly twice more at the nail to show how impossible the bet is. Now I play the "March of the Gladiators" and shortly thereafter Frau Beckmann comes rustling into the workroom in a loose salmon-colored Chinese kimono embroidered on the back with peonies and a phoenix.

She is an imposing figure, with the head of a bulldog. She has abundant, curly black hair and bright, shoe-button eyes—the rest is pure bulldog, especially the chin. Her body is huge and all of iron. Her breasts, hard as stone, project like a bulwark, then comes the comparatively slender waist and after that the famous bottom, the present point of interest. It is powerful and it, too, is hard as stone. A blacksmith is said to have failed in an attempt to pinch it when Frau Beckmann contracted her muscles; he would have broken his fingers. Karl Brill has already won bets on that subject too, just in the circle of his most intimate friends to be sure. Tonight, with the fat man present, only the other experiment will be tried: the extraction of the nail from the wall with her seat.

Everything is conducted in a very sportsmanlike and gentlemanly fashion; Frau Beckmann greets the company, of course, but is otherwise reserved and almost aloof. She regards the occasion solely from a sporting and business angle. Calmly she places her back against the wall behind a low screen, makes a few expert adjustments, and then stands still, her chin raised, serious and ready, as befits a great sporting event.

I break off the march and strike two deep quavers, which are supposed to sound like the roll of drums that heralds the death leap in Kine's circus. Frau Beckmann stiffens, then relaxes. She stiffens once more. Karl Brill grows nervous. Frau Beckmann stiffens again, her eyes turned to the ceiling, her teeth gritted. There is a tinkle and she steps away from the wall; the nail lies on the floor.

I play the "Virgin's Prayer," one of her favorites. She acknowledges it with a gracious inclination of her powerful head, says melodiously, "Good night all," pulls her kimono closer around her and disappears.

Karl Brill distributes the cash. He hands me mine. The fat man inspects the nail and the wall. "Unbelievable," he says.

I play the "Alpine Sunset" and the "Song of the Weser," two more of Frau Beckmann's favorites. She can hear them on the floor above. Karl grins over at me proudly; after all, he is the proprietor of those impressive pincers. Steinhäger, beer, and schnaps flow. I have a couple of drinks and continue to play. I want not to be alone just now. I want to think and at the same time that's the last thing in the world I want to do. My hands are full of an unaccustomed tenderness, something swirls about me and seems to press against me; the workroom disappears and the rain is there again, the mist and Isabelle and the darkness. She is not sick, I think, and yet I know that she is—but if she is sick, then all the rest of us are sicker—

A noisy altercation rouses me. The fat man has not been able to forget the figure Frau Beckmann cut. Inflamed by numerous drinks, he has made Karl Brill a triple offer— five million for afternoon tea with Frau Beckmann—one million for a short conversation now, during which he no doubt intends to invite her to an honorable dinner without Karl Brill—and two million for a couple of good grasps on the showpiece of the Beckmann anatomy, here in the workshop among brothers in happy comradeship, therefore completely honorable.

But now Karl's character asserts itself. If the fat man had no more than a sporting interest, he could perhaps have had his grasps in return for some such nominal sum as a hundred thousand marks—but such a gesture with lascivious intent strikes Karl as a serious insult. "You miserable bastard!" he roars. "I thought everyone here was a cavalier!"

"I am a cavalier," the fat man says thickly. "That's why I made the offer."

"You're a pig."

"That's true too, otherwise I wouldn't be a cavalier. You ought to be proud of the impression the lady makes—have you no heart? What can I do if my nature grows unruly? Why are you insulted? After all, you aren't married to her!"

I see Karl Brill jump as though someone had shot him. He lives in common-law marriage with Frau Beckmann, who is his housekeeper. No one knows why he does not marry her—unless perhaps it is that same stubbornness of character which makes him cut a hole in the ice so that he can go swimming in winter. Nevertheless, it is his weak point.

"If I had such a jewel," the fat man mutters, "I would carry her in my arms and clothe her in satin and silk. Silk, red silk—" He is almost sobbing and is tracing voluptuous forms in the air. The bottle beside him is empty. He is a tragic case of love at first sight. I turn away and go on playing. The picture of the fat man trying to carry Frau Beckmann in his arms is more than I can stand. "Get out!" Karl Brill shouts. "This is too much. I don't like to throw a guest out, but—"

A dreadful scream comes from the back of the room. We leap up. A little man is dancing around there. Karl jumps toward him, seizes a pair of shears and turns off one of the machines. The little man faints. "Damn it! Who would expect anyone to play with a soling machine when drunk?" Karl cries indignantly.

We examine the hand. A few threads hang out of it. The machine has caught him in the soft flesh between the thumb and index finger—fortunately. Karl pours schnaps on the wound, and the little man comes to. "Amputated?" he asks in horror, seeing his hand in Karl's paw.

"Nonsense, the arm is still attached."

The man sighs in relief as Karl shakes his arm in front of his eyes. "Blood poisoning, do you think?" he asks.

"No. Only the machine will get rusty from your blood. We'll wash your flipper with alcohol, put some iodine on it, and tie it up."

"Iodine? Doesn't that hurt?"

"It stings for a second. Just as though your hand had drunk a very strong schnaps."

The little man pulls his hand away. "I'd rather drink the schnaps myself."

He gets a not-too-clean handkerchief out of his pocket, wraps up his paw, and reaches for the bottle. Karl grins. Then he looks around uneasily. "Where's Fatty?"

No one knows. "Perhaps he's made himself thin," someone says and earns a round of laughter.

The door opens and the fat man appears. Bent double he staggers in, behind him Frau Beckmann in her salmon-pink kimono. She has twisted his arm behind him and is propelling him into the workshop. With a mighty shove she lets him go. The fat man falls on his face in the women's shoe section. Frau Beckmann makes a gesture as though dusting her hands and goes out. With a mighty leap Karl Brill is beside the fat man and yanks him to his feet. "My arm!" whimpers the rejected lover. "She has twisted it out of the socket! And my belly! Oh, my belly! What a kick!"

He doesn't need to explain. Frau Beckmann is a fair antagonist for Karl Brill, winter swimmer and first-class gymnast. She has already broken his arm twice, not to mention what she can do with a vase or a poker. One night less than six months ago she surprised two burglars who had broken into the workshop. Afterward both were in the hospital for weeks; one of them has never recovered from a blow on the skull which also cost him an ear. He still can't talk straight.

Karl drags the fat man into the light. He is white with rage, but there's nothing more he can do—the fat man is finished. It would be like beating up a typhus patient. The fat man must have received a frightful blow in the organ with which he intended to sin. He is unable to walk. Karl can't even throw him out. We lay him in the back of the shop on a pile of leather trimmings.

"The nice thing about Karl's is that it's always so jolly here," says a man who is trying to give the piano a drink of beer.

I walk homeward along Grossestrasse. My head is swimming; I have drunk too much, but that was what I intended to do. The mist sweeps past the isolated lights still burning in the show windows and weaves a golden veil around the street lamps. In the window of a butcher shop an alpine rosebush is blooming beside a slaughtered pig with a lemon gripped in its waxy snout. Sausages are arranged in a cosy circle around them. It is an affecting picture, harmoniously combining beauty with utility. I stand in front of it for a time and then wander on.

In the dark courtyard I collide with a shadow. It is old Knopf, who is once more standing in front of the black obelisk. I have run against him with my full weight and he staggers and throws both arms around the obelisk as though intending to climb it. "Sorry I ran into you," I say. "But why are you standing here? Can't you attend to your necessities in your own house? Or, if you're an exhibitionist, why not on a street corner?"

Knopf lets go of the obelisk. "Damn it, now it's down my trousers," he mutters.

"That won't hurt you. Well, you can finish up here now as far as I'm concerned."

"Too late."

Knopf staggers across to his door. I go upstairs and decide to send Isabelle a bouquet of flowers tomorrow with the money I have won at Karl Brill's. That sort of thing, to be sure, usually brings me nothing but bad luck. However, I don't know of anything else to do. For a time I stand at the window looking out into the night and then I begin very softly and somewhat shamefacedly to repeat words and sentences I would like sometime to say to somebody, but for whom I have no one except possibly Isabelle—who doesn't even know who I am. But who does know that about anyone?

Chapter Thirteen

The traveling salesman Oskar Fuchs, called Weeping Oskar, is sitting in the office. "What's new, Herr Fuchs?" I ask. "How is the grippe progressing in the villages?"

"Pretty harmless. The farmers are well fed. In the city it's different. I have two cases where Hollmann and Klotz are on the point of closing. A red granite monument, polished on one side, with two bossed socles, a yard and a half high, two million two hundred thousand marks—and a small one, forty inches high, one million three hundred thousand. Good prices. If you ask a hundred thousand less you'll get them. My commission is twenty per cent."

"Fifteen," I reply automatically.

"Twenty," Weeping Oskar declares. "I get fifteen from Hollmann and Klotz as it is. So why the betrayal?"

He is lying. Hollmann and Klotz, for whom he travels, pay him ten per cent and expenses. He gets expenses anyway; so he would be doing business with us for ten per cent extra.

"Payment in cash?"

"You'll have to see to that for yourselves. The people are well off."

"Herr Fuchs," I say. "Why don't you join us? We'd pay better than Hollmann and Klotz and we can use a first-class traveler."

Fuchs winks. "It's more fun for me this way. I'm an emotional type. When I get angry at old Hollmann I throw a job your way as revenge. If I worked for you all the time I'd get angry at you too."

"There's something in that," I say.

"What I mean is, then I would betray you to Hollmann and Klotz. Traveling in tombstones is so boring you have to do something to cheer yourself up."

"Boring? For a person who puts on such an artistic performance every time?"

Fuchs smiles like Gaston Münch of the city theater after playing the role of Karl Heinz in *Alt Heidelberg*. "One does the best one can," he concedes with colossal modesty.

"They say you have developed splendidly. Without artificial aids. Simply through intuition. Is that right?"

Oskar, who formerly had recourse to slices of raw red onions before entering a house of mourning, now maintains he can produce tears freely like a great actor. Naturally that is an enormous improvement. Now he does not have to enter a house weeping, as he did when he used the onion technique, nor, if the business lasts some time, do his tears dry up—for of course he could not use the onions while he was sitting with the mourners—on the contrary, he can now go in with dry eyes and during conversation about the departed break into natural tears, which of course produces a much stronger effect. It is like the difference between genuine and artificial pearls. Oskar maintains he is so convincing that he is often comforted and cosseted by the survivors.

Georg Kroll comes out of his room. The smoke from a streaked Havana wreathes his face and he is the picture of satisfaction. "Herr Fuchs," he says, "is it true you can weep at will, or is that just a piece of dirty propaganda on the part of our competitors to scare us?"

Instead of answering Oskar stares at him. "Well?" Georg Kroll asks. "What's the matter? Aren't you feeling well?"

"Just a minute! I must get into the right mood."

Oskar closes his eyes. When he opens them again they already look rather watery. He continues to stare at Georg and after a while there are actually heavy tears in his blue eyes. A moment later they roll down his cheeks. Oskar gets out his handkerchief and dabs at them. "How was that?" he asks, drawing out his watch. "Exactly two minutes. Sometimes I can manage it in one when there is a corpse in the house."

"Magnificent."

Georg pours out some of the cognac he keeps for customers. "You should have been an actor, Herr Fuchs."

"I have thought about that; but there are too few roles in which manly tears are required. Othello, to be sure, but aside from him—"

"How do you do it? Is there a trick?"

"Imagination," Fuchs replies simply. "Strong pictorial imagination."

"What were you picturing just now?"

Oskar empties his glass. "To speak candidly, you, Herr Kroll: with splintered arms and legs, and a swarm of rats slowly gnawing your face while you were still alive but unable to keep the creatures away because of your broken arms. I beg your pardon, but for such a quick performance I needed a very strong image."

Georg runs his hand over his face. It is still there. "Do

you imagine the same sort of pictures of Hollmann and Klotz when you're working for them?" I ask.

Fuchs shakes his head. "I picture them reaching the age of a hundred, still rich and healthy, and finally being carried off painlessly in their sleep by a heart attack—then tears of rage stream down my cheeks."

Georg pays him the commission for the last two betrayals. "I have recently developed an artificial hiccup too," Oskar says. "Very effective. It speeds up the agreement. The people feel guilty because they think it is a result of my sympathy."

"Herr Fuchs, join us!" I say again impulsively. "You belong in an establishment that is run along artistic lines—not with mere money grubbers."

Weeping Oskar smiles good-naturedly, shakes his head, and prepares to depart. "I can't just now. Without a little betrayal I would be nothing but a dripping washrag. Betrayal gives me poise. Do you understand?"

"We understand," Georg says. "We are crushed by regret but we respect personality above everything."

I note the addresses for the tombstones on a piece of paper and give it to Heinrich Kroll, who is in the courtyard, pumping up the tires of his bicycle. He looks at the slip contemptuously. To an old Nibelung like him, Oskar is a common scoundrel, though he is happy, also like an old Nibelung, to profit from him. "We never used to need this sort of thing," he exclaims. "Lucky my father didn't live to see it."

"According to what I've heard about that pioneer of the gravestone business, your father would have been beside himself with joy to play such a trick on the competition," I reply. "He was a fighter by nature—not like you, on the field of honor, but in the trenches of uncompromising business warfare. By the way, are we going to get the rest of the payment for that war memorial you sold in April? There are two hundred thousand marks still due. You know what that's worth now? Not so much as a socle!"

Heinrich mutters something and puts the slip of paper in his pocket. I go back, pleased to have taken him down a bit. In front of the house stands the piece of gutter pipe that broke off during the last rainstorm. The workmen have just finished; they have replaced the broken section. "What about the old pipe?" the foreman asks. "You don't need it. Shall we take it along?"

"Sure," Georg says.

The pipe is leaning against the obelisk, Knopf's open-air *pissoir*. It is several yards long and has a right angle at one end. Suddenly I have an inspiration. "Leave it here," I say. "We can use it."

"What for?" Georg asks.

"For this evening. You'll see. It will be an interesting performance."

Heinrich Kroll pedals off. Georg and I stand in front of the door, drinking glasses of beer that Frau Kroll has handed out through the kitchen window. The weather is very hot. Wilke, the coffinmaker, steals by, carrying bottled beer. He is on his way to take a siesta in a coffin upholstered with shavings. Butterflies play around the memorial crosses. The Knopf family's pied cat is pregnant. "Where does the dollar stand?" I ask. "Have you phoned?"

"Fifteen thousand marks higher than this morning. If it goes on like this we'll be able to pay Riesenfeld's promissory note with the price of a small headstone."

"Marvelous. Only it's too bad we haven't kept any of it. That takes away some of the necessary zest, doesn't it?"

Georg laughs. "Some of the seriousness of the business too. Except for Heinrich, of course. What are you doing this evening?"

"I'm going up the hill to see Wernicke. There, at least,

they know nothing about the seriousness and silliness of business. Up there the only stake is existence—always the whole of being, life and nothing short of life. There's no smaller wager. If you lived up there for a while, our absurd haggling over trivialities would seem insane."

"Bravo," Georg replies. "For this nonsense you deserve a second glass of ice-cold beer." He takes our glasses and hands them in through the kitchen window. *"Gnädige Frau,* the same thing again, please."

Frau Kroll sticks her gray head out. "Would you like a fresh herring and a pickle with it?"

"Absolutely! And a slice of bread. The proper *petit déjeuner* for any kind of *Weltschmerz,*" Georg replies, handing me my glass. "Do you suffer from it?"

"A respectable man of my age always suffers from *Weltschmerz,*" I reply firmly. "It's the prerogative of youth."

"I thought they'd stolen your youth in the army?"

"That's right. I'm still searching for it and I can't find it. That's why I have double *Weltschmerz.* The way an amputated foot hurts twice as much."

The beer is wonderfully cold. The sun burns the tops of our heads, and suddenly, despite all the *Weltschmerz,* there occurs another of those instants when you look at very close range into the green-gold eyes of life. I finish my beer thoughtfully. It seems all at once as though my veins had had a sunbath. "We keep forgetting that we only live on this planet for a short time," I say. "And so we have a completely crazy attitude toward the world. Like men who would live forever. Have you noticed that?"

"And how! It's humanity's cardinal mistake. That's why otherwise entirely sensible people leave millions of dollars to horrible relations instead of spending it on themselves."

"Good! What would you do if you knew you were going to die tomorrow?"

"No notion."

"No? All right, perhaps one day is too short. What would you do if you knew you'd be gone in a week?"

"Still no notion."

"But you'd have to do something! Suppose you had a month's time?"

"Very likely I'd go on living the way I do now," Georg says. "Otherwise I'd have the miserable feeling all month that I'd lived my life wrong up to then."

"You'd have a month's time to correct it."

Georg shakes his head. "I'd have a month to regret it."

"You could sell our inventory to Hollmann and Klotz, rush to Berlin, and for a month live a breathtaking life with actors, artists, and elegant whores."

"The funds wouldn't last a week. The ladies would only be barmaids. And besides, I prefer to read about it. Imagination never disappoints you. But how about you? What would you do if you knew you were going to die in four weeks?"

"I?" I say, caught off my guard.

"Yes, you."

I glance around. There lies the garden, hot and green, in all the colors of midsummer. There the swallows sail, there is the endless blue of the heavens, and upstairs old Knopf goggles down at us from his window, just emerging from his drunk and clad in suspenders and a checked shirt. "I'd have to think about it," I say. "I can't answer right away. There's too much. Right now all I have is a feeling I'd explode if I understood it all as I'd like to."

"Don't think too hard; otherwise we'll have to take you to Wernicke. And not to play the organ."

"That's it," I say. "Really that's it! If we could grasp it fully we would go mad."

"Another glass of beer?" Frau Kroll asks through the kitchen window. "There's raspberry jam here too. Fresh."

"Rescued!" I say. *"Gnädige Frau,* you have just rescued

me. I was like an arrow on its way to the sun and to Wernicke. Thank God everything is still here! Nothing has burned up! Sweet life continues to frolic around us with flies and butterflies, nothing has been reduced to ashes, it is here, it still has all its laws, even those we impose upon it like a bridle on a thoroughbred! However—no raspberry jam with beer, please! Instead, a piece of runny Harz cheese. Good morning, Herr Knopf! A fine day! What's your opinion of life?"

Knopf stares at me. His face is gray and there are sacks under his eyes. After a while he gesticulates at me angrily and closes his window. "Weren't you going to say something to him?" Georg asks.

"Yes, but not till tonight."

We go into Eduard Knobloch's restaurant. "Look over there," I say, stopping as though I had run into a tree. "Life seems to be up to its tricks here too! I should have guessed it!"

Gerda is sitting at a table in the wine room with a vase of tiger lilies in front of her. She is alone and is hacking away at a venison steak that is almost as big as the table. "What do you say to that?" I ask Georg. "Doesn't it smell of betrayal?"

"Was there anything to betray?"

"No. But what about unfaithfulness?"

"Was there anything to be faithful to?"

"Oh stop it, Socrates!" I reply. "Can't you see Eduard's fat paw at work here?"

"I see it all right. But who has betrayed you? Eduard or Gerda?"

"Gerda! Who do you think? The man's never responsible."

"Nor the woman either."

"Then who?"

"You."

"All right," I say. "It's easy for you to talk. You don't get betrayed. You are a betrayer yourself."

Georg nods with self-satisfaction. "Love is a matter of emotion," he instructs me. "Not of morality. Emotion, however, knows nothing of betrayal. It increases, disappears, or changes—so where is the betrayal? There is no contract. Didn't you deafen Gerda with your howling about your sufferings over Erna?"

"Only at the beginning. You know she was there when we had our row in the Red Mill."

"Then don't yammer now. Give up or do something."

Some people get up from a table near us. We sit down. Freidank, the waiter, veers away. "Where's Herr Knobloch?" I ask.

Freidank glances around. "I don't know—he has been here all along, at that table over there with the lady."

"Simple, isn't it?" I say to Georg. "That's where we stand now. I am a natural victim of the inflation. Once again. First with Erna, now with Gerda. Am I a born cuckold? Things like this don't happen to you."

"Fight!" Georg replies. "Nothing is lost yet. Go over to Gerda!"

"What am I to fight with? Tombstones? Eduard gives her venison and dedicates poems to her. In poems she can't see differences of quality—in food unfortunately she can. And I, fool that I am, have only myself to blame! I brought her here and aroused her appetite. Literally!"

"Then give up," Georg says. "Why fight? One can't fight about emotions anyway."

"No? Then why did you advise me to a minute ago?"

"Because today is Tuesday. Here comes Eduard—in his Sunday best with a rosebud in his buttonhole. You're done for."

Eduard is taken aback when he sees us. He peers over toward Gerda and then greets us with the condescension of a victor. "Herr Knobloch," Georg says, "is loyalty the badge of honor, as our beloved field marshal has declared, or isn't it?"

"It all depends," Eduard replies cautiously. "Today we have Königsberger meat balls with gravy and potatoes. A fine meal."

"Does a soldier strike his comrade in the back?" Georg asks, undeterred. "Does a brother strike his brother? Does a poet strike a fellow poet?"

"Poets attack each other all the time. That's what they live for."

"They live for open battle, not for stabs in the belly," I interpose.

Eduard grins broadly. "To the victor the spoils, my dear Ludwig; catch as catch can. Do I whine when you come in here with your miserable coupons that aren't worth peanuts?"

"Yes, you do," I say, "and how!"

At this instant Eduard is pushed aside. "Why, there you are, children," Gerda says affectionately. "Let's eat together! I was hoping you would come!"

"You're sitting in the wine room," I reply venomously. "We're drinking beer."

"I prefer beer too. I'll sit down with you."

"With your permission, Eduard?" I ask. "Catch as catch can?"

"What has Eduard's permission to do with it?" Gerda asks. "Why, he's delighted for me to eat with his friends, aren't you, Eduard?"

The serpent is already calling him by his first name.

Eduard stammers. "Of course, no objection, naturally, a pleasure—"

He makes a fine picture, red, raging, and making an

effort to smile. "That's a pretty rosebud you're wearing," I say. "Are you going courting? Or is it simple delight in nature?"

"Eduard has a very fine feeling for beauty," Gerda replies.

"So he has," I agree. "Did you have the regular lunch? Detestable Königsberger meat balls in some sort of flavorless German gravy?"

Gerda laughs. "Eduard, show them you're a cavalier. Let me invite your two friends to lunch! They keep saying you're dreadfully stingy. Let's prove they're wrong. We have—"

"Königsberger meat balls," Eduard interrupts her. "All right, invite them to have meat balls. I'll see that they're extra good."

"Saddle of venison," Gerda says.

Eduard now resembles a defective steam engine. "These are no friends," he declares.

"What's that?"

"We're blood brothers like Valentin," I say. "Don't you remember our last conversation at the Poets' Club? Shall I repeat it? In what verse form are you writing now?"

"What were you talking about?" Gerda asks.

"About nothing at all," Eduard replies abruptly. "These two never say a word of truth! Jokers, miserable jokers, that's what they are! Don't you ever realize the seriousness of life?"

"I'd like to know who realizes it more than we do, except gravediggers and coffinmakers," I say.

"There you go! All you know about death is its ridiculous aspect," Gerda suddenly remarks, out of a clear sky. "And that's why you don't know more about the seriousness of life."

We stare at her dumbfounded. That is unmistakably

Eduard's style! I feel I am fighting for a lost cause, but I don't give up.

"From whom did you hear that?" I ask. "From the sibyl beside the dark abysses of melancholy?"

Gerda laughs. "With you life always gets around to tombstones, the first thing. That doesn't happen so fast with other people. Eduard, for example, is a nightingale!"

A blush spreads over Eduard's fat cheeks. "Well, how about the rack of venison?" Gerda asks him.

"Well, all right, why not?"

Eduard disappears. I look at Gerda. "Bravo!" I say. "A first-rate job. What are we to make of it?"

"Don't look like a husband," she replies. "Be glad you're living."

"What is living?"

"Whatever's happening at the moment."

"Bravo!" Georg says. "And my warmest thanks for the invitation. We really love Eduard; he just doesn't understand us."

"Do you love him too?" I ask Gerda.

She laughs. "How childish he is," she says to Georg. "Can't you open his eyes a little to the fact that not everything always belongs to him? Especially when he's not around?"

"I try constantly to enlighten him," Georg replies. "The only trouble is he has a lot of internal handicaps which he calls ideals. If he ever happens to notice that they're euphemistic egoism, he'll improve."

"What is euphemistic egoism?"

"Youthful self-importance."

Gerda laughs so hard the table shakes. "I'm rather fond of that," she remarks. "But too much of it gets tiring. After all, facts are facts."

I refrain from asking her whether facts really are facts.

She sits there, honest and secure, waiting, knife in hand, for her second portion of venison. Her face is rounder than before; she has already gained weight on Eduard's food, and she beams at me without a trace of embarrassment. And why should she be embarrassed? What kind of claim do I really have on her? And just now who is betraying whom? "It's true," I say. "I am hung with egoistic atavisms like a rock with moss. *Mea culpa!*"

"Right, my pet," Gerda replies. "Enjoy your life and only think when you have to."

"When does one have to?"

"When one needs money or wants to get ahead in the world."

"Bravo," Georg says again. At this moment the venison appears and conversation comes to an end. Eduard supervises us like a mother hen with its chicks. This is the first time he has not begrudged us our food. He wears a new smile that puzzles me. He is full of fat superiority, which now and then he communicates to Gerda as though it were a clandestine note exchanged in jail. But Gerda still has her old, completely open smile which, when Eduard is looking the other way, she turns on me as innocently as a child at first communion. She is younger than I am, but I have the feeling that she has at least forty years' more experience. "Eat, baby," she says.

I eat with a bad conscience and strong misgivings; the venison, a delicacy of the first order, suddenly has no savor. "Another little piece?" Eduard asks me. "Or a little more bilberry sauce?"

I stare at him, feeling as though my former recruiting sergeant had asked me to kiss him. Even Georg is alarmed. I know that later he will maintain that the reason for Eduard's incredible openhandedness is that he has slept with Gerda—but this time I know better. She will get rack of venison only as long as she has not allowed that. Once he has had her, the most she can expect is Königsberger meat balls with German gravy. And I am perfectly sure that Gerda knows this too.

Nevertheless, I decide to go away with her after the meal. Trust, to be sure, is trust, but Eduard has too many different kinds of liqueur in the bar.

Silent and star-filled, the night hangs over the city. I am seated at the window of my room waiting for Knopf, for whose benefit I have arranged the rain pipe. It extends straight into my window and thence runs above the entrance gate to Knopf's house where the short end makes a right-angle turn in the direction of the courtyard. It cannot, however, be seen from the courtyard.

I wait, reading the newspaper. The dollar has clambered up another ten thousand marks. Yesterday there was only one suicide, but to make up for it there were two strikes. After long negotiations the government employees have finally received an increase in pay which, in the meantime, has fallen so far in value that now they can barely get an extra liter of milk a week for it. Very likely no more than a box of matches next week. The number of unemployed has risen by an additional hundred and fifty thousand. Unrest has broken out through the whole Reich. New recipes for the use of garbage in the kitchen are being recommended. The wave of grippe is still on the rise. A pension increase for the aged and infirm has been turned over to a committee for further study. Their report is expected in a few months. Meanwhile, the pensioners and invalids try to keep from starvation by begging or by borrowing from friends and relatives.

Outside, there is the sound of soft footsteps. I peer cautiously out of the window. It is not Knopf; it is a pair of lovers stealing on tiptoe through the courtyard into the garden. The season is now in full swing, and lovers' necessities are more pressing than ever. Wilke was right: where are they to go to be undisturbed? If they try to slip into their furnished rooms, the landlady lies in wait to drive them out, like an angel with a flaming sword, in the name of morality and envy—in the public parks and gardens they would be shouted at by the police or arrested—and they haven't enough money for a hotel room—so where are they to go? In our courtyard they are undisturbed. The larger memorials furnish seclusion from other couples; there they are not seen and can lean against the monuments and in their shadow whisper and embrace. The big memorial crosses are always there for stormy lovers on wet days when they cannot lie on the ground; then the girls hold onto them and are pressed close by their wooers, the rain beats upon their heated faces, mist drifts around them, their breath comes in quick pants, and their heads are held high like those of whinnying horses by their lovers' hands in their hair. The signs I have put up recently have done no good. Who worries about his toes when his whole being is aflame?

Suddenly I hear Knopf's footsteps in the alley. I look at the clock. It is half-past two; that slave driver of generations of unhappy recruits must be well loaded. I turn out the light. Inexorably Knopf steers his course straight for the black obelisk. I seize the end of the rain pipe, press my mouth close to the opening and say: "Knopf!"

It makes a hollow sound at the other end, behind the sergeant major's back, as though it came from the grave. Knopf looks around; he can't see where the voice is coming from. "Knopf!" I repeat. "You pig! Aren't you ashamed of yourself? Did I create you to get drunk and piss on tombstones, you sow?"

Knopf whirls around again. "What?" he stammers. "Who is that?"

"Filthy loafer!" I say, and it sounds ghostly and supernatural. "How dare you ask questions! Is it your place to question your superiors? Stand at attention when I address you!"

Knopf stares at his house, whence the voice comes. All the windows are dark and closed. The door, too, is closed. He cannot see the pipe on the wall. "Stand at attention, you insubordinate scoundrel of a sergeant major!" I say. "Was it for this I bestowed on you braid for your collar and a long saber, so that you could defile monuments destined to stand in God's acre?" And more sharply in a hissing tone of command: "Heels together, you worthless tombstone wetter!"

The tone of command has its effect. Knopf comes to attention, his hands at the seams of his trousers. The moon is reflected in his wide-open eyes. "Knopf," I say in ghostly tones, "you will be degraded to second-class private if I catch you at it again! You blot on the honor of the German soldier and the United Association of Retired Sergeants Major."

Knopf listens, his head extended sidewise, like a moonstruck hound. "The Kaiser?" he whispers.

"Button up your pants and vanish!" I whisper hollowly. "And mark you this! Indulge in your nastiness just once more and you will be degraded and castrated. Castrated, I say! And now off with you, you slovenly civilian! Forward march!"

In consternation Knopf stumbles toward the door of his house. Immediately thereafter the pair of lovers start up out of the garden like two startled does and rush into the street. That, of course, was no part of my plan.

Chapter Fourteen

The Poets' Club is meeting at Eduard's. The expedition to the bordello has been decided on. Otto Bambuss hopes to achieve a blood transfusion for his verse; Hans Hungermann wants to gain inspiration for his "Casanova" and for a free-verse cycle to be called "The Demon Woman"—and even Mathias Grund, the author of the "Book of Death," thinks he can pick up a few racy details for the final delirium of a paranoiac. "Why don't you come along, Eduard?" I ask.

"Don't need to," he announces in a superior fashion. "I'm well taken care of as it is."

"Really? Are you?" I know what he is trying to convey and I know it is a lie.

"He sleeps with all the chambermaids in his hotel," Hungermann explains. "If they refuse he dismisses them. He is a true friend of the people."

"Chambermaids! That's your style! Free verse, free love! Not I! Never in my own house! That's an old axiom."

"What about guests?"

"Guests." Eduard turns his eyes toward heaven. "There, of course, you often can't help yourself. The Countess von Bell-Armin, for example—"

"For example of what?" I ask as he falls silent.

Eduard demurs. "A cavalier is discreet."

Hungermann is overcome by an attack of coughing. "A fine discretion! How old is she? Eighty?"

Eduard smiles scornfully—but the next moment his smile drops from his face like a mask with a broken cord: Valentin Busch has entered. He, to be sure, is no man of letters, but nevertheless he has decided to come with us. He wants to be present when Otto Bambuss loses his virginity. "How goes it, Eduard?" he asks. "Nice that you're still alive, eh? Otherwise you wouldn't have been able to enjoy that affair with the countess."

"How do you know about it?" I ask in surprise.

"I overheard you outside in the hall. You're talking pretty loud. No doubt you've had quite a bit to drink. However, I do not begrudge Eduard the countess. I'm just happy that it was I who could rescue him for that."

"It was long before the war," Eduard declares quickly. He scents a new attack on his wine cellar.

"All right, all right," Valentin replies agreeably. "Since the war you've no doubt had some fine experiences too."

"In times like these?"

"Especially in times like these! When a person is desperate he is more open to adventure. And countesses, princesses, and duchesses are especially desperate just now. Inflation, the republic, no more imperial army, that's enough to break an aristocratic heart! How about a good bottle, Eduard?"

"I haven't time just now," Eduard replies with presence of mind. "Sorry, Valentin, but it won't do tonight. The club is making an expedition."

"Are you going along?" I ask.

"Of course! As treasurer! I have to, after all! Just didn't think of it a moment ago! Duty is duty."

I laugh. Valentin winks at me and says nothing about coming with us. Eduard smiles because he thinks he has saved himself a bottle. Thus everything is in complete harmony.

We get up and leave. It is a splendid evening. We are going to No. 12 Bahnstrasse. The city has two cat houses, but the one in Bahnstrasse is the more elegant. Situated outside the city, it is a small house surrounded by poplar trees. I know it well; I spent part of my youth there without knowing what it was. On afternoons when we had no school we used to go out of the city to fish and look for salamanders in the streams and ponds and butterflies and beetles in the fields. On one particularly hot day, in search of an inn where we could get lemonade, we arrived at No. 12 Bahnstrasse. The big taproom on the ground floor looked like any other taproom. It was cool, and when we asked for soft drinks we got them. After a while a number of women in morning gowns or flowery clothes came in too. They asked us what we were doing and what class we were in at school. We paid for our drinks and came back again on the next hot day, this time with the books we had taken with us to study outdoors beside a stream. The kindly women were there again and took a motherly interest in us. We found the place cool and agreeable, and since no one but us was there in the afternoons, we stayed and began to do our lessons. The women looked over our shoulders and helped us as though they were our teachers. They saw to it that we did our written exercises, they checked up on our marks, they listened to us recite what we had to learn by heart, and gave us chocolate when we were good or, on occasion, a gentle cuff on the ear when we were lazy. We thought nothing of it; we were still at that happy age when women mean nothing. After a short time, these ladies, smelling of violets and roses, assumed the roles of mother and teacher; they were very much interested in us, and the moment we appeared at the door one of these goddesses was likely to ask excitedly: "How did the geography class go? All right?" At that time my mother was in the hospital a great deal, and so it happened that I got part of my education in the Werdenbrück cat house, and I can only say that it was stricter than if I had got it at home. We went there for two summers, then we began to take long hikes and so had less time, and my family moved to another part of the city.

After that I was in Bahnstrasse on one other occasion, during the war. It was the day before we were to go to the front. We were just eighteen, some of us not quite eighteen, and most of us had never been with a woman. But we didn't want to be shot without knowing something about it and therefore we went, five in number, to Bahnstrasse, which we already knew from that earlier time. Business was brisk there and we were served with schnaps and beer. After we had drunk enough to feel courageous we decided to make our bid for happiness. Willy, more enterprising than the rest of us, was the first. He stopped Fritzi, the most seductive of the ladies present. "Darling, how about it?"

"Sure," Fritzi replied through the noise and smoke, without really looking at him. "Have you the money?"

"More than enough." Willy showed her his pay and the money his mother had given him to have a mass said for his safe return from the war.

"Well then! Long live the fatherland!" Fritzi said somewhat absently, looking in the direction of the beer bar. "Come upstairs!"

Willy got up and put his cap on the table. Fritzi stared

at his fiery red hair. It was of a unique brilliance and, of course, she recognized it at once even after seven years. "Just a minute," she said. "Isn't your name Willy?"

"Absolutely!" Willy declared beaming.

"And didn't you use to do your schoolwork here?"

"Right!"

"So—and now you want to come up to my room with me?"

"Of course! We already know each other."

Willy was grinning all over. The next second he received a terrific blow on the ear. "You pig!" Fritzi said. "You want to come to bed with me? That's the limit!"

"What do you mean?" Willy stammered. "All the others—"

"All the others? What do they matter to me? Have I studied the catechism with them? Have I done their homework? Have I seen to it that they didn't catch cold, you snot-nosed rascal?"

"But now I'm seventeen and a half—"

"Shut up! Why, it's like wanting to rape your mother! Out of here, you juvenile delinquent!"

"He's going to war tomorrow," I said. "Have you no patriotism?"

She looked me in the eyes. "Aren't you the one who let the snakes loose? We had to shut the place up for three days while we searched for those reptiles!"

"I didn't let them loose," I said in self-defense. "They got away from me." Before I could say any more, I, too, had been boxed on the ear. "Lousy rascals! Out with you!"

The noise brought the Madame in. Indignantly Fritzi explained the situation to her. She, too, recognized Willy instantly. "The redhead!" she gasped. She weighed two hundred and forty pounds and shook with laughter like a mountain of jelly in an earthquake. "And you! Isn't your name Ludwig?"

"Yes," Willy answered for me. "But we're soldiers now and we have a right to sexual intercourse."

"So, you have a right!" The Madame heaved with renewed laughter. "Do you still remember, Fritzi, how scared he was that his father would find out he had thrown a stink bomb in Bible class? Now he has a right to sexual intercourse! Ho ho ho!"

Fritzi couldn't see the humor of the situation. She was genuinely angry and offended. "As though my own son—"

The Madame had to be held upright by two men. Tears streamed down her face. Bubbles of saliva formed at the corners of her mouth. She held her belly with both hands. "Lemonade," she gasped. "Waldmeister lemonade! Wasn't that—" coughing, gasping—"your favorite drink?"

"We drink schnaps and beer now," I replied. "Everyone grows up sometime."

"Grows up!" a renewed attack of gasping on the part of the Madame, mad barking by her two bulldogs which heard her and thought she was being attacked. We withdrew cautiously. "Out, you thankless swine!" the irreconcilable Fritzi screamed after us.

"All right," Willy said at the door. "Then we'll just have to go to Rollstrasse."

We stood outside in our uniforms with our deadly weapons and our stinging ears. But we did not get to Rollstrasse, the city's other cat house. It was a two-hour walk, all the way to the other side of Werdenbrück, and so we had ourselves shaved instead. This, too, was for the first time in our lives, and since we had no experience of intercourse, the difference did not seem as great to us as it would later on—especially since the barber insulted us too, by recommending erasers for our beards. Later on we met more of our friends and got pretty drunk and forgot the whole thing. So it came about that we marched into the field as virgins and seventeen of us fell without ever knowing what a woman is. Willy and I lost our virginity half a year later in an *estaminet* in Houthoulst in Flanders. On that occasion Willy got a dose, was taken to the field hospital, and thus escaped the Battle of Flanders in which the seventeen virgins fell. This proved, as we could see even at that time, that virtue is not always rewarded.

We wander through the mild summer night. Otto Bambuss sticks to me as the only one who admits to knowing the cat house. The others have been there too, but act innocent, and the only one who brags that he has been an almost daily guest there, the dramatist and author of the monograph "Adam," Paul Schneeweiss, is lying: he has never been there.

Otto's hands are sweating. He expects priestesses of lust, bacchantes, and demonic beasts of prey and is not quite sure but that he will be driven back in Eduard's Opel car with his liver torn out or at least without testicles. I comfort him. "People don't get mangled in the bordello more than once or twice a week at most, Otto! And the injuries are usually not too serious. Day before yesterday Fritzi tore off a guest's ear; but so far as I know you can have an ear sewn on again or replaced by a very natural-looking celluloid one."

"An ear?" Otto stops.

"Of course there are ladies who don't tear them off," I reply. "But you'd hardly want to know *them*. What you want, after all, is the primeval woman in all her splendor."

"An ear is a pretty big sacrifice," Otto remarks, drying the lenses of his spectacles.

"Poetry demands sacrifices. With an ear torn off you would be in the truest sense a blood-drenched lyricist. Come along!"

"Yes, but an ear! Something that can be seen so easily!"

"If I had my choice," Hans Hungermann says, "I would much rather have an ear torn off than be castrated, to speak frankly."

"What's that?" Otto stops again. "You're joking! That doesn't happen!"

"It happens all right," Hungermann declares. "Passion is capable of anything. But be calm, Otto: castration is a punishable offense. The woman would get at least a couple of months in jail—and you would be avenged."

"Nonsense!" Bambuss stammers, smiling painfully. "You're just making fun of me!"

"Why should he make fun of you?" I say. "That would be mean. I recommended Fritzi to you for that very reason. She is an ear fetishist. Overcome by passion she convulsively gets hold of her partner's ears, with both hands. So you can be absolutely sure you won't be injured elsewhere. She doesn't have a third hand."

"But she still has two feet," Hungermann explains. "Sometimes they perform wonders with their feet. They let the nails grow and sharpen them."

"You're just pretending," Otto says in torment. "Don't talk nonsense!"

"Listen to me," I reply. "I don't want you to be maimed. You would profit emotionally, but your soul would be impoverished and your poetry would suffer. I have here a pocket nail file, small, handy, and made for accomplished worldlings who must always be elegant. Take it. Keep it hidden in the palm of your hand or slip it into the mattress before things start. If you see that it's getting too dangerous, a little harmless prick in Fritzi's *derrière* will be enough to do the trick. No blood need flow. Whenever anyone is bitten, even by a gnat, he lets go and reaches for the bite, that's one of the axioms of life. In the meantime you'll escape."

I take out a red leather pocket case in which there are a

comb and a nail file. It was a gift from the faithless Erna. The comb is made of artificial tortoise shell. A belated wave of rage rises in me as I take it out. "Give me the comb too," Otto says.

"You can't hack at her with a comb, you innocent satyr," Hungermann declares. "That's no weapon for the battle of the sexes. It will break on the convulsed flesh of the maenad."

"I don't want to hack at her. I want to comb my hair afterward."

Hungermann and I look at each other. It seems that Bambuss no longer believes us. "Have you a first-aid package with you?" Hungermann asks me.

"We don't need one. The Madame has a whole apothecary shop."

Bambuss stops again. "That's all nonsense! But what about venereal disease?"

"This is Saturday. All the ladies were examined this afternoon. No danger, Otto."

"You know everything, don't you?"

"We know what's necessary for life," Hungermann replies. "And usually that is something entirely different from what you learn in school and in the institutions of higher learning. That's why you're such a unique specimen, Otto."

"I was brought up too piously," Bambuss sighs. "I grew up in fear of hell and of syphilis. With such a start how can you turn into an earthy lyricist?"

"You might marry."

"That's my third complex. Fear of marriage. My mother drove my father crazy. Simply by weeping. Isn't that strange?"

"No," Hungermann and I say in unison and shake hands on it. That means we'll have seven more years to live. Good or ill, life is life; you only realize that when you have to risk it.

*

Before we enter the cozy-looking house with its poplar trees, its red lanterns, and the blooming geraniums at the windows, we fortify ourselves with a few swallows of schnaps. We have brought a bottle with us and we hand it round. Even Eduard, who has driven ahead in his Opel and has been waiting, joins us; it isn't often he gets a free drink and he enjoys it. The same drink that we are now having at a cost to ourselves of some ten thousand marks will be priced at forty thousand in the cat house—that's why we brought the bottle. Up to the doorsill we live economically —after that we're at the mercy of Madame.

At first Otto is seriously disillusioned. He expected not a taproom but an oriental setting with leopard skins, swinging lamps, and heavy perfume; instead, the ladies, lightly clad, rather resemble servant maids. He asks me in a low voice whether there aren't any Negresses or Creoles. I point to a thin, black-haired creature. "That one over there has Creole blood. She is just out of the penitentiary. Murdered her husband."

Otto doubts it. But he brightens when the Iron Horse comes in. She makes an imposing picture in high, laced boots, black underwear, a kind of lion tamer's uniform, a gray astrakhan cap, and a mouth full of gold teeth. Generations of young poets and editors have passed their examination in life on her, and she has been selected for Otto, too, by prearrangement. She or Fritzi. We have insisted that she appear in full regalia—and she has not disappointed us.

She is taken aback when we introduce Otto. No doubt she expected to be handed something fresher and younger. Bambuss looks as though he were made of paper—pale, thin, pimply, with a straggly mustache, and he is twenty-six years old. In addition, he is sweating at the moment like a salted horse-radish. The Iron Horse bares her golden fangs in a good-humored grin and nudges the shuddering Bambuss in the ribs. "Come on, stand us a cognac," she says companionably.

"What does a cognac cost?" Otto asks the waitress.

"Sixty thousand."

"What's that?" Hungermann asks in alarm. "Forty thousand, not a pfennig more!"

"Pfennig," says the Madame. "That's a word I haven't heard in a long time."

"Forty thousand was yesterday, my pet," the Iron Horse explains.

"It was forty thousand this morning. I was here this morning on behalf of the committee."

"What committee?"

"The Committee for the Rebirth of Poetry through Personal Experience."

"My pet," says the Iron Horse, "that was before the dollar quotation."

"It was after the eleven o'clock exchange."

"It was before the afternoon one," explains the Madame. "Don't be such skinflints!"

"Sixty thousand is based on the dollar exchange for day after tomorrow," I say.

"On the one for tomorrow. Every hour brings you nearer to it. Calm down! The dollar exchange is like death. You can't escape it. Isn't your name Ludwig?"

"Rolf," I reply firmly. "Ludwig did not come back from the war."

Hungermann is suddenly seized by a horrid suspicion. "And the tariff?" he asks. "How much is that? Our agreement was for two million. Undressing and a half-hour's conversation afterward included. The conversation is important for our candidate."

"Three million," the Iron Horse replies phlegmatically. "And that's cheap."

"Comrades, we have been betrayed!" Hungermann roars.

"Do you know what you have to pay now for high boots that reach almost to your bottom?" the Iron Horse asks.

"Two million and not a centime more. When agreements are no longer respected even here, what's to become of the world?"

"Agreements! What are agreements when the exchange wobbles like a drunken man?"

Mathias Grund, who as author of the "Book of Death" has been appropriately silent until now, gets up. "This is the first cat house that has been undermined by National Socialism," he announces angrily. "Treaties are scraps of paper, eh?"

"Treaties and money," the Iron Horse replies imperturbably. "But high boots are high boots and fancy black underwear is fancy black underwear. Madly expensive. Why don't you pick a cheaper class for your candidate for confirmation? The way they do with funerals—you can have them either with or without plumes. Second class is plenty good enough for him!"

There is nothing to be said to that. The discussion has reached a dead end. Suddenly Hungermann discovers that Bambuss has quietly downed both his own and the Iron Horse's cognac.

"We're lost," he says. "We'll have to pay what these Wall Street hyenas demand. You shouldn't have done that to us, Otto! Now we'll have to arrange your initiation into life in a simpler fashion. Without plumes and with only a cast-iron horse."

Fortunately at this moment Willy comes in. He is full of curiosity about Otto's transformation into a man and he pays the difference without the quiver of an eyelash. Then he orders schnaps for all of us and announces that he has made twenty-five million today on his stocks. He intends to drink up part of it. "Off with you, boy," he says to Otto. "And come back a man!"

Otto disappears upstairs.

I sit down beside Fritzi. The old quarrel has been long since forgotten; since her son was killed in the war she no longer regards us as half-children. He was a noncom and was shot three days before the armistice. We talk about the times before the war. She tells me her son studied music in Leipzig. He wanted to be an oboe player. Beside us the huge Madame is sleeping, a bulldog on her knees.

Suddenly a scream resounds from upstairs. Uproar follows and then Otto appears in his underdrawers followed by the furious Iron Horse, who is beating him over the head with a tin washbasin. Otto has good running form; he races through the front door, and three of us stop the Iron Horse. "That damned half-portion!" she wheezes. "He went to work on me with a knife!"

"It wasn't a knife," I say, realizing what has happened.

"What do you mean?" The Iron Horse turns around and points to a red spot above her black underwear.

"It's not bleeding. It was only a nail file."

"A nail file?" The Horse stares at me. "That's a new one on me! And that beggar prince pricks me instead of me pricking him! Don't my boots mean anything? And my collection of whips? I wanted to be decent to him and give him a little taste of sadism as a bonus; just a playful slap across his skinny shanks with a whip, and the deceitful, spectacled snake went to work on me with a pocket nail file! A sadist! Do I need a sadist? I, the dream girl of the masochists? What an insult!"

We quiet her down with a double kümmel. Then we go to look for Bambuss. He is standing behind a lilac bush, feeling his head.

"Come along, Otto, the danger is past," Hungermann calls.

Bambuss refuses. He asks us to throw his clothes to him. "Absolutely not," Hungermann declares. "Three million are three million! We have paid for you."

"Ask for the money back! I won't let myself be cut to pieces."

"A cavalier never asks a lady to return money. And we're going to make you into a cavalier if we have to smash your head doing it. The whip was just an act of friendship. The Iron Horse is a sadist."

"What?"

"A rigorous masseuse. We just forgot to tell you. But you should be happy to have had an experience of that kind. It's rare in small cities!"

"I'm not happy. Throw my things out here."

We succeed in luring him in again after he has dressed behind the lilac bush. We give him a drink. But we cannot get him to leave the table. He maintains that the mood is gone. Finally Hungermann reaches an agreement with the Iron Horse and the Madame. Bambuss is to have the right to return within a week without additional payment.

We go on drinking. After a while I notice that Otto seems to have caught fire despite everything. He keeps glancing across at the Iron Horse and pays no attention to the other ladies. Willy orders more kümmel. After a while we miss Eduard. He appears a half-hour later sweating, saying that he has been for a walk. The kümmel gradually produces its effect. Suddenly Otto Bambuss gets out paper and pencil and begins secretly making notes. I look over his shoulder. The title is "The Tigress." "Hadn't you better wait a while with your free verse?" I ask.

He shakes his head. "The first impression is the most important."

"But after all, you only had one slash across your bottom

with a whip and then a couple of bangs on the head with a washbasin! What's tigerish about that?"

"Just leave it to me!" Bambuss pours another kümmel through his straggly mustache. "That's where the power of imagination comes in! I am already blooming with verses like a rosebush. What am I saying? Like an orchid in the jungle!"

"Do you think you've had enough experience?"

Otto shoots a look full of lust and dread in the direction of the Iron Horse. "I don't know. But certainly enough for a small volume in boards."

"Speak up! Three million has been paid out for you. If you don't need it, let's drink it up."

"Let's drink it up!"

Bambuss tosses down another kümmel. It's the first time we've seen him like this. He has shunned alcohol like the pest, especially schnaps. His poetry thrived on coffee and elderberry wine.

"What do you make of that?" I ask Hungermann.

"It was the blows on the head with the washbasin."

"It was nothing at all," Otto howls. He has downed another double kümmel and pinches the Iron Horse on the bottom as she goes by.

The Horse stops as though struck by lightning. Then she turns around slowly and examines Otto as though he were some rare insect. We stretch out our arms to protect him from the expected blow. For ladies in high boots a pinch of this sort is an obscene insult. Otto gets up wavering, smiles absently out of nearsighted eyes, walks around the Horse, and unexpectedly lands a hearty blow on the black underwear.

Silence falls. Everyone expects murder. But Otto seats himself again unconcernedly, lays his head on his arms, and goes to sleep instantly. "Never kill a sleeping man,"

Hungermann beseeches the Horse. "The eleventh commandment!"

The Iron Horse opens her mighty mouth in a silent grin. All her gold plumbing glitters. Then she strokes Otto's thin, soft hair. "Children and brothers," she says, "to be so young and so silly again!"

We leave. Eduard drives Hungermann and Bambuss back to the city. The poplars rustle. The bulldogs bark. The Iron Horse stands in the second-story window and waves at us with her Cossack cap. Behind the cat house stands a pale moon. Mathias Grund, the poet of the "Book of Death," clambers out of a ditch. He thought he could cross it like Christ crossing the Sea of Gennesaret. It was a mistake. Willy is walking beside me. "What a life!" he says dreamily. "And to think you actually make money in your sleep! Tomorrow the dollar will be even higher and my shares will be climbing up after it like agile little monkeys!"

"Don't spoil the evening for me. Where's your car? Is it having puppies like your shares?"

"Renée has it. It looks well in front of the Red Mill. She takes her colleagues driving between performances—they burst with envy."

"Are you going to marry her?"

"We're engaged," Willy explains, "if you know what that means."

"I can imagine."

"It's funny!" Willy says. "Nowadays she often reminds me very much of Lieutenant Helle, that damned slave driver who made life so miserable for us in preparation for a hero's death. Exactly the same, in the dark. It's a scary and refined sort of pleasure to have Helle on the back of his neck defiling him. I'd never have guessed I would get fun out of something like that, you can believe me!"

"I believe you."

We walk through the dark, gloomy gardens. The scent of unrecognized flowers is borne to us. "How sweet the moonlight sleeps upon this bank," someone says, rising like a ghost from the ground.

It is Hungermann. He is as wet as Mathias Grund. "What's going on?" I ask. "It hasn't been raining here."

"Eduard put us out. We sang too loud for him—the respectable hotelkeeper! Then, when I tried to refresh Otto, we both fell into the brook."

"You too? Where is Otto? Looking for Mathias Grund?"

"He's fishing."

"What?"

"Damn it!" says Hungermann. "I just hope he hasn't fallen in. He can't swim."

"Nonsense. The brook is only a yard deep."

"Otto could drown in a puddle. He loves his native land."

We find Bambuss clinging to a bridge over the brook and preaching to the fishes.

"Are you ill, Saint Francis?" Hungermann asks.

"Yes indeed," Bambuss replies, giggling as though that were madly funny. Then his teeth begin to chatter. "Cold," he stammers. "I'm no open-air man."

Willy gets a bottle of kümmel out of his pocket. "Who's rescuing you again? Uncle Willy, the provider. Rescuing you from inflammation of the lungs and cold death."

"Too bad Eduard isn't here," Hungermann says. "Then you could rescue him, too, and found a society with Valentin Busch. Eduard's Rescuers. That would kill him."

"Spare us your bad jokes," says Valentin, who has been standing behind him. "Capital should be sacred to you, or are you a communist? I will divide mine with no one. Eduard belongs to me."

We all have a drink. The kümmel sparkles in the moonlight like a yellow diamond. "Are you going somewhere else?" I ask Willy.

"To Bodo Ledderhose's singing club. Come along. All three of you can dry out there."

"Splendid," Hungermann says.

It occurs to no one that it would be simpler to go home. Not even to the poet of death. Tonight liquids seem to have an irresistible attraction.

We walk on beside the brook. The moon shimmers on its surface. You can drink it—who was it who said that once and where and when?

Chapter Fifteen

"What a surprise," I say, "and so early on a Sunday morning!"

I had imagined I heard a burglar groping around in the dawn twilight; but on coming downstairs, at five in the morning, I've found Riesenfeld, of the Odenwald Granite Works. "You must have made a mistake," I say. "This is the Lord's day. Not even the Stock Exchange works today. Still less we simple deniers of God. Where's the fire? Or do you need money for the Red Mill?"

Riesenfeld shakes his head. "This is just a friendly visit. Had a day to spare between Löhne and Hanover. Just arrived. Why go to a hotel at this hour? I can get coffee just as well here. How is the charming lady across the street? Does she get up early?"

"Aha!" I say. "So it was lust that drove you here! Congratulations on your youthfulness. But you're out of luck. Sundays her husband is at home. An athlete and knife-thrower."

"I'm the world's champion at knife throwing," Riesenfeld replies, undisturbed. "Especially when I've had some country bacon and schnaps with my coffee."

"Come on upstairs. My room's untidy, but I can make coffee for you there. If you like, you can play the piano while the water's boiling."

Riesenfeld dismisses the idea. "I'll stay here. This combination of midsummer, early morning, and tombstones pleases me. Makes me hungry and full of zest for life. Besides, the schnaps is here."

"I have much better schnaps upstairs."

"This is good enough for me."

"All right, Herr Riesenfeld, just as you like!"

"Why are you shouting so?" Riesenfeld asks. "I haven't grown deaf since you saw me."

"It's the joy of seeing you, Herr Riesenfeld," I reply even louder, laughing noisily.

I can't very well explain that I am trying to waken Georg by my shouting and alert him to what has happened. To the best of my knowledge, the butcher, Watzek, went off last evening to a meeting of the National Socialists, and Lisa has profited by the occasion to come over and, for once, spend the whole night in her lover's arms. Without knowing it, Riesenfeld sits as guardian at the chamber door. The only way out for Lisa is through the window.

"All right then, I'll bring the coffee down," I say, running up the stairs. I take the *Critique of Pure Reason*, wrap a string around it, let it down through my window, and swing it back and forth in front of Georg's window. Meanwhile, with a colored crayon I write a warning on a sheet of paper: "Riesenfeld in the office," make a hole in the paper and let it flutter down the string and come to rest on the volume of Kant. Kant knocks a couple of times, then I see Georg's bald head. He makes a sign to me. We carry on a short pantomime in which I make it clear to him in sign language that I can't get rid of Riesenfeld. It's impossible to throw him out: he is much too important for our daily bread.

I pull the *Critique of Pure Reason* up again and lower my bottle of schnaps. A beautifully molded arm seizes it before Georg can reach it and pulls it inside. Who knows when Riesenfeld will leave? Meanwhile, the lovers will be faced by the sharp pangs of morning hunger after a wakeful night. I lower my bread and butter and a piece of liverwurst. The string comes back with a lipstick smear on the end. I hear a sighing sound as the cork is drawn from the bottle. Romeo and Juliet have been rescued for the time being.

I am serving Riesenfeld his coffee when I see Heinrich Kroll coming across the courtyard. That national businessman, in addition to his other repulsive qualities, is an early riser. He calls that opening his breast to God's great outdoors. By God, of course, he understands not a kindly legendary figure with a long beard, but a Prussian field marshal.

He gives Riesenfeld a hearty handshake. Riesenfeld is not overjoyed. "I wouldn't in the world keep you from anything," he declares. "I'm just drinking my coffee here, and then I'll doze a bit until it's time for business."

"Nothing could take me away from such a valued guest and one we see so seldom!" Heinrich turns to me. "Haven't we any fresh rolls for Herr Riesenfeld?"

"We'll have to ask the widow of the baker Niebuhr or your mother," I reply. "Apparently no baking goes on in the republic on Sundays. Reprehensible slackness! It was different in imperial Germany."

Heinrich shoots me an evil glance. "Where is Georg?" he asks abruptly.

"I am not your brother's keeper, Herr Kroll!" I reply Biblically and loudly to let Georg know about this new danger.

"No, but you're an employee of my firm! I must insist that you speak respectfully."

"This is Sunday. Sundays I am not an employee. I came down at this hour of my own free will and out of love for my profession and a friendly regard for the manager of the Odenwald Granite Works. Unshaven, as perhaps you have noticed, Herr Kroll."

"There you see," Heinrich says bitterly to Riesenfeld. "That's why we lost the war. Because of the slackness of the intellectuals and because of the Jews."

"And the bicyclists," Riesenfeld replies.

"What do you mean the bicyclists?" Heinrich asks in amazement.

"What do you mean the Jews?" Riesenfeld asks in return.

Heinrich is puzzled. "Oh, I see," he says presently, displeased. "A joke. I'll wake up Georg."

"I wouldn't do that, Herr Kroll," I remark loudly.

"Kindly spare me your advice!"

Heinrich approaches the door. I do nothing to stop him. If Georg has not locked it, it must be because he is dead. "Let him sleep," Riesenfeld says. "I have no desire for serious conversation at this hour."

Heinrich stops. "Why don't you take Herr Riesenfeld for a walk to see God's great outdoors?" I ask. "When you get back, the household will be up, eggs and bacon will be sputtering on the stove, rolls will have been baked especially for you, a vase of freshly picked gladioli will be here to relieve the dark paraphernalia of death, and Georg will be shaved and smelling of cologne."

"God forbid," Riesenfeld mutters. "I'll stay here and sleep."

I shrug my shoulders in perplexity. There's nothing I

can do to get him out of the room. "All right," I say. "In the meantime, then, I'll go and praise God."

Riensefeld yawns. "I had no idea people paid so much attention to religion here. You toss God's name around like a pebble."

"That's our misfortune! We have all become too intimate with Him. Formerly God was the familiar of emperors, generals, and politicians. At that time we were not supposed to so much as mention His name. But I'm not going to pray. Just to play the organ. Come with me!"

Riesenfeld declines. Now there is nothing more I can do. Georg must help himself. All I can do is leave—then perhaps the others will go too. I'm not worried about Heinrich; Riesenfeld will know how to get rid of him.

The city is fresh with dew. I still have more than two hours before mass. Slowly I walk through the streets. It is an unfamiliar experience. The breeze is mild and as soft as though the dollar had fallen two hundred and fifty thousand marks yesterday instead of rising that much. For a time I stare at the peaceful river, then into the show window of Bock and Sons, producers of mustard which they package in miniature casks.

A slap on the shoulder wakes me up. Behind me stands a tall thin man with watery eyes. It is the town pest, Herbert Scherz. I look at him with distaste. "Shall I say good morning or good evening?" I ask. "Is this before or after your night's rest?"

Herbert belches noisily. A stinging exhalation almost brings tears to my eyes. "All right, so it's before your rest," I say. "Aren't you ashamed? What was the occasion? Gaiety, solemnity, irony, or just desperation?"

"A founders' day," Herbert says. "Yes, a founders' day celebration," he repeats complacently. "My induction into a club. I had to entertain the executive committee." He looks at me for a while and then bursts out triumphantly: "The Veteran Riflemen's Association! You understand?"

I understand. Herbert Scherz is a collector of clubs. Other people collect postage stamps or war mementos—Herbert collects clubs. He is already a member of more than a dozen—not because he needs so much entertainment but because he is passionately interested in death and in elegant funerals. It is his ambition to have, some day, the most stylish funeral in the city. Since he cannot leave enough money for that, and no one else would pay for it, he has hit on the idea of joining every possible club. He knows that when a member dies the club provides a ribboned wreath, and that's his first goal. Besides, a delegation always follows the hearse with the club's flag, and he counts on that likewise. He has figured that with his present memberships he is already sure of two cars full of wreaths, and that's not by any means all. He is just sixty and has plenty of time to join more clubs. Of course he is a member of Bodo Ledderhose's singing club, without ever having sung a note. He is an interested inactive member of it, just as he is of the Springerheil Chess Club, the All-Nine Bowling Club, and the Aquatic and Terrestrial Pterophyllum Scalare Club. I introduced him to the Aquatic Club because I thought he would give us an advance order for his tombstone in return. He did not. So now he has managed to get into a riflemen's club. "Were you ever a soldier?" I ask.

"What need? I am a member, that's enough. A capital stroke, eh? When Schwarzkopf hears about it he'll die of rage."

Schwarzkopf is Herbert's rival. Two years ago he found out about Herbert's hobby and, as a joke, declared that he would make it a contest. Scherz took the joke so seriously that Schwarzkopf was delighted and actually joined a few clubs just to see Herbert's reaction. Presently, however, he was caught in his own net, and now he, too, has become a collector—not so openly as Scherz, but secretly and roundabout—a kind of underhanded opponent, who gives Scherz a great deal of concern.

"It takes a lot to disturb Schwarzkopf," I say to annoy Herbert.

"This will do it! This time it's not just the wreath and the club flag—my fellow members will be in uniform—"

"Uniforms are forbidden," I say mildly. "We lost the war, Herr Scherz, have you overlooked that fact? You should have joined the police club; they're still allowed uniforms."

I see Scherz making a mental note of the police idea, and I shall not be surprised if in a couple of months he appears as an inactive member of the Trusty Handcuff. At the moment he deals firmly with my skepticism. "Before I die uniforms will long since have been allowed again! Otherwise what would become of our national dignity? People can't keep us slaves forever!"

I look at the swollen face with its burst veins. Strange how people's ideas about slavery differ! The closest I ever came to slavery was as a recruit in uniform. "Besides," I say, "when a civilian dies they won't appear in dress uniform with helmets, sabers, and high boots. That's only for those on active service."

"For me too! It was specifically promised me last night! By the president himself!"

"Promised! What are promises when people have been drinking?"

Herbert appears not to have heard me. "Not only that," he whispers in demoniac triumph. "In addition there will be the most important thing of all: the salvo over my grave!"

I laugh in his dissipated face. "A salvo? With what? Soda-water bottles? Firearms are forbidden in our beloved fatherland! The Treaty of Versailles, Herr Scherz. Your salvo is wishful thinking. Forget it!"

But Herbert is not to be dismayed. He shakes his head slyly. "You have no idea! We've had a secret army for a long time! A black Reichswehr." He giggles. "I'll get my salvo all right! In a couple of years we'll have everything back again anyway. Universal military training and an army. How else are we to live?"

The wind brings the sharp smell of mustard around the corner, and suddenly the river below us throws a silver reflection across the street. The sun has risen. Scherz sneezes. "Schwarzkopf is finally beaten," he says complacently. "The president has promised me he will never be admitted to the club."

"He can join an artillerymen's club," I reply. "Then a cannon will be fired over his grave."

For a moment Scherz's right eye quivers nervously. Then he dismisses the idea. "That's a joke. There's only one shooting club in the city. No, Schwarzkopf is done for. I'll come by tomorrow and have a look at your monuments. Someday or other I'll have to make up my mind."

He has been making up his mind as long as I have been in the business. He is a perpetual Frau Niebuhr, wandering from us to Hollmann and Klotz, and from there to Steinmeyer, insisting on seeing everything, bargaining for hours, and buying nothing. We are used to such types; there are always people, mostly women, who derive a strange satisfaction from ordering their coffins, shrouds, cemetery lots, and monuments while they're still alive—but Herbert has become a world's champion at it. He finally bought his cemetery lot six months ago. It is sandy, high, dry, and has a nice view. Herbert will decay there somewhat more slowly and respectably than in the lower, moister parts of the cemetery, and he is proud of it. Every Sunday afternoon he goes out there with a Thermos of coffee, a folding stool, and a package of sugar cookies to enjoy quiet hours watching the ivy grow. But he still dangles the order for the monument in front of the snouts of the tombstone firms like a rider dangling a carrot in front of his donkey. We gallop after it but we never get it. Herbert cannot make up his mind. He is afraid he may miss some marvelous novelty, like an electric bell or a telephone in the coffin.

I look at him with distaste. He has paid me back for the cannon fast enough. "Haven't you anything new?" he asks condescendingly.

"Nothing that would interest you—aside from—but that's already as good as sold," I say, with the sudden inspiration of anger and a quick stirring of my business instinct.

Herbert bites. "What?"

"Nothing for you. Something absolutely magnificent. But as good as sold."

"What is it?"

"A mausoleum. A very important work of art. Schwarzkopf is extremely interested—"

Scherz laughs. "I know that salesman's trick. Try another."

"No. Not with an object like this. Schwarzkopf wants to use it as a kind of post-mortem clubhouse. He is already thinking of making arrangements in his will for a small, intimate yearly gathering there on the anniversary of his death. Then it will be like a new funeral every year. The room in the mausoleum is perfect for it, with its benches and stained glass. After each celebration a small collation can be served. Hard to beat, isn't it? A perpetual memorial service; no one will pay the slightest attention to the other graves!"

Scherz laughs again, but more thoughtfully. I let him laugh. Between us the sun casts weightless bands of pale silver from the river. Scherz stops. "So, you have a mausoleum like that?" he says, with the slight concern of the true collector who fears that a great opportunity may be missed.

"Forget it! It is as good as sold to Schwarzkopf. Look at the ducks on the river instead! What colors!"

"I don't like ducks. They taste too gamey. Well, I'll be around sometime to look at your mausoleum."

"Don't hurry. You'd better see it in its proper setting, after Schwarzkopf has had it installed."

Scherz laughs again, but this time rather hollowly. I laugh too. Neither of us believes the other, but each has swallowed the bait. He has swallowed Schwarzkopf, and I the possibility that this time I may catch him at last. The mausoleum is the one Frau Niebuhr ordered. She suddenly doesn't want it any more and refuses to pay. Maybe Herbert will buy it now.

I walk on. From the Altstädter Hof comes the smell of tobacco and stale beer. I wander through the gateway into the back courtyard of the inn. It is a picture of peace. The casualties of Saturday night, dead to the world, are lying there in the early sunlight. Flies buzz about in the stertorous breath of the kirsch drinkers, Steinhäger drinkers, and corn drinkers as though in aromatic trade winds from the Spice Islands; above the sleeping faces spiders climb up and down like trapeze artists, webs suspended from the wild grapevine, and a beetle is exercising in the mustache of a gypsy as though in a bamboo grove. There it is, I think—at least in sleep—the lost paradise, universal brotherhood!

I look up at Gerda's window. It is open.

"Help!" one of the figures on the ground murmurs suddenly. He says it calmly, softly, and with resignation—he does not shout, and it is just this that strikes me like an ethereal blow from some other-worldly creature. It is a weightless blow on the breast, which pierces me like an X ray, and yet robs me of breath. Help! I think. What else do we cry, audibly and inaudibly, all the time?

Mass is over. The Mother Superior gives me my honorarium. It is not worth keeping, but I cannot refuse it, for that would offend her. "I have sent you a bottle of wine for breakfast," she says. "We have nothing else to give you. But we pray for you."

"Thank you," I reply. "But how do you happen to have this excellent wine? It must be expensive."

A smile spreads over the Mother Superior's wrinkled, ivory-tinted face; she has the bloodless skin of those who live in cloisters, penitentiaries, and hospitals, and those who work in mines. "It's given to us. There's a devout wine dealer in the city. His wife was here for a long time. Now he sends us several cases each year."

I do not pause to ask why he sends them. I have remembered that Bodendiek, that warrier of God, also has breakfast after mass, and I rush off to rescue some of the wine.

The bottle is, of course, already half empty. Wernicke is there too, but he is only drinking coffee. "The bottle, out of which you have so generously helped yourself," I say to Bodendiek, "was sent to me personally by the Mother Superior as a part of my salary."

"I know," the vicar replies. "But aren't you the apostle of tolerance, you cheerful atheist? Don't begrudge your friends a drop or two. A whole bottle at breakfast would be very bad for you."

I make no reply. The churchman takes this for weakness and instantly moves to the attack. "How's your fear of life doing?" he asks, taking a hearty swallow.

"What?"

"The fear of life that oozes out of all your bones like—"

"Like ectoplasm," Wernicke throws in helpfully.

"Like sweat," says Bodendiek, who does not trust the man of science.

"If I were afraid of life, I would be a devout Catholic," I answer, pulling the bottle toward me.

"Nonsense! If you were a devout Catholic, you would have no fear of life."

"That is the famous hair-splitting of the Church fathers."

Bodendiek laughs. "What do you know about the exquisite intellectuality of our Church fathers, you young barbarian?"

"Enough to have stopped reading when I came to their argument over whether Adam and Eve had navels. The fight lasted for years."

Wernicke grins. Bodendiek makes a disgusted face. "Cheap ignorance, joining hands as usual with crass materialism," he says to us both.

"You oughtn't to be so contemptuous of science," I reply. "What would you do if you had acute appendicitis and the only surgeon within reach was an atheist? Would you pray or let the heathen operate?"

"Both, you novice at dialectic; it would give the heathen an opportunity to gain merit in the sight of God."

"You really oughtn't to let a doctor treat you at all," I say. "If it is God's will, then you should just die and not try to change it."

Bodendiek waves this aside. "Now we'll soon come to the question of free will and the omnipotence of God. Ingenious sophomores think they can use that to refute the whole teaching of the Church."

He gets up benevolently. His face is glowing with health. Wernicke and I look peaked by comparison with this blooming believer. "A benediction on our meal!" he says. "Now I must go to my other parishioners."

No one comments on the word "other." He rustles out.

"Have you ever noticed that priests and generals usually attain a good old age?" I ask Wernicke. "The tooth of doubt and care does not gnaw at them. They are in the open air a great deal, hold their jobs for life, and are not obliged to think. The one has his catechism, the other his army manual. That keeps them young. Besides, both enjoy great respect. One is in God's court, the other in the Kaiser's."

Wernicke lights a cigarette. "Have you noticed, too, what an advantage the vicar has in argument?" I ask. "We have to respect his faith, he doesn't have to respect our lack of it."

Wernicke blows smoke at me. "He makes you angry—you don't disturb him."

"That's it!" I say. "That's what enrages me so!"

"He knows it. That's what makes him so confident."

I pour out the rest of the wine. My share has been a bare glass and a half—the rest was consumed by God's warrior—a Forster Jesuitengarten 1915, a wine which should only be drunk in the evening in the company of a woman. "And you?" I ask.

"None of this touches me at all," Wernicke says. "I'm a sort of traffic policeman of the soul. I try to keep order at this particular intersection—but I am not responsible for the traffic."

"I continually feel myself responsible for everything in the world. Does that mean I'm a psychopath too?"

Wernicke bursts into insulting laughter. "You'd like that, wouldn't you? But it's not so simple! You're completely uninteresting—a wholly normal run-of-the-mill adolescent!"

I come to Grossestrasse. A protest parade is slowly pushing its way toward me from the market place. Like sea gulls fluttering before a dark cloud, the brightly clad Sunday picnickers, with their children, lunch baskets, bicycles, and colorful knickknacks, scatter before it—then it is here and blocks the street.

It is a procession of war maimed, protesting against their inadequate pensions. First, on a little gocart, comes the stump of a body with a head. Arms and legs are missing. It's no longer possible to see whether the stump was once a tall man or a short one. That cannot be estimated even from the shoulders, because the arms were amputated so high up there was no place for prostheses. The man has a round head, lively brown eyes, and a mustache. Someone must look after him every day—he is shaven, his hair and mustache have been trimmed. The little cart, which is really only a board on rollers, is being pulled by a one-armed man. The amputee sits on it very straight and attentive. After him come the wheel chairs with the legless, three abreast. The chairs have rubber-tired wheels big enough to be moved by hand. The leather aprons that cover the space where legs should be, and are usually closed, are open today. The stumps can be seen. The trousers have been carefully folded over them.

Next come the amputees on crutches. These are the strangely distorted silhouettes one sees so often—the straight crutches, with the twisted bodies hanging between them. Then follow the blind and the one-eyed. You can hear the white canes tapping the pavement and see the yellow bands with three circles on their arms. The sightless are identified by the three black circles that mark one-way streets and blind alleys—and mean "Keep Out." Many of the wounded carry placards with legends. Some of the blind do too, even though they cannot read them. "Is This the Gratitude of Our Fatherland?" one of them asks. "We Are Starving," says another.

The man on the little wagon has a stick with a sign on it thrust into his jacket. The inscription reads: "My Month's

Pension Is Worth One Gold Mark." Between two other carts flutters a white banner: "Our Children Have No Milk, No Meat, No Butter. Is This What We Fought For?"

These are the saddest victims of the inflation. Their pensions are so worthless practically nothing can be done with them. From time to time the government grants them an increase—much too late, for on the day the increase is granted, it is already far too low. The dollar has gone wild; it no longer leaps by thousands and ten thousands, but by hundreds of thousands daily. Day before yesterday it stood at 1,200,000, yesterday at 1,400,000. Tomorrow it is expected to reach two million—and by the end of the month ten. Workmen are given their pay twice a day now—in the morning and in the afternoon, with a recess of a half-hour each time so that they can rush out and buy things—for if they waited a few hours the value of their money would drop so far that their children would not get half enough food to feel satisfied. Satisfied—not nourished. Satisfied with anything that can be stuffed into their stomachs, not with what the body needs.

The procession is much slower than any other demonstration. Behind it the cars of the Sunday excursionists are piling up. It is a strange contrast—the gray, almost anonymous mass of the silent victims of war, dragging themselves along—and behind them the congested cars of the war profiteers, muttering and fuming with impatience on the heels of the war widows who, with their children, thin, hungry, woebegone, and careworn make up the end of the procession. In the cars are all the colors of summer in linen and silk—full cheeks, round arms, and round faces, the latter showing some embarrassment at being caught in so disagreeable a situation. The pedestrians on the sidewalks are better off; they simply look away, pulling their children, who would like to stay and ask questions about the maimed men. Everyone who can disappears into the side streets.

The sun is high and hot, and the wounded are beginning to sweat. It is the unhealthy, greasy sweat of the anemic that pours down their faces. Suddenly behind them there is the blast of a horn; someone has not been able to wait; he thinks he can gain a few minutes by driving past them, half on the sidewalk. All the wounded turn around. No one says a word, but they spread out and block the street. The car will have to run over them in order to pass. In it is a young man in a bright suit and straw hat, accompanied by a girl. He makes a few silly, embarrassed gestures and lights a cigarette. Each of the wounded men, as they go by, looks at him. Not in reproof—they are looking at the cigarette whose fragrant smoke drifts across the street. It is a very good cigarette; none of the wounded can afford to smoke at all. And so they sniff up as much as they possibly can while they pass.

I follow the procession to St. Mary's. There stand two National Socialists in uniform, with a big sign: "Come to Us, Comrades! Adolf Hitler Will Help You!" The procession moves around the church. Right and left the cars can now shoot by.

We are sitting in the Red Mill. A bottle of champagne stands in front of us. Its price is two million marks, more than the monthly pension of a legless man and his family. Riesenfeld has ordered it.

He is sitting where he can watch the whole dance floor. "I knew about her all along," he remarks to me. "I just wanted to watch you try to trick me. Aristocratic ladies do not live across the street from small tombstone firms, and they do not live in houses like that!"

"That's an astoundingly false conclusion for a man of the world like you," I reply. "You should know that almost all aristocrats live exactly that way nowadays. The inflation has seen to it. The days of palaces are over, Herr Riesenfeld. And if anyone still has one, he is taking in boarders. Inherited money has disappeared. Imperial highnesses live in furnished rooms, saber-rattling colonels have become embittered insurance agents, countesses—"

"Enough!" Riesenfeld interrupts me. "You're going to make me cry! Further explanations are unnecessary. But I knew about Frau Watzek from the beginning. It simply amused me to see your silly attempts to deceive me."

He looks over at Lisa, who is dancing a fox trot with Georg. I forbear to remind the Odenwald Casanova that he classified Lisa as a Frenchwoman with the sinuous walk of a panther—it would result in the immediate breaking-off of our relationship, and we urgently need a shipment of granite.

"However, that doesn't detract from the total effect in the slightest," Riesenfeld explains conciliatingly. "On the contrary, it heightens one's interest! These thoroughbreds produced by the common people! Just look at the way she dances! Like a—a—"

"A sinuous panther," I help him out.

Riesenfeld glances at me. "Sometimes you show some understanding of women," he growls.

"Learned from you!"

He drinks to me, unsuspiciously flattered.

"There's one thing I'd like to know about you," I say. "I have a feeling that at home in Odenwald you're a respectable citizen and family man—you have already shown me the photographs of your three children and your rose-covered house, in whose walls you used, out of principle, no granite at all, a fact which I as an unsuccessful poet hold greatly to your credit—why, when you are away, do you turn into such a night-club wolf?"

"In order to get greater pleasure at home out of being a citizen and family man," Riesenfeld replies promptly.

"That's a good reason. But why take the long way around?"

Riesenfeld grins. "It's my demon. The double nature of man. Never heard of it, eh?"

"Haven't I though? I am the living prototype."

Riesenfeld laughs insultingly, just like Wernicke this morning. "You?"

"The same sort of thing exists on a somewhat more intellectual level," I explain.

Riesenfeld takes a swallow and sighs. "Reality and imagination! Eternal youth and eternal discord! Or—" recovering himself he adds, ironically— "in your case, as a poet, natural yearning and fulfillment, God and the flesh, cosmos and locus—"

Fortunately the trumpets begin again. Georg comes back to the table with Lisa. She is a vision in apricot-colored crepe de Chine. After Riesenfeld found out about her plebeian background, he demanded from us as restitution that we all be his guests at the Red Mill. Now he bows in front of Lisa. "A tango, *gnädige Frau*. Would you—" Lisa is a head taller than Riesenfeld and we expect an interesting performance. But to our amazement the Granite King proves himself a magnificent master of the tango. He is not only an adept in the Argentinian, but also in the Brazilian and apparently several other varieties. Like an expert skater he pirouettes around the dance floor with the disconcerted Lisa. "How are you feeling?" I ask Georg. "Don't take it too hard. Mammon versus love! A short while ago I got several lessons in that subject myself. Even from you, piquantly enough. How did Lisa escape from your room this morning?"

"It was difficult. Riesenfeld wanted to take over the office as an observation post. He planned to keep his eye on her window. I thought I could scare him off by revealing to him who Lisa is. That did no good. He bore it like a man.

Finally I succeeded in dragging him into the kitchen for a few minutes for coffee. That was the moment for Lisa. When Riesenfeld went back to spying from the office, she was smiling graciously at him out of her own window."

"In the kimono with the storks?"

"In one with windmills."

I look at him. He nods. "Traded for a small headstone. It was necessary. Anyway Riesenfeld, bowing and scraping, shouted an invitation for this evening."

"He wouldn't have dared to when she was still called 'de la Tour.'"

"He did it respectfully. Lisa accepted because she thought it would help us in our business."

"And you believe that?"

"Yes," Georg replies happily.

Riesenfeld and Lisa come back from the dance floor. Riesenfeld is sweating. Lisa is as cool as an Easter lily. To my immense astonishment I suddenly see another figure appear among the toy balloons behind the bar. It is Otto Bambuss. He stands there, lost in confusion and about as incongruous as Bodendiek would be. Then Willy's red head bobs up beside him, and from somewhere I hear Renée de la Tour's commanding tones: "Bodmer, at ease!"

I come to. "Otto," I say to Bambuss, "what brought you here?"

"I did," Willy answers. "I wanted to do something for German literature. Otto must soon return to his village. There he will have time to grind out poems about the sinfulness of the world. At the moment, however, it is his duty to observe."

Otto smiles gently. His shortsighted eyes blink. Perspiration stands on his forehead. Willy sits down with him and Renée at the table next to ours. Between Lisa and Renée there has been a second-long, point-blank duel of eyes.

Both turn back to their tables, unbeaten, confident, and smiling.

Otto leans over to me. "I have completed the 'Tigress' cycle," he whispers. "Finished it last night. I'm already at work on a new series: 'The Scarlet Woman.' Or perhaps I'll call it 'The Great Beast of the Apocalypse' and write it in free verse. It's magnificent. The spirit has descended on me!"

"Good! But what do you expect to find here?"

"Everything," Otto replies, beaming with happiness. "I always expect everything in a place where I've never been before. I hear you really do know a circus lady!"

"The ladies I know are not for beginners to practice on," I say. "You don't seem to know anything at all, you feeble-minded camel, otherwise you wouldn't behave like such a thickhead! So, pay attention to rule number one: hands off other people's women—you haven't the right physique for it."

Otto coughs. "Aha," he says then. "Bourgeois prejudice! I wasn't talking about wives."

"Neither was I, you simpleton. With wives the rules are not so strict. But why are you so sure that I know a circus lady? I have already told you she was a ticket seller in a flea circus."

"Willy told me that wasn't true. She is a circus acrobat."

"So that's it. Willy!" I see his red head bobbing above the dancers like a buoy on the ocean. "Listen to me, Otto," I say. "It's entirely the other way around. Willy's girl is from the circus. The one with the blue hat. And she loves literature. So now's your chance! Go to it!"

Bambuss looks at me distrustfully. "I'm talking honestly to you, you half-witted idealist!" I say.

Riesenfeld is dancing with Lisa again. "What's wrong with us, Georg?" I ask. "Over there a business friend of yours is trying to cut you out with a woman, and now I have just been requested to lend Gerda in the interests of German poetry. Are we sheep, or are our ladies so desirable?"

"Both. Besides, someone else's woman is always five times as desirable as one that's unattached. It's an old moral law. But in a few minutes Lisa will come down with a bad headache. She will go out to the dressing room to get aspirin, and then she will send a waiter with the news that she has had to go home and that we are to go on having a good time."

"A blow for Riesenfeld. Then he won't sell us anything tomorrow."

"He will sell us all the more. You ought to know that. For that very reason. Where is Gerda?"

"Her engagement doesn't begin for three days. I hope she is in the Altstädter Hof. But I am afraid she's in the Walhalla with Eduard. She calls that economizing on dinner. I can't do much about it. She has such excellent reasons that I would have to be thirty years older to answer them. But you just keep your eye on Lisa. Perhaps she won't get a headache after all and can help us in our business even more."

Otto Bambuss leans over to me again. Behind his spectacles his eyes are those of a terrified herring. *"Manège* would be a good title for a volume of circus poems, wouldn't it? With reproductions of pictures by Toulouse-Lautrec."

"Why not by Rembrandt, Dürer, and Michelangelo?"

"Did they make circus drawings?" Otto asks, seriously interested.

I give him up. "Drink, my boy," I say in fatherly tones. "And enjoy your brief life, for someday soon you will be murdered. Out of jealousy, you moon-calf!"

Flattered, he drinks to me and then looks thoughtfully over at Renée, whose kingfisher-blue hat is bobbing on her blond ringlets. She looks like an animal trainer on Sunday.

Lisa and Riesenfeld come back. "I don't know what's the matter," Lisa says. "Suddenly I have a terrible headache. I'll just go and get an aspirin—"

Before Riesenfeld can spring to his feet, she has left the table. Georg looks at me with abominable self-satisfaction and reaches for a cigar.

Chapter Sixteen

"The sweet light," Isabelle says. "Why is it growing weaker? Because we are tired? We lose it every night. When we are asleep the world goes away. Where are we then? Does the world always come back, Rudolf?"

We are standing at the edge of the garden looking through the trellised gate at the landscape beyond. The early evening lies on ripening fields that extend down to the woods on either side of the chestnut *allée*.

"It always comes back," I say, and add carefully: "Always, Isabelle."

"And we? Do we too?"

We? I think. Who knows? Every hour gives and takes and alters. But I don't say it. I don't wish to be led into a conversation that will suddenly end in an abyss.

The inmates who have been working in the fields are coming back. They return like weary peasants, and on their shoulders lies the first red of sunset.

"We too," I say. "Always, Isabelle. Nothing that exists can ever be lost. Not ever."

"Do you believe that?"

"We have no choice but to believe it."

She turns around to me. She looks very beautiful on this early evening with the first clear gold of autumn in the air. "Are we lost otherwise?" she whispers.

I stare at her. "I don't know," I say finally. "Lost—that can mean so much—almost anything!"

"Are we lost otherwise, Rudolf?"

I am silent, irresolute. "Yes," I say then. "But that is when life begins, Isabelle."

"What life?"

"Our own. That's where everything begins—courage, compassion, humanity, love, and the tragic rainbow of beauty. When we realize that nothing remains."

I look at her face, illuminated by the dying light. For a moment time stands still. "You and I, don't we remain either?" she asks.

"No, we don't remain either," I reply, and look past her at the landscape full of blue and red and remoteness and gold.

"Not even if we love each other?"

"Not even if we love each other," I say, and add hesitantly and cautiously: "I think that's why people love each other. Otherwise one could not love. Love is perhaps the desire to hand on something which one cannot keep."

"Hand on what?"

I lift my shoulders. "There are many names for it. One's self perhaps, in order to rescue it. Or one's heart. Let us say our heart. Or our yearning. Our heart."

The people from the fields are arriving at the gate. The guards open it. Suddenly a man rushes past us, pushes his way through the fieldworkers, and races off. He must have been hiding behind a tree. One of the guards sees him and starts trotting in pursuit; the other stays in his place and lets the inmates through. Below us I can see the escaped man running. He is much faster than the guard. "Do you think your colleague will catch up with him at that rate?" I ask the second guard.

"He'll come back with him all right."

"It doesn't look that way."

The guard shrugs his shoulders. "It's Guido Timpe. He tries to escape at least once each month. Always runs to the Forsthaus Restaurant. Drinks a couple of beers. We always find him there. Never runs farther and never anywhere else. Just for the two or three beers. He likes dark beer." He winks at me. "That's why my colleague isn't hurrying. He just wants to keep him in sight in case of an accident. We always give Timpe time to quench his thirst. Why not? Afterward he comes back like a lamb."

Isabelle has not been listening. "Where does he want to go?" she asks now.

"He wants to drink beer," I say. "That's all! If everyone could have a goal like that!"

She doesn't hear me. She is looking at me. "Do you want to run away too?"

I shake my head.

"There's nothing to run away for, Rudolf," she says. "And no place to go. All doors are the same. And beyond them—"

She hesitates. "What's beyond them, Isabelle?" I ask.

"Nothing. They are just doors. They are always just doors and there is nothing beyond."

The guard locks the gate and lights his pipe. The sharp smell of cheap tobacco strikes me and conjures up a picture: A simple life, without problems, with an honest calling, an honest wife, honest children, honest rewards, and an honest death—all accepted as a matter of course, the day, the evening's leisure, and the night, without asking what lies beyond. For an instant I am filled with yearning, and a little envy. Then I look at Isabelle. She is standing at the gate, her hands grasping the iron bars, her head pressed against them, looking out. She stands thus for a while. The light grows fuller and redder and more golden, the woods lose their blue shadows and turn black, and the sky above us is apple-green and full of sailboats touched with rosy beams.

Finally she turns around. In this light her eyes look almost violet. "Come," she says, taking my arm.

We walk back. She leans against me. "You must never abandon me," she says.

"I will never abandon you."

"Never," she says. "Never is so short."

Incense eddies from the silver censers. Bodendiek turns, the monstrance in his hands. The nuns in their black habits are kneeling in the pews like little dark heaps of submissiveness; their heads are bowed, their hands tap their covered breasts, which must never become breasts; the candles burn; and God is in the host, surrounded by golden rays, there in the room. A woman gets up, walks down the middle aisle to the communion bench, and throws herself on the floor. Most of the patients stare motionless at the golden miracle. Isabelle is not present. She has refused to go to church. She used to go, but, for the past few days, she has not. She has explained it to me. She says she doesn't want to see the Bloody One any more.

Two nuns raise the sick woman, who has been throwing herself about and beating on the floor with her hands. I play the *Tantum Ergo*. The white faces of the inmates turn with a jerk toward the organ. I pull out the stops for the bass viols and the violins. The nuns sing.

The white spirals of incense eddy upward. Bodendiek puts the monstrance back in the tabernacle. The light of the candles flickers on the brocade of his vestments, where a large cross is embroidered, and is borne upward in the smoke to the great cross on which the bloodstained Saviour has been hanging for nearly two thousand years. I go on playing mechanically, thinking of Isabelle and what she has said. Then I think of the pre-Christian religions I was reading about last night. In those days the gods of Greece were merry, wandering from cloud to cloud, inclined to rascality, and always as faithless and changeable as the men to whom they belonged. They were incarnations and exaggerations of life in its fullness and cruelty and thoughtlessness and beauty. Isabelle is right: the pale man above me, with his beard and his bloody limbs, is not that. Two thousand years, I think, two thousand years and through all that time life with its lights, its cries of passion, its deaths, and its ecstasies has eddied around the stone structures where stand the likenesses of this pale, dying man, dim, bloody, surrounded by millions of Bodendieks—and the leaden-colored shadow of the Church has reached out over the nations, smothering the joy of life, transforming Eros, the merry, into a secret, dirty, sinful bedroom incident, and forgiving nothing despite all the sermons on love and forgiveness—for true forgiveness means to accept someone as he is and not to demand expiation and obedience and submissiveness before the *ego te absolvo* is pronounced.

Isabelle is waiting outside. Wernicke has given her permission to stay in the garden in the evenings when someone is with her. "What were you doing in there?" she asks hostilely. "Helping to cover everything up?"

"I was playing the music."

"Music covers things up too. More than words."

"There's a kind of music that tears things open," I say. "The music of drums and trumpets. It has caused a great deal of unhappiness all over the world."

Isabelle turns around. "And your heart? Isn't that a drum too?"

Yes, I think, a slow, soft drum, but it will make noise enough and bring unhappiness enough, and perhaps some day it will deafen me to the sweet, anonymous cry of life that is vouchsafed those who do not oppose a pompous self to life and do not demand explanations, as though they were righteous believers instead of what they are—brief wanderers who leave no track.

"Feel mine," Isabelle says taking my hand and laying it on her thin blouse below her breast. "Do you feel it?"

"Yes, Isabelle."

I withdraw my hand, but it is as though I had not done so. We walk around a little fountain, lamenting in the evening stillness as though it had been forgotten. Isabelle plunges her hands into the basin and throws the water into the air. "What becomes of dreams during the day, Rudolf?" she asks.

I look at her. "Perhaps they go to sleep," I say cautiously, for I know where such questions can lead.

She plunges her arms into the basin and lets them rest there. They shimmer silvery, covered with little air bubbles under the water as though they were made of some strange metal. "How can they go to sleep?" she says. "After all, they are living sleep. You only see them when you are asleep. What becomes of them during the day?"

"Perhaps they hang like bats in great, subterranean caves —or like young owls in deep holes in the trees, waiting for the night."

"And if night doesn't come?"

"Night always comes, Isabelle."

"Are you sure of that?"

I look at her. "You ask questions like a child," I say.

"How do children ask them?"

"The way you do. They keep on asking. And soon they come to a point where the grownups have no answer and so get confused or angry."

"Why do they get angry?"

"Because they suddenly realize that something is dreadfully wrong with them and they don't like to be reminded of it."

"Is something wrong with you too?"

"Almost everything, Isabelle."

"What is wrong?"

"I don't know. That's just the trouble. If one knew, that in itself would make it less wrong. One just feels it."

"Oh, Rudolf," Isabelle says, and her voice is suddenly deep and soft. "Nothing is wrong."

"It isn't?"

"Of course not. Wrong and right are something that only God knows about. But if He is God, there is no wrong or right. Everything is God. It would only be wrong if it were outside Him. But if anything could be outside Him or against Him, He would be only a limited God. And a limited God is no God at all. And so everything is right or there is no God. It's so simple."

I look at her in amazement. What she says really does sound simple and illuminating. "Then there wouldn't be any devil or hell either," I say. "Or if there were, there would be no God."

Isabelle nods. "Of course not, Rudolf. We have so many words. Who invented them all?"

"Confused human beings," I reply.

She shakes her head and points toward the chapel. "The people in there! They have captured Him in there," she whispers. "He can't get out. He would like to. But they have nailed Him to the cross."

"Who?"

"The priests. They keep Him captive."

"Those were other priests," I say. "Two thousand years ago. Not these."

She leans against me. "They are always the same, Rudolf,"

she whispers, close to my face, "don't you know that? He would like to get out, but they hold Him prisoner. He bleeds and bleeds and wants to come down from the cross. But they won't let Him. They keep Him in their prisons with the high towers, and they give Him incense and prayers and do not let Him out. Do you know why?"

"No."

Now the pale moon is hanging above the woods in the ash-colored blue. "Because He is very rich," Isabelle whispers. "He is very, very rich. But they want to keep His fortune. If He should come out, they would have to give it back, and then they would all suddenly be poor. It's like someone who has been confined up here; then the others have control of his fortune and do what they like with it and live like rich people. Just as in my case."

I stare at her. Her face is intense but betrays nothing. "What do you mean?" I ask.

She laughs. "Everything, Rudolf. But you know about it too! They brought me here because I was in their way. They want to keep my fortune. If I were to come out they would have to give it back to me. It doesn't matter; I don't want it."

I keep staring at her. "If you don't want it you can explain that to them; then there would be no reason for keeping you here any more," I say cautiously.

"Here or someplace else—after all, it's just the same. So why not here? At least they aren't here. They are like gnats. Who wants to live with gnats?" She bends forward. "That's why I disguise myself," she whispers.

"You disguise yourself?"

"Of course! Didn't you know that? You have to disguise yourself, otherwise they will nail you to the cross. But they are stupid. You can fool them."

"Do you fool Wernicke too?"

"Who is he?"

"The doctor."

"Oh, him! He just wants to marry me. He is like the others. There are so many prisoners, Rudolf. And those outside are afraid of them. But the One up there on the cross—He's the one they're most afraid of."

"Who are?"

"All those who make use of Him and live on Him. They are innumerable. They say they are good. But they bring about a great deal of evil. Anyone who is bad can do very little. You recognize him and are on your guard against him. But the good—what don't they accomplish! Oh, they're bloody!"

"Yes, they are," I say, strangely excited myself by the voice whispering in the darkness. "They have done many dreadful things. The self-righteous are merciless."

"Don't go there any more, Rudolf!" she whispers. "They must let Him go! Him on the cross. He would like to laugh again and sleep and dance."

"Do you think so?"

"Everyone would like to, Rudolf. They must let Him go. But He is too dangerous for them. He is not like them. He is the most dangerous of all—He is the kindest."

"Is that why they keep Him prisoner?"

Isabelle nods. Her breath touches me. "Otherwise they would have to crucify Him again."

"Yes," I say, looking at her. "I think so too. They would have to kill Him again; the same people who now pray to Him. They would kill Him, just as countless people have been killed in His name. In the name of justice and love of one's neighbor."

Isabelle shivers. "I don't go there any more," she says, pointing to the chapel. "They always say one must suffer. The black sisters. Why, Rudolf?"

I make no reply.

"Who makes us suffer?" she asks, pressing hard against me.

"God," I say bitterly. "If there is a God. He who created us."

"And who will punish God for that?"

"What?"

"Who will punish God for making us suffer?" Isabelle whispers. "Here, among human beings, you are put in jail or hanged if you do that. Who will hang God?"

"I never thought about that," I say. "I'll ask Vicar Bodendiek sometime."

We walk back along the *allée*. A few fireflies dart through the darkness. Suddenly Isabelle stops. "Did you hear that?" she asks.

"What?"

"The earth. It made a leap like a horse. When I was a child I used to be afraid I would fall off when I went to sleep. I wanted to be tied tight to my bed. Can you trust gravitation?"

"Yes, just as much as death."

"I don't know. Haven't you ever flown?"

"In an airplane?"

"Airplane," Isabelle says with a light contempt. "Anyone can do that. In dreams."

"Yes. But can't anyone do that too?"

"No."

"I think everyone has dreamed at some time that he was flying. It's one of the commonest dreams."

"You see!" Isabelle says. "And you trust gravitation! Suppose it stops some day? What then? Then we should fly around like soap bubbles! And then who would be Kaiser? The one with the most lead tied to his feet or the one with the longest arms? And how would you get down from a tree?"

"I don't know. But even lead wouldn't help. Then it would be light as air."

Suddenly she is all playfulness. The moon shines in her eyes as though pale fires were burning behind them. She throws back her hair, which looks colorless in the cold light. "You look like a witch," I say. "A young and dangerous witch!"

She laughs. "A witch," she whispers then. "Have you finally recognized me? How long it took!"

With a jerk she pulls open the full skirt fluttering around her hips, lets it fall, and steps out of it. She is wearing nothing but shoes and a short white blouse which she pulls open. Slender and white she stands in the darkness, more boy than woman, with pale hair and pale eyes. "Come," she whispers.

I look around. Damn it, I think, suppose Bodendiek were to come now! Or Wernicke or one of the nuns, and I am angry at myself for thinking it. Isabelle never would. She stands before me like a spirit of air that has taken on a body, ready to fly away. "You must put on your clothes," I say.

She laughs. "Must I, Rudolf?" she asks mockingly.

Slowly she comes closer. She seizes my tie and pulls it loose. Her lips are a colorless gray-blue in the moon, her teeth are chalk-white, and even her voice has lost its color. "Take that off!" she whispers, pulling open my collar and shirt. I feel her cool hands on my naked breast. They are not soft; they are narrow and hard and they hold me fast. A shudder runs over my skin. Something I had never suspected in Isabelle suddenly bursts out of her. I feel it like a strong wind and a blow; it has come from far off and has compressed itself in her as the soft winds of the open plains are suddenly compressed into a storm in a narrow pass. I try to keep hold of her hands and I glance around. She pushes my hands aside. She is no longer laughing; suddenly in her there is the deadly seriousness of the creature for whom love is superfluous byplay, who knows only one goal and for whom death is not too great a price to attain it.

I cannot hold her off. From somewhere she has gained a strength against which only brute force will avail. To avoid this I draw her to me. She is more helpless thus, but she is also closer to me, her breast pressed against mine. I feel her body in my arms and I feel her crushing herself closer to me. It won't do, I think; she is sick; it is rape, but isn't it always rape? Her eyes are close to mine, empty and without recognition, fixed and transparent. "Afraid," she whispers. "You are always afraid!"

"I'm not afraid."

"Of what? Of what are you afraid?"

I do not reply. Suddenly there is no fear any more. Isabelle's gray-blue lips are pressed against my face, cool, nothing in her is hot, but I am shivering from a cold heat, my skin contracts, only my head is glowing. I feel Isabelle's teeth; she is a small, rearing animal, a phantom, a spirit of moonlight and desire, a dead woman, one of the living, risen dead; her skin and her lips are cold. Horror and a forbidden desire whirl through me. I wrench myself away in silence and thrust her back so that she falls—

She does not get up. She cowers on the ground, a white lizard, hissing curses at me, insults, a flood of whispered truck drivers' curses, soldiers' curses, whores' curses, curses that even I have never heard, insults that cut like knives and whiplashes, words I never thought she knew, words to which the only reply is a blow.

"Be quiet!" I say.

She laughs. "Be quiet!" she mocks me. "That's all you know! Be quiet! Go to the devil!" she suddenly hisses at me more loudly. "Go, you whining dishrag, you eunuch—"

"Shut up," I say furiously. "Or—"

"Or what? Just try it!" She arches herself toward me on the ground, her hands braced behind her in a shameless posture, her mouth open in a contemptuous grimace.

I stare at her. She should be repulsive to me, but she is not. Even in this obscene position there is nothing of the whore about her, in spite of anything she does or says; there is something desperate and wild and innocent in it and in her; I love her; I would like to pick her up and carry her off, but I don't know where. I lift my hands; they are heavy; I feel bewildered and helpless and conventional and provincial—

"Get away from here!" Isabelle whispers from the ground. "Go! Go! And never come back! Don't dare come back, you senile man, you church toady, you plebeian, you gelding! Go, you simpleton, you blockhead, you soul of a salesman! Don't ever dare come back!"

She is looking at me, on her knees now, her mouth has grown small, her eyes are flat and slate-colored and wicked. With a weightless spring she is on her feet, seizes the wide, blue skirt and walks away, quick and swaying; she steps out of the *allée* into the moonlight on her long legs, a naked dancer, waving the blue skirt like a flag.

I want to run after her and shout to her to put on her clothes, but I stay where I am. I do not know what she would do next—and it occurs to me that this is not the first time that someone here has turned up naked at the entrance door. Women in particular do that often.

Slowly I walk back down the *allée*. I straighten my shirt, feeling guilty, but I do not know why.

Late at night I hear Knopf approaching. His footsteps make me realize that he is quite drunk. I am really not in the mood for it, but for that very reason I move over to the rain pipe. Knopf pauses in the gateway, and like an old soldier first surveys the field. Everything is quiet. Cautiously he approaches the obelisk. I have not expected the retired sergeant major to give up his practices after a single warning. Now he stands in readiness in front of the tombstone and pauses once more. Cautiously his head revolves. Thereupon, like an expert tactician he makes a feigned maneuver; his hand descends, but it is a bluff, he is only listening. Then, as everything continues quiet, he takes up an anticipatory pose, a smile of triumph around the Nietzsche mustache, and lets go.

"Knopf!" I howl in subdued tones through the rain pipe. "You swine, are you there again? Have I not warned you?"

The change in Knopf's face is not bad. I have always distrusted the description of eyes widened in horror; I thought one always squinted then in order to see better; but Knopf actually widens his eyes like a terrified horse when a heavy shell goes off. He even rolls them. "You are not worthy to be a retired sergeant major in the Sappers and Miners," I declare hollowly. "I herewith degrade you! I demote you to private, second class, you pisser! Dismissed!"

A hoarse bellow emerges from Knopf's throat. "No! No!" he croaks, trying to recognize the place from which God is speaking. It is the corner between the gate and the wall of his house. There is no window there, no opening; he can't understand whence the voice comes. "It's all over with the long saber, the visored cap, and the braid!" I murmur. "All over with the dress uniform! From now on you are a private, second class, Knopf, you louse!"

"No!" Knopf howls, cut to the quick. It is easier for a true Teuton to lose a finger than a title. "No! No!" he whispers, raising his paws in the moonlight.

"Adjust your clothes!" I command. And suddenly I remember all the things Isabelle screamed at me, and I feel my stomach turn, and misery descends on me like a hailstorm.

Knopf has obeyed. "Only not that!" he croaks again, his head thrown back to the little, moonlit clouds above. "Not that, Lord!"

I see him standing there like the middle figure in the Laocoön group, wrestling with the invisible serpents of dishonor and demotion. That's just about the way I was standing a few hours ago, I reflect, while my stomach begins to writhe again. Unlooked-for sympathy lays hold of me; for Knopf and for myself. I become more humane. "Very well then," I whisper. "You don't deserve it, but I will give you one more chance. You will only be demoted to lance corporal on probation. If you piss like a civilized human being until the end of September, you will be repromoted to noncom; at the end of October to sergeant, at the end of November to vice sergeant major; at Christmas you will once more become a permanent company sergeant major, retired. Understand?"

"Yes, certainly, your—your—" Knopf is groping for the right term of address. I am afraid that he is hesitating between your majesty and your divinity, and I interrupt him in time. "This is my last word, Lance Corporal Knopf! And don't think, you swine, that you can begin again after Christmas! Then it will be cold and you can't wash away the traces of your misdeeds. They will freeze solid. Stand against that obelisk once more and you will get an electric shock and inflammation of the prostate that will knock you bowlegged! Now off with you, you dung heap with chevrons!"

Knopf disappears with unaccustomed speed into the darkness of his doorway. I hear subdued laughter from the office. Lisa and Georg have witnessed the performance. "Dung heap with chevrons," Lisa giggles huskily.

A chair turns over, there is a scuffle, and the door to Georg's meditation room closes. Riesenfeld once presented me with a bottle of Holland Geneva, with the message: "For trying hours." Now I get it out. The label on the square bottle says: *Friesseher Genever van P. Bokma, Leeuwarden.* I open it and pour a big glassful. The Geneva is strong and spicy and does not curse at me.

Chapter Seventeen

Wilke, the coffinmaker, looks at the woman in amazement. "Why don't you take two small ones?" he asks. "They won't cost much more."

The woman shakes her head. "They must lie together."

"But after all, you can put them in a single grave," I say. "Then they will be together."

"No, that's not enough."

Wilke scratches his head. "What do you think?" he asks me.

The woman has lost two children. They died on the same day. Now she wants to have a common grave—she also wants one coffin for both, a kind of double coffin. That's why I have called Wilke into the office.

"The matter is simple enough for us," I say. "Tombstones with two inscriptions are used all the time. There are even family tombstones with six or eight inscriptions."

The woman nods. "That's how it must be! They must lie together. They were always together."

Wilke gets a carpenter's pencil out of his vest pocket. "It would look odd. The coffin would be too wide. Almost square; the children are still very small, aren't they? How old?"

"Four and a half."

Wilke draws. "Like a square box," he concludes. "Wouldn't you rather—"

"No," the woman interrupts. "They must remain together. They are twins."

"You can make very pretty little single coffins for twins in white lacquer. The shape is more attractive. A short double coffin would look squat—"

"That doesn't matter to me," the woman says stubbornly. "They had a double cradle and a double baby carriage and now they shall have a double coffin too. They must remain together."

Wilke sketches again. Nothing emerges but a square box, though this time decorated on top with leaves and ivy. In the case of grownups there would have been more opportunity for variation; but children are too short. "I don't even know whether it is allowed," he says as a last resort.

"Why shouldn't it be allowed?"

"It is unusual."

"It is also unusual for two children to die on the same day," the woman replies.

"That is true, especially when they are twins." Wilke is suddenly interested. "Did they have the same disease?"

"Yes," the woman replies sharply. "The same disease: they were born after the war when there was nothing to eat. Twins. I didn't even have enough milk for one—"

Wilke leans forward. "The same disease!" Scientific curiosity burns in his eyes. "They say that often happens with twins. Astrologically—"

"What about the coffin?" I ask. The woman doesn't look as though she wanted to carry on a prolonged conversation on this subject which so fascinates Wilke.

"I can try," Wilke says. "But I don't know whether it's allowed. Do you know?" he asks me.

"One could ask at the cemetery."

"How about the priest? How were the children baptized?"

The woman hesitates. "One is Catholic, the other Evangelical," she says. "We agreed on that. My husband is Catholic, I am Evangelical. So we agreed that the children should be divided."

"Then you had one baptized a Catholic and the other Evangelical?" Wilke asks.

"Yes."

"On the same day?"

"On the same day."

Wilke's interest in the marvels of existence is kindled afresh. "In two different churches, of course?"

"Of course," I say impatiently. "What did you think? And now—"

"But how could you tell them apart?" Wilke interrupts me. "I mean every day. Were they identical twins?"

"Yes," the woman says. "As alike as two eggs."

"That's just what I mean! How can you tell them apart, especially when they're so small? Could you? I mean during the first days when everything is in confusion?"

The woman is silent.

"That doesn't make any difference now," I announce, motioning Wilke to stop.

But Wilke has the unsentimental curiosity of the scientist. "It does make a difference," he replies. "After all, they have to be buried! One is Catholic and the other Evangelical. Do you know which the Catholic is?"

The woman is silent. Wilke warms to his theme. "Do you think you will be allowed to bury them together? If you have a double coffin, you'll have to, of course. Then you will have to have two ministers at the grave, one Catholic, the other Evangelical! They certainly won't agree to that! They are more jealous of God than we are of our wives."

"Wilke, that's none of your business," I say, giving him a kick under the table.

"And the twins!" Wilke cries, paying no attention to me. "The Catholic twin would have to be buried with Evangelical rites and the Evangelical twin with Catholic! Just picture the confusion! No, you won't be able to get away with a double coffin! Single coffins, that's what it will have to be! Then each religion will have its own. The men of God can turn their backs on each other and thus bestow their blessings."

Wilke apparently imagines that one religion is poison to the other. "Have you spoken to the priests about it?" he asks.

"My husband is doing that," the woman says.

"You know, I'll be really curious—"

"Will you make the double coffin?" the woman asks.

"I'll make it, of course, but I tell you—"

"What will it cost?" the woman asks.

Wilke scratches his head. "When must it be ready?"

"As soon as possible."

"Then I'll have to work through the night. Overtime. It will have to be specially designed."

"What will it cost?" the woman asks.

"I'll tell you when I deliver it. I'll keep the price down, for the sake of science. Only I won't be able to take it back if you are not allowed to use it."

"I shall be allowed."

Wilke looks at the woman in amazement. "How do you know?"

"If the priests won't bestow their blessings, we'll bury them without priests," the woman says harshly. "They were always together and they shall stay together."

Wilke nods. "Well then, agreed—the coffin will definitely

be delivered. But I won't be able to take it back."

The woman gets a black leather purse with a nickel clasp out of her handbag. "Do you want a deposit?"

"It's customary. For the wood."

The woman looks at Wilke. "One million," he says, somewhat embarrassed.

The woman gives him the bills. They have been folded and refolded. "The address—" she says.

"I'll go with you," Wilke announces. "To take measurements. They shall have a good coffin."

The woman nods and looks at me. "And a headstone? When will you deliver that?"

"Whenever you like. Generally people wait for a couple of months after the funeral."

"Can we have it right away?"

"Certainly. But it's better to wait. The grave sinks after a while. It's not advisable to put up the stone before that, otherwise it has to be reset."

"Yes?" the woman says. For an instant the pupils of her eyes seem to quiver. "Nevertheless, we'd like to have the stone right away. Can't you—isn't there some way of setting it so it won't sink?"

"To do that, we'd have to make a special foundation for the stone before the burial. Do you want that?"

The woman nods. "Their names must be there," she says. "They mustn't just lie there. It's better if their names are there from the beginning."

She gives me the number of the cemetery lot. "I'd like to pay right away," she says. "How much does it come to?"

She opens the black leather purse again. I tell her the price, as embarrassed as Wilke. "Nowadays everything is in the millions and billions," I add.

It is strange how you can sometimes tell whether people are decent and honorable by the way they fold their money.

The woman unfolds one note after the other and lays them on the table beside the samples of granite and limestone. "We saved up this money for their schooling," she says. "Now it would not be nearly enough—but for this it will just do—"

"Out of the question!" Riesenfeld says. "Have you any idea what black Swedish granite costs? It comes from Sweden, young man, and can't be bought with German marks! You have to pay in foreign exchange! Swedish kronen! We have only a few blocks left—for friends! The last ones! They are like blue-white diamonds! I'm giving you one for the evening with Madame Watzek—but two! Have you lost your mind? I might just as well ask Von Hindenburg to become a communist."

"What a thought!"

"Well, you see! Accept this rarity and don't try to get more out of me than your boss did. Since you're office boy and general manager in one, you don't need to worry about getting ahead."

"No, I don't. I'm doing it out of pure love of granite. Platonic love, as a matter of fact. I don't even intend to sell it myself."

"You don't?" Riesenfeld asks, pouring himself a glass of schnaps.

"No," I reply. "I'm thinking of changing my profession."

"What, again?" Riesenfeld pushes his chair around so he can see Lisa's window.

"Seriously this time."

"Back to schoolteaching?"

"No," I say. "I'm no longer inexperienced enough for that. Or conceited enough either. Do you know of anything I could get? You get around a lot."

"What sort of thing?" Riesenfeld asks uninterestedly.

"Anything at all in a big city. Copy boy on a newspaper perhaps."

"Stay here," Riesenfeld says. "You fit in here. I'd miss you. Why do you want to leave?"

"I can't exactly explain. If I could, it wouldn't be so necessary. Sometimes I don't even know myself; only once in a while, but then I know damn well."

"And you know now?"

"I know now."

"My God!" Riesenfeld says. "You'll wish you were back!"

"Absolutely, that's why I intend to go."

Suddenly Riesenfeld jumps as though he had laid hold of an electric wire with a wet paw. Lisa has turned on the light in her room and has stepped to the window. She appears not to see us in the half-darkened office and she slowly takes off her blouse. She is wearing nothing under it.

Riesenfeld snorts aloud. "God in Heaven, what breasts! You could easily put a half-liter stein on them with no danger of its falling!"

"That's an idea," I say.

Riesenfeld's eyes sparkle. "Does Frau Watzek do that all the time?"

"She's pretty casual. No one can see her—except us over here, of course."

"Man alive!" Riesenfeld says. "And you want to give up a position like this, you total idiot?"

"Yes," I say, and am silent while Riesenfeld steals to the window like a Würtemberg Indian, his glass in one hand, the bottle of schnaps in the other.

Lisa is combing her hair. "Once I wanted to be a sculptor," Riesenfeld says without removing his eyes from her. "With a model like that it would have been worthwhile! Damn it, the chances a man neglects!"

"Did you plan to work in granite?"

"What's that got to do with it?"

"When you use granite the models grow old before the work of art is finished," I say. "It's so hard. With a temperament like yours you should have chosen clay. Otherwise you'd have left nothing but unfinished works."

Riesenfeld groans. Lisa has taken off her skirt but has then turned out the light and gone into the next room. The head of the Odenwald Works clings to the window for a while longer, then turns around. "It's easy for you!" he growls. "You have no demon sitting on your neck. A suckling calf at most."

"*Merci*," I say. "It's not a demon in your case either; it's a billy goat. Anything else?"

"A letter," Riesenfeld announces. "Will you deliver a letter for me?"

"To whom?"

"Frau Watzek! Who else?"

I am silent.

"I'll look around for a job for you," Riesenfeld says.

I continue to be silent, watching the perspiring, disappointed sculptor. I intend to keep faith with Georg, even if it costs me my future.

"I'd have done it anyway," Riesenfeld explains hypocritically.

"I know you would," I say. "But why write? Letters never do any good. Besides, you're leaving tonight. Postpone the whole thing till you come back."

Riesenfeld finishes his schnaps. "It may seem odd to you, but one is extremely disinclined to postpone matters of this sort."

At this moment Lisa comes out of her front door. She is wearing a black tailor-made dress and the highest heels I have ever seen. Riesenfeld spies her at the same instant I do. He snatches his hat from the table and rushes out. "This is the moment!"

I watch him shoot down the street. Hat in hand, he respectfully strolls up beside Lisa, who has looked around twice. Then the two disappear around the corner. I wonder what will come of it. Georg Kroll will be certain to let me know. Quite possibly the lucky fellow will get a second Swedish-granite monument out of the business without losing Lisa.

Wilke, the coffinmaker, is coming across the courtyard. "How about a meeting tonight?" he shouts through the window. I nod. I have been expecting him to propose it. "Is Bach coming?" I ask.

"Yes. I've just been getting cigarettes for him."

We are sitting in Wilke's workshop surrounded by shavings, coffins, potted geraniums, and pots of glue. There is a smell of resin and fresh-cut pine wood. Wilke is planing down the cover for the twins' coffin. He has decided to include a garland of flowers, gratis, and to embellish it with artificial gold leaf. When his interest is aroused, he cares nothing about profit. And now it is aroused.

Kurt Bach is sitting on a black lacquered coffin with fittings of imitation bronze; I on a showpiece of natural oak in a dull finish. We have beer, sausage, bread, and cheese before us and have decided to keep Wilke company during the ghostly hour. Between twelve and one at night, the coffinmaker usually grows melancholy, sleepy, and rather scared. It is his weak hour. One wouldn't believe it, but at that time he is afraid of ghosts, and the canary that hangs over his workbench in a parrot cage is not company enough for him. It is then that he becomes discouraged, talks about the pointlessness of existence, and takes to drink. We have often found him next morning snoring on a bed of shavings in his largest coffin, the one he was so badly cheated on four years ago. The coffin was built for the giant of the Bleichfeld Circus, which was playing for a time in Werdenbrück. After a dinner of Limburger cheese, hard-boiled eggs, bologna, army bread, and schnaps, he died—apparently died, that is, for while Wilke was slaving through the night, in defiance of all ghosts, to complete the giant's coffin, the latter suddenly rose with a start from his deathbed, and, instead of informing Wilke on the spot, as a decent person would have done, finished up a half-bottle of schnaps that was left over and went to sleep. Next morning, he maintained he had no money and, besides, had not ordered a coffin for himself, an objection to which there was no answer. The circus moved on, and since no one would admit to having ordered the coffin, Wilke was left with it on his hands, and thereby acquired for a time a somewhat embittered view of the world. He was particularly incensed at young Dr. Wüllmann, whom he considered responsible for the whole thing. Wüllmann had been an army doctor and had seen two years' service; as a result he had grown venturesome. By treating so many half-dead and three-quarters-dead soldiers in the field hospital without being answerable to anyone for their deaths or misset bones, he had picked up a lot of interesting experience. For this reason he slipped in at night to have one more look at the giant and gave him an injection of some sort. He had often seen dead men come to life in the field hospital. The giant, too, promptly responded. Since that time, Wilke has had a certain prejudice against Wüllmann, which the latter has not been able to eradicate despite the fact that he has recently behaved more sensibly and has sent the families of his ex-patients to Wilke. For Wilke, the giant coffin has been a permanent warning against credulity, and I believe it was also what prompted him to go home with the twins' mother—he wanted to assure himself that the dead were not galloping around on hobbyhorses. It would have been too much for Wilke's self-respect to have been left with a square, twins' coffin, in addition to the unsalable giant coffin, and thus to have become a kind of Barnum of the coffinmaker's guild. The thing that angered him most about the Wüllmann business was that he had no chance for private conversation with the giant. He would have forgiven anything for an interview about the Beyond. After all, the giant had been as good as dead for several hours, and Wilke, as amateur scientist and dreader of ghosts, would have given a great deal to get information about existence on the other side.

Kurt Bach has no patience with all this. A son of nature, he is still a member of the Society of Freethinkers in Berlin, whose motto is: "Live and rejoice while you are here, beyond the grave there's naught to fear." It's strange that, despite this fact, he has become a sculptor of the Beyond, portraying angels, dying lions, and eagles, but that was not his original intention. As a young man he considered himself a kind of nephew to Michelangelo.

The canary is singing. The light keeps it awake. Wilke's plane makes a hissing sound. Beyond the open windows lies the night. "How are you feeling?" I ask Wilke. "Do you hear the Beyond knocking yet?"

"So-so. It's only eleven thirty. At this hour I feel as if I were out for a walk in a décolleté gown and a full beard. Uncomfortable."

"Be a monist," Kurt Bach urges. "When you don't believe in anything, you never feel especially bad. Or ridiculous either."

"Nor good, for that matter," Wilke says.

"Perhaps. But certainly not as though you had a full beard and were wearing a décolleté gown. I only feel that way when I look out the window at night and there is the sky with all its stars and the millions of light years and I am supposed to believe that over all this sits a kind of superman who cares what becomes of Kurt Bach."

The son of nature contentedly cuts himself a piece of sausage and begins to chew. Wilke is growing more nervous. Midnight is near, and at this hour he does not relish such conversation. "Cold, isn't it?" he says. "Autumn already."

"Just leave the window open," I tell him as he is about to close it. "That won't do you any good; ghosts can go through glass. Instead, take a look at that acacia out there. It's the Lisa Watzek of acacias. Listen to the wind rustling in it! Like silk petticoats rustling to the music of a waltz. But someday it will be cut down and you will make coffins out of it—"

"Not of acacia wood. Coffins are made of oak or pine with mahogany veneer—"

"All right, all right, Wilke! Is there any schnaps left?"

Kurt Bach hands me the bottle. Wilke suddenly jumps and almost cuts a finger off. "What was that?" he asks in alarm.

A beetle has flown against the electric light. "Just quiet down, Alfred," I say. "That's not a messenger from the Beyond. Just a simple drama of the animal world. A dung beetle striving toward the sun—represented for him by a one-hundred-watt bulb in the back house at No. 3 Hackenstrasse."

By agreement, from shortly before midnight until the end of the ghostly hour we call Wilke by his first name. It makes him feel more secure. After that we become formal again.

"I don't understand how anyone can live without religion," Wilke says to Kurt Bach. "What do you do when you wake up at night during a thunderstorm?"

"In the summer?"

"In the summer, of course; there aren't any thunderstorms in winter."

"You drink something cold," Kurt Bach explains, "and then go back to sleep."

Wilke shakes his head. During the ghostly hour he is not only scared but very religious.

"I used to know a man who went to a bordello during thunderstorms," I say. "He was absolutely compelled to. At other times he was impotent; thunderstorms changed that. One sight of a thunderhead and he would reach for the telephone and make an appointment with Fritzi. The summer of 1920 was the finest time of his life; there were thunderstorms all the time. Often four or five a day."

"What's become of him?" Wilke, the amateur scientist, asks with interest.

"He's dead," I say. "Died during the last and biggest thunderstorm, in October 1920."

The night wind slams a door in the house opposite. Bells ring from the steeples. It is midnight. Wilke gulps down a schnaps.

"How about a stroll to the cemetery?" asks the sometimes unfeeling atheist Bach.

Wilke's mustache quivers with horror in the wind blowing in through the window. "And you call yourselves friends!" he says reproachfully.

Immediately thereafter he is startled again. "What was that?"

"A pair of lovers out there. Stop working for a while, Alfred. Eat! Ghosts stay away from people while they're eating. Haven't you any sprats?"

Alfred gives me the look of a dog that has been kicked while answering the call of nature. "Do you have to remind me of that now? Of my unhappy love life and the loneliness of a man in his best years?"

"You're a victim of your profession," I say. "Not everyone can say that of himself. Come to *souper!* That's what this meal is called in the fashionable world."

We go to work on the sausage and cheese and we open the bottles of beer. The canary is given a lettuce leaf and breaks into a song of praise, with no thought as to whether it is an atheist or believer. Kurt Bach raises his clay-colored face and sniffs. "It smells of stars," he exclaims.

"What's that?" Wilke puts down his bottle among the shavings. "What in the world does that mean?"

"At midnight the world smells of stars."

"Cut out the jokes! How can anyone even want to go on living when he believes in nothing and yet talks like that?"

"Are you trying to convert me?" Kurt Bach asks. "You celestial inheritance hunter?"

"No, no! Or yes, if you like. Wasn't that something rustling?"

"Yes," Kurt says. "Love."

Outside we hear more cautious footsteps. A second pair of lovers vanishes into the forest of tombstones. The white blur of a girl's dress can be seen disappearing into the darkness.

"Why do people look so different when they're dead?" Wilke asks. "Even twins."

"Because they're no longer disguised," Kurt Bach replies.

Wilke stops chewing. "Disguised how?"

"By life," says the monist.

Wilke smooths his mustache and goes on chewing. "At this hour you might at least stop this nonsense! Isn't anything sacred to you?"

Kurt Bach laughs tonelessly. "You poor vine! You always have to have something to cling to."

"And you?"

"So do I." Bach's eyes in the clay-colored face gleam as though made of glass. The son of nature is usually taciturn, just an unsuccessful sculptor with broken dreams; but sometimes those latent dreams rise again as they did years ago, and then he suddenly becomes a superannuated satyr with visions.

There is a crackling and whispering in the courtyard, and once more stealthy footsteps. "Two weeks ago there was a fight out there," Wilke says. "A locksmith had forgotten to take his tools out of his pocket, and during the stormy encounter they must have got into so unfortunate a position that the lady was suddenly pricked by a sharp awl. She was up in a flash and grabbed a small bronze wreath. She beat the mechanic over the head with it—didn't you hear it?" he asks me.

"No."

"Well, she slams the bronze wreath down over his ears so hard he can't get it off. I turn on the light and ask what's going on. The fellow gallops off in terror with the bronze wreath around his skull like a Roman senator—didn't you notice the bronze wreath was missing?" he asks me.

"No."

"What a way to run a business! So he runs out as though a swarm of wasps was after him. I go down. The girl is still standing there, looking at her hand. 'Blood!' she says. 'He stabbed me. And at such a moment!'

"I see the awl on the ground and guess what has happened. I pick up the awl. 'This could give you blood poisoning,' I say. 'Very dangerous! You can put a tourniquet on a finger, but not on a buttock. Even so enchanting a one.' She blushes—"

"How could you tell in the darkness?" Kurt Bach asks.

"There was a moon."

"You can't see a blush in the moonlight. Colors don't show."

"You feel it," Wilke explains. "So she blushes, but continues to hold up her dress. It's a light dress, and blood makes spots that are hard to get out. 'I have iodine and adhesive plaster,' I say. 'And I'm discreet. Come in!' She comes in and isn't even frightened." Wilke turns to me. "That's the nice thing about your yard," he says enthusiastically. "Anyone who makes love among tombstones isn't afraid of coffins either. So it happened that, after the iodine and adhesive tape and a swallow of blended port wine, the giant's coffin served another purpose."

"It became a bower of love?" I ask to make sure.

"A cavalier enjoys his pleasures but says nothing," Wilke replies.

At this instant the moon comes out from behind the clouds, lighting the white marble and making the crosses glimmer darkly. Scattered among them we see four pairs of lovers, two on marble beds, two on granite. For a moment everyone is motionless, transfixed by surprise—there are only two courses open to them, to flee or to ignore the altered situation. Flight is not without danger; you can get away in an instant, but you may sustain such a psychic shock that it will lead to impotence. I learned that from a lance corporal who was once taken by surprise by a sergeant major when he was out in the woods with a cook—he was ruined for life, and two years later his wife divorced him.

The pairs of lovers do the right thing. Like stags scenting danger they lift their heads—then, with eyes directed at the single lighted window, ours, which was lighted before, they remain as they are, as though carved by Kurt Bach. It is a picture of innocence, a trifle ridiculous at most, just like Bach's sculptures. Immediately thereafter the shadow of a cloud obscures that part of the garden, leaving only the obelisk in the light. And who stands there, a glittering fountain? The fearlessly pissing Knopf, like that statue in Brussels which every soldier who has gone on leave in Belgium knows so well.

He is too far away for me to do anything. Besides, I don't feel like it tonight. Why should I behave like a housewife? I decided this afternoon to leave this place, and therefore life rises to meet me with double strength. I feel it everywhere, in the smell of the shavings and in the moonlight, in the tiptoeing and rustling in the courtyard and in the ineffable word September, in my hands which can move and lay hold of it, and in my eyes without which all the museums of the world would be empty, in ghosts, in spirits, in transitoriness, and in the wild career of the earth past Cassiopeia and the Pleiades, in the anticipation of boundless foreign gardens under foreign stars, of positions on great, foreign newspapers, and of rubies now crystallizing underground into lustrous gems; I feel it and it keeps me from heaving an empty beer bottle in the direction of Knopf, that half-minute fountain—

At this moment the clock strikes. It is one. The ghostly hour is past; we can speak formally to Wilke again and either go on getting drunk or descend into sleep as into a mine where there are corpses, coal, white salt palaces, and buried diamonds.

Chapter Eighteen

She is sitting in a corner of her room huddled beside the window. "Isabelle," I say.

She does not answer. Her eyelids flutter like butterflies that children have impaled alive on pins.

"Isabelle," I say. "I've come to take you out."

She gives a start and presses herself against the wall. Her posture is cramped and rigid. "Don't you know me any more?" I ask.

She remains motionless; only her eyes turn toward me, watchful and very dark. "The one who pretends to be a doctor sent you," she whispers.

It is true. Wernicke did send me. "He did not send me," I say. "I came secretly. No one knows I am here."

She frees herself slowly from the wall. "You, too, have betrayed me."

"I have not betrayed you. I could not get to you. You have not come out."

"I couldn't," she whispers. "They were all standing outside waiting. They wanted to catch me. They managed to find out that I am here."

"Who?"

She looks at me but does not answer. How frail she is! I think. How frail and alone in this bare room! She hasn't even her own self. Not even the loneliness of the ego. She has exploded like a grenade into jagged fragments of fear scattered in a strange, threatening landscape of incomprehensible dread. "No one is waiting for you," I say.

"Yes, they are."

"How do you know?"

"The voices. Don't you hear them?"

"No."

"The voices know everything. Can't you hear them?"

"It's the wind, Isabelle."

"Yes," she says with resignation. "It may be the wind. If only it didn't hurt so!"

"What hurts?"

"The sawing. They might at least cut, that would go faster, but this slow, dull sawing! Everything grows together again because they are so slow! Then they begin all over again and so it never stops. They saw through my flesh and the flesh grows together again and it never stops."

"Who saws?"

"The voices."

"Voices can't saw."

"These can."

"Where do they saw?"

Isabelle makes a gesture as though in extreme pain. She presses her hands between her thighs. "They want to saw it out so that I can never have children."

"Who?"

"The woman out there. She says she bore me. Now she wants to force me back into herself again. She saws and saws. And he holds me still."

"Who holds you?"

She shudders. "He—the one inside her—"

"Inside her?"

She groans. "Don't say it—she will kill me—I'm not allowed to know—"

I walk toward her around an easy chair upholstered in a pale rose pattern, its atmosphere of domesticity strangely inappropriate in this bare room. "What aren't you allowed to know?" I ask.

"She will kill me. I don't dare go to sleep. Why does no one keep watch with me? I must do everything alone. I am so tired," she laments like a bird. "It burns and I cannot go to sleep and I am so tired. But who can sleep when it burns and no one is keeping watch? You, too, have abandoned me."

"I have not abandoned you."

"You have been talking to them. They have bribed you. Why didn't you hold on to me? The blue trees and the silver rain. But you didn't want to. Never! You could have rescued me."

"When?" I ask, feeling something begin to tremble inside me, and I do not want it to tremble but it goes on just the same, and the room no longer seems solid; it is as though the walls were shaking and did not consist of stone and mortar and plaster but of vibrations, densely concentrated vibrations of billions of fibers that stretch from horizon to horizon and beyond and are here pressed together into a square jail of fragile nooses, hangman's nooses, in which a creature of yearning and fear is struggling helplessly.

Isabelle turns her face to the wall. "Oh, it's lost and gone—many lifetimes ago."

Suddenly twilight fills the window, spreading over it a veil of almost invisible gray. Everything is still there as before, the light outside, the green, the yellow of the roads, the two palms in the big majolica pots, the sky with its fields of cloud, the distant gray and red confusion of roofs in the city beyond the woods—and nothing is any longer the same. Twilight has isolated it. It has brushed it with the varnish of impermanence, prepared it like food, as housewives soak beef in vinegar, for the shadow wolves of the night. Only Isabelle is still there, clinging tight to the last thread of light, but she, too, is being drawn by it into the drama of the evening, which is not truly a drama and only seems so because we know it means impermanence. Only since we have known that we must die and only because we know it has the idyl turned into drama, the circle into a lance, and becoming into passing away and outcry and terror and flight and judgment.

I hold her close in my arms. She is trembling and looking at me and pressing herself against me and I hold her, we hold each other—two strangers who know nothing of one another and cling to one another because each mistakes the other for someone else: strangers who nevertheless derive a fleeting comfort from this misunderstanding which is a double and triple and endless misunderstanding and yet is the only thing that, like a rainbow, holds out the deceptive appearance of a bridge where no bridge can ever be, a reflection between two mirrors thrown onward into ever more distant emptiness. "Why don't you love me?" Isabelle murmurs.

"I love you. Everything in me loves you."

"Not enough. The others are still here. If it were enough, you would kill them."

I hold her in my arms and look over her head into the park where now shadows like amethyst waves are running up the fields and roads. Everything in me is clear and sharp, but at the same time I feel as though I were standing on a narrow platform high above a murmurous deep. "You wouldn't be able to stand it if I lived outside you," Isabelle whispers.

I don't know what to reply. Something always moves in

me when she says things like that—as though there were a deeper wisdom in them than I can recognize—as though they came from beyond the phenomenal world, from the place where there are no names. "Do you feel how cold it's getting?" she asks on my shoulder. "Each night everything dies. The heart too. They saw it to pieces."

"Nothing dies, Isabelle. Ever."

"Everything does! The stone face—it cracks into pieces. In the morning it is there again. Oh, it is no face! How we lie with our poor faces! You lie too—"

"Yes—" I say. "But I don't want to."

"You must tear away the face until there is nothing there. Only smooth skin, nothing else! But then it will still be there. It grows back. If everything stood still, one would have no pain. Why do they want to saw me away from everything? Why do they want me back? I'm not going to betray anything!"

"What could you betray?"

"The thing that blooms. It is full of mud. It comes out of the ducts."

She trembles again and presses herself against me. "They have stuck my eyes shut. With glue, and then they have run needles through them. But still I cannot look away."

"Away from what?"

She pushes me off. "They have sent you too! I will betray nothing! You are a spy. They have bought you! If I told you, they would kill me."

"I'm not a spy. And why should they kill you if you tell me? It would be much easier for them to do it before. If I know, they will have to kill me too. There would be one more who knew."

This penetrates. She looks at me again, considering. I keep so quiet that I hardly breathe. I feel that we are standing in front of a door behind which there may be freedom. What Wernicke calls freedom. A return from the maze, to normal streets, houses, and relationships. I don't know whether this will really be better, but I can't speculate about that while I have this tormented creature before me. "If you explain it to me, they will leave you in peace," I say. "And if they don't leave you in peace, I'll get help. From the police, the newspapers. They will become afraid and then you won't need to be."

She presses her hands together. "It's not just that," she manages to say finally.

"What is it then?"

In a second her face becomes hard and closed. The torment and indecision are washed away. Her mouth grows small and thin and the chin protrudes. Now there is something about her of the grim, puritanical, evil old maid. "Drop that!" she says. Her voice, too, has changed.

"All right, we'll drop it. I don't need to know."

I wait. Her eyes glitter in the last light like wet slates. All the gray of the evening seems concentrated in them; she looks at me in a superior and mocking way. "You'd like that very much, wouldn't you? Well, you have failed, you spy!"

For no reason I become furious, although I know that she is sick and that these transitions of consciousness come like lightning. "Go to hell," I say angrily. "What does all that matter to me!"

I see her face changing again; but I go out quickly, full of an incomprehensible tumult.

"And?" Wernicke asks.

"That's all. Why did you send me in to see her? It accomplished nothing. I'm no good as a nurse. You see for yourself—just when I should have spoken carefully to her, I shouted at her and ran away."

"It was better than you think." Wernicke gets a bottle

and two glasses out from behind his books and pours drinks. "Cognac," he says. "There's just one thing I'd like to know—how she senses that her mother is here again."

"Her mother is here?"

Wernicke nods. "Since day before yesterday. She hasn't seen her. She couldn't have, even from her window."

"Why not?"

"She'd have to hang out too far and have eyes like a telescope." Wernicke inspects the color of his cognac. "But sometimes patients of that sort do sense these things. Or perhaps she just guessed. I have been pushing her in that direction."

"Why?" I say. "Now she's sicker than I have ever seen her."

"No," Wernicke replies.

I put down my glass and glance at the thick books on his shelves. "She's so miserable it makes your stomach turn."

"Miserable, yes; but not sicker."

"You ought to have left her in peace—the way she was during the summer. She was happy. Now—it's horrible."

"Yes, it's horrible," Wernicke says. "It's almost as though what she imagines were really happening."

"It's as though she were in a torture chamber."

Wernicke nods. "People outside always think torture chambers don't exist any more. They exist all right. Here. Each one has his own in his skull."

"Not just here."

"Not just here," Wernicke agrees with alacrity, taking a swallow of cognac. "But there are many of them here. Do you want to be convinced? Put on a white coat. It's almost time for my evening rounds."

"No," I say. "I remember the last time."

"That was the war; it keeps right on raging here. Do you want to see more of the wards?"

"No. I remember very well."

"Not all. You only saw some of them."

"It was enough."

I recall those creatures, standing in cramped postures in the corner, motionless for weeks at a time, or continually running against the walls, clambering over beds, or groaning and shrieking, white-eyed, in strait jackets. The inaudible thunders of chaos beat down on them, and pre-existence, worm, claw, scale, writhing, footless, and slimy, the creeping things before thought, the carion existences, reach upward from below to seize their bowels and testicles and spines, to draw them down into the gray confusion of the beginning, back to scaly bodies and eyeless retchings—and, shrieking like panic-stricken monkeys, they seek refuge on the last bare branches of the brain, chattering, hypnotized by the ever-rising coils, in the final horrible dread, not of the brain, worse, the cells' dread of destruction, the scream above all screams, the fear of fears, the death fear, not of the individual, but of the veins, the blood, the subconscious entelechy that silently control liver, glands, the pulse of the blood, and the fire at the base of the skull.

"All right," Wernicke says. "Then drink your cognac, give up your excursions into the unconscious and praise life."

"Why? Because everything in it is so wonderfully arranged? Because one eats the other and then himself?"

"Because you're alive, you harmless hair-splitter! You're much too young to deal with the problem of pity, and too inexperienced. When you're old enough, you'll see it doesn't exist."

"I've had a certain amount of experience."

Wernicke dismisses the idea. "Don't be so self-important, you veteran of the wars! What you know has nothing to do with the metaphysical problem of pity—it's part of the universal idiocy of the human race. Great pity begins elsewhere—and ends elsewhere too—beyond weeping willows like you and also beyond the peddlers of comfort like Bodendiek—"

"All right, superman," I say. "Does that give you the right to let hell loose in the minds of your patients whenever you feel like it, or the fires of the stake or slimy death?"

"The right—" Wernicke replies with abysmal contempt. "How agreeable an honest murderer is in comparison with a lawyer like you! What do you know about right? Even less than about pity, you scholastic sentimentalist!"

He raises his glass, grinning, then glances contentedly into the night. The artificial light in the room falls ever more goldenly on the brown and gilt spines of the books. Light never seems so precious or so symbolic as up here where the polar night of the mind reigns. "Neither one was foreseen in the design of the universe," I say. "But I cannot reconcile myself, and if that means human inadequacy to you, I'll be glad to remain inadequate as long as I live."

Wernicke gets up, takes his hat from the hook, puts it on, then bows to me, removes it, hangs it on the hook, and sits down again. "Long live the beautiful and good!" he says. "That's what I meant. And now out with you! It's time for my evening rounds."

"Can't you give Geneviève Terhoven a sleeping pill?" I ask.

"I can, but it won't cure her."

"Why don't you let her have some peace today?"

"I am giving her peace. And I'll give her a sleeping pill too." He winks at me. "You were better for her today than a whole college of doctors. Many thanks."

I look at him uncertainly. To hell with his errands, I think. To hell with his cognac! And to hell with his godlike speeches! "A strong sleeping pill," I say.

"The best there is. Were you ever in the Orient? In China?"

"How could I have been in China?"

"I was there," Wernicke says. "Before the war. At the time of the floods and the famine."

"Yes," I say. "I can imagine what's coming now and I don't want to hear it. I've read it. Will you go to Geneviève Terhoven right away? First of all?"

"First of all. And I'll leave her in peace," Wernicke smiles. "But to even things up I'll destroy some of her mother's peace."

"What do you want, Otto?" I ask. "I'm not interested in discussing the form of the ode today! Go and find Eduard!"

We are sitting in the assembly room of the Poets' Club. I have come here in order not to think about Isabelle, but suddenly everything about the place repels me. What's the purpose of these jingles when the world reeks of fear and blood? I know this is a cheap conclusion and, in addition, a false one—but I am weary of continually catching myself in dramatized banalities. "Well, what's up?" I ask.

Otto Bambuss looks at me like an owl fed on buttermilk. "I was there," he says reproachfully. "Again. First you drive me there and then you don't even want to hear about it!"

"That's life for you. Where were you?"

"In Bahnstrasse, in the bordello."

"What's new about that?" I ask, without really hearing him. "We were all there together, we paid for you, and you ran away. You want us to put up a statue to you for that?"

"I went again," Otto says. "Alone. Please listen to me, won't you?"

"When?"

"After the evening in the Red Mill."

"So what?" I ask without interest. "Did you run away from the facts of life again?"

"No," Otto explains. "Not this time."

"My respects! Was it the Iron Horse?"

Bambuss blushes. "That doesn't matter."

"All right," I say. "Why are you talking about it then? It's not exactly a unique experience. A good many people in the world sleep with women."

"You don't understand. It's the consequences."

"What consequences? I'm sure the Iron Horse isn't sick. People always imagine that sort of thing, especially at first."

Otto has a tormented expression. "That's not what I mean! You know why I did it. Everything was going fine with both my cycles, especially with 'The Scarlet Woman,' but I thought I needed even more inspiration. I wanted to end that cycle before I had to go back to the village. That's why I went to Bahnstrasse again. Properly, this time. And, just imagine, since then nothing! Nothing! Not a line! It's as though it had been cut short! The opposite should have happened!"

I laugh, although I'm not in the mood for laughter. "That's just artist's luck!"

"It's all right for you to laugh," Bambuss says excitedly, "but consider my position! Eleven faultless sonnets, and this misfortune while I'm working on the twelfth! It simply won't move any more! My imagination has gone! It's all over! I'm done for!"

"It's the curse of fulfillment," says Hungermann, who has come up to us and obviously knows about the matter. "It leaves nothing over. A hungry man dreams of food. A satisfied man is repelled by it."

"He will get hungry again and his dreams will return," I reply.

"They will for you, but not for Otto," Hungermann explains with great satisfaction. "You are superficial and normal, Otto is profound. He has replaced one complex by another. Don't laugh—perhaps it's the end of him as a writer. It is, as one might say, a funeral in a house of joy."

"I'm empty," Otto says despondently. "Emptier than I have ever been. I have ruined myself. Where are my dreams? Fulfillment is the enemy of yearning. I should have known!"

"Write something about it," I say.

"Not a bad idea!" Hungermann says, getting out his notebook. "I had it first, as a matter of fact. Besides, it's nothing for Otto; his style isn't hard enough."

"Then he can write it as an elegy. Or a lament. Cosmic despair, stars dropping like golden tears, God Himself sobbing because He has made such a mess of the world, the autumn wind harping a requiem—"

Hungermann is writing busily. "What a coincidence!" he says as he writes. "I said exactly the same thing in almost the same words a week ago. My wife heard me."

Otto has pricked up his ears slightly. "Besides all that, I am afraid I may have caught something," he says. "How long does it take before you know?"

"With a dose three days, with lues four weeks," Hungermann, the married man, replies promptly.

"You haven't caught anything," I say. "Sonnets don't get lues, but you can take advantage of your state of mind. Put the rudder hard over! If you can't write for, write against! Instead of a hymn to the woman in scarlet and purple, a biting satire. Pus drips from the stars, Job writhes with boils, probably the first syphilitic, amid the shards of the universe, the Janus face of love, smiling sweetly on one side, nose eaten away on the other—" I see Hungermann writing again. "Did you say that to your wife, too, a week ago?" I ask.

He nods beaming.

"Why are you writing it down then?"

"Because I'd already forgotten it. I often forget these small inspirations."

"It's easy for you to make fun of me," Bambuss says, offended. "I can't write *against* anything. I am a hymn writer."

"Then write hymns to virtue, purity, the monastic life, loneliness, absorption in the nearest and farthest thing there is, one's self."

Otto listens for a moment with his head on one side like a hunting dog. "I've already done that," he says, cast down. "Besides, it's not altogether my style."

"To hell with your style! Don't make so many demands!"

I get up and go into the next room. Valentin Busch is sitting there. "Come and drink a bottle of Johannisberger with me," he says. "That will annoy Eduard."

"I don't want to annoy anyone today," I reply, leaving him.

As I come out into the street, Otto Bambuss is standing there, staring dejectedly at the plaster Valkyries that adorn the entrance to the Walhalla. "What a misfortune!" he says aimlessly.

"Don't cry," I tell him in order to get rid of him. "Apparently you belong among those who reach their peak early, Kleist, Bürger, Rimbaud, Büchner, the finest stars in the firmament of poets—so don't take it to heart."

"But they all died young!"

"You can still do that too if you like. Besides, Rimbaud lived for many years after he had stopped writing. As an adventurer in Abyssinia. What about that?"

Otto looks at me like a doe with three legs. Then he stares once more at the thick bottoms and busts of the plaster Valkyries. "Listen," I say impatiently. "Write another cycle: The Temptations of Saint Anthony! There you have both lust and renunciation, and a lot of other things as well."

Otto's face lights up. A moment later he is concentrating as much as is possible for an astral sheep with sensual desires. Apparently for the moment German literature has been saved, for I am clearly much less important to him already. Absently he waves to me and hurries down the street toward his writing desk. I look after him enviously.

The office is dark and empty. I switch on the light and find a note: "Riesenfeld gone. You have tonight off. Use the time to polish your buttons, improve your mind, cut your fingernails, and pray for Kaiser and Reich. Signed Kroll, Sergeant Major and human being. P.S. He who sleeps sins too."

I go up to my room. The piano shows its white teeth at me. Books by dead men stare down coldly from the shelves. I toss off a succession of sevenths. Lisa's window opens. She stands in the warm light; her dressing gown hangs open, and she is holding up a wagon wheel of flowers. "From Riesenfeld," she shouts. "What an idiot! Have you any use for these vegetables?"

I shake my head. If I sent them to Isabelle, she would think her enemies were attempting something underhanded—and I haven't seen Gerda in so long a time she would misinterpret the gesture. There's no one else I know.

"Really not?" Lisa asks.

"Really not."

"You bird of bad luck! But don't take it too hard! I think you're going to grow up."

"When is one grown up?"

Lisa considers this for a moment. "When you think more of yourself than of others," she croaks, slamming the window.

I toss another succession of sevenths, this time in a minor key, through the window. They have no visible effect. I close the piano and wander downstairs again. Wilke's light is still on. I climb up to his shop. "How did the problem of the twins turn out?" I ask.

"Tiptop. The mother won. The twins were buried in

their double coffin. In the municipal cemetery, not the Catholic, to be sure. Funny that the mother bought a grave in the Catholic cemetery first—she ought to have known it wouldn't work when one of the twins was Evangelical. Now she has the first grave on her hands."

"The one in the Catholic cemetery?"

"Of course. It's excellent—dry, sandy, with a lot of aristocrats lying nearby. She's lucky to have it!"

"What for? For herself and her husband? She'll want to be buried in the municipal cemetery because of the twins."

"As a capital asset," Wilke says, impatient at my stupidity. "Today a grave is a first-class asset, everyone knows that! She could make a profit of a couple of million right now if she wanted to sell. Commodities are rising like mad!"

"Right. I'd forgotten about that for the moment. Why are you still here?"

Wilke points to a coffin. "For Werner, the banker. Cerebral hemorrhage. Expense no object, solid silver fittings, finest workmanship, real silk, overtime price—how about helping me out? Kurt Bach isn't here. In return you can sell them a monument tomorrow morning. No one knows about it yet. It happened after business hours."

"Not tonight. I'm dead tired. Go to the Red Mill a little before midnight, come back at one o'clock and finish up then—that will solve the problem of the ghostly hour."

Wilke thinks it over. "Not bad," he announces. "But won't I need a tuxedo?"

"Not even in your dreams."

Wilke shakes his head. "Out of the question just the same! That one hour would cost me more than I'll make in the whole night. But I might go to a bar."

He looks at me gratefully. "Put down Werner's address," he says.

I write it down. Strange, I think, this is the second time tonight that someone has taken my advice—only I haven't any for myself. "It's odd you're so afraid of ghosts," I say, "when you're something of a freethinker."

"Only during the day. Not at night. Who is a freethinker at night?"

I point toward Kurt Bach's room below us. Wilke shakes his head. "It's easy to be a freethinker when you're young. But at my age, with a rupture and encapsulated tuberculosis—"

"Do a turnabout. The Church loves repentant sinners."

Wilke lifts his shoulders. "Then what would become of my self-respect?"

I laugh. "You have none at night, eh?"

"Who has any at night? You?"

"No. But perhaps a night watchman, or a baker who plies his trade at night. Do you absolutely have to have self-respect?"

"Naturally. After all, I am a human being. Only animals and suicides haven't any. It's a miserable thing, this division! However, tonight I'm going to try Blume's Restaurant. The beer there is excellent."

I wander back across the dark courtyard. In front of the obelisk there is a pale shimmer. It is Lisa's wreath of flowers. She has put it there before going to the Red Mill. For a moment I stand undecided; then I pick it up. The thought that Knopf might desecrate it is too much. I take it to my room and put it in a terra-cotta urn I bring up with me from the office. The flowers at once take over the whole room. There I sit with the brown and yellow and white chrysanthemums that smell of earth and of the cemetery as though I were about to be buried! But in fact haven't I buried something?

By midnight the scent is too much for me. I see that Wilke has gone out to spend the ghostly hour in the bar. I pick up the flowers and take them into his workroom. The door is open. The light is still on so that the ghost dreader will not be terrified when he comes back. A bottle of beer is standing on the giant's coffin. I drink it, put glass and bottle on the window sill and open the window so that it will look as though some ghost had grown thirsty. Then I strew the chrysanthemums all the way from the window to Banker Werner's half-finished coffin, and at the end I set down a handful of valueless thousand-mark notes. Let Wilke make what he can of that! If it results in Werner's coffin not being ready on time, that won't matter—the banker used the inflation to cheat dozens of small householders out of their meager possessions.

Chapter Nineteen

"Would you like to see something that will touch your heart almost like a Rembrandt?" Georg asks.

"Go ahead."

He unfolds his pocket handkerchief and lets an object fall ringing on the table. It takes me a while to recognize it. I gaze at it with emotion. It is a gold twenty-mark piece. The last time I saw one was before the war. "Those were the days!" I say. "Peace reigned, security prevailed, insults to His Majesty were still punishable by imprisonment, the steel helmet was unknown, our mothers wore corsets and their blouses had high, whalebone-stiffened collars, dividends were paid, the mark was as untouchable as God, and every quarter you contentedly clipped the coupons from your government bonds and were paid in gold. Let me kiss you, you glittering symbol of a vanished era!"

I weigh the gold piece in my hand. It bears the likeness of Wilhelm II, who is now sawing wood in Holland and growing a pointed beard. On the coin he still wears the proudly waxed mustache which once meant: It has been achieved.

It certainly has been achieved. "Where did you get it?" I ask.

"From a widow who inherited a whole chest of them."

"Good God! What're they worth?"

"Four billion paper marks apiece. A small house, or a dozen beautiful women. A week at the Red Mill. Eight months' pension for one of the severely wounded war—"

"Enough—"

Heinrich Kroll enters, the bicycle clips on his striped pants. "This will enchant your loyal, subservient heart," I say, sending the golden bird spinning to him through the air. He catches it and stares at it with tear-filled eyes. "His Majesty," he says with emotion. "Those were the days! We still had our army!"

"Apparently they were different days for different people," I reply.

Heinrich looks at me reproachfully. "You'll have to admit they were better days than these!"

"Possibly!"

"Not possibly! Certainly! We had order, we had a stable currency, we had no unemployed, but a thriving economy instead, and we were a respected people. Won't you agree to that?"

"At once."

"Well then! What have we today?"

"Disorder, seven million unemployed, a false economy, and we are a conquered people," I reply.

Heinrich is taken aback. He hadn't thought it would be so easy. "Well then," he repeats. "Today we are sitting in the muck and then we were living on the fat of the land. Even you can probably draw the logical conclusion, can't you?"

"I'm not sure. What is it?"

"It's damn simple! That we must have a Kaiser and a decent national government again!"

"Hold on!" I say. "You've forgotten something. You've forgotten the important word *because*. That is the heart of the evil. It's the reason that today millions like you raise their trunks again and trumpet this nonsense. The little word *because*."

"What's that?" Heinrich asks blankly.

"Because!" I repeat. "The word *because!* Today we have seven million unemployed and inflation and we have been conquered *because* we had the national government you love so much! *Because* that government in its megalomania made war! *Because* we had your beloved blockheads and puppets in uniform as our government! And we must *not* have them back to make things go better; instead we must be careful that they don't come back, *because* otherwise they will drive us into war again and into the muck again. You and your friends say: Yesterday things went well; today they are going badly—so let's have the old government back. But in reality it should be: Today things are going badly *because* yesterday we had the old government—so to hell with it! Catch on? The little word *because!* That's something your friends like to forget! Because!"

"Nonsense!" Heinrich splutters in rage. "You communist!"

Georg breaks into wild laughter. "For Heinrich everyone is a communist who isn't on the extreme right."

Heinrich inflates his chest for an armored retort. The image of the Kaiser has made him strong. At this moment, however, Kurt Bach comes in. "Herr Kroll," he asks Heinrich, "is the angel to stand at the right or left of the text: 'Here lies Master Tinsmith Quartz'?"

"What's that?"

"The bas-relief angel on Quartz's tombstone."

"On the right, of course," Georg says. "Angels always stand on the right."

Heinrich exchanges the role of national prophet for that of tombstone salesman. "I'll come with you," he announces ill-humoredly and puts the gold piece back on the table. Kurt Bach sees it and picks it up. "Those were the days!" he says enthusiastically.

"So, for you too," Georg replies. "What sort of days were they, then, for you?"

"The days of free art! Bread cost pfennigs, schnaps a fiver, life was full of ideals, and with a couple of those gold pieces you could travel to the blessed land of Italy without any fear that they would be worthless when you got there."

Bach kisses the eagle, lays the coin back, and grows ten years older. Heinrich and he disappear. As a parting shot Heinrich calls from the door, a darkly threatening look on his fat face: "Heads will roll yet!"

"What was that?" I ask Georg in amazement. "Wasn't it one of Watzek's favorite phrases? Are we, perhaps, about to see the embattled cousins joining forces?"

Georg stares thoughtfully after Heinrich. "Perhaps," he says. "Then it will become dangerous. Do you know what's so hopeless? In 1918 Heinrich was a rabid opponent of the war. Since then he has forgotten everything that made him oppose it, and the war has become a jolly adventure." He puts the twenty-mark piece into his vest pocket. "Everything you survive becomes an adventure. It makes one sick! And the more horrible it was, the more adventurous it seems in recollection. Only the dead could really judge the war; they alone experienced it completely."

He looks at me. "Experienced?" I say. "Expired."

"They and the ones who have not forgotten it," he goes on. "But there are very few of them. Our damnable memory is a sieve. It wants to survive. And survival is only possible through forgetfulness."

He put his hat on. "Come along," he says. "We'll see what

sort of days our gold bird will call up in Eduard Knobloch's memory.

"Isabelle!" I say deeply astonished.

I see her sitting on the terrace in front of the pavilion for the incurables. There is no trace of the twitching, tormented creature I saw last time. Her eyes are clear, her face is calm, and she seems to me more beautiful than I have ever seen her—but this may be because of the contrast to last time.

It has rained during the afternoon and the garden is glistening with moisture and sunlight. Above the city, clouds float against a pure, medieval blue, and the whole fenestrated front of the building has been transformed into a gallery of mirrors. Unconcerned about the hour, Isabelle is wearing an evening dress of very soft black material and her golden shoes. On her right arm hangs a bracelet of emeralds—it must be worth more than our whole business, including the inventory, the buildings, and the income for the next five years. She has never worn it before. It's a day of rarities, I think. First the golden Wilhelm II and now this! But the bracelet does not move me.

"Do you hear them?" Isabelle asks. "They have drunk deep and well and now they are calm and satisfied and at peace. They are humming deeply like a million bees."

"Who?"

"The trees and all the bushes. Didn't you hear them screaming yesterday when it was so dry?"

"Can they scream?"

"Naturally. Couldn't you hear it?"

"No," I say, looking at her bracelet, which sparkles as though it had green eyes.

Isabelle laughs. "Oh, Rudolf, you hear so little!" she says tenderly. "Your ears have grown shut like a boxwood hedge.

And then you make so much noise too—that's why you hear nothing."

"I make noise? How do you mean?"

"Not with words. But in other ways you make a dreadful amount of noise, Rudolf. Often one can hardly stand you. You make more noise than the hydrangeas when they are thirsty, and they're really terrific screamers."

"What is it in me that makes the noise?"

"Everything. Your wishes, your heart, your dissatisfaction, your vanity, your uncertainty—"

"Vanity?" I say. "I'm not vain."

"Of course you are—"

"Absolutely not!" I reply, knowing that what I'm saying is untrue.

Isabelle kisses me quickly. "Don't make me tired, Rudolf! You're always so precise with words. Besides, you're not really named Rudolf, are you? What is your name?"

"Ludwig," I say in surprise. It is the first time she has asked me.

"Yes, Ludwig. Aren't you sometimes tired of your name?"

"To be sure. Of myself too."

She nods as though it were the most natural thing in the world. "Then go ahead and change it. Why not be Rudolf? Or someone else. Take a trip. Go to another country. Each name is a different country."

"I happen to be called Ludwig. How can I change that? Everyone here knows it."

She appears not to have heard me. "I, too, am going to go away soon," she says. "I feel it. I am weary and weary of my weariness. Everything is beginning to be a little empty and full of leave-taking and melancholy and waiting."

I look at her and suddenly feel a quick fear. What does she mean? "Doesn't everyone change continually?" I ask.

She looks over toward the city. "That's not what I mean,

Rudolf. I think there is another kind of change. A greater one. One that is like death. I think it is death."

She shakes her head without looking at me. "It smells of it everywhere," she whispers. "Even in the trees and the mist. It drips at night from Heaven. The shadows are full of it. And there is weariness in one's joints. It has slipped in unobserved. I don't like to walk any more, Rudolf. It was nice with you, even when you did not understand me. At least you were there. Otherwise I should have been quite alone."

I do not know what she means. It is a strange moment. Everything is suddenly very quiet, not a leaf moves. Only Isabelle's hand with its long fingers swings over the arm of the cane chair and the green stones of her bracelet ring softly. The setting sun gives her face a tint of such warmth that it is the very opposite of any thought of death—and yet it seems to me as though a coolness were spreading like a silent dread, as though Isabelle may no longer be there when the wind begins to blow again—but then it suddenly moves in the treetops, it rustles, the ghost is gone, and Isabelle straightens up and smiles. "There are many ways to die," she says. "Poor Rudolf! You know only one. Happy Rudolf! Come, let's go into the house."

"I love you very much," I say.

Her smile deepens. "Call it what you like. What is the wind and what is stillness? They are so different and yet both are the same thing. For a while I have ridden on the painted horses of the carrousel and I have sat in the golden gondolas that are lined with blue satin and turn round and round and move up and down at the same time. You don't like them, do you?"

"No, I used to prefer the varnished stags and lions. But with you I would ride in the gondolas."

She kisses me. "The music!" she says softly. "And the

lights of the carrousel in the mist! What has become of our youth, Rudolf?"

"Yes, what?" I say, suddenly feeling tears in my eyes without understanding why. "Did we have one?"

"Who knows?"

Isabelle gets up. Above us there is a rustling in the leaves. In the glowing light of the late sun I see that a bird has let fall its droppings on my jacket. Just about where the heart is. Isabelle sees it too, and doubles up with laughter. I use my handkerchief to wipe away the excrement of the sarcastic chaffinch. "You are my youth," I say. "I know that now. You are everything it ought to be. Also that one only recognizes it when it is slipping away."

Is she slipping away from me? I think. What am I talking about? Have I, then, ever possessed her? And why should she slip away? Because she says so? Or because there is suddenly this cool, silent fear? She has said so much before and I have so often been afraid. "I love you, Isabelle," I say. "I love you more than I ever knew. It is like a wind that rises, and you think it is only a playful breeze and suddenly your heart bows down before it like a willow tree in a storm. I love you, heart of my heart, single quietude in all this confusion. I love you, you who can hear when the flowers are thirsty and when time is weary like a hunting dog in the evening. I love you and love streams out of me as though through the just-opened gate of an unknown garden. I do not altogether understand it and I am amazed at it and am still a little ashamed of my big words, but they tumble out of me and resound and do not ask my leave; someone whom I do not know is speaking out of me, and I do not know whether it is a fourth-class melodramatist or my heart, which is no longer afraid—"

With a start Isabelle has stopped walking. We are in the same *allée* through which, that other time, she walked back naked in the night, but everything now is different. The *allée* is full of the red light of evening, full of unlived youth, of melancholy, and of a happiness that trembles between sobbing and jubilation. It is no longer an *allée* of trees; it is an avenue of unreal light, where trees bend toward each other like dark fans striving to contain it, a light we stand in as though we were almost weightless, soaked in it, like cakes on Sylvester's Eve drenched in rum until they are ready to fall apart. "You do love me?" Isabelle whispers.

"I love you and I know I shall never love anyone else the way I love you because I shall never again be as I am at this moment, which is passing while I speak of it and which I cannot keep even if I were to give my life—"

She looks at me with great, shining eyes. "Now at last you know!" she whispers. "Now at last you have felt it—the nameless happiness and the sadness and the dream and the double face! It is the rainbow, Rudolf, and you can walk across it, but if you have doubts you will fall! Do you believe that at last?"

"Yes," I murmur, knowing that I believe it and that a moment ago I believed it too, and that I already do not quite believe it. The light is still strong, but at the edges it is already gray; dark patches push slowly forward and the contagion of thought breaks out again beneath them, just covered over, but not healed. The miracle has passed me by; it has touched but not changed me; I still have the same name and I know I will probably bear it to the end of my days; I am no phoenix; resurrection is not for me; I have tried to fly but I am tumbling like a dazzled, awkward rooster back to earth, back behind the barbed wires.

"Don't be sad," Isabelle says, watching me.

"I can't walk on the rainbow, Isabelle," I say. "But I should like to. Who can?"

She brings her face close to my ear. "No one," she says.

"No one? Not even you?"

She shakes her head. "No one," she repeats. "But it's enough to have the longing."

The light is rapidly becoming gray. Once before everything was like this, I think, but I cannot remember when. I feel Isabelle near me and suddenly I take her in my arms. We kiss as if we were desperate and accursed, like people being torn apart forever. "I have failed in everything," I say breathlessly. "I love you, Isabelle."

"Quiet!" she whispers. "Don't speak!"

The pale patch at the end of the *allée* begins to glow. We walk toward it and stop at the park gate. The sun has disappeared and the fields are colorless; but in contrast a mighty sunset hangs over the woods and the city looks as though its streets were burning.

We stand for a time. "What arrogance," Isabelle says suddenly, "to believe that a life has a beginning and an end!"

I do not immediately understand her. Behind us the garden is already settling itself for the night; but in front, beyond the iron lattice, a wild alchemy flames and seethes. A beginning and an end? I think, and then I comprehend her meaning; it is arrogant to try to isolate and define a tiny existence in this seething and hissing and to make our meager consciousness the judge of its own duration, whereas it is at most a snowflake briefly floating on its surface. Beginning and end, invented words for an invented concept of time and the vanity of an amoeba-like consciousness unwilling to be submerged in a greater one.

"Isabelle," I say. "You sweet, beloved life, I think I have finally felt what love is! It is life, nothing but life, the highest reach of the wave toward the evening sky, toward the paling stars and toward itself—the reach that is always in vain, the mortal reach toward what is immortal—but sometimes Heaven bends down to the wave and they meet for an instant and then it is no longer piracy on the one hand

and rejection on the other, no longer lack and superfluity and the falsification of the poets, it is—"

I break off. "I don't know what I'm saying," I tell her. "It's like a rushing stream and perhaps part of it is lies, but if so they are lies because words are deceptive and like cups used to catch a fountain—but you, you will understand me even without words; it is so new for me I can't express it; I didn't know that even my breath can love and my nails can love and even my death, and to hell with how long it lasts and whether I can hold on to it or express it—"

"I understand," Isabelle says.

"You understand?"

She nods with sparkling eyes. "I was worried about you, Rudolf."

Why should she be worried about me? I wonder. After all, I'm not sick. "Worried?" I say. "Why worry about me?"

"Worried," she repeats. "But now I'm not any more. Farewell, Rudolf."

I look at her and hold her hands tight. "Why do you want to go? Have I said something wrong?"

She shakes her head and tries to free her hands. "Yes, I have!" I say. "It was false! It was arrogant, it was words, it was a speech—"

"Don't spoil it, Rudolf! Why do you always have to spoil the things you want the minute you have them?"

"Yes," I say. "Why?"

"The fire without smoke or ashes. Don't spoil it. Farewell, Rudolf."

What is this? I think. It is like a play, but it cannot be one! Is this farewell? But we have often said farewell, every evening. I hold Isabelle tight. "We'll stay together," I say.

She nods and lays her head on my shoulder and I suddenly feel her crying. "Why are you crying?" I ask. "After all, we're happy!"

"Yes," she says and kisses me and frees herself. "Good-by, Rudolf."

"Why are you saying good-by? This is not a leave-taking! I'll come again tomorrow."

She looks at me. "Oh, Rudolf," she says as though again there were something she could not make clear to me. "How is one ever to be able to die when one cannot say good-by?"

"Yes," I say. "How? I don't understand that either. Neither the one nor the other."

We are standing in front of the pavilion where she lives. No one is in the hallway. A bright scarf is lying on one of the cane chairs. "Come," Isabelle says suddenly.

I hesitate for an instant, but now I cannot say no again and so I follow her upstairs. She walks into her room without looking around. I stand in the doorway. With a quick gesture she kicks off her light gold shoes and lays herself on the bed. "Come, Rudolf!" she says.

I sit down beside her. I do not want to disappoint her again, but I do not know what to do nor what I am to say if a nurse or Wernicke comes in. "Come," Isabelle says.

I lean back and she lays herself in my arms. "At last," she murmurs, "Rudolf." And after a few deep breaths she falls asleep.

The room grows dark. The window is pale in the oncoming night. I hear Isabelle's breath and now and again murmurs from the next room. Suddenly she wakes with a start. She thrusts me from her and I feel her body go rigid. She holds her breath. "It is I," I say. "I, Rudolf."

"Who?"

"I, Rudolf. I have stayed with you."

"You have slept here?"

Her voice has changed. It is high and breathless. "I have stayed here," I say.

"Go!" she whispers. "Go at once!"

I do not know whether she recognizes me. "Where is the light?" I ask.

"No light! No light! Go! Go!"

I stand up and feel my way to the door. "Don't be afraid, Isabelle," I say.

She twists about on the bed as though trying to pull the blankets over her. "Do go!" she whispers in her high, altered voice. "Otherwise she'll see you, Ralph! Quick!"

I close the door behind me and go down the stairs. The night nurse is sitting in the hall. She knows I have permission to visit Isabelle. "Is she quiet?" she asks.

I nod and walk across the garden to the gate through which the sick and the well come and go. What was that now? I think. Ralph, who can he be? She has never called me that before. And why did she think I must not be seen? I have often been in her room in the evening.

I walk down toward the city. Love, I think, and my high-flown speeches recur to me. I feel an almost unbearable longing and a faint horror and something like a desire to escape. I walk faster and faster toward the city with its lights, its warmth, its vulgarity, its misery, its commonplaceness, and its healthy revulsion against secrets and chaos, whatever names they may go by.

During the night I am awakened by voices. I open the window and see Sergeant Major Knopf being carried home. It is the first time this has happened; he has always got back under his own power even when schnaps was running out of his eyes. He is groaning loudly. Lights go on in a few windows.

"Damned drunkard!" a voice screeches from one of them. It is the widow Konersmann, who has been lying in wait there. She has nothing to do and is the neighborhood snoop. I have had reason to suspect that she is spying on Georg and Lisa too.

"Shut your trap!" an anonymous hero answers from the dark street.

I don't know whether he knows the widow Konersmann. In any case, after a few seconds of silent indignation such a deluge of abuse descends upon him, upon Knopf, upon the customs of the city, of the country, and of humanity that the street re-echoes.

Finally the widow stops. Her last words are that Hindenburg, the bishop, the police, and the employer of the unknown hero will be informed. "Shut your trap, you disgusting old hag!" replies the man, who seems, under cover of darkness, to possess unusual staying power. "Herr Knopf is seriously ill. I wish it was you."

The widow immediately bursts forth again with redoubled energy, a thing no one would have thought possible. With the aid of a pocket flashlight she is trying to identify the malefactor from her window, but the beam is too weak. "I know who you are!" she screeches. "You are Heinrich Brüggemann! Imprisonment is what you'll get for insulting a helpless widow, you murderer! And as for your mother—"

I stop listening. The widow has a good audience. Almost all the windows are open now. Grunts and applause come from them. I go downstairs.

Knopf is just being brought into the courtyard. He is white, perspiration is running down his face, and the Nietzsche mustache hangs moistly over his lips. With a scream he suddenly frees himself, reels forward a few steps, and unexpectedly springs at the obelisk. He embraces it with both arms and legs like a frog, presses himself against the granite and howls.

I look around. Behind me stands Georg in his purple pajamas, behind him old Frau Kroll without her teeth, in a blue bathrobe, with curling papers in her hair, and behind her Heinrich, who, to my astonishment, is in pajamas without either steel helmet or decorations. However, the pajamas are striped in the Prussian colors, black and white.

"What's the trouble?" Georg asks. "Delirium tremens? Again?"

Knopf has already had it a few times. He saw white elephants coming out of the wall and airships that go through keyholes. "Worse," says the man who has held his ground against the widow Konersmann. It is in fact Heinrich Brüggemann, the plumber. "His liver and kidneys. He thinks they have burst."

"Why are you bringing him here then? Why not to St. Mary's Hospital?"

"He won't go to the hospital."

The Knopf family appear. In front Frau Knopf, behind her the three daughters, all four rumpled, sleepy, and terrified. Knopf howls aloud under a new attack. "Have you telephoned for a doctor?" Georg asks.

"Not yet. We had our hands full getting him here. He wanted to jump into the river."

The four female heads form a mourning chorus around the sergeant major. Heinrich, too, has gone up to him and is trying to persuade him as a man, a comrade, a soldier, and a German to let go of the obelisk and go to bed, especially since the obelisk is swaying under Knopf's weight. Not only is Knopf in danger from the obelisk, Heinrich explains, but the firm would have to hold him responsible if anything happened to it. It is costly, highly polished SS granite and will certainly be damaged if it falls.

Knopf cannot understand him; with wide-open eyes he is whinnying like a horse who has seen a ghost. I hear Georg in the office telephoning for a doctor. Lisa enters the courtyard in a slightly rumpled evening dress of white satin. She is in blooming health and smells strongly of kümmel. "Cordial greetings from Gerda," she says to me. "She wants you to show up some time."

At this instant a pair of lovers shoots at a gallop from behind the crosses and out of the courtyard. Wilke appears in raincoat and nightgown; Kurt Bach, the other freethinker, follows in black pajamas with a Russian blouse and belt. Knopf continues to howl.

Thank God it is not far to the hospital. The doctor appears shortly. The situation is hurriedly explained to him. It is impossible to pry Knopf loose from the obelisk. And so his comrades pull down his trousers far enough for his skinny rear cheeks to be bared. The doctor, accustomed to difficult situations by his war experience, swabs Knopf with cotton dipped in alcohol, hands Georg a small flashlight, and drives a hypodermic into Knopf's brilliantly lighted posterior. Knopf half looks around, lets go a resounding fart, and slides down from the obelisk. The doctor has jumped back as though Knopf had shot him. Knopf's escorts pick him up. He is still holding on to the foot of the obelisk with his hands, but his resistance is broken. I understand why he rushed to the obelisk in his dread; he has spent beautiful, carefree moments there free of renal colic.

They carry him into the house. "It was to be expected," Georg says to Brüggemann. "How did it happen?"

Brüggemann shakes his head. "I've no idea. He had just won a bet against a man from Münster. Named correctly a schnaps from Spatenbräu and one from Blume's Restaurant. The man from Münster brought them in his car. I was umpire. Then while the man from Münster is fiddling with his wallet, Knopf suddenly gets white as a sheet and begins to sweat. Right after that he is on the floor writhing and vomiting and howling. You've seen the rest. And do you know the worst of it? In all the confusion that fellow from Münster ran off without paying the bet. None of us knows him and in the excitement we didn't get his license number."

"That is indeed horrible," Georg says.

"Fate is what I'd call it."

"Fate," I remark. "If you want to avoid your fate, Herr Brüggemann, then don't go back by way of Hackenstrasse. The widow Konersmann is checking the passers-by; she has borrowed a strong flashlight and she has that in one hand and a beer bottle in the other. Isn't that right, Lisa?"

Lisa nods energetically. "It's a full bottle. If she cracks you on the skull with that, you'll be cooled off for good."

"Damn it!" Brüggemann says. "How can I get out? Is this a blind alley?"

"Fortunately not," I reply. "You can work your way through the back gardens to Bleibtreustrasse. I advise you to leave soon; it's getting light."

Brüggemann disappears. Heinrich Kroll is examining the obelisk for damage, then he likewise disappears. "Such is man," Wilke says rather platitudinously, nodding up at Knopf's windows and over at the garden through which Brüggemann is creeping. Then he starts to move up the stairs again to his workshop. Apparently he is sleeping there tonight and not working.

"Have you observed more floral manifestations on the part of spirits?" I ask.

"No, but I have ordered some books on the subject."

Frau Kroll has suddenly realized that she has forgotten her teeth and takes flight. Kurt Bach is devouring Lisa's bare, brown shoulders with the eye of a connoisseur, but moves on when he finds no answering look.

"Is the old man going to die?" Lisa asks.

"Probably," Georg replies. "It's a wonder he hasn't been dead long since."

The doctor comes out of Knopf's house. "What's the trouble?" Georg asks.

"His liver; it's been due for a long time. I don't think he'll make it this time. Everything wrong. A day or two and it will be all over."

Knopf's wife appears. "You understand, not a drop of alcohol!" the doctor tells her. "Have you searched his bedroom?"

"Thoroughly, Herr Doctor. My daughter and I. We found two more bottles of that devil's brew. Here!"

She gets the bottles, uncorks them and is about to empty them. "Stop!" I say. "That's not entirely necessary. The important thing is that Knopf shouldn't have any, isn't that right, Doctor?"

"Of course."

A strong smell of good schnaps arises. "What am I to do with them in the house?" Frau Knopf complains. "He'll find them anywhere. He's a terrific bloodhound."

"We can relieve you of that responsibility."

Frau Knopf hands one bottle to the doctor and one to me. The doctor throws me a glance. "One man's destroyer is another's nightingale," he says, leaving.

Frau Knopf closes the door behind her. Only Lisa, Georg, and I remain outside. "The doctor thinks that he's going to die, doesn't he?" Lisa asks.

Georg nods. His purple pajamas look black in the late night. Lisa shivers and stands still. *"Servus,"* I say and leave them alone.

From above I see the widow Konersmann like a shadow on patrol in front of her house. She is still on the lookout for Brüggemann. After a while I hear a door being gently closed downstairs. I stare into the night, thinking of Knopf and then of Isabelle. Just as I am getting sleepy I see the widow Konersmann crossing the street. No doubt she believes Brüggemann is hiding and she runs the beam of her flashlight around our courtyard. In front of me on the window sill rests the old rain pipe I used to terrify Knopf. Now

I almost regret it. But then I catch sight of the circle of light wavering across our courtyard and I cannot resist. Cautiously I bend forward and breathe into the pipe in a deep voice: "Who disturbs me here?" and add a sigh.

The widow Konersmann stands still as a post. Then the circle of light begins to dance frantically across the courtyard and the tombstones. "May God have mercy on your soul too—" I breathe. I should like to imitate Brüggemann's style of talking, but control myself. On the strength of what I have said so far the widow Konersmann cannot file a complaint if she should find out what has happened.

She does not find out. She steals along the wall to the street and rushes across to her door. I can hear her begin to hiccup, then all is silent.

Chapter Twenty

Gently I get rid of Roth, the former postman. During the war this little fellow made deliveries in our section of the city. He was a sensitive man and took it very much to heart in those days that he was so often the unwilling bearer of ill tidings. In all the years of peace people had eagerly looked forward to his arrival with the mail, but during the war he became increasingly a figure of fear. He brought army draft notices and the dreaded official envelopes containing the announcement: "Fallen on the field of honor." The longer the war lasted the more he brought, and his appearance became the signal for lamentation, curses, and tears. Then one day he had to deliver one of the dreaded envelopes to himself, and a week later a second. That was too much for him. He grew silent and went quietly mad; the Post Office Department had to pension him off. That meant, for him as for so many others during the inflation, being condemned to death by slow starvation. However, a few friends looked after the lonely old man, and a couple of years after the war he began to go out again. But his mind remains confused. He thinks he is still a postman and goes about in his old visored cap, bringing people fresh news; but now, after the tidings of disaster, he wants to bring only good news. He collects old envelopes and post cards wherever he can find them and delivers them as messages from Russian prison camps. Men believed dead are still alive, he announces. They have not been killed. Soon they will come home.

I look at the card he has thrust upon me. It is a very ancient printed notice, advertising the Prussian lottery—an empty joke in these days of the inflation. Roth must have fished it out of a wastebasket somewhere; it is addressed to a butcher named Sack, who has been dead for years. "Many thanks," I say. "This is wonderful news!"

Roth nods. "They'll soon be back from Russia, our soldiers."

"Yes, of course."

"They will all come home. It will just take time. Russia is so big."

"Your sons too, I hope."

Roth's faded eyes light up. "Yes, mine too. I've already had word."

"Once again, many thanks," I say.

Roth smiles without looking at me and moves on. At first the Post Office Department tried to keep him from his rounds and even asked that he be imprisoned; but the townspeople opposed this, and now he is left in peace. In one of the rightist inns, to be sure, some of the regular patrons recently hit on the idea of sending Roth around to their political enemies with scurrilous letters—and to unmarried women with salacious messages. They thought it a side-splitting notion. Heinrich Kroll, too, considered it robust, earthy humor. Among his equals in the inn Heinrich is, by the way, a quite different man; he is even considered a wit.

Roth has naturally long since forgotten which houses

have suffered bereavement. He distributes his cards at random and, although one of the nationalistic beer drinkers went with him to point out from a distance the houses for which the abusive letters were intended, now and again mistakes occurred. So it was that a letter addressed to Lisa was delivered to Vicar Bodendiek. It contained an invitation to sexual intercourse, in exchange for a payment of ten million marks, at one o'clock in the morning in the bushes behind St. Mary's. Bodendiek crept up upon the observers like an Indian, suddenly appeared among them, seized two of them, knocked their heads together, without asking questions, and gave a fleeing third such a mighty kick that he shot into the air and barely succeeded in getting away. Only then did Bodendiek, that expert collector of penitents, put his questions to the two captives, re-enforcing them by blows on the ear with his huge peasant fist. The confessions were quickly forthcoming, and since both captives were Catholic, he asked for their names and ordered them to appear next day either at confession or at the police station. Naturally they preferred confession. Bodendiek gave them the *ego te absolvo* and in doing so followed the procedure the cathedral pastor had used with me—he ordered them not to drink for a week and then to appear at confession again. Since both feared excommunication, they turned up again, and Bodendiek mercilessly ordered them to come each ensuing week and not to drink. Thus he made them into abstemious, ill-tempered, first-class Christians. He never discovered that the third sinner was Major Wolkenstein, who, as a result of the kick he received, had to undergo treatment for his prostate, and, in consequence, became more belligerent politically and finally joined the Nazis.

The doors of Knopf's house are open. The sewing machines are humming. This morning bolts of black cloth were brought home, and now mother and daughters are at work on their mourning weeds. The sergeant major is not yet dead, but the doctor has said it can only be a matter of hours or, at most, days. He has given Knopf up. Since the family would consider it a serious blow to their reputation to enter the presence of death in bright clothes, hasty preparations are under way. At the moment Knopf draws his final breath, the family will be provided with black garments, a widow's veil for Frau Knopf, thick black stockings for all four, and black hats as well. Bourgeois respectability will have its due.

Georg's bald head floats toward me like half a cheese above the window sill. He is accompanied by Weeping Oskar.

"How's the dollar doing?" I ask as they enter.

"Exactly one billion at twelve o'clock," Georg replies. "We can celebrate it as a jubilee if you like."

"So we can. And when are we going broke?"

"When we have sold out. What will you have to drink, Herr Fuchs?"

"Whatever you have. Too bad there's no vodka in Werdenbrück!"

"Vodka? Were you in Russia during the war?"

"And how! I was commandant of a cemetery there, as a matter of fact. What fine days those were!"

We stare at Oskar questioningly. "Fine days?" I ask. "You say that when you're so sensitive you can weep on request?"

"They were fine days," Weeping Oskar announces firmly, sniffing at his schnaps as though he thought we intended to poison him. "Lots to eat and drink, agreeable duties far behind the front—what more can you ask? A fellow gets used to death fast enough, the way you do to a contagious disease."

Oskar sips his schnaps in a dandified fashion. We are a

little confused by the profundity of his philosophy. "Some people get used to death the way you do to a fourth man in a game of skat," I say. "Liebermann, the gravedigger, for instance. For him a job in the cemetery is like working in a garden. But an artist like you!"

Oskar smiles in a superior way. "There's a tremendous difference! Liebermann lacks true metaphysical sensitivity. Awareness of eternal death and recurrence."

Georg and I look at each other in amazement. Are we to consider Weeping Oskar a poet *manqué*. "Do you have that all the time?" I ask. "This awareness of death and recurrence?"

"More or less. At least unconsciously. Don't you have it, gentlemen?"

"We have it rather sporadically," I reply. "Principally before meals."

"One day word came that His Majesty was going to visit us," Oskar says dreamily. "God, what excitement! Fortunately there were two other cemeteries nearby and we could trade."

"Trade what?" Georg asks. "Tombstones? Or flowers?"

"Oh, all that was taken care of. True Prussian efficiency, you know. No, corpses."

"Corpses?"

"Corpses, of course! Not because they were corpses, of course, but for what they had once been. It goes without saying that every cemetery had lots of privates as well as lance corporals, noncoms, vice sergeant majors, and lieutenants—but trouble began when it came to higher commissioned officers. My colleague at the nearest cemetery, for example, had three majors; I had none. But to make up for that I had two lieutenant colonels and one colonel. I traded him one of my lieutenant colonels for two majors. I got a fat goose out of the deal besides; my colleague felt it was such a disgrace not to have any lieutenant colonels. He didn't see how he could meet His Majesty without a single dead lieutenant colonel."

Georg hides his face in his hand. "I dare not think of it even now."

Oskar nods and lights a thin cigar. "But that was nothing compared to the other cemetery commandant," he remarks contentedly. "He didn't have any brass at all. Not even a major. Lieutenants, of course, in quantity. He was in despair. I had a well-balanced assortment but just to be obliging I finally traded him one of the majors I got for my lieutenant colonel in exchange for two captains and a full sergeant major. I had captains myself, but a full sergeant major was rare. You know those swine always sat way behind the front and almost never got killed; that's why they were such beastly slave drivers—well, I took all three to be agreeable and because it gave me joy to have a full sergeant major who couldn't shout at me."

"Didn't you have a general?" I ask.

Oskar raises his hands. "A general! A general killed in action is as rare as—" He searches for a comparison. "Are you beetle collectors?"

"No," Georg and I reply in chorus.

"Too bad," Oskar says. "Well, as the giant stag beetle, Lucanus Cervus, or, if you are butterfly collectors, as the death's head moth. Otherwise, how could there be wars? Even my colonel died of a stroke. But this colonel—" Suddenly Weeping Oskar grins. It produces a strange effect; from so much weeping his face has acquired as many folds as a bloodhound's and usually wears the same look of sad solemnity. "Well, the other commandant naturally had to have a staff officer. He offered me anything I wanted, but my collection was complete; I even had my full sergeant major, to whom I had given a nice corner grave in a conspicuous spot. Finally I gave in—for three dozen bottles of the best vodka. I gave him my colonel, to be sure, not my lieutenant colonel. For thirty-six bottles! Hence, gentlemen, my present taste for vodka. Of course you can't get it here."

By way of compensation Oskar pours himself another glass of schnaps. "Why did you go to so much trouble?" Georg asks. "You had to transfer all the bodies. Why didn't you simply put up a few crosses with fictitious names and let it go at that. You could even have had a lieutenant general."

Oskar is shocked. "But, Herr Kroll!" he says in mild reproof. "How could we risk that? It would have been forgery. Perhaps even desecration of the dead—"

"It would only have been desecration if you had given a dead major some lower rank," I say. "Not if you promoted a private to general for a day."

"You could have put fictitious crosses on empty graves," Georg adds. "Then it would not have been desecration of the dead at all."

"It would still have been forgery. And it might have been discovered," Oskar replies. "Perhaps through the gravediggers. And what then? Besides—a false general?" He shudders. "His Majesty surely knew his generals."

We let it rest at that. So does Oskar. "You know the funniest thing about the whole affair?" he asks.

We are silent. The question can only be rhetorical and requires no answer.

"On the day before the inspection the whole thing was called off. His Majesty did not come at all. We had planted a field of primroses and narcissuses."

"Did you give back the corpses?" Georg asks.

"That would have been too much work. Besides, the papers had been changed. And the families had been notified that their dead had been transferred. That often happened. Cemeteries came under fire and then everything had to be rearranged. The only one who was furious was the commandant who had given me the vodka. He and his chauffeur even tried to break in and get the cases back, but I had found an excellent hiding place. An empty grave." Oskar yawns. "Yes, those were the days! I had several thousand graves under me. Today—" he takes a paper out of his pocket—"two medium-sized headstones with marble plaques, Herr Kroll, that, alas, is all."

I am walking through the darkening gardens of the asylum. Isabelle was at devotion today for the first time in a long while. I am looking for her, but can't find her. Instead, I run into Bodendiek, who smells of incense and cigars. "What are you at the moment?" he asks. "Atheist, Buddhist, skeptic, or already on the way back to God?"

"Everyone is constantly on the way to God," I reply, weary of argument. "It just depends on what you mean by that."

"Bravo," Bodendiek says. "Wernicke is looking for you, I believe. What makes you fight so stubbornly about something as simple as faith?"

"Because there is more rejoicing in heaven over one fighting skeptic than over ninety and nine vicars who have been singing hosannas since childhood," I reply.

Bodendiek looks pleased. I don't want to get into a fight with him; I remember the kick in the bushes behind St. Mary's. "When will I see you at confession?" he asks.

"Like the two sinners of St. Mary's?"

That startles him. "So, you know about them? Well, no, not like that. You will come of your own free will! Don't wait too long!"

I make no reply and we part cordially. As I walk toward Wernicke's room falling leaves flutter through the air like bats. Everywhere there is the smell of earth and autumn. What has become of the summer? I think. It was hardly here!

Wernicke pushes a pile of papers aside. "Have you seen Fräulein Terhoven?" he asks.

"In church. Not since."

He nods. "Don't meet her any more for the time being."

"Fine," I say. "Any further orders?"

"Don't be a fool! Those aren't orders. I'm doing what I consider best for my patient." He looks at me more closely. "You aren't by any chance in love?"

"In love? With whom?"

"With Fräulein Terhoven, who else? She's pretty, after all. Damn it, that's a factor in the situation I hadn't thought about."

"Neither had I. And what situation?"

"Then it's all right." He laughs. "Besides, it wouldn't have been bad for you at all."

"Really?" I reply. "Up to now I had thought that only Bodendiek was God's representative here. Now we have you as well. You know exactly what's bad and what's good, eh?"

Wernicke is silent for a moment. "So it really happened," he says presently. "Well, what does it matter? Too bad I couldn't have listened to you two! Those must have been fine mooncalf dialogues! Take a cigar. Have you noticed that it's autumn?"

"Yes," I say. "That's something I can agree with you about."

Wernicke offers me the cigar box. I take one just in order not to hear, if I refuse, that this is a further sign of being in love. I am suddenly so miserable I want to vomit. Nevertheless, I light the cigar.

"I owe you an explanation," Wernicke says. "Her mother! She has been here twice. She finally broke down. Husband died early; mother pretty, young; friend of the family, with whom the daughter was obviously infatuated; mother and family friend careless, daughter jealous, surprises them, perhaps has been observing them for some time—you understand?"

"No," I say. All this is as repulsive to me as Wernicke's stinking cigar.

"Well then, we've got that far," Wernicke continues with gusto. "Daughter hates mother for it, revulsion complex, escape through a splitting of the personality—typical flight from reality and recourse to a dream life. Mother then marries the family friend, which brings the whole thing to a crisis—understand now?"

"No."

"But it's so simple," Wernicke says impatiently. "The only hard thing was to get to the heart of the matter, but now—" He rubs his hands. "Besides, by good fortune the other man, the former family friend called Ralph or Rudolf or something of the sort, is no longer in the way. Divorced three months ago, killed in the last couple of weeks in an automobile accident. So the cause has been eliminated, the road is free—now at last you must catch on?"

"Yes," I say and would like to slap a chloroform mask on the cheerful scientist's mouth.

"Well, you see! Now we have to face the solution. Suddenly the mother is no longer a rival, the meeting can happen, carefully prepared for—I've been working on it for a week already and everything's going well; you've seen for yourself, Fräulein Terhoven went to devotion this evening—"

"You mean you've converted her? You, the atheist, and not Bodendiek?"

"Nonsense!" Wernicke says, irritated by my dullness. "That's not the point at all! I mean that she has become more open, more accessible, freer—didn't you notice that the last time you were here?"

"Yes."

"Well, you see!" Wernicke rubs his hands again. "Coming after the first severe shock, that was a very cheering result—"

"Was the shock, too, a result of your treatment?"

"It was in part."

I think of Isabelle in her room. "Congratulations," I say.

In his absorption Wernicke does not notice my irony. "The first short meeting and the treatment naturally brought everything back; that was the intention, of course —but since then—I have great hopes! You understand that right now I don't want anything to distract—"

"I understand. You don't want me."

Wernicke nods. "I knew you would understand! You, too, have a certain amount of scientific curiosity. For a time you were useful, but now—what's wrong with you? Are you too hot?"

"It's the cigar. Too strong."

"On the contrary!" the tireless scientist explains. "These Brazilians look strong—but they're the mildest of all."

That's true of many other things, I think, laying the weed aside.

"The human mind!" Wernicke says enthusiastically. "When I was young I wanted to be a sailor and adventurer and explorer of primeval forests—ridiculous! The greatest adventure lies here!" He taps his forehead. "I guess I explained that to you once before."

"Yes," I say. "Often."

The green husks of the chestnuts rustle under my feet. In love like a mooncalf! I think. What does that fact-finding beetle mean? If it were only as simple as that! I walk to the gate and almost bump into a woman coming slowly from the opposite direction. She is wearing a fur stole; she does not belong to the institution. I see a pale, faded face in the darkness, and the scent of perfume lingers behind her. "Who was that?" I ask the watchman at the exit.

"Someone to see Dr. Wernicke. Been here a couple of times before. I believe she has a patient here."

Her mother, I think, hoping it is not true. I stop outside and stare up at the buildings. A sudden rage seizes me, anger at having been ridiculous and then a contemptible self-pity—but in the end all that is left is helplessness. I lean against a chestnut tree and feel the cool trunk and do not know what to do or what I want.

I go on and as I walk I feel better. Let them talk, Isabelle, I think, let them laugh at us as mooncalves. You sweet, beloved life, flying untrammeled, walking safely where others sink, skimming where others tramp in high boots, but caught and bleeding in webs and on boundaries the others cannot see, what do they want of you? Why must they so greedily pull you back into their world, into our world; why won't they permit you your butterfly existence beyond cause and effect and time and death? Is it jealousy? Is it insensibility? Or is it true, as Wernicke says, that he must rescue you from something worse, from nameless fears that would come, fiercer than those that he himself conjured up, and finally from decline into toadlike idiocy? But is he sure he can? Is he sure that he will not break you with his attempts at rescue or force you more quickly into what he wants to save you from? Who knows? What does this butterfly collector, this scientist, know of flying, of the wind, of the dangers and ecstasies of the days and nights outside space and time? Does he know the future? Has he drunk the moon? Does he know that plants scream? He laughs at that. For him it is all just a retreat reaction caused by a brutal experience. But is he a prophet who can see in advance what is going to happen? Is he God to know what must happen? What did he know about me? That it would be quite all right if I were a little in love? But what do I myself know about that? It bursts forth and streams and has no end; what intimation did I have of it? How can one be so devoted to someone else? Didn't I myself constantly reject it during those weeks that are now as unattainable as the sunset on the far horizon? But why do I lament? What am I afraid of? May not everything turn out all right and Isabelle be cured and—

There I stop short. What then? Will she not leave? And then her mother will be part of the picture, with a fur stole, with discreet perfume, with relations in the background and ambitions for her daughter. Isn't she lost to me, somebody who can't even scrape together enough money to buy a suit? And is that perhaps the reason I am so confused? Out of stupid egoism—and all the rest is just decoration?

I step into a cellar café. A few chauffeurs are sitting there; behind the buffet a wavy mirror reflects my haggard face, and in front of me in a glass case lie a half-dozen dry rolls and some sardines that have turned up their tails with age. I drink a schnaps and feel as though my stomach had a deep, tearing hole in it. I eat the rolls and sardines and some old, cracked Swiss cheese; it tastes awful, but I stuff it into me and then devour some sausages that are so red they can almost whinny, and I feel more and more unhappy and more and more hungry and as if I could eat the whole buffet.

"Boy, you have a wonderful appetite," says the owner.

"Yes," I say. "Have you anything else?"

"Pea soup. Thick pea soup; if you just break some bread into it—"

"All right, give me the pea soup."

I devour the pea soup, and the owner brings me as a gift another slice of bread with lard on it. I polish it off too, and am hungrier and more unhappy than before. The chauffeurs begin to take an interest in me. "I once knew a man who could eat thirty hard-boiled eggs at a sitting," one of them says.

"That's impossible. He would die; that's been proved scientifically."

I stare at the scientist angrily. "Have you seen it happen?" I ask.

"It's a fact," he replies.

"It's not a fact at all. The only thing that has been scientifically proved is that chauffeurs die young."

"Why would that be?"

"Because of the gasoline fumes. Slow poisoning."

The owner appears with a kind of Italian salad. A sporting interest has prevailed over his sleepiness. Where he got the salad and mayonnaise is a puzzle. Surprisingly, it is fresh. Perhaps it is part of his own supper that he has sacrificed. I consume it too, and leave—with a burning stomach that still feels empty—and no whit comforted.

The streets are gray and dimly lighted. There are beggars everywhere. They are not the familiar beggars of other times—now they are amputees and the dispossessed and the unemployed and quiet old people with faces that look as though they were made of rumpled, colorless paper. I am suddenly ashamed that I have eaten so thoughtlessly. If I had given what I have devoured to two or three of these people, they would be filled for a night and I would be no hungrier than I am. I take what money I have with me out of my pocket and give it away. It is not much and I am not impoverishing myself; by ten o'clock tomorrow morning, when the dollar is announced, it will have lost a quarter of its worth. This fall the German mark has had tenfold galloping consumption. The beggars know it and disappear immediately, since every minute is costly; the price of soup can rise several million marks in an hour. It all depends on whether the proprietor has to market tomorrow or not—and also on whether he is businesslike or himself a victim. If he is a victim, then he is manna for the smaller victims because he raises his prices too late.

I walk on. Some people are coming out of the city hospital. They are clustered around a woman whose right arm is in a sling. A smell of disinfectants comes from her. The hospital stands in the darkness like a mountain of light. Almost all the windows are bright; every room seems to be occupied. In the inflation people die fast. That's something we have noticed too.

In Grossestrasse I go to a delicatessen store that is usually open after the official closing time. We have made a deal with the woman who owns it. She received a medium-sized headstone for her husband, and we in return have a credit of six dollars at the exchange rate of September 2. Trading has long since become the style. People trade old beds for canaries and knickknacks, jewelry for potatoes, china for sausages, furniture for bread, pianos for hams, old razor blades for vegetable parings, old furs for remade military blouses, and the possessions of the dead for food. Four weeks ago Georg had a chance to acquire an almost new tuxedo in exchange for a broken marble column and foundation. He gave it up with a heavy heart simply because he is superstitious and believes that in a dead man's possessions something of the departed lingers for a long time. The widow explained to him that she had had the tuxedo chemically cleaned; therefore it was really completely new and one could assume that the chlorine fumes had driven the departed out of every seam. Georg was sorely tempted, for the tuxedo fitted him, but in the end he gave it up.

I press the latch of the door, but it is locked. Naturally, I think, staring hungrily at the display in the window. At last I walk wearily homeward. In the courtyard stand six small sandstone plaques, still virginal, no names engraved on them. Kurt Bach has turned them out. It is really a prostitution of his talent, being considered stonemason's work, but at the moment we have no commissions for dying lions or war memorials in bas-relief—therefore Kurt has been turning out a supply of very small inexpensive plaques, which we can always use—especially in the fall when, as in the spring, we can count on a large number of deaths. Grippe, hunger, bad food, and lowered resistance will see to that.

The sewing machines behind Knopf's door hum quietly. Light from the living room where the mourning clothes are being sewn shines through the glass. Old Knopf's window is dark. Probably he is already dead. We ought to put the black obelisk on his grave, I think, like a sinister stone finger pointing from earth toward heaven. For Knopf it would be a second home, and two generations of Krolls have failed to sell the dark accuser.

I go into the office. "Come in here!" Georg shouts from his room.

I open the door and stop in amazement. Georg is sitting in his easy chair, with illustrated magazines strewn in front of him as usual. The Reading Club of the Elegant World, to which he subscribes, has just supplied him with new provender. But that is not all—he is wearing a tuxedo with a starched shirt and a white vest to boot, a perfect magazine version of the fashionable bachelor. "After all!" I say. "You disregarded the warnings of instinct and succumbed to worldly self-indulgence. The widow's tuxedo!"

"Not at all!" Georg preens himself complacently. "What you see is evidence of woman's superiority in the matter of inspiration. It is a different tuxedo. The widow traded hers to a tailor for this one, and so I get paid without injury to my sensibilities. Look at this—the widow's tuxedo was lined in satin—this one has pure silk. It fits me better, too, under the arms. The price was the same in gold marks because of the inflation; the suit is more elegant. Thus, by exception, sensibility has paid out."

I look at him. The tuxedo is good but not altogether new. I avoid injuring Georg's feelings by pointing out that this suit in all likelihood comes from a dead man too. What, after all, doesn't come from the dead? Our language, our customs, our knowledge, our despair—everything. During the war, especially in the last year, Georg wore so many dead men's uniforms, sometimes still showing faded bloodstains and mended bullet holes, that his present disinclination is more than neurotic sensibility—it is rebellion and the wish for peace. For him peace means, among other things, not to have to wear dead men's clothes.

"What are the movie actresses up to—Henny Porten, Erika Morena, and the imcomparable Lia de Putti?" I ask.

"They have the same problems we do!" Georg explains. "To turn their money into commodities as fast as possible —cars, furs, tiaras, dogs, houses, stocks, and film productions —only it's easier for them than for us."

He glances lovingly at a picture of a Hollywood party. It is a ball of incomparable elegance. The gentlemen are wearing tuxedos like Georg's or tails. "When are you going to get a dress suit?" I ask.

"After I've been to my first ball in this tuxedo. I'll skip off to Berlin for that! For three days! Some time when the inflation is over and money is money again and not water. Meanwhile, I'm making preparations, as you see."

"You still need patent-leather shoes," I say, irritated to my own surprise at this self-satisfied man of the world.

Georg takes the gold twenty-mark piece out of his vest pocket, tosses it into the air, catches it, and puts it back without a word. I watch him with gnawing envy. There he sits, with no cares to speak of, in his vest pocket a cigar that will not taste like gall, as Wernicke's Brazilian did, across the street lives Lisa, who is infatuated with him simply because his family were businessmen when her father was a day laborer. She idolized him when he was a child wearing a white collar and a sailor cap on his curls while she traipsed about in a dress made from one of her mother's old skirts—and this admiration has endured. Georg need do nothing more; his glory is secure. I don't believe Lisa even knows he is bald—for her he is still the merchant prince in a sailor suit.

"You're lucky," I say.

"I deserve to be," Georg replies, closing the copies of the reading circle *Modernitas*. Then he takes a box of sprats from the window seat and points to a half-loaf and a piece of butter. "How about a simple supper and a glance at the night life of a medium-sized city?"

They are the same sort of sprats that made my mouth water when I saw them in the store in Grossestrasse. Now I can't bear the sight of them. "You amaze me," I say. "Why are you eating here? Why aren't you dining on caviar and sea food in the former Hotel Hohenzollern, now the Reichshof?"

"I love contrast," Georg replies. "How else could I exist, a tombstone dealer in a small city with a yearning for the great world?"

He stands in full splendor at the window. Suddenly from across the street comes a husky cry of admiration. Georg turns full face, his hands in his trouser pockets to show the white vest to full advantage. Lisa dissolves, as far as that is possible for her. She draws her kimono around her, executes a kind of Arabian dance, unwraps herself, suddenly stands naked and dark, silhouetted in front of her lamp, throws the kimono on again, puts the lamp at her side and is once more warm and brown, wrapped in flying cranes, her white smile like a gardenia in her greedy mouth. Georg accepts this homage like a pasha and grants me a eunuch's share. In a single moment he has consolidated for years to come the position of the lad in the sailor suit who so impressed the tattered girl. Tuxedos are nothing new to Lisa, who is at home among the profiteers in the Red Mill; but Georg's, of course, is something entirely different. Pure gold. "You're lucky," I say again. "And how easy! Riesenfeld could burst a blood vessel, compose poems, and ruin his granite works without accomplishing what you have done by just being a mannequin."

Georg nods. "It's a secret! But I'll reveal it to you. Never do anything complicated when something simple will serve as well. It's one of the most important secrets of living. Very hard to apply. Especially for intellectuals and romanticists."

"Anything more?"

"No. But don't pose as an intellectual Hercules when a pair of new trousers will produce the same result. You won't irritate your partner and she won't have to exert herself to follow you; you remain calm and relaxed, and what you want will fall, figuratively speaking, into your lap."

"Be careful not to get grease on your silk lapels," I say. "Sprats are drippy."

"You're right," Georg takes off his coat. "One must never press one's luck. Another important rule."

He reaches once more for the sprats. "Why don't you write mottos for a calendar company?" I inquire bitterly of that cheerful purveyor of worldly wisdom. "It's a shame to waste them on the universe at large."

"I present them to you. For me they're a stimulus, not platitudes. Anyone who is melancholy by nature and has to work at a business like mine must do all he can to cheer himself up and mustn't be choosy about it. Another maxim."

I see that I cannot get the better of him and withdraw into my room as soon as the box of sprats is empty. But even there I can find no relief—not even at the piano, because of the dead or dying sergeant major—and as for funeral marches, the only possible thing to play, I have enough of them in my head as it is.

Chapter Twenty-one

In the window of old Knopf's bedroom a ghost suddenly rises. The sun, striking the panes of our window keeps me for a time from recognizing the sergeant major. So he is still alive and has dragged himself from his bed to the window. His gray head protrudes woodenly from his gray nightgown. "Just look," I say to Georg. "He doesn't intend to die between sheets. The old war horse is going to have a last look at the Werdenbrück Distilleries."

We gaze at him. His mustache hangs in a sorry tangle over his mouth. His eyes are leaden. He stares out for a while, then turns away.

"That was his last look," I say. "How touching that even such a soulless slave driver should want to gaze at the world once more before leaving it forever. A theme for Hungermann, the poet of social consciousness."

"He's taking a second look," Georg replies.

I abandon the Presto mimeographing machine, on which I have been turning out catalogue pages for our salesmen, and go back to the window. The sergeant major is standing there again. Beyond the sun-struck pane I see him raise something to his lips and drink. "His medicine!" I say. "To think that even the most hopeless wreck still clings to life! Another theme for Hungermann."

"That's not medicine," Georg replies, who has sharper eyes than mine. "Medicine doesn't come in schnaps bottles."

"What?"

We open our window. The reflection disappears, and I see that Georg is right: old Knopf is unmistakably drinking out of a schnaps bottle. "What a good idea!" I say. "His wife has filled a schnaps bottle with water so it will be easier for him to drink. There's no liquor in his room, you know; everything has been thoroughly searched."

Georg shakes his head. "If that was water he'd have hurled the bottle out of the window long ago. For as long as I've known the old man he's only used water for washing—and grudgingly at that. What he has there is schnaps; he has kept it hidden somewhere in spite of the search, and you, Ludwig, have before you the edifying spectacle of a man courageously going to meet his fate. The old sergeant major intends to fall on the field of honor with his hand at the enemy's throat."

"Oughtn't we to call his wife?"

"Do you think she could take the bottle away from him?"

"No."

"The doctor has only given him a few days at best. What difference does it make?"

"The difference between a Christian and a fatalist. Herr Knopf!" I shout. "Sergeant Major!"

I don't know whether he has heard me—but he makes a gesture as though waving to us with the bottle. Then he puts it to his mouth again. "Herr Knopf!" I shout. "Frau Knopf!"

"Too late!" Georg says.

Knopf has lowered the bottle. He makes another circular

motion with it. We wait for him to collapse. The doctor has declared that a single drop of alcohol will be fatal. After a while he fades backward into the room like a corpse sinking beneath the water. "A fine death," Georg says.

"Oughtn't we to tell the family?"

"Leave them in peace. The old man was a pest. They'll be happy that it's all over."

"I don't know; attachment sometimes takes strange forms. They could get his stomach pumped out."

"He'd fight that so hard he'd get a stroke. But telephone the doctor if your conscience is bothering you. Hirshmann."

I reach the doctor. "Old Knopf has just drunk a small bottle of schnaps," I say. "We saw it from our window."

"In one gulp?"

"In two, I believe. What has that to do with it?"

"Nothing. It was just curiosity. May he rest in peace."

"Isn't there anything to be done?"

"Nothing," Hirshmann says. "He'd have died anyway. As a matter of fact, I'm surprised he held out till today. Give him a tombstone in the shape of a bottle."

"You're a heartless man," I say.

"Not heartless, cynical. You ought to know the difference! Cynicism is heart with a minus sign, if that's any comfort to you. Have a drink in memory of the departed schnaps thrush."

I put down the telephone. "Georg," I say, "I believe it's really high time I changed my profession. It coarsens one too much."

"It doesn't coarsen, it only dulls the sensibilities."

"Even worse. It's not the thing for a member of the Werdenbrück Poets' Club. What becomes of our profound wonder, horror, and reverence in the face of death when one measures it in money or in monuments?"

"There's enough left," Georg says. "But I understand

what you mean. Now let's go to Eduard's and drink a silent toast to the old twelve-pointed stag."

In the afternoon we return. An hour later screams and cries resound from Knopf's house. "Peace to his ashes," Georg says. "Come on, we must go over and speak the customary words of comfort."

"I only hope they all have their mourning clothes ready. That's the one comfort they need at this moment."

The door is unlocked. We open it without ringing and stop short. An unexpected picture greets us. Old Knopf is standing in the room, his walking stick in his hand, dressed and ready to go out. His wife and daughters are cowering behind the three sewing machines. Knopf is screeching with rage and striking at them with his cane. Grasping the neck of the nearest sewing machine with one hand for a firm stance, he rains blows with the other. They are not very heavy blows, but Knopf is doing the best he can. Round him on the floor lie the mourning clothes.

It's easy to see what has happened. Instead of killing him, the schnaps has so enlivened the sergeant major that he has got dressed, probably with the intention of going on his usual round through the inns. Since no one has told him he is sick unto death and his wife has been too terrified of him to summon a priest to prepare him for his passage into blessedness, it has never occurred to Knopf to die. He has already survived a number of attacks and, as far as he is concerned, this is just one more. It is not hard to see why he is enraged—no one enjoys seeing that his family has written him off so completely that they are laying out precious money for mourning weeds.

"Accursed crew!" he screeches. "You were celebrating already, were you? I'll teach you!"

He misses his wife and gives a hiss of rage. She clings to

his cane. "But Father, we had to make preparations; the doctor—"

"The doctor is an idiot! Let go of my stick, you devil! Let go, I tell you, you beast!"

The little, roly-poly woman lets the stick go. The hissing drake in front of her swings it and hits one of his daughters. The three women could easily disarm the weak old man, but he has the upper hand, like a sergeant major with his recruits. The daughters are now holding onto the cane and trying tearfully to explain. Knopf will not listen. "Let go of my stick, you devil's brood! Wasting money, throwing it away, I'll teach you!"

The cane is released, Knopf strikes again, misses, and falls forward on one knee. Bubbles of saliva hang in the Nietzsche mustache as he gets up and continues to follow Zarathustra's precept by beating his harem. "Father, you'll kill yourself if you get so excited!" cry the weeping daughters. "Please be calm! We're overjoyed that you're alive! Shall we make you some coffee?"

"Coffee? I'll make you coffee! I'll beat you to a pulp, that's what I'll do, you devil's brood! Squandering all that money—"

"But Father, we can sell the things!"

"Sell! I'll sell you, you damned spendthrifts—"

"But Father, it hasn't been paid for yet!" screams Frau Knopf in utter despair.

That penetrates. Knopf lets the cane sink. "What's that?"

We step forward. "Herr Knopf," Georg says. "My congratulations!"

"Kiss my ass!" the sergeant major replies. "Can't you see I'm occupied?"

"You are overexerting yourself."

"Well? What's that to you? I'm being ruined by my family here."

"Your wife has just done a splendid bit of business. If

she sells the mourning clothes tomorrow, she will make a profit of several billion through the inflation—especially if the material hasn't been paid for."

"No, we haven't paid for it yet!" cry the quartet.

"Then you should be happy, Herr Knopf! While you've been ill the dollar has been rising fast. Without knowing it you've made a profit in your sleep."

Knopf pricks up his ears. He knows about the inflation because schnaps has become constantly more expensive. "Well, a profit," he mutters. Then he turns to his four ruffled sparrows. "Have you bought a tombstone for me too?"

"No, Father!" cry the quartet in relief—with a warning glance at us.

"And why not?" Knopf screeches furiously.

They stare at him.

"You geese!" he shouts. "Then we could sell it too! At a profit, eh?" he asks Georg.

"Only if it had been paid for. Otherwise we'd simply take it back."

"That's what you think! Then we'd sell it to Hollmann and Klotz and pay you out of the proceeds!" The sergeant major turns back to his brood. "You geese! Where's the money? If you haven't paid for the cloth, you still have the money! Bring it here!"

"Come on," Georg says. "The emotional part is over. The financial part is no concern of ours."

He is mistaken. A quarter of an hour later Knopf is standing in our office. A penetrating smell of schnaps surrounds him. "I've found out everything," he says. "Lies won't help you. My wife has confessed. She bought a tombstone from you."

"She didn't pay for it. Remember that. Now you don't have to take it."

"She bought it," the sergeant major declares threateningly. "There are witnesses. Don't try to crawl out! Yes or no?"

Georg looks at me. "All right. But it was an inquiry rather than a purchase."

"Yes or no?" Knopf snorts.

"Because we've known each other so long, let it be as you like, Herr Knopf," Georg says to quiet the old man.

"All right then. Give it to me in writing."

We look at each other. This worn-out martial skeleton has learned fast. He is trying to outsmart us.

"Why in writing?" I ask. "Pay for the stone and it's yours."

"Be silent, you betrayer!" Knopf shouts at me. "In writing!" he screeches. "For eight billion! Much too much for a piece of stone!"

"If you want it, you must pay for it immediately," I say.

Knopf fights heroically. It takes us ten minutes to defeat him. He produces eight billion of the money he has taken from his wife and pays. "In writing, now!" he growls.

He gets it in writing. Through the window I see the ladies of his family standing in their doorway. Timidly they look over at me and make signs. Knopf has robbed them of their last measly million. Meanwhile, he has been handed his receipt. "So," he says to Georg. "And now what will you pay me for the stone? I'll sell it."

"Eight billion."

"What? You double-dealer! Eight billion is what I have paid myself. What about the inflation?"

"The inflation is here. Today the stone is worth eight and a half billion. I pay you eight as the purchase price. We have to make a half-billion profit on the sale."

"What? You usurer! And I? Where's my profit? You'll just pocket that, eh?"

"Herr Knopf," I say. "If you buy a bicycle and sell it again an hour later, you won't get the full purchase price back. That's one of the facts of business; our economy rests on it."

"The economy can kiss my ass!" the incensed sergeant major declares. "A bicycle that has been bought is a used bicycle, even if you haven't ridden it. But my headstone is new."

"Theoretically it's used too," I say. "Speaking in a business way. Besides, you can't ask us to take a loss simply because you're still alive."

"Frauds! That's what you are!"

"Just keep the headstone," Georg advises him. "It's a good investment. Some time or other you'll have use for it. No family is immortal."

"I'll sell it to your competitors. To Hollmann and Klotz if you don't give me ten billion for it immediately!"

I pick up the telephone. "Come on, we'll save you the trouble. Here, call them up. Number 624."

Knopf becomes uncertain and refuses. "The same sort of shysters as you! What will the stone be worth tomorrow?"

"Perhaps a billion more. Perhaps two or three billion."

"And in a week?"

"Herr Knopf," Georg says. "If we knew the dollar exchange in advance we wouldn't be sitting here haggling with you about headstones."

"It's easily possible that you will be a trillionaire in a month," I explain.

Knopf considers this. "I'll keep the stone," he growls finally. "Too bad I've paid for it already."

"We'll buy it back any time."

"You'd like that, wouldn't you! I wouldn't dream of it without making a profit! I'll keep it as a speculation. Give it a good place." Knopf looks anxiously out of the window. "Perhaps it will rain."

"Rain doesn't hurt headstones."

"Nonsense! Then they're no longer new! I demand that mine be kept in the shed. On straw."

"Why don't you put it in your house?" Georg asks. "Then it will be protected from the cold during the winter."

"You're completely crazy, aren't you?"

"Not in the least. There are lots of admirable people who keep their coffins in their homes. Holy men, principally, and South Italians. Some even use them for beds. Wilke upstairs always sleeps in his giant coffin when he has drunk so much that he can't get home."

"It won't work!" Knopf decides. "The women! The stone is to remain here. Untouched! You'll be responsible! Insure it! At your own expense!"

By now I have had enough of this military tone. "How about holding a review every morning?" I inquire. "See to it that the polish is first class, that the tombstone is precisely lined up with the ones in front, that the base is properly drawn in like a belly, that the bushes around are standing at attention, and, if you insist, Herr Heinrich Kroll can report every day in uniform. He would certainly enjoy that."

Knopf looks at me somberly. "The world would be a better place if there were more Prussian discipline in it," he replies, and belches frighteningly. The smell of Roth schnaps is pervasive. The sergeant major has probably had nothing to eat all day. Knopf belches again, this time more softly and melodiously, stares at us for a while with the pitiless eye of a full sergeant major in retirement, turns around, almost falls, catches himself, and then wavers purposefully out of the courtyard toward the left—in the direction of the first inn, in his pocket his family's remaining billions.

Gerda is standing in front of her gas ring, making cabbage *roulades*. She has a pair of worn-down green bedroom slippers on her feet and a red checked kitchen towel draped over her right shoulder. The room smells of cabbage, fat, powder, and perfume; outside, the red leaves of the wild grapevine swing in front of the window, and autumn stares in with blue eyes.

"It's nice that you came again," Gerda says. "I'm moving out of here tomorrow."

"You are?"

She stands unconcernedly in front of the gas ring, confident of her own body. "Yes," she says. "Does that interest you?"

She turns around and looks at me. "It does interest me, Gerda," I reply. "Where are you going?"

"To the Hotel Walhalla."

"To Eduard?"

"Yes, to Eduard."

She shakes the pan with the cabbage *roulades*. "Have you anything against that?" she asks presently.

I look at her. What can I have against it? I think. I wish I did have something against it! For a moment I am tempted to lie, but I know she will see through me. "Aren't you staying on at the Red Mill?" I ask.

"I finished up there long ago. You didn't bother to find out, did you? No, I'm not going to continue. People starve in our profession. But I'll stay in this city."

"With Eduard," I say.

"Yes, with Eduard," she repeats. "He's turning the bar over to me. I'll be the barmaid."

"And you'll live in the Walhalla?"

"I'll live in the Walhalla, upstairs under the rafters, and I'll work in the Walhalla. I'm not as young as you think; I have to look for some kind of security before I find myself with no more engagements. Nothing came of the circus either. That was just a last try."

"You can go on finding engagements for years, Gerda," I say.

"You don't know anything about that. I know what I'm doing."

I glance at the red vine leaves swinging in front of the window. For no reason I feel like a shirker. My relationship with Gerda has been no more than that of a soldier on leave, but for one of every pair it is always something different.

"I wanted to tell you myself," Gerda says.

"You wanted to tell me it's all over between us?"

She nods. "I play fair. Eduard is the only one who has offered me something secure—a job—and I know what that's worth. I'm not going to cheat." She laughs suddenly. "Farewell to youth. Come, the cabbage *roulades* are done."

She puts the plates on the table. I look at her and am suddenly sad. "Well, how is your heavenly love affair getting on?" she asks.

"It's not, Gerda. Not at all."

She serves the meal. "The next time you have a small affair," she says, "don't tell the girl anything about your other loves. Do you understand?"

"Yes," I reply. "I'm sorry, Gerda."

'For God's sake, shut up and eat!"

I look at her. She is eating calmly and matter-of-factly, her face is clear and firm, she has been used from childhood on to living independently, she understands her existence and has adjusted herself to it. She has everything I lack, and I wish I were in love with her and that life were clear and foreseeable and one always knew what one needed to know about it—not very much but that little with certainty.

"You know, I don't want much," Gerda says. "I grew up among blows and then was thrown out. Now I have had enough of my profession and I'm going to settle down. Eduard is not the worst."

"He is vain and stingy," I declare and am at once angry at myself for having said it.

"That's better than being slovenly and extravagant, if you're going to marry someone."

"You're going to get married?" I ask in amazement. "Do you really believe that? He'll exploit you and then marry the daughter of some rich hotel owner."

"He hasn't promised me anything. I just have a contract for the bar, for three years. In the course of those years he will discover that he can't get along without me."

"You have changed," I say.

"Oh, you sheep! I have just made up my mind."

"Soon you will join Eduard in cursing at us about those coupons."

"Do you still have some?"

"Enough for another month and a half."

Gerda laughs. "I won't curse. Besides, you paid for them properly at the time."

"It was our one successful financial transaction." I watch Gerda as she clears away the plates. "I'll turn them all over to Georg," I say. "I'll not be coming to the Walhalla any more."

She turns around. She is smiling, but her eyes are not. "Why not?" she asks.

"I don't know. It's the way I feel. But perhaps I shall, after all."

"Of course you'll come! Why shouldn't you?"

"Yes, why not?" I say dispiritedly.

From below come the subdued tones of the player piano. I get up and walk to the window. "How fast this year has gone!" I say.

"Yes," Gerda replies, leaning against me. "Idiotic!" she murmurs, "when once you find someone you like, it has to be somebody like you, somebody who just doesn't fit." She pushes me away. "Now go—go to your divine love—God, what do you know about women?"

"Not a thing."

She smiles. "Don't try to either, baby. It's better this way. Now go! Here, take this with you."

She gets a medal and gives it to me. "What's that?" I ask.

"A man who carries people through the water. He brings luck."

"Has he brought you luck?"

"Luck?" Gerda replies. "That can mean many different things. Perhaps. Now go."

She pushes me out and closes the door behind me. I walk down the stairs. In the courtyard two gypsy women meet me. They are on the program at the inn. The lady wrestlers have long since gone. "Your future, young gentleman?" asks the younger of the gypsies. She smells of garlic and onions.

"No," I say. "Not today."

At Karl Brill's the tension is extreme. A pile of money lies on the table; there must be trillions there. The opposing bettor is a man with a head like a seal and very small hands. He has just tested the nail in the wall and is coming back. "Another two hundred billion," he offers in a clear voice.

"Done," Karl Brill replies.

The opponents lay down the money. "Anyone else?" Karl asks.

No one speaks. The wagers are too high for all of them. Karl is sweating in clear drops, but he is confident. The odds stand at forty to sixty in his favor. He has allowed the seal to give a last tap with the hammer; in return the odds of fifty-fifty have been changed to forty-sixty. "Will you play the 'Bird Song at Evening'?" Karl asks me.

I sit down at the piano. Presently Frau Beckmann appears in her salmon-colored kimono. She is not so imperturbable as formerly; her mountainous breasts heave as though an earthquake were raging beneath them, and her eyes have a different expression. She does not look at Karl Brill.

"Clara," Karl says, "you know the gentlemen here except for Herr Schweizer." He makes an elegant gesture. "Herr Schweizer—"

The seal bows with an astonished and rather worried expression. He glances at the money and then at this four-square Brünhilde. The nail is wrapped in cotton, and Clara takes up her position. I play the double trill and stop. Everyone is silent.

Frau Beckmann stands there, calm and concentrated. Then two quivers pass through her body. Suddenly she casts a wild glance at Karl Brill. "Sorry!" she grits through clenched teeth. "It won't go."

She moves away from the wall and leaves the workroom. "Clara!" Karl screams.

She does not reply. The seal emits a burst of oily laughter and begins to pick up the money. The drinking companions are as though struck by lightning. Karl Brill groans, rushes over to the nail, and comes back. "Just a minute!" he says to the seal. "Just a minute, we're not through yet! We bet on three tries. These were just the first two!"

"There were three."

"You're no judge of that! You're new here. It was two!"

Sweat is now running down Karl's skull. The drinking companions have found their tongues again. "It was two," they asseverate.

An argument ensues. I do not listen. I feel as though I were sitting on an alien planet. It is a brief, intense, and horrible feeling, and I am happy when I can follow the voices again. The seal has exploited the situation; he will grant a third try if there is a further wager thirty-seventy in his favor. Sweating, Karl agrees to everything. As far as I can see, he has wagered half his workshop, including the soling machine. "Come here!" he whispers to me. "Come upstairs with me! We must change her mind! She did that on purpose."

We climb the stairs. Frau Beckmann has been waiting for Karl. She is lying on her bed in the kimono decorated with a phoenix, excited, marvelously beautiful to anyone who likes big women, and ready for battle. "Clara!" Karl whispers. "Why this? You did it on purpose."

"So?" Frau Beckmann says.

"Of course you did! I know it! I swear to you—"

"Don't swear anything! You beast, you slept with the cashier at the Hotel Hohenzollern! You disgusting swine!"

"I? What a lie! How do you know about it?"

"You see, you admit it!"

"I admit it?"

"You have just admitted it! You asked how I knew. How could I know it, if it isn't true?"

I look with sympathy at Karl Brill, the breast-stroke expert. He has no fear of water no matter how cold, but here he is out of his depth. On the stairs I have advised him not to get into an argument but simply to plead with Frau Beckmann on his knees and beg her forgiveness, without, of course, admitting anything. Instead, he is now reproaching her with a certain Herr Kletzel. Her answer is a fearful blow in the nose. Karl leaps backward, feels his snout to see whether it is bleeding, and then with a cry of rage moves forward in a crouch like an experienced fighter to seize Frau Beckmann by the hair, pull her out of bed, place one foot on the back of her neck, and go to work on her mighty hams with his braces. I give him a fairly stiff kick in the rear. He turns around, ready to attack me too, sees my warning glance, my raised hands, and my silently whispering mouth and awakens from his thirst for blood. Human reason shines once more from his brown eyes. He nods briefly, with blood now gushing from his nose, turns around, and sinks down on his knees beside Frau Beckmann's bed with the cry: "Clara! I have done nothing, but forgive me!"

"You pig!" she screams. "You double pig! My kimono!"

She jerks the precious garment aside. Karl is bleeding onto the sheets. "Damned liar!" she trumpets. "And lying still!"

I notice that Karl, a simple, honorable man, who expected an immediate reward for falling on his knees, is about to get up again in rage. If he starts another boxing match while his nose is bleeding, all is lost. Perhaps Frau Beckmann will forgive him for the cashier at the Hohenzollern, but never for ruining her kimono. I step on his foot from behind, holding him down with one hand on his shoulder, and say: "Frau Beckmann, he is innocent! He sacrificed himself for me."

"What?"

"For me," I repeat. "That happens often among old war comrades—"

"What? You and your damned war camaraderie, you liars and cheaters—and you expect me to believe something like that!"

"Sacrificed himself!" I say. "He introduced me to the cashier, that was all."

Frau Beckmann straightens up with flaming eyes. "You want me to believe that a young man like you would hanker after an old worn-out bag like that cadaver at the Hohenzollern!"

"Not hanker after, *gnädige Frau*," I say. "But when needs must, the devil eats flies. If loneliness has you by the throat—"

"A young man like you could surely do better!"

"Young, but poor," I reply. "Nowadays women want to be taken to expensive bars. And while we're speaking about it, you'll have to admit that if you doubt that a bachelor like me living alone and caught in the storm of the inflation could be interested in the cashier, it would be completely absurd to suspect anything of the sort of Karl Brill, who enjoys the favors of the most beautiful and interesting woman in all of Werdenbrück—undeservedly, I admit—"

This last makes an impression. "He's a beast!" Frau Beckmann says. "And undeservedly is right."

Karl takes a hand. "Clara, you are my life!" he moans hollowly from the bloody sheets.

"I'm your bank account, you cold-blooded devil!" Frau Beckmann turns back to me. "And what about that half-dead she donkey at the Hohenzollern?"

I dismiss the creature. "Nothing, not a thing! It came to nothing at all! She turned my stomach."

"I could have told you that in advance!" she declares with deep satisfaction.

The battle has been decided. We are now engaged in a rear-guard action. Karl promises Clara a sea-green kimono with lotus blossoms, and swansdown slippers. Then he goes to bathe his nose in cold water, and Frau Beckmann gets up. "How high are the bets?" she asks.

"High," I reply. "Trillions."

"Karl!" she shouts. "Cut Herr Bodmer in for two hundred and fifty billion."

"Of course, Clara!"

We stride down the stairs. Below sits the seal, guarded by Karl's friends. We find out that he has tried to cheat while we were away, but Karl's drinking companions tore the hammer away in time. Frau Beckmann smiles haughtily, and thirty seconds later the nail lies on the floor. Majestically she stalks out to the accompanying strains of "Alpine Sunset."

"A friend in need is a friend indeed," Karl says to me emotionally later on.

"Question of honor! But what's all this about the cashier?"

"What's a man to do?" Karl replies. "You know how you feel sometimes in the evenings! But to think the bitch talked! I'm going to withdraw my patronage from those people. But you, dear friend—choose whatever you like!" He points to his array of leathers. "A first-class pair of shoes made to order as a gift—whatever you like: black buckskin, brown, yellow, patent leather, doeskin—I'll make them for you myself—"

"Patent leather," I say.

As I come home I see a dark figure in the courtyard. It is actually old Knopf, who has arrived just before me and, just as though he had not already been pronounced dead, is making ready to desecrate the obelisk. "Sergeant Major," I say, taking him by the arm, "now you have a headstone of your own for your childish necessities. Make use of it!"

I lead him over to the stone he has bought, and wait at the door so that he can't return to the obelisk.

Knopf stares at me. "You mean my own headstone? Are you crazy? What's it worth now?"

"According to the latest exchange, nine billion."

"And you want me to piss on that?"

Knopf's eye wanders about for a few seconds, then he reels muttering into his house. What no one has been able to achieve has been accomplished by the simple concept of property! The sergeant major is making use of his own toilet. Let them talk about communism! It is possessions that produce a feeling for order!

I stand for a while, reflecting on the fact that it has taken nature millions of years, from the amoeba up through fish, frog, vertebrates, and monkeys, to achieve old Knopf, a creature compounded of physical and chemical marvels, with a circulatory system that is a work of genius, a heart mechanism one can only regard with awe, a liver and two kidneys by contrast with which the I.G. Farben factories are ridiculous journeyman workshops—and all this, this perfect miracle carefully elaborated over millions of years, called during his short time on earth full Sergeant Major Knopf, simply for the purpose of making life miserable for young recruits and afterward, on a moderate pension from the state, of giving itself up to drink! Truly God sometimes takes a great deal of trouble for nothing!

Shaking my head I turn on the light in my room and stare into the mirror. There I see another miracle of nature that hasn't been able to make much of itself. I turn the light off and undress in the dark.

Chapter Twenty-two

A young lady comes toward me through the *allée* of chestnut trees. It is Sunday morning; I saw her earlier in church. She is wearing a light gray, beautifully tailored suit, a small gray hat, and gray suède shoes; her name is Geneviève Terhoven and she is a complete stranger to me.

Her mother was with her in church. I've seen them and I've seen Bodendiek, and Wernicke as well, visibly exuding pride at his success. I have walked around the garden and already given up hope; now all at once Isabelle is walking toward me alone between the lines of almost leafless trees. I stop. She approaches, slender and light and elegant, and suddenly all my yearning returns, heaven and the surging of the blood. I cannot speak. Wernicke has told me she is well, that the shadows have dispersed, and I realize that myself; all at once she is here, changed, but wholly here; no trace of sickness any longer stands between us; love in all its power springs from my hands and eyes, and dizziness rises like a silent whirlwind through my veins into my brain. She looks at me. "Isabelle," I say.

She looks at me again, a small crease between her eyebrows. "Yes?" she says.

I do not understand right away. I think I must remind her. "Isabelle," I repeat. "Don't you know me? I am Rudolf—"

"Rudolf?" she repeats. "Rudolf—what is it, please?"

I stare at her. "We have often talked to each other," I say then.

She nods. "Yes, I have been here a long time. But I have forgotten a great deal, please forgive me. Have you been here a long time too?"

"I? I've never been here! I only come to play the organ! And then—"

"Oh yes, the organ," Geneviève Terhoven replies politely. "In the chapel. Yes, I remember now. Excuse me for letting it slip my mind. You played very well. Many thanks."

I stand there like an idiot. I don't know why I do not leave. Obviously Geneviève doesn't know either. "Excuse me," she says. "I still have a lot to do; I'm leaving soon."

"You're leaving soon?"

"Yes," she replies in surprise.

"And you don't remember anything? Not even the names that are shed at night and the flowers that have voices?"

Isabelle raises her shoulders in bewilderment. "Poems," she exclaims presently, smiling. "I've always loved them. But there are so many! You can't remember them all."

I give up. My foreboding has come true! She is cured, and I have slipped out of her mind like a newspaper dropping from the hands of a sleepy woman. She remembers nothing any more. It is as though she had awakened from an anesthetic. The time up here has been wiped from her memory. She has forgotten everything. She is Geneviève

Terhoven and she no longer knows who Isabelle was. She is not lying, I can see that. I have lost her, not as I feared I would, not because she comes from a different social world and is going back to it, but far more completely and irrevocably. She has died. She is alive and breathing and beautiful, but at the moment when the strangeness of her sickness was removed she died, drowned forever. Isabelle, whose heart flew and blossomed, is drowned in Geneviève Terhoven, a well-brought-up young lady of good family who someday will unquestionably marry a rich man and will no doubt become a good mother.

"I must go," she says. "Many thanks again for the organ music."

"Well?" Wernicke asks. "What have you to say?"

"To what?"

"Don't act so dumb. Fräulein Terhoven. You must admit that in the three weeks since you last saw her she has become a quite different person. Complete success!"

"Is that what you call success?"

"What would you call it? She is going back into life, everything is in order, that earlier time has disappeared like a bad dream, she has become a human being again—what more do you want? You've seen her, haven't you? Well then?"

"Yes," I say. "Well then?"

A nurse with a red peasant face brings in a bottle and glasses. "Are we to have the additional pleasure of seeing His Reverence Vicar Bodendiek?" I ask. "I don't know whether Fräulein Terhoven was baptized a Catholic, but since she comes from Alsace I assume so—His Reverence, too, will, then, be full of joy at having retrieved a lamb for his flock from the great chaos."

Wernicke grins. "His Reverence has already expressed his

satisfaction. Fräulein Terhoven has been attending mass daily for the past week."

Isabelle, I think. Once she knew that God still hangs on the cross and that it was not just the unbelievers who crucified Him. "Has she been to confession too?" I ask.

"I don't know. It's possible. But is it necessary for someone to confess what he has done while mentally ill? That's an interesting question for an unenlightened Protestant like me."

"It depends on what you mean by mentally ill," I say bitterly, watching that plumber of souls drain a glass of Schloss Reinhartshausener. "No doubt we have different views on the subject. Besides, how can one confess what he has forgotten? No doubt Fräulein Terhoven has suddenly forgotten a good deal."

Wernicke fills his glass again. "Let's finish this before His Reverence arrives. The smell of incense may be holy, but it ruins the bouquet of a wine like this." He takes a sip, rolling his eyes, and says: "Suddenly forgotten? Was it so sudden? There were signs long ago."

He is right. I, too, noticed it earlier. There were moments when Isabelle seemed not to recognize me. I remember the last occasion and drain my glass angrily. Today the wine has no flavor for me.

"It's like an earthquake," Wernicke explains contentedly, beaming with self-satisfaction. "A seaquake. Islands, even continents, that formerly existed disappear and others emerge."

"What about a second seaquake? Does that have the reverse effect?"

"That, too, happens sometimes. But almost always in cases of a different kind; those associated with increasing hebetude. You've seen examples here. Is that what you'd like for Fräulein Terhoven?"

"I want the best for her," I say.

"Well then!"

Wernicke pours the rest of the wine. I remember the hopelessly sick, standing or lying in the corners, with spittle dribbling from their mouths, soiling themselves. "Of course I hope she will never be sick again," I say.

"It is to be assumed that she will not. Hers was one of those cases that can be cured once the causes are eliminated. Everything went very well. Mother and daughter now feel, as sometimes happens in such instances when a death occurs, that in some vague way they have been betrayed—and so they are like orphans and thereby brought closer together than before."

I stare at Wernicke. I have never heard him speak so poetically. But he doesn't mean it altogether seriously. "You'll have a chance to see for yourself at noon," he remarks. "Mother and daughter are coming to lunch."

I want to leave, but something compels me to stay. Anyone given to self-torture does not readily miss a chance for it. Bodendiek appears and is surprisingly human. Then mother and daughter come in, and a commonplace, civilized conversation begins. The older woman is about forty-five, a trifle stout, inconsequentially pretty, and full of light, polished phrases which she scatters effortlessly. She has an unreflective answer for everything.

I watch Geneviève. Sometimes, fleetingly, I think I perceive in her features that other beloved, wild, and disturbed countenance, rising toward the surface like the face of a drowning woman; but it is instantly submerged in the ripples of the conversation about the modern facilities of the sanitarium—neither lady calls it anything else—the pretty view, the old city, various uncles and aunts in Strasbourg and in Holland, the difficulty of the times, the necessity of faith, the merits of Lothringian wines, and the beauty of

Alsace. Not a word of what so overwhelmed and excited me. It is gone as though it had never existed.

Soon I take my leave. "Good-by, Fräulein Terhoven," I say. "I hear you are leaving this week."

She nods. "Are you coming back this evening?" Wernicke asks me.

"Yes, for the evening devotion."

"Then come up to my room for a drink. You'll join us too, won't you, ladies?"

"With pleasure," Isabelle's mother replies. "We were going to evening devotion anyway."

Geneviève does not reply. There is a small crease in her forehead as though she were brooding over something.

The evening is even worse than noon. There is something traitorous about the soft light. I saw Isabelle in chapel; the glow of the candles hovered over her hair. She hardly moved. The faces of the patients swung around at the sound of the organ like bright, flat moons. Isabelle was praying; she was well.

Afterward it gets no better. I succeed in meeting Geneviève at the door of the chapel and walking alone with her for a way. We go along the *allée*. I do not know what to say. Geneviève pulls her coat around her. "How cold the evenings are already," she says.

"Yes. So you are leaving this week?"

"That's what I plan. It has been a long time since I was home."

"Are you glad?"

"Certainly."

There is nothing more to say. But I can't help myself—her walk is the same, her face in the darkness, the soft presentiment—"Isabelle," I say as we are about to emerge from the *allée*.

"I beg your pardon?" she asks in amazement.

"Oh," I say. "That was just a name."

For a moment she looks at me. "You must be mistaken," she replies then. "My first name is Geneviève."

"Yes, of course. Isabelle was someone else's name. We talked about her occasionally."

"So? Perhaps. One talks of so much," she remarks apologetically. "Then you forget this and that."

"Oh yes."

"Was it someone you knew?"

"Yes, that was it."

She laughs softly. "How romantic. Forgive me for not remembering at once. Now I recall."

I stare at her. She remembers nothing, as I can see. She is lying to be polite. "So much has happened in the last weeks," she says lightly and in a slightly superior way. "Everything gets a little confused." And then, once more out of courtesy, she asks: "How has it been going recently?"

"What?"

"What you were telling me about Isabelle—"

"Oh that! It is over! She died."

She stops horrified. "Died? I am so sorry. Forgive me, I didn't know—"

"It makes no difference. I only knew her slightly anyway."

"Died suddenly?"

"Yes," I reply. "But in such a way that she didn't even know it. That counts for something."

"Of course." She extends her hand to me. "It really makes me very sad."

Her hand is firm and narrow and cool—no longer feverish. It is the hand of a young lady who has been guilty of a slight *faux pas* and has rectified it. "A beautiful name, Isabelle," she says. "I used to hate my given name."

"And now you don't?"
"No," Geneviève says in a friendly way.

She remains friendly too. It is the odious courtesy to people in a small city whom you meet in passing and will soon forget. Suddenly I am aware of being clad in an ill-fitting suit, made by Sulzblick, the tailor, out of my old uniform. Geneviève, on the other hand, is beautifully dressed. She always was, but it has never struck me so forcibly. Geneviève and her mother have decided to go to Berlin for a few weeks before returning home. Her mother is all consideration and affection. "The theater! And the concerts! It's always so stimulating to be in a real metropolis. And the shops! The new styles!"

She pats Geneviève's hand. "We'll just spoil ourselves thoroughly for once, won't we?"

Geneviève nods. Wernicke beams. They have caught her in their net. But just what have they caught? I wonder. Perhaps it is something that is buried, hidden in each of us, but what, in fact, is it? And is it then in me too? Has it, too, been caught in a net or was it never free? Does it exist; is it something that existed before me and will exist afterward, something more important than I? Or was it only a moment of confusion that seemed profound, a distortion of the senses, an illusion, nonsense that seemed like wisdom, as Wernicke maintains? But then why did I love it; why did it leap upon me like a leopard leaping on an ox; why can I not forget it? Was it not, despite Wernicke, like opening a door in a locked room so that you could see rain and lightning and the stars?

I get up. "What's the matter with you?" Wernicke asks. "Why, you're as jumpy as—" he pauses and then goes on—"as the dollar exchange."

"Oh, the dollar," Geneviève's mother says with a sigh. "What a misfortune! Luckily Uncle Gaston—"

I do not listen to what Uncle Gaston has done. Suddenly I am outdoors. I only remember saying to Isabelle, "Thanks for everything," and her surprised reply: "But for what?"

Slowly I walk down the hill. Good night, sweet, wild heart, I think. Farewell, Isabelle! You have not drowned! You have flown away, or rather you have suddenly become invisible, like the ancient gods; a wave length has changed; you are still here, but you are no longer to be touched; you will always be here and you will never disappear. Everything is always here; nothing is ever destroyed. It's just that light and shade pass over it; it is always here, the countenance before birth and after death, and sometimes it shines through what we call life and dazzles us for an instant and afterward we are never the same!

I notice that I am walking faster. I breathe deeply and then break into a run. I am wet with sweat; my back is wet. I come to the gate and then go back. I still have the same feeling; it is like a mighty liberation; every axis suddenly runs through my heart, birth and death are only words, the wild geese have been flying over me since the beginning of the world, and there are no longer any questions or any answers! Farewell, Isabelle! *Salute,* Isabelle! Farewell, Life! *Salute,* Life!

Much later, I notice it is raining. I lift my face to the drops and taste them. Then I walk to the gate. A tall figure, smelling of wine and incense, is waiting there. We walk through the gate together. The watchman closes it behind us. "Well?" Bodendiek asks. "Where have you been? Searching for God!"

"No. I have found Him."

He squints at me suspiciously from under his broad-brimmed hat. "Where? In nature?"

"I don't know where. Is He to be found in special places?"

"At the altar," Bodendiek rumbles and then, pointing to the right, "This is my way. And yours?"

"All of them are right," I reply.

"Surely you haven't drunk that much," he growls behind me, somewhat startled.

As I near home someone jumps on me from behind our door. "Now I've got you, you swine!"

I shake him off, thinking it some kind of joke. But he is on his feet again instantly and butts me in the stomach with his head. I fall against the obelisk but manage to plant a kick in his belly: a weak kick because I am falling. The man leaps on me again, and I recognize the horse butcher Watzek. "Have you gone crazy?" I ask. "Can't you see who I am?"

"I see all right!" Watzek seizes me by the throat. "I see you well enough, you bastard! But this is the end of you."

I don't know whether he is drunk, but I have no time to consider the question. Watzek is smaller than I, but he has the muscles of a bull. I succeed in carrying him over backward and pinning him against the obelisk. He lets go halfway. I throw myself and him to one side and knock his head against the foundation. He lets go completely. To make sure, I give him a blow under the chin with my shoulder, get up, go to the gate, and turn on the light. "What's the meaning of all this?" I say.

Watzek gets up slowly. He is shaking his head, still somewhat dazed. I watch him. Suddenly he runs at me again with his head aimed at my stomach. I step to one side, put out my leg, and he hits the obelisk again with a dull thud, this time between the socles. Anyone else would have been knocked silly; Watzek hardly reels. He turns around with a knife in his hand. It is his long, sharp, butcher's knife, as I can see in the electric light. He has drawn it from his boot and now he is running at me. I indulge in no superfluous heroism; it would be suicide against a man like the horse butcher, who knows how to use a knife. I spring behind the obelisk; Watzek after me. Fortunately I am quicker and lighter on my feet than he. "Are you crazy?" I hiss. "Do you want to be hanged for murder?"

"I'll teach you to sleep with my wife!" Watzek gasps. "Blood will flow!"

Finally I realize what is happening. "Watzek!" I shout. "You're murdering an innocent man!"

"Shit! I'll slit your throat!"

We race around the obelisk. It doesn't occur to me to call for help. Everything is happening too fast; besides, who could really help me? "You're deceived!" I gasp. "What's your wife to me?"

"You're sleeping with her, you devil!"

We continue to run—first to the right, then to the left. Watzek, wearing boots, is clumsier than I. Damn it! I think. Where is Georg? I'll be slaughtered for him while he sits in his room with Lisa. "Ask your wife, you idiot!" I gasp.

"I'll slaughter you!"

I look about for a weapon. There is nothing. Before I could lift a small headstone, Watzek would have my throat cut. Suddenly I see a piece of marble about the size of my fist shimmering on the window sill. I seize it, dance around the obelisk and hurl it at Watzek's skull. It hits him on the left side. Right away blood streams over one eye so that he can only see with the other. "Watzek! You're mistaken!" I say. "I've had nothing to do with your wife! I swear it to you!"

Watzek is slower now, but he is still dangerous. "To do that to a friend!" he growls. "What foulness!"

He makes a lunge like a miniature bull. I spring aside, grab the piece of marble again and throw it at him. Unfortunately it misses and lands in the lilac bush. "Your wife doesn't matter a shit to me!" I hiss. "Understand that, man! Not a shit!"

Watzek goes on chasing me in silence. Now he is bleeding profusely on the left side; I run to the left so that he can't see me clearly. At a dangerous moment I succeed in catching him with a good kick in the knee. At the same instant he stabs, but only slices the sole of my shoe. The kick has its effect. Watzek stops, bleeding, his knife ready. "Listen to me!" I say. "Stay where you are! Let's have an armistice for a minute! After that you can start again right away, and I'll knock your other eye out! Pay attention, man! Try, you imbecile!" I stare at Watzek as though trying to hypnotize him. Once I read a book about that. "I—have—not—had—anything—to—do—with—your—wife—" I chant distinctly and slowly. "She doesn't interest me! Hold on!" I hiss as Watzek makes a new move. "I have a woman of my own—"

"All the worse, you goat!"

Watzek takes up the chase, but collides with the foundation of the obelisk on too close a turn; he stumbles, and I give him another kick, this time in the shin. He is wearing boots, but this kick does the trick. Watzek halts, his legs apart, unfortunately still holding the knife. "Stop this, you ass!" I say in the impressive tones of a hypnotist. "I'm in love with an entirely different woman! Hold on! I'll show her to you! I have her photograph here!"

Watzek makes a silent lunge. We make another half-turn around the obelisk. I succeed in getting my wallet out. Gerda at parting has given me a picture of herself. I fumble desperately for it. A few billion marks slide colorfully to the ground; then I find the photo. "Here!" I say, warily pushing it toward him along the obelisk so that he can't hack at my hand. "Is this your wife? Look at it! Read the inscription!"

Watzek squints at me with his uninjured eye. I place Gerda's picture on the foundation of the obelisk. "So—there you have it! Is that your wife?"

Watzek makes a halfhearted attempt to catch me. "You camel!" I say. "Just look at the photograph! Do you think anyone with something like that would run after your wife?"

I've gone almost too far. The insult provokes a lively lunge. Then he stands still. "Somebody is sleeping with her!" he announces uncertainly.

"Nonsense!" I say. "Your wife is true to you!"

"Then why is she here all the time?"

"Where?"

"Here!"

"I have no idea what you mean," I say. "She may have come here a few times to telephone, that's possible. Women like to telephone, especially when they're alone a lot. Get her a telephone!"

"She's here at night too!" Watzek says.

We are still standing facing each other with the obelisk between us. "She was here for a few minutes the night a while back when they brought Sergeant Major Knopf home seriously ill," I reply. "Aside from that she has been working at the Red Mill."

"That's what she says—but—"

The knife is hanging. I pick up Gerda's photograph and walk around the obelisk to Watzek. "So," I say. "Now you can stab me as much as you like. But we can talk to each other too. What do you want to do? Murder an innocent man?"

"Not that," Watzek says after a pause. "But—"

It transpires that the widow Konersmann has been talking to him. I am mildly flattered that she believes I am the only one in the house who could be the culprit. "Man," I say to Watzek, "if you knew where my thoughts are, you wouldn't suspect me. And besides, just compare the figure. Don't you notice something?"

Watzek gapes at Gerda's photograph and the inscription: "For Ludwig with love from Gerda." What could he possibly notice with his one eye? "Similar to your wife's," I say. "Same size. Besides, hasn't your wife a loose coat, rust-red, something like a cape?"

"Sure," Watzek replies, once more growing dangerous. "She has. What of it?"

"This lady has one too. You can get them in all sizes at Max Klein's in Grossestrasse. They're the style just now. Well, old Konersmann is half blind—there we have the solution."

Old Konersmann has eyes like a hawk, but what won't a cuckold believe if he wants to? "She has confused them," I say. "This lady has been here a few times to visit me. Which she has a perfect right to do, don't you think?"

I am making it easy for Watzek. He need only say yes or no. This time he need only nod. "All right," I say. "And for this a fellow almost gets stabbed to death in the dark."

Watzek lowers himself painfully to the doorstep. "Comrade, you treated me pretty rough too. Just look at me."

"Your eye is still there."

Watzek touches the black, congealing blood. "You'll be in the penitentiary before long if you go on this way," I say.

"What am I to do? It's my nature."

"Stab yourself if you have to stab someone. That would spare you a lot of unpleasantness."

"Sometimes a man would like to do just that! Comrade, what am I to do? I'm crazy about my wife. And she can't stand me."

Suddenly I feel touched and weary; I lower myself onto the step beside Watzek. "It's my profession," he says in despair. "She hates it. You know, a man smells of blood if he spends all his time slaughtering horses."

"Haven't you another suit? One you could put on before leaving the slaughterhouse?"

"That won't do. The other butchers would think I was putting on airs. Besides, the smell would come through. It clings."

"What about a bath?"

"A bath?" Watzek asks. "Where? In the municipal baths? They're closed when I come home from work at six in the morning."

"Isn't there a shower at the slaughterhouse?"

Watzek shakes his head. "Only hoses to wash down the floors. It's too cold now to stand under them."

I can understand that. Ice-cold water in November is no pleasure. If Watzek were Karl Brill, it wouldn't bother him at all. Karl is the man who chops a hole in the river ice so he can go swimming with his club. "What about toilet water?" I ask.

"What?"

"Perfume, to drown out the smell of blood."

"I can't try that. The others would take me for a pansy. You don't know those fellows at the slaughterhouse!"

"How about changing your profession?"

"I don't know any other," Watzek says sadly.

"Horse dealer," I suggest. "That's the same line."

Watzek dismisses the idea. We sit for a time in silence. What does he matter to me? I think. And how can anyone help him? Lisa is in love with the Red Mill. It's not so much Georg; it's her aspiration to rise above her horse butcher. "You must become a cavalier," I say finally. "Do you make good money?"

"Not bad."

"Then you're in luck. Go to the municipal baths every other day and buy a new suit to wear only at home. A couple of shirts, a tie or two—can you manage that?"

Watzek broods. "You think that would help?"

I remember my evening under the critical eye of Frau Terhoven. "You'll feel better in a new suit," I reply. "I've had that experience myself."

"Really?"

"Really."

Watzek looks at me with interest. "But your clothes are always first-class."

"That depends. To you, perhaps. Not to certain others. I have noticed that."

"Have you? Recently?"

"Today," I say.

Watzek's mouth flies open. "Think of that! Then we're almost like brothers. It's amazing!"

"I read somewhere that all men are brothers. That's even more amazing when you look at the world."

"And we almost killed each other!" Watzek says happily.

"Brothers often do."

Watzek gets up. "I'm going to the baths tomorrow." He feels his left eye. "I really intended to order an SA uniform. They've just been put on sale in Munich."

"A natty, double-breasted dark gray suit would be better. There's no future for your uniform."

"Many thanks," Watzek says. "But perhaps I'll manage both. And don't hold it against me, comrade, that I tried to knife you. Tomorrow I'm going to send you a big dish of first-class horse sausage to make up for it."

Chapter Twenty-three

"The cuckold is like a domestic animal," Georg says, "an edible one, a chicken, let's say, or a rabbit. You eat it with pleasure provided you don't know it personally. But if you grow up with it, play with it, feed and protect it—then only a barbarian could relish it as a roast. That's why one should never know cuckolds."

Silently I point at the table. There between the samples of stone lies a thick, red sausage—horse sausage—a gift Watzek left for me this morning. "Are you going to eat it?" Georg asks.

"Of course I'm going to eat it. I've eaten worse horse meat before, in France. But don't dodge the issue! There lies Watzek's gift. I am in a dilemma."

"Only because you love dramatic situations."

"All right," I say. "I grant that. Nevertheless, I saved your life. Widow Konersmann is going to keep on spying. Is the affair worth it?"

Georg gets a Brazilian out of the cupboard. "Watzek considers you his brother now," he replies. "Is that what causes your conflict of conscience?"

"No. Besides, he's still a Nazi—that cancels out this one-sided brotherhood. But let's stick to the subject."

"Watzek is my brother too," Georg announces, blowing the white smoke of the Brazilian into the face of a painted plaster image of Saint Catherine. "Lisa, you must know, is deceiving me as well."

"Are you making that up?" I ask in amazement.

"Not a bit of it. Where do you think she gets all those clothes and jewels? Watzek, her husband, never gives them a thought—I, however, do."

"You?"

"She confessed to me herself without my asking. She explained she didn't want any kind of deception between us. She meant it honestly too—not as a joke."

"And you? You betray her with the fascinating creatures of your imagination and your magazines."

"Of course. What does betrayal mean anyway? The word is never used except by those to whom it is happening at the moment. Since when has feeling had anything to do with morality? Is that all you've learned from the postwar education I've given you here among the symbols of mortality? Betrayal—what a vulgar word for the everlasting, sensitive dissatisfaction, the search for more, always more—"

"Granted!" I interrupt him. "That short-legged, muscular fellow with a bump on his head you just saw turning into his house is the freshly bathed butcher Watzek. His hair has been cut and is still damp with bay rum. He is trying to please his wife. Don't you find that touching?"

"Of course. But he will never please his wife."

"Then why did she marry him?"

"That was during the war when she was very hungry and he could provide plenty of meat. Since then she has grown six years older."

"Why doesn't she leave him?"

"Because he has threatened to kill her whole family if she does."

"Did she tell you all this?"

"Yes."

"Dear God," I say. "And you believe it!"

Georg blows an artistic smoke ring. "If you ever get to be as old as I am, you proud cynic, I hope you will have found out that some beliefs are not only convenient but often justified as well."

"All right," I say. "Meanwhile, what about Master Butcher Watzek and the sharp-eyed Widow Konersmann?"

"Disturbing," he replies. "Besides, Watzek is an idiot. At the moment he has an easier life than ever before—because Lisa is deceiving him she treats him better. Just wait and listen to his screams when she is true to him again and makes him pay for it. Now come along, let's eat! We can consider this case another time."

Eduard almost has a stroke when he sees us. The dollar has risen to nearly a trillion marks, and we still seem to have an inexhaustible supply of coupons. "You're printing them!" he asserts. "You're counterfeiters! You print them secretly!"

"We'd like to have a bottle of Forster Jesuitengarten after our meal," Georg says with dignity.

"Why after your meal?" Eduard asks suspiciously. "What are you trying to get away with now?"

"The wine is too good to drink with what you've been serving these past weeks," I explain.

Eduard swells with rage. "To eat on last winter's coupons at a miserable six thousand marks per meal and then criticize the food—that's going too far! I ought to call the police!"

"Call them! One more word out of you and we'll eat here and have our wine at the Hotel Hohenzollern!"

Eduard looks as though he were about to explode, but he controls himself because of the wine. "Stomach ulcers," he mutters, hurriedly withdrawing, "stomach ulcers is what I've got because of you! Now all I can drink is milk!"

We sit down and look around. Covertly and guiltily I search for Gerda, but do not see her. Instead, I become aware of a familiar, grinning face moving toward us through the middle of the room. "Do you see what I see?" I ask Georg.

"Riesenfeld! Here again! 'Only the man acquainted with longing—'"

Riesenfeld greets us. "You've come at exactly the right time to express your gratitude," Georg says to him. "This young idealist here fought a duel for you yesterday. An American-style duel, knives against chunks of marble."

"What?" Riesenfeld asks, seating himself and calling for a glass of beer. "How's that?"

"Herr Watzek, the husband of Lady Lisa, whom you are pursuing with flowers and chocolates, assumed that these items came from my friend here and lay in wait for him with a long knife."

"Wounded?" Riesenfeld asks abruptly, examining me.

"Only the sole of his shoe," Georg says. "Watzek is slightly injured."

"Are you two lying again?"

"Not this time."

I look at Georg with admiration. His impudence is incomparable. But Riesenfeld is not easy to upset. "He must go at once!" he decrees like a Roman emperor.

"Who?" I ask. "Watzek?"

"You!"

"I? Why not you? Or both of you?"

"Watzek will do battle again. You are his natural victim.

He won't think of us at all. We have bald heads. So you must go. Understand?"

"No," I say.

"Didn't you want to leave anyway?"

"Not on Lisa's account."

"I said anyway," Riesenfeld explains. "Didn't you want to plunge into the wild life of a big city?"

"As what? You aren't fed for nothing in a big city."

"As a newspaper employee in Berlin. At first you won't earn much, but it will be enough to live on. Then you can look around."

"What?" I say breathlessly.

"You've asked me a couple of times whether I couldn't find something for you! Well, Riesenfeld has connections. I have found something for you. That's why I came by. You can begin on January 1, '24. It's a small job but in Berlin. Agreed?"

"Hold on!" Georg says. "He has to give me five years' notice."

"Then he'll just run away without giving notice. That taken care of?"

"How much will he make?" Georg asks.

"Two hundred marks," Riesenfeld replies calmly.

"I thought all along it was a joke," I say angrily. "Do you enjoy disappointing people? Two hundred marks! Does a ridiculous sum like that still exist?"

"It does again," Riesenfeld says.

"Indeed?" I ask. "Where? In New Zealand?"

"In Germany! Rye marks. Haven't you heard about them? Renten marks!"

Georg and I look at each other. There has been a rumor that a new currency was to be issued. One mark to be worth a certain quantity of rye; but in recent years there have been so many rumors that no one believed it.

"This time it's true," Riesenfeld explains. "I have it on

the best authority. Then the rye marks will be converted into gold marks. The government is behind it."

"The government! It's responsible for the whole devaluation!"

"Possibly. But now things are changing. The government has got rid of its debts. One trillion inflation marks will be valued at one gold mark."

"And then the gold mark will start slipping, eh? And the dance will begin all over again."

Riesenfeld drains his beer. "Do you want the job or don't you?" he asks.

The restaurant suddenly seems very quiet. "Yes," I say. It is as though someone next to me had said it. I don't trust myself to look at Georg.

"That's sensible," Riesenfeld declares.

I look at the tablecloth. It seems to be swimming. Then I hear Georg say: "Waiter, bring us the bottle of Forster Jesuitengarten at once."

I glance up. "After all, you saved our lives," he says. "That's what it's for!"

"Our lives? Why ours?" Riesenfeld asks.

"A life is never saved singly," Georg replies with great presence of mind. "It is always bound up with others."

The moment has passed. I look at Georg gratefully. I betrayed him because I had to, and he has understood. He will stay behind. "You'll visit me," I say. "Then I'll introduce you to the great ladies and all the movie actresses in Berlin."

"Children, what plans!" Riesenfeld says. "Where's the wine? After all, I've just saved your life."

"Who's saving whom?" I ask.

"Everyone saves someone at least once," Georg says. "Just as he kills someone at least once. Even though he may not know it."

The wine is standing on the table. Eduard appears. He is pale and upset. "Give me a glass too."

"Make yourself scarce!" I say. "You sponger! We'll drink the wine ourselves."

"You don't understand. This bottle is on me. I'll pay for it. But give me a glass. I have to have a drink."

"You're going to treat us to this? Think what you're saying!"

"I mean it." Eduard sits down. "Valentin is dead," he declares.

"Valentin? What happened to him?"

"Heart attack. I've just heard about it by telephone."

He reaches for his glass. "And you want to drink to that, you scoundrel?" I say indignantly. "Because you're rid of him?"

"I swear to you that's not the reason! After all, he saved my life."

"What?" Riesenfeld asks. "You too?"

"Yes of course. Who else?"

"What's going on here?" Riesenfeld asks. "Are we a life-savers' club?"

"It's the times," Georg replies. "During these last years lots of people have been saved. And lots haven't."

I stare at Eduard. He actually has tears in his eyes; but what can you tell about him? "I don't believe you," I say. "You've wished him dead too often. I've heard you. You wanted to save your damned wine."

"I swear to you that's not true! I may have said it occasionally, the way you do. But not in earnest!" The drops in his eyes have grown bigger. "He actually saved my life, you know."

Riesenfeld gets up. "I've had enough of this lifesaving nonsense! Will you be in the office this afternoon? Good!"

"Don't send her any more flowers, Riesenfeld," Georg warns him.

Riesenfeld assents and disappears with an indecipherable look on his face.

"Lets drink to Valentin," Eduard says. His lips are trembling. "Who would have thought it! He got through the whole war and now suddenly he's lying dead, from one second to the next."

"If you're going to be sentimental, do it in style," I reply. "Fetch a bottle of the wine you always begrudged him."

"The Johannisberger, yes indeed." Eduard gets up quickly and waddles away.

"I believe he's honestly grieved," Georg says.

"Honestly grieved and honestly relieved."

"That's what I mean. Usually you can't ask for more."

We sit in silence for a time. "There's rather a lot going on just now, isn't there?" I say finally.

Georg looks at me. *"Prost!* You'd have had to go sometime. And as for Valentin, he has lived quite a few years longer than anyone would have expected in 1917."

"So have we all."

"Yes, and for that reason we should make something of it."

"Isn't that what we're doing?"

Georg laughs. "You're making something of life if you don't want anything at any particular moment beyond what you've got."

I salute him. "Then I've made nothing of mine. And you?"

He grins. "Come along, let's get out of here before Eduard comes back. To hell with his wine!"

***

"Tender one," I murmur, my face turned toward the dark wall. "Tender and wild one, whiplash and mimosa, how foolish I was to want to possess you! Can one lock up the wind? What would become of it? Stale air. Go now, go your way, go to the theaters, the concerts, go and marry a reserve officer, a bank director, a conquering hero of the inflation, go, miracle of a gale that has become a calm, go, Youth who abandons only those who wish to abandon you, banner that flutters but cannot be seized, sail against many blue skies, fata morgana, fountain of sparkling words, go, Isabelle, go, my late-recovered, somewhat too knowing and too precocious youth, snatched back from beyond the war, go both of you, and I, too, will go. We have nothing to reproach ourselves for; our directions are different, but that, too, is only an appearance, for no one can betray death, one can only endure it. Farewell! We die a little each day, but each day we have lived a little longer too; you have taught me that and I will not forget it; nowhere is there annihilation, and he who does not try to hold on to anything possesses everything; farewell, I kiss you with my empty lips, I embrace you with my arms that cannot and will not hold you; farewell, farewell, you are in me and will remain there as long as I do not forget you—"

I have a bottle of Roth schnaps in my hand and I am sitting on the last bench in the *allée,* facing the asylum. In my pocket crackles a check for sound foreign exchange, thirty whole Swiss francs. Marvels have not ceased: a Swiss newspaper, which I have been bombarding with my poems for two years, has suddenly accepted one and sent me a check for it. I have already been to the bank to inquire—it's perfectly good. The bank manager immediately offered me a quantity of black marks for it. I am carrying the check in my breast pocket next to my heart. It came a few days too late. With it I could have bought a new suit and a white shirt and cut a respectable figure in the eyes of the ladies Terhoven. Too late! The December wind whistles, the check crackles, and I sit here in an imaginary tuxedo, wearing a pair of imaginary patent-leather shoes, which Karl Brill still owes me, and I praise God and worship you, Isabelle! A handkerchief of finest batiste flutters from my breast pocket, I am a capitalist on a pleasure trip; if the whim strikes me the Red Mill lies at my feet, in my hand sparkles the fearless drinker's champagne, the tipple of Sergeant Major Knopf with which he put death to flight —and I drink to the gray wall behind which are you, Isabelle, Youth, and your mother, and God's bookkeeper, Bodendiek, and Wernicke, Reason's major, and the great confusion and the eternal war; I drink and see opposite me on the left the District Lying-in Hospital, with a few windows still lighted, where mothers are giving birth, and I am struck for the first time by its proximity to the insane asylum—I recognize it, as indeed I should, for I was born there and until today I had not thought of that! Salutations to you, too, familiar home, beehive of fruitfulness; they took my mother to you because we were poor and there was no charge for a delivery if it took place with a class looking on; thus from the very start I was useful to science! Salutations to the unknown architect who placed you so suggestively close to the other building! Very likely he intended no irony, for the good jokes in the world are always made by serious practical men. Nevertheless—let us praise reason, but let us not be too proud of it and not too sure! You, Isabelle, have yours back again, that gift of the Greeks, and up there sits Wernicke rejoicing—and he is right. But each time you are right you are one step closer to death. He who is right all the time has turned into a black obelisk! His own monument!

The bottle is empty. I throw it as far away as I can, and it makes a dull thud in the soft, plowed field. I get up. I have had enough to drink and now I am ready for the Red Mill. Riesenfeld is giving a farewell party there tonight— a farewell and lifesaving party. Georg will be there and so will Lisa. I, too, am going, but I had my few private farewells to attend to, and after all of it we are going to celebrate a terrific and general farewell—the farewell to the inflation.

Late at night we move like a drunken funeral procession along Grossestrasse. The scattered street lamps flicker. We have buried the year a little prematurely. Willy and Renée de la Tour have joined us. Willy and Riesenfeld got into a heated argument; Riesenfeld swore to the end of the inflation and the beginning of the rye mark era—and Willy explained that he would be bankrupt then and so it couldn't be true. At this Renée de la Tour grew thoughtful.

Through the windy night we see in the distance another procession. It is coming toward us up Grossestrasse. "Georg," I say. "Suppose we leave the ladies a little way behind; this looks like a fight."

"Agreed."

We are near New Market. "If you see we're getting the worst of it, run straight to the Café Matz," Georg instructs Lisa. "Ask for Bodo Ledderhose's singing club and say we need them." He turns to Riesenfeld: "It would be better for you to pretend you aren't with us."

"Run, Renée," Willy remarks. "Keep away from the shooting!"

The other procession has reached us. Its members are wearing boots, the pride and joy of German patriots; with one or two exceptions they are all twenty years old. On the other hand, they are twice as many as we.

We start by. "There's that red dog!" someone shouts suddenly. Even at night Willy's shock of hair is conspicuous. "And the bald pate!" a second shouts, pointing at Georg. "After them!"

"Get going, Lisa!" Georg says.

We see her heels flash. "The cowards are going to call the

police," shouts a bespectacled towhead, starting after Lisa. Willy sticks out his foot and the towhead pitches forward. After that we're in a fight.

There are five of us, not counting Riesenfeld. Really four and a half. The half is Hermann Lotz, a war comrade, whose left arm was amputated at the shoulder. He and little Köhler, another comrade, ran into us in the Café Central. "Watch out, Hermann, or they'll knock you down!" I shout. "Stay in the middle. And you, Köhler, if they get you on the ground bite!"

"Backs to the wall!" Georg commands.

The order is a good one, but the wall behind happens to be the big show window of Max Klein's clothing store. The German patriots are attacking in full force, and who wants to be pushed through a glass window? You're sure to get your back cut to ribbons, and, besides, there's the question of damages for the window. We'd certainly be stuck with them if we were found sitting among the ruins. We couldn't escape.

For a moment we stay close together. The window is half lighted, and so we can see our opponents clearly. I recognize a middle-aged man; he is one of those we had a row with in the Café Central. Following the maxim of getting the leader first, I shout to him: "Come here, you coward. You ass with ears!"

He wouldn't dream of it. "Haul him out!" he orders his guards.

Three of them rush at me. Willy cracks one on the head and he falls. The second has a blackjack with which he hits me on the arm. I can't reach him, but he can reach me. Willy sees what is happening, leaps forward, and twists his arm. The blackjack falls to the ground. Willy tries to pick it up but is knocked down. "Grab the blackjack, Köhler!" I shout. Köhler dives into the melee on the ground where Willy in his light gray suit is already fighting.

Our battle line has been broken. I get a kick that sends me flying against the window so hard that it rings. Fortunately the glass does not break. Windows fly open above us. Behind us, from the depths of the show window, Max Klein's elegantly attired mannequins stare out at us. They stand motionless, clad in the latest winter fashions, like strange voiceless versions of the wives of the ancient Germans, cheering on their warriors from the wagon fort.

A big pimply youngster has me by the throat. He smells of herring and beer, and his head is as close to me as though he were trying to kiss me. My left arm is lame from the blackjack blow. With my right thumb I try to gouge his eye, but he prevents me by keeping his head pressed tight against my cheek as though we were a pair of unnatural lovers. I can't kick him either because I am too close, and so he has me pretty much at his mercy. Just as my breath begins to fail and I am about to lunge downward with all my strength, I see what strikes me as an illusion of my failing senses—a geranium in full bloom sprouting from the pimply youth's skull as though out of an especially potent dung heap. At the same time his eyes take on a look of mild surprise, his grip on my throat relaxes, fragments of the flowerpot rain down around us, I dive, get free, shoot up again, and feel a sharp crack; I have caught him under the chin with my skull, and he goes down slowly onto his knees. Strangely, the roots of the geranium that was dropped on us from above have fixed themselves so firmly to the head of this pimply Ancient German that he sinks to his knees with flowers on his head. It makes him more attractive than his forebears, who wore ox horns as their headgear. On his shoulders rest, like the remnants of a shattered helmet, two green majolica shards.

It was a big pot, but the patriot's skull seems to be made of iron. I feel him, still on his knees, trying to get at my genitals, and I seize the geranium along with its roots and the earth sticking to them and jam the dirt into his eyes. He lets go, rubs his eyes, and since at the moment I can do nothing with my fists, I pay him back by a kick in the balls. He doubles up and lowers his paws to protect himself. I thrust the sandy tangle of roots into his eyes once more and expect him to bring up his hands so that I can repeat the process. But his head sinks forward as though he were making an oriental salaam, and the next instant everything around me is ringing. I have not been alert and have received a terrific blow from the side. Slowly I edge along the show window. Heroic in size and completely disinterested, a mannequin with painted eyes and a beaver coat stares out at me.

"Break through to the *pissoir!*" I hear Georg shout.

He is right. We need a better cover for our rear. But it's easier said than done; we're wedged in. The enemy has been reinforced, and it looks as though we will end up with broken heads among Max Klein's mannequins.

At that instant I see Hermann Lotz kneeling on the ground. "Help me get this sleeve off!" he gasps.

I reach over and pull off the left sleeve of his jacket. His gleaming artificial arm comes free. It is made of nickel and ends in a black-gloved hand of artificial steel. Because of it, Hermann has the nickname Götz von Berlichingen of the Iron Hand. Quickly he frees the arm from his shoulder, seizes the artificial hand with his real one and gets up. "Gangway! Götz is coming!" I shout from below. Georg and Willy make room for him so that he can get through. He swings his artificial arm around him like a threshing flail and with the first blow lays the leader low. The attackers draw back for an instant. Hermann springs among them and whirls in a circle with his artificial arm outspread. Then in a trice he reverses it so that he now holds it by the shoulder piece and can attack with the steel hand. "Get moving! To the *pissoir!*" he shouts. "I'll cover you!"

It is a remarkable thing to see Hermann go to work with his artificial hand. I have often watched him fight that way, but our opponents have not. They stand gaping for a moment as though the devil had fallen in their midst, and that gives us our chance. We break through and race toward the *pissoir* in New Market. As I rush by I see Hermann land a beautiful blow on the open snout of the second ringleader. "Quick, Götz!" I shout. "Come along! We've got through!"

Hermann takes one more swing. His empty coat sleeve flutters, he makes wild motions with the stump of his arm to keep his balance, and two booted enemies in his path gape at him with amazement and horror. One gets a cut in the chin, the other, as he sees the artificial black hand hurtling toward him, screeches with terror, shuts his eyes, and runs.

We reach the attractive, square sandstone building and take refuge on the women's side. It is easier to defend. On the men's side they might climb in through the window and take us in the rear; on the women's side the windows are small and high.

Our enemies have followed us. There must be at least twenty of them by now; they have been reinforced by some Nazis. I can see a few of their shit-colored uniforms. They are trying to break in on the side where Köhler and I are standing. But amid the confusion I see help coming. A moment later Riesenfeld is bringing his rolled-up brief case, full of samples of granite I hope, down on someone's skull, while Renée de la Tour has taken off one of her high-heeled shoes, seized it by the toe, and is flailing away with the heel.

As I watch all this someone butts me in the stomach with his skull and my breath shoots out of my mouth with a bang. I strike about me feebly and wildly, and have at the same time a feeling of being in a familiar situation. Automatically I raise my knee, expecting the billy goat to attack again. At that instant I see one of the loveliest sights imaginable in such a situation: Lisa, like the Victory of Samothrace, is storming across New Market, beside her Bodo Ledderhose and behind him his singing club. At the same instant I feel the billy goat again and see Riesenfeld's brief case descend like a yellow flag. Simultaneously Renée de la Tour makes a lightning downward stroke which is followed by a shriek of anguish from the billy goat. Renée shouts in her vibrant voice of command: "Halt, you swine!" A number of our attackers involuntarily jump. Then the singing club goes into action and we are free.

I straighten up. It is suddenly quiet. Our attackers have fled, dragging their wounded with them. Hermann Lotz is coming back. He has pursued the fleeing foe like a centaur and has succeeded in landing one more good crack. We have got off not badly. I have a fair-sized bump on my head and I feel as though my arm were broken. It is not. But I feel very sick. I have drunk too much to enjoy blows in the stomach. Once more I am tormented by that tantalizing, familiar memory which I cannot place. What was it? "I wish I had a schnaps," I say.

"You'll get one," Bodo Ledderhose replies. "Come along now, before the police turn up."

Just then there is the sound of a resounding slap. We turn around in surprise. Lisa has hit someone. "You damned drunkard!" she says with dignity. "So this is the way you look after your home and wife—"

"You—" the figure gurgles.

Lisa's hand descends again. And now, suddenly, the knots of memory are released. Watzek! There he stands, oddly grasping his behind.

"My husband!" Lisa says to New Market in general. "That's the man I'm married to."

Watzek makes no reply. He is bleeding profusely. The

old wound I gave him has opened again. In addition, blood is running out of his hair. "Did you do that with your brief case?" I ask Riesenfeld softly.

He nods, watching Watzek attentively. "What odd places people meet!" he says.

"What's the matter with his rear end?" I ask. "Why is he holding onto it?"

"A wasp sting," Renée de la Tour replies, replacing a long hat pin in her ice blue satin cap.

"My respects!" I bow low before her and go over to Watzek. "So," I say, "now I know who was butting me in the stomach! Is this the thanks I get for my instruction in a finer way of life?"

Watzek stares at me. "You? I didn't recognize you! My God!"

"He never recognizes anybody," Lisa explains sarcastically.

Watzek makes a sorry picture. And yet I notice that he has actually followed my advice. He has had his mane cut, with the result that Riesenfeld's blow was all the more effective; he is also wearing a new white shirt, on which the bloodstains show up clearly. He really is a bad-luck bird.

"Back home with you! You pig's foot, you brawler!" Lisa says, departing. Watzek follows her at once. They wander across New Market, a strange pair. No one follows them. Georg helps Lotz adjust his artificial arm.

"Come along," Ledderhose says. "We can still get a drink in my inn. A private party!"

We sit for a while with Bodo and his club. Then we start homeward. The gray of dawn is crawling across the streets. A newspaper boy comes by. Riesenfeld motions to him. The big headlines on the front page read: INLATION ENDS! ONE MARK FOR A TRILLION!

"Well?" Riesenfeld says to me.

I nod.

"Children, I may actually be broke," Willy announces. "I've kept on playing it short." He looks ruefully at his gray suit and then at Renée. "Well, easy come, easy go—it was only money anyway."

"Money is very important," Renée replies coolly. "Especially when you haven't got it."

Georg and I walk along Marienstrasse. "Strange that Watzek got his beating from me and Riesenfeld," I say, "not from you. It would have been more natural if you and he had fought."

"More natural, perhaps, but not more fair."

"Fair?" I ask.

"In a complicated sense. I'm too tired now to disentangle it. Men with bald heads oughtn't to fight. They ought to philosophize."

"Then you'll have a lonesome life. The times look like fighting."

"Maybe not. Some kind of horrid carnival has come to an end. Doesn't today feel like a cosmic Ash Wednesday? A huge soap bubble has burst."

"And?" I say.

"And?" he replies.

"Someone will blow a new and bigger one."

"Perhaps."

We stop in the garden. The milky light of morning is streaming like a gray flood around the crosses. The youngest Knopf daughter appears, sleepy-eyed. She has been waiting up for us. "Father says you can buy back the headstone for twelve trillion."

"Tell him we offer eight marks. And the offer only holds until noon today. Money will be very short."

"What's that?" Knopf asks from his bedroom window, where he has been listening.

"Eight marks, Herr Knopf. And after noon today only six. Prices are going down. Who would ever have expected that, eh? Instead of up."

"I'd rather keep it through all eternity, you damned grave robbers!" Knopf screeches, slamming the window.

Chapter Twenty-four

The Werdenbrück Poets' Club is holding a farewell party for me in the Old German Room at the Walhalla. The poets are uneasy; they pretend deep feeling. Hungermann is the first to come up to me. "You know my poems. You yourself said they were one of your deepest poetical experiences. Deeper than Stefan George."

He looks at me intently. I never said anything of the sort. It was Bambuss who said it; in return Hungermann said that he considered Bambuss more significant than Rilke. But I do not correct him. I look expectantly at the poet of Casanova and Mohammed.

"Well then," Hungermann goes on, but his attention is distracted. "By the way where did you get that new suit?"

"I bought it today with a Swiss honorarium," I reply with all the modesty of a peacock. "It's the first new suit I've had since I was a soldier of His Majesty. No remade uniform. Real civilian clothes! The inflation is over!"

"A Swiss honorarium? So you're already internationally known? Well, well," Hungermann says, surprised and instantly rather vexed. "From a newspaper?"

I nod. The author of "Casanova" makes a deprecatory gesture. "I thought so! Of course my things are not for the daily press! Only for first-rate literary magazines, if at all. Unfortunately a volume of my poems was published by Arthur Bauer here in Werdenbrück three months ago. An outrage!"

"Were you forced to do it?"

"Yes, morally speaking. Bauer lied to me. He said he was going to launch a terrific publicity campaign, he was going to enlarge his press and publish not only my work but Mörike, Goethe, Rilke, Stefan George, and, above all, Hölderlin. He hasn't done any of it."

"He published Otto Bambuss," I reply.

Hungermann frowns. "Bambuss—between us, a bungler and imitator. That did me harm. Do you know how many copies of my work Bauer has sold? No more than five hundred!"

I know from Bauer that the entire printing consisted of two hundred and fifty copies; twenty-eight have been sold and nineteen of these were bought secretly by Hungermann. And it was not Hungermann who was forced to publish but Bauer. Hungermann blackmailed him with the threat of recommending another book dealer to the high school where he teaches.

"Now that you're going to be on a newspaper in Berlin," Hungermann goes on, "you know, friendship among artists is the noblest thing in the world!"

"I know. The rarest too."

"So it is." Hungermann draws a slender volume out of his pocket. "Here—with a dedication. Write something about it in Berlin. And send me two proofs. On my side, I will keep faith with you here in Werdenbrück. And if you find a good publisher up there—the second volume is in preparation."

"Agreed."

"I knew I could rely on you." Hungermann solemnly shakes my hand. "Aren't you going to publish something soon?"

"No. I've given it up."

"What?"

"I'm going to wait a while," I say. "I want to look around in the world a bit."

"Very wise!" Hungermann exclaims with emphasis. "If only more people would do that instead of publishing immature stuff and getting in the way of their betters!"

He looks sharply around the room. I expect at least a wink, but he is all seriousness. I have turned into a business opportunity and his sense of humor has abandoned him. "Don't tell the others about our arrangement," he adds with emphasis.

"Certainly not," I reply and see Otto Bambuss stalking me.

An hour later I have in my pocket a copy of Bambuss's "Voices of Silence" with a flattering dedication, and, in addition, a carbon copy of the sonnet sequence "The Tigress," which I am to get published in Berlin; from Sommerfeld a copy of the "Book of the Dead" in free verse, from other members a dozen additional works—and from Eduard a carbon of his "Paean on the Death of a Friend" in 186 lines, dedicated to "Valentin, Comrade, Fellow Warrior, and Man." Eduard works easily and quickly.

Suddenly it all seems remote. As remote as the inflation, which died two weeks ago—or my childhood which was smothered overnight in a uniform. As remote as Isabelle.

I look at the faces around me. Are they still the faces of awestruck children, confronted by chaos and miracle, or are they already the faces of conscientious club members? Is there still something in them of Isabelle's rapt and terrified countenance, or are they mere imitators, noisily exploiting that tenth of a talent which every youth possesses, whose disappearance they boast of and enviously celebrate instead of cherishing it in silence and trying to preserve some bit of it for the future?

"Comrades," I say. "I hereby resign from your club."

All faces turn toward me. "Impossible! You'll be a corresponding member in Berlin," Hungermann declares.

"I'm resigning," I say.

For an instant the poets are silent. They look at me. Am I mistaken or do I see something like the fear of discovery in the faces of some? "Do you really mean it?" Hungermann asks.

"I really mean it."

"All right. We accept your resignation and we hereby make you an honorary member."

Hungermann glances around. There is resounding applause. The faces relax. "Unanimously passed!" says the poet of Casanova.

"I thank you," I reply. "This is a proud moment. But I cannot accept. It would be like being turned into a statue. Or a gravestone. I do not want to go into the world as the honorary member of anything—not even of our establishment in Bahnstrasse."

"That's not a nice comparison," says Sommerfeld, the poet of Death.

"Give him leave," Hungermann decrees. "Well then, how do you want to go into the world?"

I laugh. "As a spark of life struggling to avoid extinction."

"Dear God," Bambuss says, "isn't there something like that in Euripides?"

"Possibly, Otto. Then there must be something to it. Besides, I don't intend to write about it; I'm going to try to be it."

"It isn't in Euripides," Hungermann, the academician,

announces with a triumphant glance at Bambuss, the village schoolmaster. "So you intend—" he says to me.

"Last night I made a fire," I say. "It burned well. You know the old marching order: travel light."

They nod eagerly. They have long since forgotten it, I suddenly realize. "All right then," I say. "Eduard, I still have twelve luncheon coupons. The inflation has overtaken them, but I believe I would still have the legal right, even if I had to go to court about it, to demand food from you. Will you trade two bottles of Reinhartshausener for them? We want to drink them now."

Eduard makes a lightning calculation, counting in Valentin as well as the poem about Valentin in my pocket. "Three," he says.

Willy is sitting in a small room. He has exchanged his elegant apartment for this. It is a terrific fall in the world, but Willy is bearing it well. He has saved his suits, and some of his jewelry; with these he will be able to play the elegant cavalier for some time to come. The red car had to be sold. He had speculated too recklessly on continued depreciation. The walls of his room are papered with notes and worthless bonds of the inflation. "It was cheaper than wallpaper," he explains. "And more entertaining."

"And now?"

"I'll probably get a small job in the Werdenbrück bank." Willy grins. "Renée is in Magdeburg. She writes that she's having a big success in 'The Green Cockatoo.'"

"It's nice that she goes on writing at least."

Willy makes an expansive gesture. "None of it matters, Ludwig. Out of sight, out of mind! Besides, for the last month I haven't been able to persuade Renée to play the general at night. So it was only half the fun. The only time lately that she shouted a command was during that memorable battle at the *pissoir* in New Market. Farewell, youth! As a going-away present—" he opens a bag full of bonds and paper money. "Take anything you like! Millions, billions—it was a dream, wasn't it?"

"Yes," I say.

Willy accompanies me to the street. "I've saved a few hundred real marks," he whispers. "The fatherland is not yet lost! Now it's the turn of the French franc. I'm going to speculate on its falling. Would you like to take a small flier with me?"

"No, Willy. From now on I'm only speculating on rises."

"Rises," he says as though he were saying Popocatepetl.

I am sitting alone in the office. It is my last day. I am leaving tonight. As I leaf through a catalog, wondering whether to include Watzek's name on one of the tombstones I have drawn, the telephone rings.

"Are you the one called Ludwig?" a husky voice inquires. "The one who used to collect frogs and slowworms?"

"Could be," I reply. "It depends on the reason. Who's speaking?"

"Fritzi."

"Fritzi! Of course it's me! What has happened? Has Otto Bambuss—"

"The Iron Horse is dead."

"What?"

"Yes. Last evening. Heart attack. While at work."

"A beautiful death," I say. "But too young!"

Fritzi coughs. Then she says: "You're in some sort of monument business, aren't you? You told me about it once!"

"We have the best monument business in the city," I reply. "Why?"

"Why? My God, Ludwig, I'll give you three guesses! The Madame naturally wants to give the order to a client. And, besides, it was on the Iron Horse that you—"

"Not I," I interrupt. "But possibly my friend Georg—"
"No matter, a client is to have the order. Come on out here! But come soon! A salesman for your competitors has been here already—he kept weeping and saying it was on the Horse that he—"

Weeping Oskar! Not a doubt of it! "I'm coming at once!" I say. "That blubberer was lying!"

The Madame receives me. "Do you want to see her?" she asks.

"Is she laid out here?"

"Upstairs, in her room."

We go up the creaking stairs. The doors are open. I see the girls getting dressed. "Are you going to be open tonight?" I ask.

The Madame shakes her head. "Not tonight. The ladies are just getting dressed anyway. Habit, you know. Being closed is no great loss. Now that the mark is the mark again, our business has gone to pot. All the sinners are broke. Funny, isn't it?"

It is not funny; it is true. The inflation has turned straight into deflation. Where billions were once thrown about, calculations are again being made in pfennigs. There is a general shortage of money. The horrible carnival is over. A spartan Ash Wednesday has come.

The Iron Horse lies on her bier among green potted plants and lilies. Her face is now severe and old; I recognize her only by one gold tooth just visible at one corner of her lips. The mirror, in front of which she has so often made up, is hung with white tulle. The room smells of stale perfume, evergreens, and death. On the bureau stand a few photographs and a crystal ball, with one flat side where a picture is glued. If you shake the ball the people in the picture look as if they were in a snowstorm. I know it well; it is one of the finest memories of my childhood. I longed to steal it in the days when I used to do my schoolwork in Bahnstrasse. "She was a kind of stepmother to you, wasn't she?" the Madame asks.

"Say rather a kind of mother. Without the Iron Horse I would probably have become a biologist. But she loved poems; I had to keep bringing her new ones and finally I forgot about biology."

"That's right," says the Madame. "You always had salamanders and fishes with you!"

We go out. On the way I see the Cosack cap lying on the dressing table. "Where are her high boots?" I ask.

"Fritzi has them now. Fritzi is no longer interested in anything else. Wielding the whip is less exhausting. And brings in more. In fact, we'll soon have to find an understudy. We have quite a little circle of clients for a strenuous masseuse."

"How did it really happen to the Horse?"

"In line of duty. She always took too much interest in the matter, that was the real reason. We have a one-eyed Dutch businessman, a very fine gentleman; he doesn't look the part at all but the only thing he wants is beating and he comes every Sunday. Crows, when he's had enough, like a rooster, very droll. Married, has three sweet children, but can't, of course, order his wife to beat him—so he's a permanent client, with foreign exchange in his wallet, pays in gulden—we almost worshiped that man—and his *valuta*. Well, so that's how it happened yesterday. Malvina got too excited—and suddenly she fell over, whip in hand."

"Malvina?"

"That's her first name. You didn't know, did you? What a shock for the gentleman to be sure! He won't come again," says the Madame woefully. "What a client! Pure sugar! We could always buy meat and baked stuffs for a whole month with his foreign exchange. How does it stand now, by the way?" She turns to me. "Not worth what it used to be, is it?"

"A gulden is worth just about two marks."

"Is it possible! And a little while ago it was worth trillions! Well, then it's not so bad even if our client should stay away. Won't you take some trifle with you as a memento of the Horse?"

For a moment I think of the glass ball with its snowstorm. But one oughtn't to carry along keepsakes. I shake my head.

"All right," says the Madame. "Then we'll have a nice cup of coffee downstairs and pick out the monument."

I have been figuring on a small headstone, but it turns out that, thanks to the Dutch businessman, the Iron Horse had amassed considerable savings. She put the gulden notes away in a strongbox. Now they represent an impressive sum. The businessman has been her loyal client for years. "Malvina had no family," the Madame says.

"Then of course," I reply, "we can turn to the important class of tombstones. Marble or granite."

"Marble is not the thing for the Horse," Fritzi says. "That's more for children, isn't it?"

"Not always, by any means! We have laid generals to rest under marble columns."

"Granite," says the Madame. "Granite is better. Suits her iron nature."

We are sitting in the big room. The coffee is steaming, there are home-baked cakes with whipped cream and there is a bottle of curaçao. I feel almost as though I had been spirited back to the old times. The ladies are looking over my shoulder at the catalogue just as they used to look at my schoolbooks.

"Here's the finest thing we have," I say. "Black Swedish granite, a memorial cross with a double socle. There aren't more than two or three like it in the whole city."

The ladies examine the drawing. It is one of my last. I have put Major Wolkenstein in the inscription—as having fallen in 1915 at the head of his troop—which would certainly have been a blessing for the carpenter in Wüstringen.

"Was the Horse Catholic?" Fritzi asks.

"A cross is not just for Catholics," I reply.

The Madame scratches her head. "I don't know whether she would have cared for anything as religious as that. Isn't there something else? Something more like a natural rock?"

For an instant my breath leaves me. "If you want something of that sort," I say, "I have just the thing. Something extraordinary! An obelisk!"

It is a shot in the dark, I know. My fingers suddenly trembling with the excitement of the chase, I search for the drawing of the veteran and lay it on the table.

The ladies study it in silence. I hold back. Sometimes there is a kind of beginner's luck that accomplishes with a child's touch things that would baffle the expert. Fritzi suddenly laughs. "Really not bad for the Horse," she says.

The Madame smiles too. "What does the thing cost?"

For as long as I have been in the business, no price has ever been put on the obelisk, since everyone knew it was unsalable. I calculate quickly. "A thousand marks is the official price," I say. "For you, as friends, six hundred. For the Horse, as my teacher, three hundred. I can take the chance of making this ridiculous price because this is my last day in the office—otherwise I'd be fired. Cash payment of course! And the inscription extra."

"Well, why not?" Fritzi says.

"It's all right with me!" the Madame nods.

I can't trust my ears. "Then it's a deal?" I ask.

"A deal," the Madame replies. "How much is three hundred marks in gulden?"

She begins to count out the notes. A bird shoots out of the cuckoo clock on the wall and chirps the hour. It is six o'clock. I put the money in my pocket. "A schnaps to Malvina's memory," says the Madame. "She'll be buried tomorrow morning. We need the place again for the evening."

"Too bad I can't stay for the funeral," I say.

We all drink cognac with a dash of crème de menthe. The Madame wipes her eyes. "It touches me deeply," she remarks.

It touches us all. I get up and say good-by. "Georg Kroll will install the monument," I say.

The ladies nod. I have never met so much loyalty and good faith as here. They wave to me from the windows. The bulldogs bark. I walk quickly along the brook back toward the city.

"Impossible!" Georg says. Silently I take the Dutch gulden out of my pocket and spread them on the desk. "What have you sold for all that?" he asks.

"Just a minute."

I have heard the tinkle of a bicycle bell. Immediately thereafter there is the sound of an authoritative cough at the front door. I pick up the bills and put them back in my pocket. Heinrich Kroll appears in the doorway, the cuffs of his trousers somewhat soiled by the dust of the roads. "Well," I ask, "sold anything?"

He stares at me venomously. "Go out and try to sell something yourself! There's a state of general bankruptcy. No one has money! And anyone who has a couple of marks holds onto them!"

"I was out," I reply, "and I sold something."

"Did you? What?"

I turn so that I have both brothers in front of me and say: "The obelisk."

"Nonsense!" Heinrich says curtly. "Go make your jokes in Berlin!"

"I have nothing more to do with the business, of course," I explain, "inasmuch as my employment terminated at twelve o'clock today. Nevertheless, I wanted to show you how simple it is to sell tombstones. A kind of vacation job really."

Heinrich swells with rage, but restrains his anger. "Thank God we won't have to listen to this sort of nonsense much longer! Have a good trip! They'll teach you to talk respectfully in Berlin."

"He has actually sold the obelisk, Heinrich," Georg says.

Heinrich stares at him incredulously. "Prove it!" he barks at length.

"Here!" I say, letting the gulden notes flutter down. "Even in foreign exchange!"

Heinrich gapes at the notes. Then he seizes one of them, turns it over and examines it to see whether it is genuine. "Luck," he snaps finally. "Fool's luck!"

"We can use such luck, Heinrich," Georg says. "Without this sale we couldn't have paid the note that's due tomorrow. You ought to thank him warmly. It's the first real money we've seen. We need it damned badly."

"Thank him? I'd rather die!"

Heinrich disappears, slamming the door—a genuine, honest German who owes thanks to no one. "Do we really need the money so badly?" I ask.

"Badly enough," Georg replies. "But now let's do some figuring. How much have you?"

"Enough. I was given traveling expenses third class. I'm going fourth class and so will save twelve marks. I sold my piano—I couldn't take it with me. The old box brought a hundred marks. That is, all told, one hundred and twelve marks. I can live on that till I get my first pay."

Georg takes thirty Dutch gulden and offers them to me. "You worked as a special agent. That means you have a right to a commission just like Weeping Oskar. For extraordinary services, five per cent additional."

A short argument ensues; then I take the money, as an anchor to windward in case I am fired during the first month. "Do you know yet what you're going to have to do in Berlin?" Georg asks.

I nod. "Report fires, describe thefts, review unimportant books, fetch beer for the editors, sharpen pencils, correct proof—and try to get ahead in the world."

The door is kicked open. Like a ghost Sergeant Major Knopf stands in the doorway. "I demand eight trillion," he croaks.

"Herr Knopf," I say. "You have not yet altogether awakened from a long dream: the inflation is over. Two weeks ago you could have got eight trillion for the stone you paid eight million for. Today the price is eight marks."

"You rat! You did it on purpose!"

"What?"

"Stopped the inflation! To exploit me! But I won't sell! I'll wait for the next one!"

"What?"

"The next inflation!"

"All right," Georg says. "We'll have a drink on that."

Knopf is the first to reach for the bottle. "Want to bet?" he asks.

"On what?"

"That I can tell by taste where this bottle came from."

He pulls out the cork and sniffs. "It's impossible for you to tell," I say. "With schnaps from a cask, perhaps—we know you're the greatest expert in the district—but with schnaps in bottles never."

"How much will you bet? The price of the headstone?"

"We're suddenly impoverished," Georg replies. "But we'll risk three marks. To oblige you."

"All right. Give me a glass."

Knopf smells and tastes. Then he demands a second and a third glassful. "Give up," I say. "It's impossible. You don't have to pay."

"This schnaps is from Brockmann's Delicatessen Store in Marienstrasse," Knopf says.

We stare at him. He is right. "Hand over the money!" he croaks.

Georg pays the three marks, and the sergeant major disappears. "How was that possible?" I say. "Has the old schnaps thrush second sight?"

Georg laughs suddenly. "He tricked us!"

"How?"

He lifts the bottle. On the back at the bottom is a tiny label: J. Brockmann, delicatessen, 18 Marienstrasse. "What a sharpie!" he says with amusement. "And what eyes he has!"

"Eyes!" I say. "Day after tomorrow he won't trust them —when he comes home and finds the obelisk gone. His world, too, will collapse."

"Is yours collapsing?" Georg asks.

"Daily," I reply. "How else could one live?"

Two hours before train time we hear tramping feet outside and the sound of voices raised in song.

Then at once a four-part harmony rises from the street: "Holy night, oh pour the peace of Heaven upon this heart—"

We go to the window. On the street stands Bodo Ledderhose's club. "What's this all about?" I ask. "Turn on the light, Georg!"

In the glow falling from our window, we recognize Bodo. "It's about you," Georg says. "A farewell song from your club. Don't forget you're a member still."

"Grant the weary pilgrim peace, soothing ointment for his pain—" they roll on loudly.

Windows fly open. "Quiet!" Widow Konersmann screams. "It's midnight, you drunken dogs!"

"Brightly shine the stars on high like lamps in the distant blue—"

Lisa appears in her window and bows. She thinks the song is for her.

In short order the police arrive. "Disperse!" an authoritative voice commands.

The police have changed with the deflation. They have grown strict and energetic. The old Prussian spirit is back again. Every civilian is a permanent recruit.

"Disturbance of the peace!" growls the uniformed music hater.

"Arrest them!" howls the widow Konersmann.

Bodo's club consists of him and twenty steadfast singers. Opposed to them stand two policemen. "Bodo," I shout in alarm, "don't lay hands on them! Don't defend yourselves! Otherwise you'll be in jail for years!"

Bodo makes a reassuring gesture and goes on singing wide-mouthed: "Might I but depart with thee—on thy way to Heaven."

"Quiet, we want to sleep!" the widow Konersmann screams.

"Hey there!" Lisa shouts to the policemen. "Just leave the singers alone! Why aren't you out catching thieves?"

The policemen are perplexed. They order everyone to accompany them to the police station, but no one moves. Bodo begins the second stanza. The policemen finally do the best they can—each arrests one of the singers. "Don't defend yourselves!" I shout. "It's resisting the law!"

The singers offer no resistance. They let themselves be led away. The rest go on singing as though nothing had happened. The station is not far. The police come back on the run and arrest two more. The others go on singing, but they have become very weak in first tenors. The police are making their arrests from the right; on the third trip Willy is taken away and with that the first tenors are silenced. We hand bottles of beer out of the window. "Hold out, Bodo!" I say.

"Don't worry! To the last man!"

The police come back and arrest two second tenors. We have no more beer and begin handing out our schnaps. Ten minutes later only the basses are left. They stand there, disregarding the arrests. I have read somewhere that herds of walruses will remain unconcerned in just this way while hunters bludgeon their neighbors to death—and I have seen whole nations behave the same way in war.

After another fifteen minutes Bodo Ledderhose is standing there alone. The angry, sweating policemen come galloping up for the last time. They take Bodo between them. We follow him to the station. Bodo goes on humming alone. "Beethoven," he says briefly and starts humming again, a lonely musical bee.

But suddenly it is as though aeolian harps were accompanying him from afar. We prick up our ears. It sounds like a miracle—angel voices are actually accompanying him—angels in first and second tenor and in both basses. They weave their flattering and deceptive strains around Bodo and grow clearer as we advance. When we round the church, we can actually understand the fleeting, disembodied voices. They are singing: "Holy night, oh pour the peace of Heaven—" and at the next corner we recognize whence they come—from the police station, where Bodo's arrested friends are unconcernedly going on with their song. Bodo takes his place as leader, as though it were the most natural thing in the world, and continues: "Grant the weary pilgrim peace—"

"Herr Kroll, what's the meaning of this?" the desk sergeant asks in perplexity.

"It is the power of music," Georg replies. "A farewell song for a man who is going out into the wide world. It's harmless and really ought to be encouraged."

"Is that all?"

"That's all."

"It is disturbance of the peace," protests one of the men who made the arrests.

"Would it have been disturbance of the peace if they had been singing *'Deutschland, Deutschland über alles'*?" I ask.

"That would have been different!"

"Throw them out!" shouts the sergeant. "But they're to keep quiet from now on."

"They'll keep quiet. You're not a Prussian, are you?"

"Franconian."

"That's what I thought," Georg says.

We are at the station. It is windy and there is no one on the platform but us. "You will visit me, Georg," I say. "I'll do all I possibly can to meet the women of your dreams. Two or three will be there for you if you come."

"I'll come."

I know he will not. "You owe it to your tuxedo at least," I say. "Where else could you wear it?"

"That's true."

The train bores through the darkness with two glowing eyes. "Keep the colors flying, Georg! We're immortal you know."

"So we are. And you, don't let them get you down. You've been saved so often it's your duty to survive."

"Sure," I say. "If only because of the others who weren't saved."

"Nonsense. Simply because you're alive."

The train roars into the station as though five hundred people were waiting for it. But only I am waiting. I look for a compartment and get in. The compartment smells of sleep and people. I open the window in the passageway and lean out. "When you give up something, you don't have to lose it," Georg says. "Only idiots think that."

"Who's talking about losing?" I reply as the train begins to move. "Since we lose in the end anyway, we can give ourselves the luxury of winning beforehand like the spotted monkeys of the forest."

"Do they always win?"

"Yes—because they don't know what winning is."

The train is already rolling. I feel Georg's hand. It is too small and too soft and there is an unhealed scar on it from the Battle of the *Pissoir*. The train moves faster, Georg is left behind and suddenly he is older and paler than I thought. Now I can only see his pale hand and pale head and then nothing more but the sky and the fleeing dark.

I go into the compartment. A commercial traveler with eyeglasses is wheezing in one corner; a woodsman in another. In the third a fat man with a mustache is snoring; in the fourth a woman with sagging cheeks and a hat askew on her head is emitting quavering sighs.

I feel the sharp hunger of sorrow and open my bag, which is in the luggage net. Frau Kroll has provided me with sandwiches for the trip. I fumble for them unsuccessfully and get the bag down out of the net. The quavering woman with the tilted hat wakes up, looks around furiously and goes back challengingly to her quavers. I see now why I could not find the sandwiches. Georg's tuxedo lies on top of them. Very likely he put it in my bag while I was selling the obelisk. I look at the black cloth for a while, then I get out the sandwiches and begin to eat. They are admirable sandwiches. The whole compartment wakes up for a moment at the smell of bread and liverwurst. I pay no attention and go on eating. Then I lean back in my seat and look out into the darkness, where now and again lights fly past, and I think of Georg and the tuxedo and then I think of Isabelle and Hermann Lotz and of the obelisk that was pissed on and that saved the firm in the end, and finally I think of nothing at all.

Chapter Twenty-five

I never saw any of them again. Occasionally I planned to take a trip back, but something always interfered and I thought I had plenty of time. Suddenly there was no more time. Night broke over Germany, I left it, and when I came back it lay in ruins. Georg Kroll was dead. The widow Konersmann had gone on spying and had found out that Georg and Lisa had had an affair; in 1934, ten years later, she revealed this fact to Watzek, who was then *Sturmführer* in the SA. Watzek had Georg thrown into a concentration camp, despite the fact that he himself had divorced Lisa five years before. A few months later Georg was dead.

Hans Hungermann became Cultural Guardian and *Obersturmbannführer* in the new party, which he celebrated in glowing verses. For this reason he lost his position as educational director in 1945 and was in difficulties for a time. Since then, however, his pension application has been approved by the State and he is living in comfortable idleness, like countless other party members.

Kurt Bach, the sculptor, was in a concentration camp for seven years and came out an unemployable cripple. Today, ten years after the collapse of the Nazis, he is still fighting for a small pension, like innumerable other victims of the regime. If he is successful he will get an income of seventy marks a month—about one-tenth of what Hungermann receives and also about one-tenth of what the new democratic State has been paying for years to the first chief of the Gestapo—the man who organized the concentration camp in which Kurt Bach was crippled—not to mention, of course, the substantially higher pensions and indemnities paid to generals, war criminals, and prominent former party officials. Heinrich Kroll, who got through this period handsomely, looks upon all this with pride as proof of the incorruptible justice of our beloved fatherland.

Major Wolkenstein had a distinguished career. He joined the party, had a hand in the Jewish decrees, lay low for a few years after the war, and today, along with many other party members, is employed in the Department of Foreign Affairs.

For a long time Bodendiek and Wernicke kept a number of Jews hidden in the insane asylum. They put them in the cells for incurables, shaved their heads, and taught them to behave like madmen. Later Bodendiek was packed off to a small village because he had had the temerity to protest when his bishop accepted the title of Counselor of State from a government that regarded murder as a sacred duty. Wernicke was discharged because he refused to give lethal injections to his patients. Before that he had succeeded in smuggling out his hidden Jews and sending them on their way. He was sent to the front and fell in 1944. Willy fell in 1942, Otto Bambuss in 1945, Karl Brill in 1944. Lisa was killed in an air raid. So was old Frau Kroll.

Eduard Knobloch survived it all; he served the just and the unjust with impartial excellence. His hotel was destroyed, but it has been rebuilt. He did not marry Gerda, and no one knows what has become of her. Nor have I ever heard anything of Geneviève Terhoven.

Weeping Oskar had an interesting career. He went to Russia with the army and for a second time became commandant of a cemetery. In 1945 he was an interpreter with the occupation forces, and, finally, for several months he was burgomaster of Werdenbrück. After that he went back into business, this time with Heinrich Kroll. They founded a new firm and prospered greatly—tombstones at that time were in almost as great demand as bread.

Old Knopf died three months after I left Werdenbrück. He was run over one night by a car. A year later, to everyone's surprise, his wife married Wilke, the coffinmaker. It has been a happy marriage.

During the war the city of Werdenbrück was so demolished by bombs that hardly a house remained intact. It was a railroad junction and so was bombed repeatedly. A year afterward I was there for a few hours between trains. I looked for the old streets but lost my way in the city I had lived in so long. There was nothing left but ruins, nor could I find any survivors of that earlier time. In a little shop of rough boards near the station I bought some picture post cards with views of the city in the time before the war. That was all that was left. Formerly, if one wanted to remember his youth he went back to the place where he had spent it. One can hardly do that in Germany today. Everything has been destroyed and rebuilt and is strange. Picture post cards have to take its place.

The only buildings that have remained completely undamaged are the insane asylum and the lying-in hospital—principally because they stand some distance outside the city. They were immediately filled to capacity again and are still full. Indeed, they even had to be substantially enlarged.